"OVER ON YOUR

She complied, lowering her cheek to the floor, as ritual demanded. Directly behind her she heard the door open and the servant slip out. Then she heard mumbled conversation, the voices of two men. Clenching her jaw, she crawled forward. Reaching the foot of the bed, she raised herself on her palms and pulled herself slowly up onto the bed. There, the prince and another man sat on satin pillows, waiting for her, grinning, the scent of perfume heavy in the air.

She felt herself go limp with fear, bedclothes dropping from under her. She was vaguely aware of hands touching her, fingers exploring her body, warm lips pressing against her mouth, till she knew she must cry out, even if it meant her life!

BOOKS BY BARBARA RIEFE

THIS RAVAGED HEART
FAR BEYOND DESIRE
AULDEARN HOUSE
BARRINGER HOUSE
ROWLESTON

FIRE AND FLESH

BARBARA RIEFE

PLAYBOY PRESS
PAPERBACKS

FIRE AND FLESH

Copyright © 1978 by Barbara Riefe.

Cover illustration by Betty Maxey: Copyright © 1978 by Playboy

All rights reserved. No part of this book may be reproduced, stored in a retrieval system or transmitted in any form by an electronic, mechanical, photocopying, recording means or otherwise without prior written permission of the author.

Published simultaneously in the United States and Canada by Playboy Press, Chicago, Illinois. Printed in the United States of America. Library of Congress Catalog Card Number: 78-55738. First edition.

Books are available at quantity discounts for promotional and industrial use. For further information, write our sales-promotion agency: Ventura Associates, 40 East 49th Street, New York, New York 10017.

ISBN: 0-872-16480-2

TO MARTHA SUSAN VATALARO
WITH LOVE

BOOK I   THE FORBIDDEN CITY   **11**

BOOK II   JOURNEY TO DESPAIR   **129**

BOOK III   THE EYES OF THE DRAGON   **229**

BOOK IV   BITTER TRIUMPH   **333**

Who can find a virtuous woman?
for her price *is* far above rubies.

Strength and honour *are* her clothing;
and she shall rejoice in time to come.

She openeth her mouth with wisdom;
and in her tongue *is* the law of kindness.

Her children arise up, and call her blessed;
her husband *also,* and he praiseth her.

—PROVERBS 31

BOOK ONE
THE FORBIDDEN CITY

I

The bitter wind whirling down from the deserts of Mongolia grieved restlessly as it discovered the small house in Hibiscus Lane. Circling it, binding it snugly about its eaves, it then relented and relaxed, flinging free, whipping across the yard, tearing the flame in the brazier in passing. Its voice rose, becoming shrill. The sound startled Deirdre and she sat straight up in bed, awakening on the instant to the nightmare of reality.

The lilies scattered in profusion across the crimson background of her silk pajamas reflected the wan white light of the sun filtering through the window. Under the k'ang brick bed upon which she sat, the warming fire had reduced itself to ashes, and she trembled slightly, half imagining that the wind that had roused her had left its chill behind to slip beneath the eaves through the frame edge of the window into the room.

The room itself presented the delicate scent of rose petals, her pillow filled with them and perforated, permitting the fragrance to escape. The bed hangings were of pink satin and apricot crepe, woven with a design of apulownia and paper trees, their somber stateliness contrasting sharply with the laughing thrushes flitting among them. Impeding a yawn with the palm of her hand, Deirdre stretched, threw aside the coverlet and, searching briefly with her toes, located her slippers. Rising, she glanced about; the *chaise percée* on which she was washed every night before retiring dominated the furnishings. It stood before the teakwood *étagère,* its shelves crowded with bottles and flasks containing perfumes, toiletries and cosmetics, with lovely dragon vases, porcelain stem-cups and other pottery and stone pieces interspersed among them. An ancestral portrait concealed most of the wall opposite the foot of the bed, a mandarin, his hands concealed in his cuffs, their weight draping them to within inches of his shoes. His mouth was sealed, his skin lineless and without blemish but typically sallow, his eyes dark and questioning, his entire expression seeming to inquire the reason for her presence.

A concern she herself shared. What *was* a foreigner, an American, doing living among these people, the Han Chinese and the Manchus, that remarkable minority whose vital presence in the Middle Kingdom served to elevate everyone's existence?

Rising from the bed, she glided soundlessly over the tile floor to her mirror and sat before it, her slender fingers, the nails grown to nearly four inches, touching her pale cheeks. Her eyes were as green as the beautiful jade phoenix on the second shelf of the *étagère;* her hair was flaming red. In a crowd of 10,000 Chinese, it alone made her stand out like fire in a forest of fir.

She quelled the urge to close her eyes and yield her mind to memory—but for moments only. Soon the past, loathsome and terrifying, came sweeping across the screen of her mind, a panorama of bestiality and cruelty. Her eyes misted, blurring vision of her face in the glass. Once more she saw the slave ship and the foul, rat-infested hold in which she and the two Franeker girls had been shackled with the other captives. Once more she recalled the living hell of the long voyage from Batavia to Chefoo on the Yellow Sea. Their captors had stripped them naked in near-freezing weather; they had raped and tortured them day and night, endlessly, so it had seemed, until she had lost the ability to feel, to recognize and to react to pain. She drew in her breath, and the sweet scent of the rose petals was supplanted by the fulsome stench of human feces combined with that of the putrid gruel fed them, forced upon them, and the stink of sweat and of dead, rotting vermin. Her shackles had chafed her wrists and ankles, and the scars still faintly purpled the whiteness of her flesh. To bear the unbearable, to suffer as no human dead or alive or yet to be born would ever suffer, and to relive it in recollection infused her with nausea and a momentary giddiness. She braced herself with both hands on the vanity to keep from falling forward against the glass.

The face came back to her, the identical expression worn by 20, 30 different men. It was the grin of Satan, eyes fired with lust, teeth bared, the hoarse, panting sound escaping the throat, the hands reaching . . . The same horrible mask repeated, stamped upon the darkness rising in a semicircle above her. Down came many hands pinning her arms and legs to the damp floor, spreading her legs. Her attacker went to his knees, his organ in his hand, erect, ready, thrusting forward.

Her hands flew to her face. She winced and cried out, wrenching her pounding heart within her.

A knock.

"Hwŏy'an . . ."

"Flame"—her Chinese name for her red hair. Deirdre Dandridge turned at the sound, grateful for the interruption to her thoughts, the manner in which it erased the scenes flooding her imagination. The door opened, revealing a middle-aged man. Slender and of medium height, he was bald, his pate gleaming like polished citrine. The restricted ravages of smallpox marred the skin of his face, a crescent of pits following the outer circle of his left cheek partway, a constellation of "celestial flowers." Three of his front teeth gathered as one, his lip stretched to accommodate the forward thrust. Supporting his mouth was his small, unobtrusive chin, so typical of the Confucian scholar, the solemn, dispassionate literate. His name was Kuo-cheng. This was his house. She had come to know him as a kindly, considerate man, highly principled and moral: a gentleman from pate to black satin boots; the man to whom she owed her life.

"I was passing the door. You cried out."

She nodded. "Good morning, Kuo-cheng."

"Another nightmare?" His concern was genuine, she knew, his every reaction as authentic as his devotion to learning.

"The same one, always, asleep, awake . . ."

He came to her, putting his arm around her shoulder in avuncular fashion. She rested her cheek against the back of his hand. In spite of her circumstance, the cage of bamboo imprisoning the bird that didn't belong, her heart opened to this quiet, homely, gentle man, not alone for what he had given her, but for what he was apart from his magnanimity. In spite of which she constantly thought of escape, every day, every night, magnetically drawn by her homesickness, her desperate yearning, to the temptation to try to return to her parents. If only she could; if only the gods would pluck her out of this place, wing her across the seas and set her down where she belonged.

As to escape, the second it crossed her mind, she dismissed the idea—every time. Dwelling on the impossible only made it more painful. And impossible it was, without money, this far from the nearest port. Without a miracle in her behalf, she wouldn't get as far as the Marco Polo Bridge, just outside the city. She stood up.

Kuo-cheng smiled and took hold of her upper arms. "But you slept reasonably well? Warm enough?"

"Yes."

"You must have slept: You look radiant. And so you should on this day of all days."

Sighing, she averted his eyes.

"Now, now, Hwŏy'an . . ."

" 'Deirdre,' please. You're the only one here who has ever called me that. Don't stop now."

"Deirdre." He slurred the r's slightly. "As you wish.

My dear, you must not fritter away the hour. You must make your toilet. Tang-yü will bring in hot water and towels."

"Not right away. We must talk."

His smile faded. "Deir-dre . . ."

"Please."

"Very well."

"Kuo-cheng, I have always done as you asked, without question, without hesitating, cheerfully, gladly. But this is different. I know how much it means to you, but I've thought it over and I don't want to go through with it. I just don't want to leave here." She extended her hands. "This is the only home I've known for such a long time. Why force me to leave? Have I offended you? Are you displeased with me?"

The desperate intensity of the three questions run together surprised him.

"Why turn me out?" she continued.

"What words you choose. I'm not displeased with you. I'm not turning you out. My child, I'm giving you a splendid opportunity, a chance to do something with your life. Would you rather stay in this house until you're as old and wrinkled as Tang-yü, until I am dead and buried?"

"I don't want to leave you! You've been so kind to me. If I go, we shall never see each other again."

"You don't understand. To be selected to serve in the Forbidden City is an honor every girl dreams of. To be a concubine in the court of the empresses—"

"*I* don't dream of it; I don't want it!"

She was beginning to work along the edge of his patience; his expression and his tone betrayed it. "We have been through this so many times. My dear, it's all arranged."

"Without your even asking me. Because you knew I'd protest." She cupped her hands over her face, shielding her eyes. "When I think back to the brothel those animals sold me to in Chefoo—a nightmare upon a nightmare; how you bought me. You gave me back my life, Kuo-cheng. If you hadn't come along, sooner or later I would have killed myself, like Hendrickja Franeker and the others. Eight out of twenty-two dead on that awful ship, even before we reached Chefoo; Hendrickja and three others taking their own lives. And the brothel was just as bad, only less filthy. But the same faces, the same slobbering, disgusting animals, the pain, the humiliation, the degrading things they forced us to do . . ." She shuddered. "I don't understand you. You saved me from drowning in despair; you gave me all this, your friendship, your protection. Now you turn me away, back into prostitution."

"Nonsense! A concubine is not a prostitute. Wherever did you get such a foolish notion? Virgins are selected to serve as concubines. Many live their whole lives, die at ninety and never even see a man, let alone share one's bed. The eunuchs will protect you. You have nothing to fear. You'll be safer than you are in the streets of the city." He went on at his persuasive best, trotting out all his arguments.

She closed her ears. When she spoke, her words came measured, with all the deliberation of a carefully rehearsed confession, her eyes fixed on the toes of his boots. "I want to go home to my parents, to Providence. I've asked you before, and you don't listen or you change the subject or you make some excuse, always a different one but never any that makes sense. I ask you this, and be honest: If you put me out, why should you care where I go? What's the difference if I go home? Would it hurt you, deprive you? Please, Kuo-cheng, let me go. You'll be rid of me forever. Please, I beg you." Sinking to her knees, she threw her arms around his legs, pressing her cheek against his knee. "I'll do anything you ask; just let me go home. Say you will, please, please . . ."

"Deir-dre."

Shooting to her feet, she seized his hands, squeezing

them, pleading with him. "Is it so much to ask? Whatever I borrow, I promise I'll pay you back. My father will; he's very rich. He'll pay you ten times what you advance me, a *hundred* times." Hope welled in her heart, hurrying her words. "I wouldn't need much. If I could get to Shanghai, I could board a ship—American, British, anything—to San Francisco, even to Australia. From there—"

"Be quiet!" he snapped. "Stop babbling like a fool. You're not leaving and that's final. I've explained, you've listened, you understand, you're not stupid. Accept it. Be realistic. If you tried to get to the coast, you'd be kidnaped, your throat cut before you even reached Tientsin."

"Not if you were with me. Or if you can't go, some friend going to Shanghai, Hong Kong—"

"Enough!" His sallowness was giving way to the red of anger, his small jaw jutting forward, his eyes blazing.

Deirdre had never seen him lose his temper before. It was as if he had no such emotion, as if surrendering to such a display were beneath him. It frightened her to see him so.

Flinging his arms about, he began striding up and down, yelling, citing her stupidity, her ingratitude, criticizing himself for being softhearted, overly generous, wasting his consideration, his kindness. "You owe me the air you breathe! Have you no conscience? Answer me!"

"You know how grateful I am. How many times have I told you?"

"If this is gratitude, I am a coolie—better, a coolie's donkey—a brainless fool who has done everything in his power to give you happiness and security. Ten thousand girls in Peking alone would give their eyes to take your place."

"Please stop shouting."

He was about to continue, reconsidered and, with a supreme effort of will, managed to get control of himself, pounding his thighs with his fists to achieve it. Turning his back on her, he spoke quietly. "I am a scholar, Hwŏy'an, a teacher of the classics, a learned man approaching his fifty-fifth year but with very little to show for my dedication and effort." He half-laughed bitterly. "All I own in this world is this house and the furnishings, such as they are. Measured by the standards of the Imperial Court, I am the height of a brick above poverty and the dismal insignificance poverty breeds. But, with a little luck, it could all change."

He turned to her; a smile that impressed her as almost apologetic drew his lips away from his teeth. His eyes brightened and a faraway look filled them. "If I were to be appointed to office, perhaps made *Sieuquen* of a city of the third order . . . not even that, just to be appointed to the eighth class, to be able to wear the button of brass gilt, to reach out and grasp the ladder, from such a position I could move up on merit." He shook his head sadly. "Were I a Tatar, I could have had such an honor at the age of five or six. Instead, I am a Chinese, a nameless, faceless scholar cursed by the absence of hereditary influence. The years go by; I sink deeper and deeper into the mass of people, no father to pull me up, no son whose courage and heroism in battle might elevate me. All I have is you."

"So why force me into slavery?"

"Not slavery, child, the court. You will be in the service of Tz'u Hsi herself. Far removed from the throne, perhaps, but inside the golden circle nevertheless, reflecting her smile. She has a soft spot in her heart for concubines. She herself was one once. Don't you understand, child? You'll be where a word in the right ear, a subtle suggestion—"

"I should have known," she said. "I *am* stupid, deaf and dumb. I should have stopped to think. I would have realized that my kindly benefactor had an ax to grind. Doesn't everybody?"

"I don't like that," he said testily. "Mind your tongue."

"Forgive me: Kuo-cheng's candor is so praiseworthy it's contagious. So I'm to become a concubine to help you to the ladder and up it. As if I, the *wàigworén** of Hibiscus Lane, could possibly do anything."

"You could."

"Her Majesty Tz'u Hsi detests foreigners—everybody knows that—the Americans, the British, the French, even the Japanese."

He nodded. "True. But how could she hate you?"

"How could anyone hate a pretty prostitute?"

Back came his anger, like a whip cracking in her face. "You must never say that word! Never tell a living soul where I found you. Not a whisper about that ship, Chefoo, any of it. As far as anyone knows, you are the daughter of my American trader friend in Chefoo. Your father died of fever and left you orphaned. His last request was that I bring you up as my own daughter. I warn you, Deirdre, if anyone ever learns the truth, the two of us will be lucky if we're decapitated instead of beaten to death. To foist off a prostitute for service as a royal concubine would be an outright insult to Her Majesty, worse than slandering her to her face. Do you understand me?"

"Yes."

"You will give me your solemn word never to tell— *never.*"

She nodded, sighing wearily.

He softened his tone. "I have given you everything I have to give in preparation for this," he went on. "You have been an apt pupil, cooperative, a good daughter. In exchange, I ask only that you use your position in my behalf. There is nothing devious about such a . . . policy. Everyone who can does it. You can be sure I'll be a credit to the judgment of the official who recommends my appointment."

* "Foreigner."

It was disarmingly simple, she thought; one hand washes the other. Under the circumstances he'd created, how could he possibly help her to get out of China, this kindly, considerate, so very moral man who had saved her life?

He smiled enigmatically. It was intended to reassure her, but for the first time in the eight months she had known him, she saw something in his eyes other than kindliness: the clearly discernible glint of ambition. She clasped her hands in front of her, lowering her eyes in an attitude of submission, fatalistic surrender. He covered her hands with his own and kissed her on the forehead.

"I will send in Tang-yü."

He left the room, and she turned back to her mirror. As soon as the door was closed, she was overcome by a wave of listlessness of the sort she imagined old people felt, their spent bodies burdened too long with too great a weight; a peculiar, unfamiliar exhaustion that crushed her spirit and spread sadness through her heart as the bed pillow spread the scent of roses to the corners of the room.

She felt so very much older than her 16 years.

II

Tang-yü shuffled in, bearing a large bronze basin of hot water and wet and dry towels. Deirdre responded to her greeting and, removing her pajamas, stepped into the basin, permitting Tang-yü to bathe her, then dry and massage her with rose petals, scented herbs and precious essences. She sat naked in a towel on the *chaise percée,* and her scalp was rubbed with oils and pomades under her flowing red hair. Then, putting on her favorite robe of orange silk emblazoned with flights of swallow-tailed butterflies, she returned to her vanity. Her hair was gathered up from the nape into an enormous, weighty decoration of jewels, shaped like flowers and insects fanning outward on either side and hung with tassels of pearl. Her face was sprayed with a mixture of glycerine and honeysuckle, blush added to her eyelids, and her eyes outlined with kohl. The long nails of her third and little fingers on both hands were then shielded with jade, and she was dressed in beautiful dragon robes.

Tang-yü babbled without letup in her shrill, tinderdry voice. She was a tiny creature, her shoulders perpetually sagging, her little face overrun with lines and wrinkles, deep, shadowed furrows abutting each other down the planes of her cheeks, across her throat and around the visible portion of her neck.

Her daughter, Nalute, a younger physical version of Tang-yü, came in bringing breakfast: a bowl of hot milk sweetened with honey and almonds, and lotus-root porridge. Deirdre was not hungry, and her response to the two women's urgings to eat was to down less than half the contents of each bowl.

"You seem sad, Hwǒy'an," said Tang-yü, searching her eyes. "This day you should not be sad. To live at the Imperial Court in the Purple City—"

"In the light of Susie's radiant smile, I know," interrupted Deirdre, smiling wistfully at her corruption of the empress's name. She turned to Nalute, who was fussing with the pearls in her hair, and took her by the wrist. "You go in my place, Nalute."

"You joke," said the girl, freeing her arm. "Common servants can never hope to see the inside of the Forbidden City. You are the first I have ever known to go and live there."

"I wish one of you could come with me."

"We will, but only through the Gate of the Zenith," said Tang-yü. "Then we will be replaced by eunuchs."

"How can men serve a woman?"

Nalute tittered behind her hand, and her mother slapped it. "Quiet, you silly cow. Hwǒy'an knows that the eunuchs are not men. A eunuch leaves his manhood on the edge of the surgeon's knife outside the gate."

"For six taels* they become crows." Nalute tapped her throat with her fingertips, cawing loudly. Tang-yü tittered.

"Why do they do it?" asked Deirdre. "It makes no more sense than binding the feet, crippling oneself for life."

"A eunuch becomes a eunuch to become as rich as a prince," said Tang-yü. "Can you think of a better reason?"

"Rich? At ten taels a month, their food and a place to sleep?"

Tang-yü's response to this was a patronizing smirk.

* *Chinese money of account equivalent to 575.8 grains of silver; approximately 70 cents in 1867.*

With the patient indulgence a mother would accord a small child, she explained: "There are more than three thousand eunuchs serving in the Forbidden City. They have great power and influence. Most become as rich as princes. Which is the real reason they choose the surgeon's knife, to escape the misery and poverty in which so many of our people spend their lives.

"Works of art, antiques, silk, fur, jade and jewels come into their hands in an endless stream. Nobody in the royal family pays any attention. Then, too, a palace eunuch can legally take a percentage of all the money that passes through his hands. If his job is to purchase rice or grain or wood for construction or the services of craftsmen or laborers, he takes his cut, which can be thousands of taels.

"The concubines cannot leave the city, but eunuchs can, as long as they return by sunset when the gates are closed. Some of them buy and keep homes in Peking. Some even take wives and adopt children to save face; for everyone, except those they serve, despises them and makes fun of them," she said, closing her disquisition.

Discussion of the eunuchs, gossip and ribald humor regarding them continued as Tang-yü and Nalute primped and fussed over Deirdre's hair, robes and jewels. She encouraged the conversation, not out of curiosity alone, but to take her mind off the events pending and the future in store for her. Her eyes strayed to her bed, and her heart sank at the thought that she would never sleep in it again. Never again would she see this room, this house, Kuo-cheng and the servants —nor anything outside the walls of the Forbidden City.

She was sitting here, being exquisitely done up, from hair to jeweled slippers, awaiting her escort and the short journey by sedan chair through the many gates into the city. All that she could remember of the world outside of China was already beginning to fade. The last she had seen of her mother had been down at the docks in Batavia. Closing her eyes, divesting the women's chatter of her attention, she envisioned her mother standing at the rail of the *Sea Urchin,* waving, blowing kisses as the whistle shrilled and the paddle wheels began churning, the black water raising catherine wheels of foam, pushing the little vessel away from the dock and westward toward the Sunda Strait; heading for Tasmania and Macquarie Harbor in search of her father.

At the time, watching the little vessel grow smaller and smaller against the sun-bleached sky, she knew that it would be ages before she saw her mother and father again—if she were to see her father ever.

The days had become weeks and Deirdre had waited patiently in Batavia with Anna and Hendrickja Franeker at the family's rubber plantation outside the city—to everyone's ultimate regret, because when the followers of Dipå Negörå in Batavia suddenly rose in revolt, the plantation had been one of the first areas attacked. The buildings and trees were burned, the men and older boys murdered, the women and girls seized, ravaged and left for dead or sold. Deirdre and Hendrickja and Anna were sold to the Chinese pirates whose ship lay at anchor in the bay, pirates who had temporarily forsaken the pillaging of ships and seaside towns and villages in favor of a fling at the prosperous slave trade.

Who would have heard her story and not have said that she was lucky to be alive? Was she? Or was Hendrickja, who had been raped and tortured so viciously, pummeled and punished, beaten about the breasts and buttocks with slender bamboo rods until the thread of reason anchoring her mind had snapped, and madness as stark and unreasoning as that afflicting a rabid dog had taken possession of her?

With the others, Deirdre had looked on helplessly as Hendrickja had sunk her teeth into first one wrist, then the other, the blood spurting forth. Screaming in frustration, they had watched as she held her hands over her head, allowing the crimson flow to spill down upon her upturned face. Within minutes she had slumped over dead. When two of the slavers came to feed them and discovered her, they were as concerned as a drunken carriage driver who had accidentally run over a stray cat. Unshackling the poor creature, they had carried her up the stairs to the afterdeck and flung her over the gunwale, leaving a pool of blood circled by her empty shackles. Her sister Anna began sobbing continuously, hour after hour, day and night, all the way up the South China Sea, week after wearyingly wretched week, until her voice became as thin as a baby bird's. She was still whimpering when the ship reached Chefoo, their captors unshackled them, they put on the filthy rags that had once been their clothing and were hurried up to the auction block set up on deck. To whom Anna was sold, what had happened to her, where she was now, whether she was alive or dead, Deirdre would never know. But bought and paid for and led away, she had still been whimpering.

Tang-yü and Nalute were continuing to hover about her like two hummingbirds about a succulent flower when Kuo-cheng opened the door. Beaming broadly, he clapped his hands and announced the arrival of the imperial heralds. Deirdre could hear the growing clamor in the street as the crowd gathered outside the shaded window. Kuo-cheng raised the shade, revealing the imperial-yellow carts of the carriers.

The Empress Tz'u Hsi was choosing for her nephew, the young prince, his harem for the day, and Hwǒy'an, the *waìgworén*, was among those fortunates commanded to appear. His thin chest threatening to burst the buttons and seams of his waistcoat with pride, Kuo-cheng took Deirdre by the hand and led her out of the room to the street door. The assembling crowd had grown so large, the entire lane was blocked in both directions to the corners and beyond. A courier unrolled his scroll and read aloud in Chinese in a bored voice, completing the summons, rolling up his scroll and gesturing her with it into her waiting chair.

She sat cross-legged, her lovely robes pulled snugly about her against the freezing air. The sky was bleak overhead, the glowering gray of an angry sea, as if the gods were indicating disapproval of the mortal goings-on below. Kuo-cheng smiled and waved, and the heralds pushed forward, separating the gawking onlookers. The procession resumed its walk through the city. Intruding itself upon the horizon from a plain situated among vast groves of white pines, Peking was located less than 100 miles south of the Great Wall. From Prospect Hill, the heavily wooded city stretched toward the White Dagoba, reaching cloudward like a gigantic bobbin and dominating the purple-walled Imperial City. Into Hung-wei-Lu, a considerably broader street but no less crowded, the procession headed, threading its way out of the Chinese City toward the Tatar City contiguous to it. Locked into the surging mass of people, the column pressed onward in the direction of Chíen Men, the central gate of the Tatar City. Passing through the gate, they entered upon the broad central street of the city, where the crowd thinned slightly and a feverish turbulence, encouraged by the relative spaciousness of the street, was initiated. The odors of tobacco and garlic, meats boiling and roasting, soy and ginseng stabbed at her nostrils. Barrows and carts trundled along, thudding against one another. Mules and donkeys staggered past, their masters thrashing them with sticks, oblivious of the wall of humanity slowing progress and the back-breaking loads all but crushing the creatures. Fat-lipped, stupid-eyed camels plodded by, their massive bellies swaying against pedestrians, jamming them into tight little knots that sprang loose once the beast had passed. Flanking both sides of the street were unbroken lines of stalls and mat-shed booths clustered three and four deep, their pennants, proclaiming their wares, streaming grandly in the breeze. Beggars abounded, infecting the crowd like maggots attacking meat. Peddlers supporting yokes with panniers piled with fans and paper toys, clay figures, silk handkerchiefs, tea, thread and needles, candies, rice cakes and doughnuts cried out, whistled, thumped small drums and tooted pipes to engage the attention of passersby. Night-soil merchants, their heavy jars filled with human and animal waste balanced on their shoulders, added their foul odor to the awesome stench. Quack doctors and scribes squatted at their little tables; jugglers and acrobats in curiously odd and imaginatively contrived costumes displayed their talents; puppeteers and storytellers, barbers and soup sellers, astrologers, poets, fortune-tellers and uniformed police, menders of everything from porcelain to fractured bones jostled and shoved and lent their voices to the indistinguishable chorus rising into the winter sky.

Mandarins' attendants preceding their masters cleared the way, flicking their bamboo rods. Higher officials, princes and ministers rode in sedans of various colors, every conceivable color but imperial yellow.

The street over which they traveled, like all the streets of the city, was cleansed of its sewage by flushing down day and night and by spring and autumn rains, but the squalor survived, creating a slovenliness that was enough to turn the stomach of any onlooker not inured to the sight. Most of the buildings appeared on the verge of collapse. Vehicles were old, dilapidated, creaky-wheeled and in need of paint and repair. The people were, for the most part, ragged and wretched-looking, malnourished, diseased, continually picking lice from their hair and shabby clothing.

And yet, time and again, Kuo-cheng had insisted that from the convenient height of Prospect Hill, Peking resembled a fairyland overflowing with flowering trees and lovely shrubbery, with the dazzlingly bright gold of the imperial-yellow tiles of the Forbidden City, the full spectrum of colors displayed in the enamels of the palaces, gatehouses and temple roofs, the azure and emerald and scarlet of pavilions and artistically fashioned upturned eaves. The city was, he assured her, comparable to a royally robed mendicant seen from afar; close up, his filthy face and hands, the noxious odors of his body, his rotten teeth and foul breath immediately dispelled the first impression.

The sedan chair jounced along under the grip of her four bearers, and the commingling of rot and beauty, raggedness, poverty, wealth and grandeur, faded from awareness. It was cold even for early March, the harsh winter's lingering presence still manifest in the icy wind gathered in the Gobi, sweeping over the Khingan mountain range, scaling the Great Wall and assaulting the city. Snow crusted the rooftops; frozen brown and yellow slush lined the pavement against the walls. It was winter outside Deirdre's eyes and inside her heart and soul. The knifelike wind whipped through the rounded corridors of her heart, chilling her blood, filling her body with its frigidity, sending a tremor soundlessly crackling up her spine.

The cities were Chinese boxes, one inside the other, inside another. Within the Tatar City, slightly off center in relation to it, stood the Imperial City, the doors and windows and special stone for its palaces fetched from the plundered former capital of Kaifeng, brought to their present site in hundreds of single wagons pulled by as many as 500 men. The smaller Forbidden City was built inside the Imperial City, enclosed within 36-foot-high walls surrounded by a moat and rendered accessible by gates on all four sides.

Now the procession made its way slowly over the ice-shielded waters of the moat surrounding the Imperial City, passing through the T'ien an Men and down the spaciously wide and beautiful I-ho-yüan-Lu, through a maze of pagodas and garden retreats, pavilions, temples and living quarters, to a second moat, beyond which rose the open Gate of the Zenith, set with four impressive towers. Crossing over the second moat, the procession entered the Forbidden City.

Despite her downcast mood, it was to Deirdre an awesome sight. The buildings, each one seemingly more imposing and magnificent than the other, stood on individual raised terraces of marble. Fringed by covered balustrades and facing the broad courtyards of Yunnan marble, close-up sight of them seized her breath—as it did that of both Tang-yü and Nalute, standing on either side of her chair. A swarm of palace eunuchs were gathered at one side; two approached Deirdre, the two women giving way to them.

"Farewell, Hwŏy'an," whispered Tang-yü in a tone that threatened to crack as each syllable issued from her mouth. Nalute did not echo her mother's words. Instead, she hung her head, finding the corner of one eye with a knuckle.

And like wisps of smoke caught by an errant breeze, they were gone, slipping through the massed eunuchs who by now had surrounded the concubines-elect. Deirdre had obeyed the command to relinquish her chair and stand. She turned around and called after Tang-yü and Nalute; but they either failed to hear her or pretended not to. Sighing, she turned back and surveyed the Supreme Imperial Gate directly ahead beyond the bridges over the solidly frozen River of Golden

Water. To the left stood the Imperial Storehouses, to the right the Halls of Literary Glory. Crystal-armored, ground to roofs, with snow, the area within the scope of her vision appeared as beautiful and formidable a prison as the mind of man could conceive.

Her prison, for the rest of her days.

III

The rain rattled against the oriel window looking out upon the winter-ravaged rose garden. The elderly man sat stiffly on the window seat, ramrod straight, thumb and index fingertips massaging the inner corners of his eyes, his spectacles in his other hand, resting on one knee. His companion, half his age, tall, his sweat-stained shirt stretched to its limit over the sinewy expanse of his chest, ran a hand through his hair and resumed pacing.

"I wish you'd sit, Ross," said the older man, restoring his glasses to his nose and fixing him with a look of authority. "You're tiring me out."

"I'm glad you're able to find something amusing in all this, Alex."

"Oh, shut up! You're not talking to one of your shipyard slaves. I'm as concerned, as involved in this, as you are."

Ross exhaled in a manner suggesting his breath carried with it some small portion of the frustration besetting him, relieving some of the pressure. "I'm sorry."

"Sit."

Ross complied, slumping wearily into a chair directly across from Alexander Craven. snatching up his brandy and emptying the glass in one gulp.

"Does that help?" asked Craven.

"I have one cloudy, unpolishable facet of character, Alex: I can't stand feeling helpless. It makes me want to break things. Standing by, my hands hanging, staring, watching my wife bend one way then the other, like a bulrush in the wind. Worst of all is not knowing when

33

the lucid stage is to end. Sometimes I think that when she's making sense, when she can smile and laugh and respond and talk clearly, when she's not staring or hiding her cheek in the pillow when you speak to her . . . God in heaven, I don't even know what I said to start this!" Up on his feet again, he resumed pacing.

Dr. Craven made no comment. He swiveled on his seat to look out over the garden beyond the wall to the narrow, twisting path leading to the foothills a quarter-mile distant. A woodchuck trundled across the path, patently oblivious of the downpour, and disappeared into the pines.

"I'm going up!" snapped Ross.

"No you don't!"

So forceful was the doctor's tone, so unexpectedly commanding coming from one so small and unimposing in appearance, Ross caught himself and stared. "Alex . . ."

"Give him another five minutes, please. And ring for some brandy." Craven held up his empty glass.

Ross went to the bell cord and jerked it once. Thursby appeared almost immediately, his watery-blue eyes peering out of his albescent face threaded with tiny veins.

"Bring in the decanter, Thursby, please."

"Yes, sir." He floated away.

Craven watched him go in amusement. Oddly, whenever he thought of Blackwood, the maples marshaled protectingly around this great and sprawling insinuation on the landscape, as he privately called it, Dandridge "Castle" crowning the hill overlooking Providence, Thursby was the first resident to appear in his mind. Probably because Thursby most always opened the front door for him. The two of them had served the Dandridges, grandfather, father, son, wives, relatives, Ross and Lisa's daughter, Deirdre, and the lesser members of the household staff for nearly 40 years. He and the wraith that walked like a man had something very much in common, mused Craven, this family Dandridge, what was left of it. He and Ross Dandridge likewise shared something in common: the omnipresent, devilishly infuriating feeling of utter and abject helplessness in the face of the present crisis.

Searching Ross out halfway around the world, with the help of the captain and crew of a small Dutch freighter, Lisa had plucked him out of the icy waters at the Gates of Hell in Macquarie Harbor and brought him back to Batavia. Within days Ross's health, mind and body, had been completely restored. The two of them had only to return to Batavia in Java, where their 15-year-old daughter, Deirdre, waited in the captain's home. But during their absence an insurrection had taken place in Batavia, and upon returning, they were told that their daughter had been taken away by slavers.

On top of the long and exhausting search and Ross's eventual rescue, the strain of losing Deirdre had proven too much for Lisa. The crushing pressures with which fate had burdened her suddenly became more than she could tolerate. Her mind had given way. And Ross, himself only just recovered, had had no alternative but to get her home as speedily as sail could carry them.

It had been a decision he had not hesitated to make, which made it no less difficult. But, he had reasoned, to begin searching for Deirdre immediately, to leave Lisa under a doctor's care and go thrashing off into the black wilderness of the Orient, would have been foolhardy. Captain Franeker had agreed. Everyone with whom he had talked had agreed: told him with their eyes that it would have been foolhardy because Deirdre was already dead. *That* he hadn't been able to accept. His decision therefore rankled him, and continued to as he'd sailed for San Francisco with Lisa.

The mind unhinged, as Alex Craven had recently observed, was a curious entity. As speedily as a human can embrace madness, he or she can exchange it for sanity. At least temporarily it was to happen to Lisa. On the voyage, a week out of the East Indies, she began to emerge from the grip of the monster and behaved normally for long periods, frequently days at a time, before sinking back.

During those early stretches of sanity, realizing that Deirdre had vanished, she had insisted they turn back, return to Batavia and initiate a search. Quietly but firmly, Ross had argued against such a course, with the result that by the time the ship had reached San Francisco, Lisa, when lucid, was no longer speaking to him. This he accepted.

By the time he was able to get her home to Blackwood, she was badly run down, nervous, moody, wrenching back and forth between normalcy and acute melancholia. Only Craven's periodic injections kept her from going off the deep end completely.

He had examined her on their first day back. Most of the symptoms of melancholia were present—malaise, insomnia, indigestion, constipation, with little appetite. However, she was constantly thirsty. Craven had then called in Dr. Howard Cairns, of the Butler Hospital for the Insane in Providence, to corroborate his findings. Cairns was upstairs with her now.

Thursby returned with the brandy, pouring for both of them, going out, closing the door. Ross was becoming more and more restless, glancing at his watch, heaping muttered damnation upon the weather, taking a book down from a shelf, opening it in one hand, slamming it shut just as quickly, putting it back and bolting his brandy as if it were ice water.

"What in hell is taking so long?" he barked. "And why aren't you up there with him? Shouldn't you be?"

Craven frowned. "Ask Howard your first question when he comes down. You know the answers to the other two."

"He sees to her mind; you see to her body. Very commendable, but I should think you'd occasionally want to compare notes."

"We do!" exclaimed Craven testily. "We're not *competing* with each other." For the first time he hurled down his brandy. "We just don't trespass on each other's territory. We agreed at the start and we're sticking to it."

"I wish to God it would stop raining. It seems like it's been going on for six weeks. It's so damp in this mausoleum I can almost feel water running down my back."

"It's nervous perspiration. You shouldn't need a doctor to tell you that."

Striding to the bell cord, Ross jerked it twice.

"Pull it loose, why don't you?"

"Mind your own goddamned—"

The door opened. Thursby held his chin up affectedly, his thin lips pursed, his eyes blinking. Ross shrunk him with a frown.

"Light the fires, will you?"

"They're lit, sir, all four. And cook has both stoves on. It's very damp. Shall I leave this door open?"

A gentle creaking sound was audible overhead. Dr. Cairns descended the stairs, sliding his impressively large red hand down the polished banister. A big man, twice Craven's size and less than half his age, he looked to Ross more like an overweight athlete stuffed into a cassimere suit two sizes too small for him. He was from Maine, and his down-east accent lingered, converting horse to "huss," road to "rud," and conveying the impression of a well-dressed feed-and-grain salesman rather than the foremost alienist in the east, as Craven consistently described him.

Exercising the discretion of his calling, Thursby withdrew.

"How is she?" asked Ross.

"Better, better. Alex, I took the liberty of giving her something to get her to sleep." He looked at Craven for approval and got a noncommittal grimace from him, his lower lip forcing upward, arching his mouth. "She's putting on weight. Her color's improving."

Ross resisted commenting. He offered him a brandy. Cairns declined.

"We had a long talk about your experiences, what happened to your daughter. The first time we really got into that part of it. Lisa wants very much to go back to the Orient to look for her."

Ross thrust out his arm, dismissing the idea. "That's all she talks about. I wish there was some way we could get it out of her head. It's what's holding her back from recovery."

Cairns sat down in the window seat alongside Craven. The wind suddenly caught the rain, lifting it horizontally, shooting it against the glass like buckshot. Cairns stared at Ross.

"I agree, Mr. Dandridge. Have you thought about looking for your daughter?"

The question offended Ross. "I've been in constant touch with the State Department since the day we got back. Senator Evan Brockway is a close personal friend. He's worked like a Trojan. He assures me inquiries have been made in virtually every city and town, from Wellington, New Zealand, to Vladivostok. If she's alive—"

" 'If'?" Cairns stared.

"Doctor, she was taken in slavery. I don't have to draw pictures for you. So, under the circumstances, I have to be realistic. There's one chance in a thousand she's still alive, one in ten thousand. But, of course, as long as there's any chance at all, we'll continue to search." His voice took on a bitter edge. "Strangely enough, it isn't the odds or even that there's practically half the world to cover."

"She's got to be in China," said Craven, interrupting. "And regardless of how terrible her situation, keep in mind she's more valuable to them alive than dead. Common sense—"

"Don't mention common sense to me," said Ross

irritably. "I've come to believe there's no such animal."
He shrugged. "Still, if Deirdre is alive, as I was about to
say, it isn't the odds or the expanse of area that's got to
be covered; the biggest stumbling block is turning out
to be China. We can't seem to move an inch there. They
hate Americans with a passion. British, French, any
foreigners. Evan Brockway claims they all talk in circles, as pleasant, as mannerly as can be—but completely uncooperative. I hate that country so, I get sick
to my stomach talking about it. It's gotten so every
time I pass an Oriental on the street, I want to grab
him and wring his neck. Do you two know I never even
saw her? Not since she was a baby!"

"Your wife insists she's alive and in China," said
Cairns.

"I know; I've heard her say it a hundred times."

"Being one of your doctors, I can't help thinking
what would be best for our patient, outside of treatment. medication. Obviously. the best thing of all would
be to restore her peace of mind. Have you thought about
going back to look for your daughter?"

"Didn't you ask me that already? Doctor, what in the
world do you take me for? She's my flesh and blood. I'd
give my life to get her back here. I'd go in a minute but
for Lisa. I can't leave her; I can't bring myself to. Joining the navy during the war when I didn't even have to
was the biggest blunder of my life the stupidest thing
I've ever done. All this started with that decision. If it
hadn't been for her, her grit, her tenacity, loyalty . . .
God in heaven, she was amazing. That's the only word
for it. I'd be dead and buried in that hellhole in Tasmania. I swore when I got my memory back, even
before this rotten business with Deirdre, I'd never let
Lisa out of my sight again. But don't imagine I don't
have any feelings for my daughter. This nightmare is
tearing me to pieces!"

"I think I'll have a bit of brandy now," said Dr.
Cairns, "if I may."

Ross poured him a glass, refilling his own and Craven's. Cairns sipped and eyed Ross over the rim of his glass. "Delicious. Benedictine?"

"Don't ask me. Whatever it is, it's hot, goes down smoothly and loosens some of the knots."

Cairns cleared his throat, his heavy pink features arranging themselves in a grim expression. "When I said 'you' before, I meant you *and* Mrs. Dandridge. The two of you going back to look for your daughter."

"You're not serious."

"Perfectly."

Ross drank, turning from Cairns as he did so. "Alex . . ."

"Let him say what he has to, Ross. Dig down and bring up a little patience for a change."

"Dr. Cairns, my wife is in no condition for travel, not to Boston, let alone halfway around the world. It was hard enough getting her back here. You can't imagine how much it took out of her."

"I can imagine," said Cairns. "Please bear with me. Call me a fool when I'm finished, but let me talk. Putting aside the problem of your daughter and any trip back for the moment, let's talk about your wife. She's ill; she's well. She's lucid; she's rambling or withdrawn and unresponsive. She has her faculties or they slip away."

"You say she's getting better."

"She improves; she slips back. It's as if she were walking down a narrow hallway so dark she can't see. She bumps her left shoulder, bumps her right. Disturbed, normal, disturbed, normal. We can't anticipate what her condition will be from one day to the next. Most unfortunate of all, it's possible the hallway can stretch all the way to the end of her days."

"I don't believe that!"

"I don't want to, but it could happen. Alex . . ." Cairns turned to Craven.

"He's right, Ross."

"She's an unusual human being," continued Cairns. "To be honest, I've never seen a patient with so much self-discipline, so powerful a will." He made a fist before his face. "When her mind is in her grasp, when it's working for her instead of against her, she wants to be well, to heal, to hang onto normalcy—which makes her the best doctor she can have, with the most cooperative patient. The sticky thing is that, by its very nature, her condition refuses to permit her to get the best of it. It fights back. It wins, it loses, but it stubbornly resists eradication. To get rid of it, regardless of how hard she fights, she has to have help."

"Taking her back there won't help her. If anything, it'll push her over the edge."

"I disagree," said Cairns quietly. "Most emphatically. She wants to go. You must remember, she's a mother. There's a yearning there, a driving urge so powerful there isn't a man alive who can measure it accurately, who can even understand it. It's peculiarly female, as if the umbilical cord is never actually severed."

Ross cut in. "But be realistic, man! Say we do go back. We start looking, buttonholing officials, traipsing from town to town, moving heaven and earth to get an audience with the empress—which, believe me, is impossible. What happens if we search for ten years, for the rest of our lives, and never find her? Can you imagine the effect that would have on Lisa?

"Or what if lightning should strike, what if by some miracle we *were* able to track Deirdre down? What if it turns out she's dead? It has to be the probability. Common sense—"

"There's no such animal," said Craven.

Ross paid no attention to him, bulling forward, flinging his hands for emphasis, his face a sullen mask. "Oh, I can see that hope and anticipation, getting on a ship, getting over there, all of it could lift her up. But the higher she's lifted, the farther she can fall. And that fall could kill her! Don't tell me it couldn't. Is that the chance the two of us are supposed to take? Does it come down to one toss of a coin?"

Cairns set his empty glass on the tray beside the decanter and studied the floor. When he spoke, he avoided Ross's eyes, continuing to pretend he was examining the carpet. "Mr. Dandridge, *you* can make the decision or you can sidestep it. avoid it altogether. Unfortunately for you, she refuses to."

"She brought it up and you encouraged the idea, is that it?"

"That's not it." The doctor's florid features deepened in color. "You don't have a very lofty opinion of me, do you? Or is that how you feel about doctors in general?" He turned to the window. "It seems to be letting up. I've got to get back."

"Ross . . ." Craven began.

"I apologize," said Ross. "I had no right implying . . . I'm sorry. I know you're doing the best you can."

"Aren't we all?" asked Cairns. "Except your wife. Not that she isn't trying. If she had a smidgen of cooperation . . ."

"Touché," said Ross.

"She's suggested going back to you, hasn't she?" Cairns asked Ross.

"You know she has," he replied. "Many times. Look, maybe I *am* being overly protective. but what you're asking seems so . . . radical and dangerous. I think it's the worst possible thing we could do."

"I think it makes sense," said Craven airily. Ross fixed him with a look that said "You would." Craven pretended not to notice. He went on: "If she sticks to her diet, if we see that she continues to get enough sleep, even if induced—the Veronal—keep a close watch on her temperature and pulse rate, I would say, from strictly the physical standpoint, there's no reason not to go back."

"Not tomorrow," said Cairns. "But if you decided

now to leave in a month or six weeks, I'll bet my bottom dollar you'd see tremendous improvement. Hope is one of nature's most versatile medicines. It can work wonders."

Ross pondered his words. "We'll see. We've got to talk a lot more. We have to consider every possible angle. It still scares me out of my shoes."

Cairns smiled. "Let's have another brandy, and talk."

IV

The flowers strewn across the generous expanse of the toile canopying the bed threatened to tear free and tumble down upon the counterpane, so Lisa imagined staring up at them through eyelids flickering, willingly surrendering to sleep. Blessed sleep, beautiful sleep, mercifully introduced into her stubborn consciousness by Dr. Cairns. This will help you sleep—sleep only, no nightmares, no chilling incubi this time. She was so exhausted; she wanted so to sleep, sleep. . . .

The wide walnut tester bed slowly elevated itself, floating, the footposts renouncing their solidity, the walls of the room swimming, the windows, slightly ajar, admitting fresh air and the steady patter of the rain, dissolving into a blur that brightened, then faded, giving way to a black cloud. It rolled into the room, shaping itself to the corners. Erased by its arrival were the walls and furnishings, the bedposts, the canopy, the flowers. The cloud gathered about her. The rain grew louder, louder, like sticks rattling snare drums thumping in unison. Closer, louder still. The cloud seeped into her brain, the rain drilling, pounding louder, louder. . . .

Rising, threatening to puncture her eardrums, the sound suddenly began losing its loudness, becoming fainter, fading, reducing itself to silence. Darkness. Blackness so impenetrable it seemed like stone moved in on all sides, closing around her, head to foot. Shrinking, tightening, an adamantine envelope surrounding her, cutting off the last breath. Choking, gurgling deep down.

Her brain burst. A horrendous crashing sound. The

stone shattered, uncasing her, falling away, the blackness rushing in. Silence.

In the distance a purple dot appeared against the blackness. It came closer, enlarging, a face taking shape. Eyes opened to the hideous stare of a cockatrice, horrifying, chilling, a skull floating, hovering over her, its eyes impaling her, setting her to trembling with fear. She tried to close her eyes and could not—could not turn her head; could not lift her hands to block out the sight; could not move her arms or legs.

Light gleamed directly overhead, the blade of a knife catching illumination from some unseen source poised above her, preparing to drive downward. Screaming silently, she tore her eyes from it, looking down the length of her prostrate body. Her stomach rose; she was pregnant. The pains began lancing through her. The baby stirred, the stretched-taut flesh of her stomach yielding to the pressure from within. The pain was becoming increasingly severe, like hot irons thrusting and probing inside her. Down came the knife, down, down, down, with agonizing slowness. The point pricked her flesh. Blood spurted upward, crimsoning the gleaming length of the blade, sliding back down it. She blinked her eyes and the blade vanished, replaced by a scalpel.

It entered her; she could feel it twisting about, probing. Agonizing pain raced through her, filling her. She screamed as the blood gushed straight upward in a fountain, splashing down, spreading over her helpless body.

The scalpel vanished. Skeletal hands descended, entering her, digging, loosening, lifting, the blood continuing to gush out of her. Between the hands, cradled in them was her heart. The skull and hands attached themselves to a body, the heart pulsing and twisting between the hands. The terrifying eyes turned away, the hands clutching the heart swinging about.

The tight, forced, choking cry of a baby. Instantly

the blood was gone, and the pain. The hands came back into view holding a child kicking, screaming. A healthy little girl, wispy red hairs darting from her scalp, her face wizened and pink. Little legs and arms thrusting, jerking, eyes bright, blinking . . . The hands bearing her came toward Lisa, closer. closer. And now she could lift her own arms. Raising her hands above her, she accepted the child. But as she lowered her arms to bring it to her breast, it vanished, replaced by her heart writhing, contorting, fighting like a fish to free itself from her hold.

From the center of the top of its skull, the creature leaning over her split with a cracking sound, dividing itself in two, falling away on either side. Stuffing the heart inside the bloodless gaping hole in her chest, she raised herself on both elbows, then fell back exhausted, but managing a glance at her breasts. No incision, no blood, only her naked breasts glistening with perspiration.

Her eyelids became leaden, dropping, snapping shut. The thick black cloud gathered about her, closed round, shrinking, tightening, an adamantine envelope surrounding her, cutting off sight, sound, air. Suffocation, crash, pain, silence. A purple dot . . .

And again. Again. Between the dreaded, painful re-enactment, she summoned resistance, drawing it from within, amassing it, shaping it, raising and thickening a wall against the purple dot to block its approach and the hideous consequences. Thrashing about on the bed, she loosened the covers, perspiration bursting from her flesh, drenching her body as well as the bedclothes. Fighting, fighting for sleep without pain, without horror . . . Her heart restored to her chest, she raised herself, examined her breasts and fell back as before. And fought. Up went the wall to block sight of the dot in the darkness. Shutting out its coming, screening it from recognition. Her hands flew to her face. locking her eyes closed with the tips of her fingers. Willing, willing . . .

At length the cloud softened, slowly losing its blackness, a grayness that neither bound nor smothered her replacing it. The screen of her mind gone blank abruptly filled itself with a familiar sight: the cabin of the *Olympia,* the ship on which she and Ross had journeyed to the United States 17 years before—their honeymoon voyage. She saw once more interior walls paneled in rosewood and richly ornamented with imitation inlaid gold. The ceiling surrounding the large, unlit copper lamp swinging lazily overhead was as white as spume and framed with handsomely wrought molding with gilded beads. Two overstuffed chairs, with stout mahogany legs to match the sideboard and bedstead, occupied the open corners on either side of a lowboy attached, as was the sideboard, to a wall in the event of heavy seas.

Upon the silk-sheeted bed they lay naked, Lisa Allworth now Dandridge and her Ross, her curly-haired giant with his mischievous, ever-dancing brown eyes, his smile crinkling his eyes, stretching the tawny skin of his cheeks. A smile that sent out invisible waves of love that searched out and enfolded her heart in embrace. He kissed her breasts gently, ever gently, lovingly warming her body.

She slid her hands up his back, finding the long, narrow depression of his spine with the tips of her fingers, traveling it slowly to the nape of his neck, seizing his head above her, bringing his mouth down upon her own. Their lips met, firming in a passionate kiss, mouths working one against the other. His chest pressed her breasts; his hand slipped behind her back, turning her slowly toward him as he moved to the side. Now they lay on their sides facing each other, the kiss still joining them. Her free hand cupped the back of his head, then began stealing down his body, the warm expanse of his naked flesh. She could feel his member stiffening against her, its length throbbing. The fire in her loins quickened in anticipation. Their tongues drove through their open mouths, finding each other's, thrashing. Drinking love from his mouth, feeling his member, his desire infecting her, pushing tiny needles into her thighs, she freed his mouth, moving her lips to his cheek, kissing. His kiss traversed her chin, moving down her throat to her shoulder. She squealed as his teeth gripped and bit into the exposed flesh.

Now she was over on her back, the sinewy length of his powerful body suspended above her. Gripping his head, she again crushed his mouth against hers. And quivered as his throbbing member descended into the valley between her thighs, slipping slowly, deliberately forward, forward, touching, touching.

Ross, Ross . . .

She slept, without nightmare, without dreams of any sort, deep and sonorous abandonment of consciousness, divesting herself of her weariness, refilling the wells of her strength. Sleep . . . sleep . . . A day and a year. Beautiful, tender, affectionate sleep.

"Lisa darling." The gauze of slumber stripped itself from her eyes and she awoke. The rain had stopped; the breeze fluttered the curtains setting them to dancing like wraiths in the pale light of the moon. He was sitting in a chair drawn up to the bed, his face somber, his eyes wide with worry and the indelible glimmer of hope.

"Lisa, Lisa . . ."

She lifted her arms and he leaned forward, embracing her. She kissed his forehead and his cheek, and their mouths met in a long, luxurious kiss that fired every fiber of her body. She pulled herself up to a sitting position.

"What are you doing?" he asked anxiously. "Lie down"

"What time is it?"

"About ten o'clock. You've been asleep hours and hours."

"The best sleep I've had in months!" She described

its awful beginning and the sweet dreams that followed. And subsequent sleep with no dreams, terrifying or pleasant. "Darling, did Dr. Cairns tell you what we talked about? Deirdre, China, we're going back, you and I. We're going to find her. We'll start in Singapore. We'll map strategy; we'll turn the world inside out if we have to. She's alive, Ross, I know it, I feel it—as surely as I feel my heart pounding."

"Wait."

"No! We've waited too long, almost a year."

"Lisa, please, don't make it more difficult than it is already." He got up tiredly as if, she noted, lifting the weight of their problem on his broad shoulders. Going to the window, he positioned himself between the dancing curtains, staring at the starless night, continuing in a low voice.

"Cairns brought it up. Alex supports him. We three discussed it most of the afternoon."

"Discussed, or argued about it?"

"I don't like it, Lisa; I can't see it. I try, I really do. I've listened to both of them. They're very convincing, but it won't wash."

"Darling . . ."

"Let me finish, please. It comes down to two things: I can't leave you and I can't take you with me. You're in no condition to travel, you know that."

Flinging the coverlet aside, she got out of bed, joining him at the window. "Your mind's made up, is that it?"

"Lisa."

"Which is automatically supposed to make up mine. Well, it doesn't. That, Ross, is what 'won't wash.' It comes down to *one* thing: Deirdre. I refuse to go on living under a question mark like a sword hanging overhead. I'm sick to death of having my heart wrenched about, this terrible frustration welling up inside me, filling my throat, drowning me. Ross, I'm going back. Come if you like. If you don't want to, don't."

"Oh, that's marvelous! So very charitable of you.

Goddamnit, do you think I feel any less miserable about it than you? You think I don't feel any pain, any heart wrenching, any frustration? I reached a point long ago where I hate myself so much for not going after her I can't stand the sight of my face in the mirror. I see one of her baby pictures, I crumble to bits inside! Why do you suppose I carry on so, raving like an idiot, drinking myself into a stupor night after night?"

"We're going back!"

He took her in his arms. She yielded as he kissed her, dissolving in embrace.

"I'm better, Ross. Much better."

"You're not well."

"I will be. I promise."

"When you are. When the two of them can look me in the eye and tell me so, back we'll go, as fast as the wind can carry us. Until that time, we have no choice but to rely on Evan Brockway and the State Department and—"

"Please! Stop before you start on that. Ten people, a thousand, it makes no difference. They all fail; they'll continue to fail—for the same reason private detectives and money alone would have failed to get you out of Macquarie Harbor. We're the only two in this world who can find her, and we can't put it off any longer. Every day counts, every hour. Dr. Cairns said that at the rate I'm improving, in another month I'll be a hundred percent!"

"He hopes."

"We can spend that month traveling. It'll take over two months to get to Singapore; it's halfway round the world. To St. Louis, down to New Orleans, across the gulf to Vera Cruz, across Mexico, up the coast to San Francisco, nine thousand miles to Singapore . . ." She searched his eyes. "Are you coming with me, Ross? Do you want to help me find her?"

"What a lovely way to put it! My darling, it's ridiculous. We'd get to Singapore and you'd be so exhausted you'd be back in bed to stay—probably fighting for your life!"

"Please, spare me the dramatics. Darling, if I *don't* go I'll end up fighting for my life."

He kissed her and sighed. Outside the window, in the heart of a colossal cloud, thunder jarred the heavens.

"I'm getting better, Ross. I'm starting to climb out of the pit." She balled her hands into fists and slammed them against her chest. "I feel it in here, where you can't lie to yourself. You can't talk yourself into things that aren't true. It's in me, this truth, it's growing. I'm going to beat it, with Cairns's help and Alex's. And yours. Don't slow me down. Bear with me and help me, darling. I'm coming back." She grasped his hands and held them tightly.

His eyes brightened with sympathy.

"You are, I can see it, honestly. Give yourself one more month."

"Do you know what you're asking?"

"Thirty days."

She sighed and smiled enigmatically but said no more about it, instead turning the conversation to discussion of late dinner and, for a welcome change, of how famished she was.

V

A week later, Ross received a letter from Senator Evan Brockway. As he sat in the library reading the lines and between them, the undisguisable discouragement all but made him groan aloud. Appeals to the Chinese government through the State Department requesting an audience with Prince Kung had been rebuffed. According to Brockway, they had elected to approach the prince for two reasons: his known tolerance of the presence of foreigners on Chinese soil, and his powerful influence with the empress. Failing to enlist his help, other high officials had been approached. None appeared interested in even discussing the matter. In the senator's view, their recalcitrance was directly traceable to an unfortunate incident that had taken place the previous year. In 1866 an American vessel had been attacked and burned in the Yellow River and her entire crew murdered. The reaction in Washington had been instantaneous. So incensed had President Johnson been that for a brief time there was talk of declaring war. Despite this threat, China had refused satisfaction. The empress's xenophobia, earlier spawned and nurtured by the aggressive behavior of English traders and French missionaries, was becoming increasingly obsessive. Every foreign nation, including neighboring Japan, was the target of her scorn. In the wake of the Yellow River incident, the United States had severed relations with the court in Peking. It was this widening abyss that Ross and Lisa or someone would be obliged to bridge, according to Brockway in his letter.

As for Lisa, in seven days her condition had im-

proved remarkably, notwithstanding Ross's lingering
concern over how well she would be able to tolerate
the rigors of a long journey. He decided that Brockway's letter could only fuel the fires of her determination. Reading it, he had been briefly tempted to destroy
it rather than show it to her. But should he neglect to,
sooner or later either the Brockways would visit them,
as they normally did when the senator came home to
Providence, and the subject of the situation in China—
and his letter—would come up, or Lisa, overcome by
curiosity as to the state of matters, might even contact
him in Washington. Furthermore, he, Ross, couldn't
possibly justify deceiving her by claiming it was in her
best interests.

She came downstairs for dinner for the second time
that week, insisting that she was up to it. It was, he
knew, a ploy to stimulate his optimism. She confessed
as much while they sat at opposite ends of the long table
in the high-backed Venetian-style chairs. attacking their
fruit compote and conversing down the line of candles
steadily consuming their wicks without a flicker.

She wore her emerald-and-white French Penang shirt-
waist, with the gathered puff-top sleeves and turn-down
collar, and a plain black Henrietta skirt, velvet-bound
and rustle-lined. Her hair hung loose, the waves framing
her beautiful face catching the candle glow and deepening its natural fire.

"You look magnificent tonight, my darling."

"Thank you, sir," she said. "And healthy?"

"You do look healthy." He narrowed his eyes, affecting suspicion. "Are your cheeks real or rouged?"

"A little of each, thank you. I saw the mail come this
morning. Anything of interest?"

"We got a letter from Evan. Sort of a summation of
all the obstacles."

"May I read it?"

"It's in the library. Later . . ."

Thursby materialized in the doorway with the serving

maid and their salad. He beamed. "May I say, madam, I'm . . . we're delighted to see you downstairs again. Permit me to say you're looking absolutely splendid."

"Permission granted. There's a letter in the library. Would you get it for me?"

"Yes, madam."

She finished the letter before her salad, nibbling at her aspic disinterestedly, engrossed in Brockway's words. Folding the letter and laying it alongside her napkin ring, she made a face and stared at her wineglass without seeing it. If she was disappointed, however, her features failed to show it. Instead she appeared to Ross to be sinking deep into thought.

"That really settles it," she said.

"I'm afraid it doesn't help a great deal."

"I mean if you want anything done, you must do it yourself." She raised her eyes and smiled thinly. "Find out the schedule for the first through train New York to St. Louis. We'll start packing tonight."

"We have only three weeks to go."

"No, Ross, tomorrow."

"All right, all right. Before we start arguing, before we say or do anything, before we set one foot out the door, Cairns and Alex will have to examine you. The decision is theirs, not yours, not mine. Agreed?"

She hesitated, her eyes narrowing, her lips turning up slightly in the suggestion of a smile. "We'll see."

"Damnit! You have to have it that way, don't you!"

"What way?"

"You and me head to head, locking horns."

"Females with horns?" She thought a moment. "I'll tell you what: I'll meet you halfway. We'll take a doctor along with us. That should make you feel better."

"*I* don't happen to be ill. We've discussed taking a doctor; the question is, who? Alex? He's going on eighty. I wouldn't have the heart to ask him, or the gall. As for Cairns, you can't expect him to drop his practice and tag along to Singapore as if it were an afternoon jaunt to Westerly. No decent doctor is going to be willing to shelve his patients for what could easily turn into three or four years. Still, we're going to have to beat the bushes looking for one."

"No we don't. We don't need one, darling. If I take my medicine like a good girl, stay on my diet, get plenty of rest . . ."

He ignored her change of mind. "You'll have to have a complete physical examination, of course."

"Then it's settled!" she burst brightly, dropping her spoon with a clatter.

"There's still *when*. We defer to Alex's and Cairns's judgment on that. *And* on the business of taking a doctor. As far as I'm concerned, that's an absolute must."

She got up from the table and came striding down to him. bending, kissing him warmly on the mouth. "First thing in the morning—my examination, I mean."

He sighed in capitulation, throwing up his hands. "I'll send somebody from the yard to get Alex."

"Don't bother; I'll go to his office."

"Darling . . ."

"If I can't make it to his office, I can hardly make it to Singapore!"

"You are a backbreaker, do you know that, Mrs. Dandridge?" He grinned. "You wear me down to the bone."

VI

Ross's halfhearted concession that, pending the doctors' approval, she and he would leave for the Orient proved heady wine for Lisa, despite her suspicion that he was counting on both doctors to delay departure for at least three more weeks. Since their return from Batavia, she had perforce been sleeping alone, although Ross had spent a good part of every night with her, sitting by the bed talking, dosing her with optimism, kindness and love. Neither had any liking for sleeping in separate bedrooms, but Alex Craven had insisted.

She lay in bed staring up at Ross fondly, dimly aware of the night sounds signaling the early onset of spring. He trimmed the climax burner in the vase lamp, setting it on the nightstand, straightening the silken edge of the blanket under her chin, bending and kissing her. She held him tightly, savoring his love.

"Sleep here tonight," she said softly.

A mock animal sound escaped his throat, announcing his frustration, but he shook his head. "Alex would have my hide."

"What he doesn't know . . ."

His hand cradled her cheek, gliding down her neck, pulling back the blanket and sheet, slipping over her rib cage to her breast rising under the medici lace, his fingers edging beneath it, finding and holding her breast, warming it with ardor. She covered his hand with her own, encircling his neck with her free arm, bringing his lips down upon hers, igniting them with the smoldering embers of her passion.

"Lisa, I love you, I worship you."

They disrobed each other. His skin took on a gleaming golden cast in the feeble glow of the lamp. Sight once again of his strength, tightly bound by the flesh of his shoulders, arms and massive chest, thrilled her, taking her breath, rousing her dormant desire. Tenting the sheet and blanket to let him slip beneath, she trembled as his warm body came in contact with her own, his chest against her breast, his leg contiguous to hers, his arms stealing about her. Now his wandering fingers found the inner planes of her thighs, stroking them gently, barely touching, describing small circles over their silken-smooth surface. Touching, caressing, kissing with his fingertips, setting her heart to thundering. Upward his hand traveled, firing her flesh, stroking, fondling. Down came his lips kissing her stomach, exploring her thighs, driving her wild!

Throwing back the covers, he lowered his head, kissing her legs rapidly, gently, like flower petals touching, his burning lips barely making contact, traveling upward, across her stomach, and back down. Her hips, stomach, arms and breasts all surrendered in turn, and the flame within her rose and raged until she began writhing and moaning. Only then did he embrace her and kiss her roughly, passionately, abandoning all control of his hunger for her, driving her into a paroxysm of carnal lust.

She smothered him with kisses as he mounted her and his rigid member began its slow and steady passage between her throbbing thighs.

She slept without nightmares, her mind's eye closed, blind to the images of her fancy. The sound awakened her, a shutter outside the window loosened by the wind that was clattering loudly against the front of the house. She had no idea what time it was. Rising, she went to the window, drawing her nightgown tightly about her breasts with one hand and reaching out to relatch the shutter. The moon was full, seemingly shattered into fragments by the naked branches crisscrossing its pallid face. The wind arriving from below was visible through the trees, groups yielding in turn to its bullying force. It was cold and angry, reaching the house and thrashing about boisterously. Shuddering she pulled both windows shut and went back to bed. She was preparing to lie down, adjusting the covers when sudden pain struck her like a stone in the forehead penetrating, stabbing through to the left side of her head. Her hand went to the spot, pressing it. She blinked in astonishment. Against the bedroom door stood a pillar, its top rounded, a deathly pale specter that as she stared in wonderment and horror began assuming human form. A face materialized. She gasped. Familiar features: red hair, green eyes, magnificent white skin overcast with a faint pink blush, full lips slender neck. It was as if she were seeing her own reflection.

"Mother . . ."

"Dear God . . . my darling, my baby!" Jumping up, she ran to the apparition, her arms reaching, groping, embracing. Nothingness. The air. No face, no form, nothing.

Covering her face with her hands, she began sobbing softly. She returned to the bed getting into it, her eyes irresistibly drawn to the door. Instantly the phantom reappeared, more clearly discernible.

"Mother, help me, please help me. It's awful, hideous. If they don't kill me, I shall kill myself. I must; I can't go on. Help me, help me."

As Lisa gazed in horror, other figures took shape, men without faces, naked, their bodies gleaming with sweat, their members erect. Their hands reached out for her daughter, clawing at her. The sound of cloth ripping was audible. Lisa screamed:

"Stop!"

Sitting on the edge of the bed, one leg raised upon it, she tried to bring it down to get up and run to rescue

Deirdre from them, but she could not move. It was as if she had suddenly turned to stone.

"Mother . . ."

"Deirdre, darling!"

She watched in horror as they threw her down and one by one raped her, her screams knifing into Lisa's heart. On and on they ravaged her, wild beasts feeding the fires of their lust, their laughter underscoring her pitiful screams. Now she began groaning and crying out, pleading for mercy, begging:

"Mother, Mother, Mother, Mother . . ."

Unable to move, Lisa shrieked, a single, long, heart-rending cry. At once an enormous web materialized before her eyes, a crimson net separating her from the horrible scene assaulting her eyes. She screamed and screamed and screamed, and with each effort the web joining walls and ceiling and floor pulsed and brightened.

"Mother . . . Mother . . ."

The door flew open, slamming against the wall. At the sound, the vision vanished and Lisa half rose from her bed, then fell back. In rushed Ross.

"Lisa, darling . . ."

VII

Alex Craven was awakened by his housekeeper. He dressed hurriedly and rushed up the hill to Blackwood. The deep-blue night sky was losing its somber look, fading to gray; fleecy, storm-hearted cumulus clouds flocking about the horizon, the wind up, the sun seemingly reluctant to rise by the time he completed his examination.

He put Lisa back to sleep, a deeply troubled sojourn into unconsciousness, conjectured Ross, studying her strained features. He and Craven stood on opposite sides of the bed, staring down at her. Then the doctor drifted to the cabriole table in the corner upon which his bag rested.

"She'll sleep most of the morning, to ten o'clock at least," he said. "There's nothing more we can do now."

"This settles it," said Ross; "the trip. Maybe it's fate or luck or a little of each."

"I suppose. If it had happened halfway to Singapore . . ." Craven paused and shook his head. "Of course, with a doctor on board—"

Ross cut in. "I don't get it, Alex. She was doing wonderfully all week. Every day brighter-looking, feeling better. I could see the improvement. The idea of going back seemed to pick her up by the bootstraps."

"Maybe her progress was too hurried. You must remember, the direct exciting cause of the condition is due to the accumulation of waste products in the tissues. They get into the bloodstream and work on the cells and fibers of the brain. Toxicity is still present; how much, how powerful, it's difficult to guess, but it's obviously there in sufficient quantity to . . . upset her."

"She was hallucinating again. It must be three weeks since the last time."

"The last time for conscious hallucinating. She's still complaining of nightmares."

"How could you and Cairns even think she was on the mend enough to go back? Putting the idea in her head . . ."

"Hold everything, Ross. Howard didn't put it there, nor I."

"He agreed with it, and you with him. It amounts to the same thing."

"I still believe it's a good idea. What I'm saying is, the benefits outweigh the drawbacks, temporary relapse being one. Of course, you'll have to have somebody experienced in dealing with acute melancholia along."

"Sure." Ross's eyes wandered to the window reopened by Craven upon his arrival. The breeze set the curtains to flapping lightly and, further invading the room, gently fluttered the bed canopy. "I think I'll stay home from work today. Keep an eye on her."

"That won't be necessary."

"I'd rather. Damn!"

"What?"

"Today's the day Frazier and the rest of those bank people are coming down from Boston. We're in the process of changing over, you know, to steam."

"Completely?"

Ross nodded. "Please, I know what you're thinking."

"You do?"

"That this Dandridge is sacrificing the family heritage for the almighty dollar. That Grandfather and Father built the finest clipper ships in the world, and when it all comes into my grubby, incompetent hands, I'm tossing it away in favor of stinking, dirty, noisy steam."

Craven's smirk lifted his face so suddenly it popped his spectacles off his nose. He caught them easily, as if he were well practiced at it. Then he poked Ross's hand with one finger. "Grubby? Incompetent?"

"I'm swimming with the tide Alex. There's no market for clipper ships anymore. It's too small a market for anybody but toymakers. Like the dinosaurs and Genghis Khan, they had their day and it's past. Still, if Cyrus and Gray had lived to see this . . ."

"If it bothers you that much. why change over?"

"It's either that or close down. sell the works. To somebody lucky enough not to be burdened with the Dandridge heritage, the Dandridge conscience . . ."

"You certainly don't need the money."

"It's the employees. Some of the men worked under Cyrus, most of them under Gray. We had a meeting, all seventy-eight of us, even the watchmen. At first, everybody shouted down the idea of converting. It was like asking a staunch Baptist to change to Mohammedanism. But when they began to see that it was the only way to save their jobs, they changed their minds. I'm doing it for them, Alex. But please, don't spread it around town."

"I won't."

"Word of honor?"

"I won't have to; they will. Relax, Ross; you were never cut out to be a robber baron. You're much too good-hearted."

"We'll build good sound vessels. We already have. I learned a great deal from John Ericsson working on the *Monitor* during the war. But . . ."

"You're heart isn't in it, right?"

Ross nodded. "Give me time. I'll come around." Turning from the window, he glanced at Lisa sleeping. "I'll stay with her."

"No need; she'll be fine. You go to the yards. Go tangle with your banker friends and beat them to their knees. Bring good news home to her. It'll do her a sight more good than your hanging around like a third cousin at the reading of the will."

"I could settle matters before noon and get back here."

"Do so."

Ross left for the yards in a buggy drawn by the big bay brought up from the stables by Enos Pryne, a dried and bent little anchorite past 80 but doggedly clinging to the job Grandfather Cyrus had given him nearly 50 years earlier.

It was 8:30 as Ross descended the hill, leaving Blackwood rising above the black maples snugging it round, its roof slates dully reflecting the ascending sun, its upper windows staring blankly after him. Cyrus's "Castle," he mused, built, burned and rebuilt atop the hill at the virtual geometric center of 800 acres of woodland, lush valleys and lovely hills. If only Cyrus himself could have been rebuilt; and Gray.

The clacking of iron shoes against gravel gave way to a steady clopping as the road became dirt deeply rutted by the rain, undulating through the trees down into town. Ross cast a look back over his shoulder at the house gaping after him. He pictured Lisa slumbering in her bed, and consciousness of his inability to do anything more for her than stare at her, hold her hand and reassure her of his devotion settled a stone in the pit of his stomach, a stone that seemed to gain weight as he continued to dwell on the situation. An idea occurred to him. If Alex was too old to make the trip- -and he was—so be it. But what if he could be persuaded to move into Blackwood to be by her side day and night? He could still maintain his practice, working out of Blackwood. Most important, it would free his favorite patient's husband to sail to the Orient and start searching. Lisa wouldn't like it; he could almost hear her protesting, demanding he take her along, but that he'd never allow. She belonged where she was, at home with Thursby and the staff and under Craven's care.

He would write her upon his arrival in Singapore or

Hong Kong, wherever they put in, and send daily word of his progress. That should buoy her spirits, providing he made any progress.

Two chimney swifts, snapping their short, spiny tails, rode the breeze overhead with practiced ease, angling and crossing his path. They had followed him down from the roof of the house, two tiny guardians ostensibly, from their interest in him, disapproving of his departure. Circling above him twice they gave it up at last and flew back toward the house, back to sentry duty.

Within 20 minutes he had reached the first drab and neglected little homes that served to circle the city, passing among them, crossing the bridge and entering the yards. Foreman Tom Overstreet hailed him laying hold of the cheekpiece of his horse bridle a grin of greeting brightening his ruddy features. Thank God for this man, mused Ross, getting down, stretching and following Overstreet to the office, the gate guard taking over the horse and buggy.

The office was a helter-skelter of stools and drafting boards, a stove, a curtain-top desk the clutter entire surrounded by bare walls and salt-scaled windows looking out upon the yards.

In 20 years the office had not changed, not a stick. Not so the yards themselves however. Vanished were the tall-masted clipper ships and the small mountains of white oak, rock maple and the softer woods designated for deck planking bulwarks and trim. Standing staring out the window Ross envisioned the yards before the war, the workmen stretching the oaken keels on the blocks, raising the frames from the keelsons, laying in the lower and upper decks chipping into the masts to accommodate long spars, the booms, the gaffs. And the glorious launchings mauls driving in the iron wedges splitting the keel blocks, the hull settling upon the cradle with a gargantuan groan. Then the trigger released by a single blow, and cradle and ship sliding down the ways into the water. The lines brought in, the blocks rattling the sheaves, creaking as the boom swung indolently across the newly varnished deck.

Tom Overstreet, whom Ross had induced to relinquish retirement in favor of two more years with Dandridge Shipbuilding, stood by his side, puffing his omnipresent pipe. "It's all gone, Ross," he said, reading his thoughts.

"Like a sand castle dissolving in front of a wave."

"Progress. We cling to the past and reach for the future at the same time. Building clippers and steamships together, phasing one out in favor of the other."

"Progress. Everybody thinks it's so marvelous, but it can certainly treat a man's pride shabbily."

"You still feel you're sweeping your heritage out the door?"

"Don't you?"

"I do not. Perhaps I ought to, but when you get as old as I, you have little choice but to be realistic."

Gulls swooped over the newly constructed forge shed, its corrugated iron roof already beginning to rust. Clipper ships didn't rust, reflected Ross; that was the difference between metal and wood. Wood and white canvas breathed, lived; metal just lay there or stood there insensitive, inert, rusting. Beyond the shed, three empty ways climbed out of the dark water. He envisioned all the Dandridge clippers lining up out in the sea, heading in, sailing one by one up the ways, positioning themselves in the yards, stacking one against the other, filling the area, hundreds upon hundreds of vessels reclaimed from the sea. Only there were no longer hundreds; more than half sent out now lay at the bottom, where one day every Dandridge clipper ever built would end. Progress.

Dalton Frazier, board chairman of the First Commercial Bank of Boston, arrived with two briefcase-toting assistants. Frazier resembled a bull walrus, ponderously heavy-set, particularly from the waist down, bald and bewhiskered. At times, when the light was right and imagination given full rein, all that seemed to be lacking was an ice floe for him to squat upon.

The First Commercial Bank was preparing to loan Dandridge Shipbuilding an unconscionably large sum to complete the revamping and retooling of the yards. Needed were rolling machines for straightening and bending plates, for fairing and bending beams and angle bars; shaping and slotting machines; lathes and milling machines; heavy planing machines, shops and storage buildings furnished with racks and shelving. The list seemed endless, as did the list of now obsolete tools and equipment necessary to the creation of clipper ships. Ross would have preferred to finance the purchases out of pocket, but Muybridge & Muybridge, the company's law firm, had counseled against it.

The Muybridges, father and son, arrived. The two were look-alikes a generation apart. Junior was tall, prematurely gray, athletic-looking, an avid earner of letters and praise for his exploits on the playing fields of Brown; a talkative young man who strode through life in his father's footsteps both proudly and neatly, taking care never to enlarge the imprint. His father displayed all of Junior's physical characteristics aged 30 years, paunched and jowled, bespectacled and white-haired.

Ross's attention wavered as Frazier and the two lawyers droned at each other and at him and Tom Overstreet. At Muybridge Senior's direction, he signed line after dotted line on document after document mechanically, his thoughts straying back to Lisa. The more he considered it, the more merit his idea gained. Move Alex into Blackwood and leave. After he'd concluded this business and begged out of lunch, he would handshake Frazier and his attendants out of his life, run across town to the doctor's office and put it to him.

The meeting dragged on, finally concluded, and Ross fled, heading straight for Craven's office on Academy Avenue, near Roger Williams Hospital. Arriving, he was told by Craven's nurse that the doctor was at the hospital delivering a baby. Ross left word for Craven to get in touch with him, grabbed a sandwich at Straydecker's and drove home.

Thursby answered the door before he was able to knock. He stared at Ross with what was for Thursby an extraordinarily vacuous expression.

Ross hurriedly shucked his gloves, hat and surtout. "How is she? Awake?"

"Sir . . ." Thursby looked away, then past him at the empty buggy parked on the gravel turnaround awaiting Enos Pryne's arrival from the stable.

"Thursby . . ."

"Sir, I'm sorry to have to tell you that madam is . . . gone."

Ross blanched, started to say something, changed his mind and charged off, sprinting up the stairs.

"Mr. Dandridge, sir, wait."

Stopping halfway up, Ross turned. Thursby stood at the foot of the stairs, waving an envelope. Ross came back down, snatching it from him, ripping it open, reading:

My darling,
By the time you read this, I'll be on my way—after her. I beg you, don't try to stop me. You'd only be wasting your time. I know what I'm doing.
I can no longer stand living on tenterhooks, going on biding precious time waiting for the bad dreams and hallucinations to pass. This will finish them, or should at least help to.
Please believe me when I say I shall be all right. I promise I'll take very good care of me. This is the only way, Ross, the only solution. Even as I write

this, my heart is beginning to lift, knowing that I'm putting the wheels in motion, however slowly at first. Trust me, darling. I found you; I mean to find her. I shall be in touch.

I love you forever.

Lisa

VIII

To the north lay the labyrinthine apartments of the two empresses, Tz'u Hsi and Tz'u An, and their 3,000 eunuchs. To the west lay the lovely wilderness of the Sea Palaces, planted tree by tree, situated on the shores of three artificial lakes and dotted with pleasure domes. To the south, the source of the empress's celestial energy, stood the Gate of the Zenith, guarded by four imposing towers.

But to Deirdre's eyes, all the visible beauty without and within, the splendor and grandeur of her surroundings were as unimpressive as the night-soil pile behind Kuo-cheng's house. For this was her prison and nothing more. Purple walls, gray walls, it was their height, thickness and impenetrability that mattered, not their color. And it promised to be a more secure prison than any ordinary one, barred round, as she was, with Chinese and Manchus, eunuchs, concubines, maids and officials, the lone Occidental in their midst, a kernel of wheat lodged in a sack of rice.

Considering her plight for the dozenth time that day alone, her heart seemed to dissolve inside her, drop by drop slipping slowly into her veins, leaving an empty space. No heart, no place for hope. Too many walls within walls reducing hope to a ridiculous sham. To get through all three gates across the moats and out of Peking down to the sea, to a boat and escape to Korea, Japan, the Philippines, anywhere, called for a miracle of the highest order.

With the other concubines-elect, she had left her sedan chair behind and, escorted by the eunuchs, had

proceeded on foot across the wide courtyard up a side
flight of marble stairs. The main stairway, with its delicately carved floating marble carpet on which the imperial five-clawed dragon, wreathed in clouds, pursued
the ever-fleeing jewel of omnipotence, was reserved, as
were all the central gates, for the exclusive use of their
majesties. On either side rose the vermilion, uptilting
temples to the Tutelary Gods and the Imperial Ances-
tors, where the Daughters of Heaven sacrificed on every
anniversary of the past ruler's birth and death. The
buildings blazed with color, their rafters carved with
feng, the legendary phoenix, female complement of the
male dragon. Cranes, symbols of longevity; flying bats,
emblems of happiness; snarling, ugly lion-dogs—*ch'i-
ling*—guarded the thresholds against evil spirits. The
interiors were decorated with embroidered hangings of
peonies in full blossom, overripe pomegranates and
luscious peaches, spiky blossoms and lotus, all signify-
ing good fortune. And the winter sun filtering through
lattice screens was reflected in cloisonné urns and
bronze incense burners.

Over the snow-encrusted courtyards, across the River
of Golden Water, which separated the southern area of
the Forbidden City in a flowing arc, over one of the
bridges spanning it they walked. Through the Gates of
Correct Conduct to the west of the T'ai Ho Men, the
Gate of Supreme Harmony, and onward they strolled,
across the enormous courtyard, the largest within the
Forbidden City, to the Throne Hall of Supreme Harmony standing on the Dragon Pavement Terrace, its
columns and massive tiered roofs elevated above an
expanse of pure white marble, open to the heavens and
approached by a triple flight of gradually rising stairs.

Deirdre and the others were led to the left into the
Nei Wu Fu, the offices of the Imperial Household. Here,
amid sumptuous surroundings distinguished by screens
depicting the war and hunting exploits of the Ming
emperors, the five lucky characters of each candidate's

birth comprising her horoscope were studied. Then Deirdre and the others were stripped naked and carefully examined for defects, blemishes and illnesses by three elderly court physicians. Poking and prodding Deirdre from head to foot, the doctor then placed the scab of a recent smallpox victim in one of her nostrils so that, in inhaling, she would ward off the disease.* Sixteen girls were rejected by the physicians, and the remaining 39, including the *wàigworén,* were accepted for service as royal concubines to the Empress Dowager Tz'u Hsi's nephew, Pao-chu.

Following their physical examination, they were measured for court robes and shoes and given jewelry and ornaments. Then they were led back to the Dragon Pavement Terrace and into the Throne Hall of Supreme Harmony. Two luxuriously upholstered thrones were placed side by side, their backs against a ponderous immobile screen, its scrolled top burdened with intricate carvings of lion-dog faces and writhing dragons. Seated on the thrones, surrounded by golden urns and gold and ivory figures set upon mahogany tables, were the two empresses. As the concubines-to-be and their eunuchs entered group by group, they fell to their knees in the kowtow at the shrill command of Li Lien-ying, the Chief Eunuch. Court ritual prescribed three separate kneelings, each followed by full prostration with the forehead meeting the floor.

"Kneel, fall prostrate, rise to your knees!" crowed the Chief Eunuch once, twice, a third time, and everyone he included kowtowed to the two rulers.

As Deirdre regained her feet, her eyes, like everyone else's, went to both Tz'u Hsi and Tz'u An. They wore identical imperial-yellow dragon robes embroidered in seed pearls and coral, the hem stripes dyed a rich royal purple and the breast and sleeves adorned with the

---

* *Variolation; the introduction of variolus material from an infected individual into the body of a healthy individual was an early form of vaccination originating in China.*

characters for wedded bliss—bats and other symbols and emblems—sable hats and high Manchu shoes. But there the resemblance ended. Their features reflected the sharpest imaginable contrast.

Tz'u An, the late Emperor Hsien-feng's widow, was placid, bovine-looking, dreamy-eyed, as if unaware she was sitting upon the throne of her people. But, as everyone rose, a smile brightened her face. It almost seemed to Deirdre that in the next moment she would reach out and gather in her new daughters in motherly pride. But royal restraint prevailed.

Tz'u Hsi, on the other hand, appeared anything but motherly. Her expression was as inscrutable as a stone mask, her lips loosely sealed, her jowls sagging, the fleshy gatherings under each eye creating shadowy inverted cusps contrasting with the slender horizontal lines painted on to replace her shaved eyebrows. Her hands glittered with rings, and the six-inch fingernails of her fourth and third fingers were protected by woven gold shields inlaid with kingfisher feathers. Although Deirdre had seen paintings and drawings of "Sue-Ann" and "Susie," she had never been impressed with the strength and forcefulness in the latter's face, in the set of her jaw, in her eyes. Sight of her in the flesh made a remarkable difference.

The book of Tz'u Hsi's history was open to every Chinese, every Manchu and no small number of foreigners, British and French in particular, those in commerce and Protestant and Catholic missionaries on Chinese soil. She enjoyed a reputation for ruthlessness, maliciousness and deceit second to that of no European ruler past or present. She was as well opportunistic, cruel and xenophobiacal in the extreme. Her hatred of foreigners amounted to a mania. But for all her failings of character, she was a thoroughly fascinating personality, as individualistic and indomitable as the Great Khan. The kowtowing ordered by the Chief Eunuch was to her, not to "motherly" Tz'u An, who cheerfully deferred to Tz'u Hsi's judgment in all matters of state, permitting their relationship to be as free of strain and disagreement as any such relationship could possibly be.

The august ceremony of induction followed. The 39 concubines were accepted into the Imperial Household, a family consisting of the empresses, 3,000 eunuchs, as many female servants and maids and Pao-chu, the 18-year-old prince. Other males—officials, army officers, guards, tradesmen and laborers—were rarely permitted within the walls of the Forbidden City after sundown. Essentially, Deirdre and the other new concubines joining with those already residing there comprised the world's largest seraglio. All were instructed in the rigid sumptuary laws and rituals, and late in the afternoon they were escorted to the apartments assigned them. Two of Deirdre's personal eunuchs left her on the way, leaving the remaining two to complete their duties.

The one-room apartments boasted a typical wooden-framed k'ang bed delicately draped and with warming embers beneath, a vanity, a marble bath, a stool, chairs and an armoire. Inner doors opened to the apartments immediately adjacent, and Deirdre was introduced to her new neighbor, the apartment on the opposite side being unoccupied. Her neighbor's name was Li-Sing. Next door to Li-Sing was An Te-si. Li-Sing was a Man-chu, a distant relative of the renowned statesman Prince Kung. She was a chubby, cheerful girl of 19, who, Deirdre was quick to discover, doted upon gossip, feasting on rumors and the popular lies of the day with all the eagerness of a child attacking sweets. Li-Sing's second and third loves proved to be sweets and beautiful clothes.

An Te-si was her opposite in personality as well as appearance. She was a tall, exotic-looking girl a few months older than Deirdre. An Te-si was the daughter of a well-to-do wheat dealer from Ch'eng-te, a city northwest of Peking.

No sooner had the eunuchs finished explaining the

rules governing the conduct of concubines in the Imperial Household and taken leave to summon the maids than Deirdre's inner door burst open and in rushed Li-Sing and An Te-si.

Li-Sing bounced upon her bed, wrinkling her round face in a frown. "This is much more comfortable than mine. Mine's so hard I think it's filled with salt. Did you see her—Tz'u Hsi? Isn't she scary? *Brrr.* They say she smokes opium, has a frightful temper and plays sex games with one of the eunuchs."

"Don't be ridiculous!" snapped An Te-si. "How on earth could any eunuch satisfy her?"

"It's true! One—I can't think of his name—dresses her hair and bathes and massages her. He puts his fingers in her private parts and pokes about until she reaches climax."

"Well, I'm very sure Prince Pao-Chu doesn't use his fingers," snapped An Te-si, leering. "And if I were you two, I'd start preparing for his summons. Li Lien-ying will come knocking very soon."

"The Chief Eunuch?" asked Deirdre, seating herself before her mirror. She began removing her headdress.

An Te-si nodded and produced a slender book from her sleeve. "After all, that's what we're here for. Prince Pao-Chu writes the name of the concubine he wishes to sleep with on a jade tablet and gives it to Li Lien-ying. He comes to your apartment, undresses you, wraps you in a scarlet rug and carries you to the prince's bed. Then he lays you down and takes away the rug."

"And you get up and get in bed," burst Li-Sing. "So?"

"That's how much you know. You don't dare. You crawl across the floor up to his feet and he gives you orders. He may only want you to kiss the bottom of his feet. It's all in here." She showed the book. *"The Art of the Bedchamber,* with all the secret codes. It was written by Lady Mystery. It describes all the methods."

"Let me see that," said Li-Sing, reaching for the book.

An Te-si pulled it back. "Get your own. I need this. I'm memorizing it from cover to cover."

"What makes you think the prince will summon you?" asked Li-Sing. "He has more than seventy concubines, many favorites."

An Te-si narrowed her eyes, and a cryptic smile softened her ruby-red mouth. "Sooner or later my name will go down upon the jade tablet. I will be dumped at his feet. I will sleep with him and give him such pleasure as he could never imagine."

"Good for you," said Deirdre dryly.

"Scoff all you like, Hwǒy'an, but how do you think Tz'u Hsi became empress dowager? In bed; no place else." She ran a hand haughtily down her cheek and across her shoulders. "If you're blessed with beauty, you must have brains enough to use it."

"She's right about Tz'u Hsi," said Li-Sing. "Everybody knows. The Emperor Hsien-feng was being carried by his eunuchs in the royal sedan chair when he saw her sitting under a wutung tree by a small pond. He was struck by her beauty and commanded her to bathe him. She was very beautiful when she was younger, you know. That very night two eunuchs of the Imperial Bedchamber Affairs came to summon her for the royal favor. She stripped herself in front of them, and they rolled her up in the rug and carried her to one of the palaces where the emperor was staying for the night. When they got there, he had just finished drinking a bowl of deer's blood, so he was very virile and filled with lust. He took her without a word. She was very clever, giving her all, whispering sweet words of love and pretending to enjoy everything he did to her. When he was finished, the same two eunuchs came back in to carry her away. The emperor ordered them not to squeeze the royal sperm out of her vagina. The very next morning she was made a Royal Consort. Can you imagine? Nine months later she gave birth to a baby boy."

"T'ung Chih," said An Te-si, obviously eager to contribute something to Deirdre's edification.

"He died," added Li-Sing wistfully.

"But that didn't stop her. And look where she is now." An Te-si held up her book. "When my turn comes, I shall be as well prepared, so loving and adoring I will be made a Royal Consort in the morning. Wait and see."

"Are you a virgin?" asked Deirdre.

The question shocked An Te-si, but she quickly recovered her aplomb. "Why do you ask such a silly question?"

"If you aren't, you should be able to bring a lot more to his bed than anything any book has to advise."

"We're all virgins!" exclaimed An Te-si petulantly. "And those who aren't need only carry a little chicken blood."

"Is that in the book?" asked Deirdre.

"It's what a prostitute uses when her customer demands a virgin," said Li-Sing.

Deirdre stared grimly. "Oh."

The maids arrived scurrying about the apartments, bowing and scraping and informing all three that they would be taking dinner within the hour. And that their eunuch would be coming to take them to the tables set in one of the palaces by the Gate of Spiritual Valor.

Li-Sing's demands to see An Te-si's copy of *The Art of the Bedchamber* finally wore the other girl down, and she grudgingly handed over the book. Li-Sing and Deirdre pored through it. Lady Mystery's nine basic methods for copulation were descriptively named and clearly detailed. Li-Sing read aloud, to the embarrassment of the maids within earshot.

" 'The Fish Interlock Their Scales: The man lies flat on his back. The woman sits on his body, her thighs open, and he enters her slowly, no deeper than two inches.

" 'The Cranes Entwine Their Necks: The man sits on the bed, bending his knees so that the soles of his feet face each other. The woman opens her legs and sits on his thighs, holding his neck with both hands. He enters her as deeply as two inches and holds her hips to help her move rhythmically.

" 'The Phoenix Hovers: The woman lies with her face upward and holds her legs apart. The man kneels between her thighs and pushes his jade stem into her up to four inches. This will make her move rhythmically. He thrusts twenty-four times, and she will be exceedingly satisfied.

" 'The Cicada Clings: The woman lies on her stomach, stretching herself, and opens her legs. The man lies on her back and raises her hips slightly. Then he pushes his jade stem into her and thrusts fifty-four times.

" 'The Monkey Wrestles: The woman lies on her back, and the man places her legs on his shoulders and pushes her knees over her breasts. She arches her back and raises her hips to a suitable angle for him to push his jade stem into her jade doorway, as deep as three inches. The woman moves and shakes. He keeps on thrusting vigorously until she is contented.' "

Deirdre got up and began combing her hair. "It all gets a little boring," she said quietly.

"There are lots more: 'The Fish Eye to Eye, The Unicorn Shows Its Horn, The Swallows of One Heart, The Roc in the Firmament, The Phoenix Saunters in the Crimson Cave . . .' "

"Would you mind reading it to yourself?" said Deirdre.

"Are you a virgin?" asked An Te-si bluntly.

"Yes," lied Deirdre. "Why?"

"Your face; you seem to be displeased. Do you dislike men?"

"No."

"She's saving herself for her husband," said Li-Sing.

An Te-si's laugh was as hollow as the bronze urn on the windowsill. "Concubines do not take husbands. You can die a virgin at ninety in the Forbidden City. It's happened. But it won't happen to me."

"Or to her," said Li-Sing. "She's much too beautiful." She handed the book back to An Te-si. Their escorts arrived and they went to dinner.

IX

She lay in bed in darkness, inhaling the pleasant scent of incense mingled with that of jasmine, a slender vase of yellow blossoms standing on her vanity. Upon first arriving at the apartment, she had disposed of the small-pox scab lodged in her nostril by the doctor. It nauseated her and she refused to leave it there. Let them beat her to bleeding when they caught her without it, she didn't care. There was nothing better for a crushed ego than a show of defiance.

She sniffed. Surely this had to be the sweetest-smelling prison in all the world. When the last gate had clanged shut behind her, hope, like a linnet, had been instantly imprisoned in a small cage—where it would remain until it died. Her thoughts wandered back to Kuo-cheng, her savior and benefactor. And manipulator. Had she been less grateful and more perceptive, she would have questioned his motives all along. Nobody takes in a total stranger, let alone a foreign prostitute, without some hope of profit or betterment in mind.

She thought about the nightmare weeks in the brothel in Chefoo in Lotus Street, the brazen little lanterns flaunting their colors swinging from the eaves outside, mutely announcing the services available within. She could see the dirty pallet lying on the floor in her cubicle with the single sheet drawn over its rips and smudges, the beaded curtain only partially concealing the interior from curious eyes looking in. The overpowering odor of cheap perfume. The dreadful nights never knowing when the next man would pull aside the curtain and leer down at her—even worse, what he

79

would do to her, by what perverted method he would take his pleasure.

There was the middle-aged doctor, the very proper gentleman, who came on the average of once every five days and would beat her mercilessly about the thighs with a knotted rope until she screamed. To his heart's content. Satisfied, he would throw his rope aside and enter her immediately.

And the preposterously vulgar fat Japanese who delighted in crushing her with his body, pinning her to the pallet so that she could not move, could scarcely get her breath. Usually drunk on *sam shui*, a fiery Chinese wine, he would roar like a bull at climax, bringing Madame Ching running in cheering and applauding his success.

Once a French sailor had bought her. He too was drunk, sickening her with his foul breath, fumbling at her vagina, making a disgusting spectacle of himself. She had pleaded with him to take her away, buy her freedom or even go and return for her early in the morning when the other girls and Madame Ching slept. But she knew no French and he could not understand English, and after he had abused her he went away, never to return.

In all the time she had spent under Madame Ching's watchful eyes, only one opportunity to get away presented itself. An Englishman, a sandy-haired, puny, sexually frustrated clerk in the employ of a trading company in Tsingtao, down the coast, had paid for her services, only to spend the next 40 minutes attempting and failing to gain an erection. He had finally lost his temper, slapping her viciously, blaming her for her failure to arouse him. On that occasion Madame Ching had come to her rescue with Harka, the giant boatman employed as the brothel "policeman." Among his duties he was required to evict troublemakers, anyone who might bring the law down on Madame Ching's infamous palace of pleasure.

The Englishman had managed to get control of his temper and had apologized. Madame Ching and Harka had left the two of them in privacy, and Deirdre had immediately begun begging him to take her away. Completely flustered, he had stammered a promise to help and had left. She neither saw nor heard from him again. She was still waiting, praying he would come back with the police, with British soldiers, anybody who might deliver her from her private hell, when Kuo-cheng had appeared.

He had paid Madame Ching nearly 200 taels for her. He had brought her new clothes and shoes and had taken her to a hotel on the other side of the city, where she was able to bathe in privacy and in reasonably decent surroundings. And she had accompanied him to Peking to live in the house in Hibiscus Lane.

So overwhelmed with relief and gratitude had she been, she could not find the words to express herself. It had been a miracle. The endless parade of filthy, vulgar, drunken and diseased men, the perverts and sadists who had assaulted her in the name of pleasure, began to fade in memory. The disgusting spectacles Madame Ching had arranged, forcing the girls to perform indecent acts with one another, with Harka and with animals, gradually began passing from her thoughts as her life turned the corner and she came under Kuo-cheng's benign guardianship.

Had she only known, she would have run away the very day they returned to Peking, and taken her chances in the city. Still, had she done so, she would have been dead by now. Without money, without the help of friends, without a clever disguise, she would not have made it as far as the Marco Polo Bridge across the Hun River, down which she would have been obliged to travel to Tientsin. From Tientsin, the Pei River would take her to the Gulf of Chihli. There, if she made it, she could smuggle herself aboard a ship—bound for anywhere.

As she reflected upon her situation, the slender shaft of an outrageously wild idea beamed across her mind into a corner, establishing itself and taking shape.

Kuo-cheng. He had put her into this bed in this apartment in this Forbidden City. Could he not take her out? Perhaps he could be pressured into doing so. He wanted an office, his pride demanded it, his ego was willing to practically risk his life for a precious button. But should anyone in authority in the Forbidden City suspect for an instant that his *wàigworén* had been a lowly prostitute in Chefoo, he would have been seized like a common criminal, fined, beaten with bamboo rods, imprisoned and eventually either exiled or executed, pounded to death with cudgels. Common people, even Confucian scholars, simply did not embarrass the Daughter of Heaven; did not slap the Royal cheek.

Closing her eyes, she could see his eyes as he cautioned her never to mention Chefoo or Madame Ching's palace of pleasure. His eyes and his tone both betrayed his deathly fear that she might impetuously divulge the truth. His only assurance that she would not lay in the fact that the consequences of such a slip would be as harsh for her as for him.

Not quite, she thought. If she could bluff him into believing that she no longer cared what they did to her, that all that really mattered to her was to get out of China, that disgrace and punishment, regardless of how severe, would be small payment for the privilege of being banished, concern for his reputation and his skin might well override his ambition.

But suppose it did: Would he be able to deliver her from this place now that she was an established member of the Imperial Household? By what means—through bribery? Through some inspired subterfuge? A moot point that, but a point unreachable if she failed to at least attempt reversal of her situation by threatening to expose him.

There was a slender-tipped camel's-hair brush and

some sheets of rice paper in one of the vanity drawers, but no paint. She would have to get some from somebody, perhaps one of the eunuchs, the tall, sad-looking one who had shown her her apartment. He had impressed her as more sensitive, more private a person than the other three, with their ostentatious mincing about and endless gabbling.

One thing was certain: She would need all the friends she could make to get out of the Forbidden City.

In the year 1404, the corpulent and canny Ming emperor, Yung Lo, commanded the reconstruction of Peking, which had been devastated by invaders at the close of the previous century. Also to be built by imperial decree was the Forbidden City. Designed as a perfect rectangle, the dimensions of this man-made Eden approximated 1,000 yards from north to south and 800 yards from east to west. Surrounded by a moat, its 36-foot-high walls were interrupted by four individual gates. Its interior was divided into two major sections, the first containing the principal state buildings, the second the residential section. The West Flowery Gate and the East Flowery Gate were situated with uncharacteristic asymmetry in the southern section devoted to official buildings thereby providing access to them without disturbing the emperor's privacy.

From the south gate, the Wu Men, the south-north axis continued across a courtyard separated by the undulating length of the River of Golden Water. Shaped like a Tatar bow, this artificial stream was spanned by five marble bridges, each of which symbolized one of the five virtues. To the left of the Meridian Gate adjacent the southern wall were located the servants and eunuchs' quarters. To the right, diagonally opposite the East Flowery Gate, stood the secretarial offices.

The southernmost interior entryway, the Supreme Imperial Gate, separated the Imperial Storehouses and the Hall of Literary Profundity, which embraced the Imperial Library, the Halls of Literary Glory and the Hall of Proclaimed Intellect. Between the Supreme Imperial

Gate and the centrally located Gate of Heavenly Purity were various halls, offices and palaces beautified by gardens and the archery grounds. In proceeding northward from the Gate of Heavenly Purity, the Imperial Residential Buildings began to predominate, continuing up to the wall through which entrance into the Imperial City is gained by way of the Gate of Divine Military Genius.

The rebuilding of Peking and construction and landscaping of the Forbidden City required 16 years, from 1404 to 1420. Rising on slender columns of lacquered wood, the golden roofs of the halls and palaces surmounted the purple walls like an enormous multifaceted jewel in the setting of the Imperial City, itself lodged in the city of Peking.

In the days that followed the concubines' arrival, So-leng, the eunuch upon whom Deirdre fixed her eyes and her hopes, came daily to her apartment to wait upon her and assist her with her hair and toilet. It was he who, apart from showing her about the place, explained the rules governing the conduct of concubines in the Imperial Household. She had seen eunuchs before in Peking, and her impression was that one and all were effeminate, simpering creatures, pretentious and silly, fittingly nicknamed "crows," with their high-pitched, cawing voices. So-leng's voice was as high as the other eunuchs' but his manner curiously less effeminate. To Deirdre, it appeared, as he was familiarizing her with the furnishings in the apartment, that he was straining to control his rasping falsetto and effeminate gestures and indicate in as masculine a manner as he was capable of. She had never met anyone so discouraged and downtrodden-looking. His clenched face, boasting extraordinarily high cheekbones, eyes like black pearls and complexion as fulvous as the lion-dogs guarding the entrances to many of the buildings, appeared frozen in glumness. But she imagined she saw something like sympathy in his expression as he stared at her, following Tang-yü's and Nalute's departure inside the entrance to the Forbidden City.

Deirdre and he were standing on the veranda of the apartment one early afternoon when she rashly seized the initiative. "Would you do me a small favor?" she asked.

"If I can."

"I need some writing paint."

"What for? Are you so taken by all this splendor and luxury you're inspired to write poetry?"

"I want to send a note to my guardian, Kuo-cheng, in Hibiscus Lane. Would you deliver it for me? I understand you're allowed to go into Peking during the day."

"I'm sorry, I can't help you."

"If it's money you want . . ."

He shook his head, frowning. "I don't want your money. If you really want to know, you'd be wasting your time. Let me guess what you'd say in your note. You'd ask him to help you get out of the Forbidden City."

"You're quite wrong."

"Am I? I've been watching you, the way you stare at the wall and the gates as if you want to crumble them with your eyes. Face up to it: You're in here to stay for the rest of your life."

The unexpected harshness of his words and the matter-of-fact manner in which he delivered them, all but tossing them off with a shrug, made her heart sink.

"You don't understand; I shouldn't even *be* here. What do they want with a *hwàwàirén?** They hate the sight of my hair, my eyes, my skin. It makes no sense!"

"It makes all the sense in the world. Whether you realize it or not, you're one of the spoils of her highness's undeclared war with the foreigners."

* "Barbarian."

"You make me feel like a trained bear in a king's court."

"Empresses, and not a trained bear; more like a live toy." He smiled sympathetically. "I'm sorry, I have no right to tease, but you must be practical. Now that you're in here, there is no longer any 'out there.' As far as you concubines are concerned, the rest of the world disappeared the moment your chair bearers stepped inside the Wu Men Gate."

"Then you won't help me."

"It's not that I won't; I can't. Your guardian might as well be dead. The rules are clear. I'm sorry."

Her hands folded at her waist, she walked in silence with him down the steps toward the Well of the Pearl Concubine within sight of the barracks and stables. They sat on a marble bench under a thuya tree, its loveliness ravaged by the cold weather.

"How long have you been here?" she asked.

"Ten thousand years. Now you're going to ask me if I like it, if I like being a crow." The word was uttered with manifest disdain.

"I wasn't thinking of that."

"Of course you were." His brittle chuckle drew her eyes to his face. "Don't bother to spare my feelings. Feelings are a luxury we eunuchs do without. One gets used to the jokes about teapots without spouts, dogs without tails."

"You sound bitter."

"Why should I be?"

"If you chose to become a eunuch . . ."

"Did I?"

"Don't all of you?"

He laughed mirthlessly. "Who told you that?"

"Everybody says—"

"Everybody talks too much, particularly about the things they know the least about. I'm afraid it's not as black and white as all that. In my case, I had nothing like a choice in the matter. I was castrated when I was seven years old."

She gasped. "How terrible! How cruel . . ."

"And painful."

"Didn't your parents—"

"My parents had no choice. At least I try to persuade myself they didn't. My father was a soldier in the war with the French and English. He was at the siege of the Taku forts. When it was all over, he left the army and became a construction worker. He never called himself a laborer." So-leng swept his outstretched arms upward, taking in the walls. "He was working, repairing these very walls." He pointed toward the Meridian Gate. "There. There was an accident. Part of the wall collapsed and he was pinned under a mass of rubble. They called a doctor and he cut off one of his legs. The other went two days later. We were very poor to begin with. With my father out of work, a useless cripple, we became destitute. He turned to begging, my mother to prostitution."

"How awful!"

"To spare each other's feelings, neither told the other what he was up to. When they finally confessed to each other, there was a terrible row. Each one made the other swear to stop what he was doing, which was all well and good, very laudable, even noble, but failed to solve the original problem—how to put rice on the table. To make matters even more interesting, in a very short time my father came to despise me."

"Why?"

"Why do you think? Because I could walk and he could not. One day, without my mother knowing, he took me to the T'ien An Men Gate outside the Imperial City. He had six taels borrowed from a friend, the surgeon's standard fee. It all happened very fast, though not quite fast enough; the pain was excruciating. Even now, fourteen years later, there are times I imagine I still feel it."

FIRE AND FLESH 89

"Good God."

"For three days afterward I was forbidden to drink, but on the night of the third day I found I was able to pass water, so it seemed the operation was a success. And I was doomed to recover. Three months later the wound was completely healed."

"How terrible for you."

"And for them. When my mother found out, she nearly killed him. She left him. She died a year later. He died two years ago, of a broken heart, so they say. A perilously slow breaking process, eh? So you see, your presumption is false; not all eunuchs are eunuchs by choice."

Apart from establishing Deirdre's sympathy for him, So-leng's story eased her disappointment at his refusal to help her. But alone in her apartment later in the day, she decided that anyone who had been so heartlessly treated as he could hardly fail to appreciate her own predicament. Despite his unwillingness to take her note to Kuo-cheng, she resolved to work on him; there was, after all, no risk on his part. He need merely drop the note off at the door. Kuo-cheng would never know who delivered it.

XI

Early that evening she was lying in her bed staring at the canopy, carefully examining Kuo-cheng's armor for chinks and considering how best to phrase her note, when Li-Sing came bursting in.

"Hwŏy'an, Hwŏy'an! Come see, he's here!"

Deirdre raised herself on her elbows and stared. "Who? What are you talking about?"

"The Chief Eunuch! He's come for An Te-si. The prince has inscribed her name on the jade tablet!"

Deirdre got up and followed Li-Sing into her apartment. Pressing their ears to the inner door, they could hear the Chief Eunuch instructing An Te-si as he disrobed her in preparation for carrying her out wrapped in the scarlet rug. Giddy with excitement, she continually interrupted him, rousing his anger.

"Be silent, chatterbox! Pay attention. You will be carried to his room and laid upon the floor inside the door. As soon as the rug is removed, you will flatten yourself upon the floor face down. You must not raise your eyes to look at him. You will lie still until he commands you to approach him. When you do so, you will crawl on your stomach to the foot of his bed, up over the end of it into the bed. You will not speak unless spoken to. Whatever you are ordered to do you will do instantly, without hesitation, without question; do you understand?"

"Yes."

"Are you familiar with the thirty positions of lovemaking from heaven and earth?"

"Yes, yes, I know them by heart. I'm learning all sixty-five. You may test me."

"Foolish virgin! How stupid you are. Is it your intention to deny his highness the pleasure of teaching you his favorite positions?"

"I . . . no, no . . ."

"If a grain of intelligence rests in the hollow of your skull, you will pretend to total innocence, you understand?"

"Yes, yes . . ."

"His highness may not be in the mood to enter your jade doorway. Instead, he may order you to play his flute. Do you understand what playing the flute is?"

"I—"

"You will learn. One more thing: Be prepared for his highness to Shoot the Arrow While Galloping. You stand against the wall, knees slightly bent, legs spread apart. His highness will run toward you from the other side of the room and aim to enter you at first try. I warn you there will be some discomfort. But you are not to cry out. Freeze your smile upon your face. Pretend that you are overcome with joy, if you know what's good for you."

"I will, I will!"

"Let's look at you. Your breasts are small but high. Yes, yes . . . your skin is without blemish. Hips round, firm. He may enjoy you; pray that he will."

"I have prayed, I will pray."

"Lie down on the rug."

Li-Sing and Deirdre padded softly to Li-Sing's front door and, easing it open a crack, watched as Li-Lien-ying emerged from the next apartment with An Te-si wrapped in the scarlet rug slung over his shoulder. Down the front steps he padded, around the corner in the direction of the Nine Dragon Screen and, beyond it, the Palaces of the Young Princes.

"The lucky thing!" exclaimed Li-Sing, closing the door and pouting.

"Lucky?"

"Certainly!" Together they sat down on the edge of her bed. "Don't you think so? To sleep with the prince. She was right, you know: If she does her best, if he's impressed with her, she could be named a Royal Consort." She threw up her hands. "There'll be no living with her then. She's the vainest hen in the yard already. If she wins his favor, she'll be intolerable. Lucky, lucky, lucky . . ."

However, Li-Sing's estimation of An Te-si's immediate future turned out to have no basis in fact. Less than an hour later she was brought back to her apartment by two eunuchs and dumped into her bed. In came the elderly physician who had examined Deirdre on the day she had come to the Forbidden City. Again Li-Sing called her into her room to listen. But this time there was no conversation. Not a syllable passed between the doctor and An Te-si. Indeed, the only sound emanating from the apartment was a subdued and pitiful moaning.

"What do you suppose happened?" asked Li-Sing, her eyes wide with bewilderment.

"Wait until the doctor leaves," cautioned Deirdre.

He continued to minister to An Te-si for a few more minutes, then left. The instant the door clicked shut behind him, Li-Sing and Deirdre rushed into the room. They stopped short, blanching and gasping at the sight that met their eyes.

An Te-si lay on the bed naked to the coverlet at her waist. Her eyes were black and blue and so swollen the pupils were barely visible between the lids. Her bloodied nose displayed a painful-looking bruise angling from the bridge down her left cheek. Her mouth was cut and bleeding and her trembling hands held a damp cloth to it, moving it to her nostrils and down to her chin in an effort to stanch the bleeding. She trembled visibly as she stared at them, moaning and sobbing.

"What did he do?" asked Li-Sing, aghast.

"Take a good look!" exclaimed Deirdre in annoyance.

"I . . . lay face down on the . . . floor," whispered An Te-si hoarsely. "When he called to me, I crawled up to the foot of the bed and . . . into it. He . . . he showed me his . . . jade stem and grabbed me by . . . by the hair and forced my mouth down upon it. When . . . when it spit, it made me nauseous. I gagged and . . . and . . ." She stopped abruptly and turned her cheek to the pillow, unable to go on.

Li-Sing stared at Deirdre inquiringly.

"It sounds like she threw up on his royal highness," said Deirdre quietly. Her eyes strayed to the night table. Upon it lay An Te-si's favorite book, *The Art of the Bedchamber*.

"The poor thing," murmured Li-Sing. "Isn't there anything we can do for her?"

Deirdre shook her head. "Sleep is the best thing. The bleeding seems to be stopping itself. If she stays in bed, she'll be all right in a few days. 'Lucky, lucky, lucky,' eh?"

Li-Sing, turning from the sight of the now sleeping girl, pretended not to hear. But Deirdre could not look away. If, she thought, there was anything resembling lingering doubt in her mind regarding escape, this served to banish it completely. She would penetrate Kuo-cheng's armor. If her threat failed, she would think of something else. She would go on thinking, planning, trying to get away until she succeeded or died in the attempt.

XII

An Te-si slept fitfully that night, or so Li-Sing assured Deirdre the next morning.

"She woke me at least five or six times with her screaming. Didn't you hear her?"

Deirdre wrinkled her nose, eyeing her balefully. "Through two doors with your apartment between?"

They were standing on Deirdre's veranda, watching their maids file toward them as they came around the corner of the Inner Court.

"The doctor's with her now," continued Li-Sing. "He wouldn't let me in to see her."

"She doesn't need visitors; she needs rest."

The early-morning air was chilly, the wind curling down from the distant Bell Tower to the north in the Tatar City. The little doll maids padding toward them, chattering like magpies, hastened their steps, intent on reaching the apartments before they began shivering. Leaving her door ajar, Deirdre sat before her mirror. One by one the maids shuffled in, nodding greeting. The incident involving An Te-si and Prince Pao-chu provided sufficient grist for the gossip mill to honor it as the sole subject for discussion. Opinion tended to excuse the prince and condemn An Te-si for all sorts of imagined foolish acts, from resisting his amorous advances to insulting him in various ways. The female servants of the Forbidden City generally disliked their concubine mistresses, Deirdre noted, the jade-eyed monster in them rousing itself to criticize the concubines' significantly loftier station and the luxuries it guaranteed: jewels, expensive clothing, privacy and the services of the eunuchs.

Deirdre had not yet had words with any of her maids, but she nevertheless detected the presence of a subdued animosity as they gabbled on, fussing over her robes and about the apartment, attending to her makeup and her hair, skillfully surmounting the lovely waves with strings of pearls.

So-leng appeared, his waxen features announcing a sleepless night caused, she surmised, by conscientious dedication to drunkenness and debauchery. Waving his arms vigorously, he sent the maids scurrying out and closed the door.

"Good morning," she said, suppressing a smile. He groaned and sat down hard on a satin-covered stool, dropping his head into his hands and shaking it with exaggerated slowness. "Too much *jau?*"

"How can something so enjoyable cause so much misery?"

She laughed.

"Not so loud, please, my poor melon . . ."

Opening the vanity drawer, she took out an envelope. "When I got up this morning, I wrote this note to Kuocheng. I didn't have any paint, so I dipped the brush in kohl mixed with water." Grasping his wrist, she eased one of his hands down from the side of his head and placed the envelope in it. "Hibiscus Lane."

He dropped it to the floor and looked up at her. "I'm telling you, you're wasting your time. He put you in; he won't lift a finger to get you out."

"It's worth a try."

"It's not."

"He thinks I'm going to ask somebody to help get him an appointment. He does this to me and he actually thinks I'd do him a favor!"

"Because he thinks he's doing you one." So-leng laughed, winced and restored the tips of his fingers to his temples. "Besides, you don't have to say anything to anybody. The fact that he presented you as a gift to the Imperial Court is all the bribe he needs."

"In the note, I've warned him I'll spill the beans to everybody."

So-leng failed to understand the term but let it pass. Picking up the envelope, she tucked it inside his tunic. "Kuo-cheng, Hibiscus Lane."

"I told you I don't want to get involved."

"You're not."

"What do you call it?"

She sighed and smiled and began rubbing his temples gently, affectionately, to soothe the pain. She began recounting his sorry history and artfully, with neither bitterness nor self-pity, revealing her own and comparing the two. If, she insisted, people so unfortunate, so badly abused by the fates didn't help each other, to whom could they turn? Moreover, if their positions were reversed, he knew in his heart that she would help him without hesitation, particularly in light of the total absence of risk.

She assailed him with irrefutable arguments for better than an hour, but when he finally capitulated, agreeing to deliver the note, she couldn't be sure if she'd won him over or worn him down, reducing his determination to refuse to a point where he would have agreed to deliver the note to the moon if it would stop her tongue.

"You wear me out!" he exclaimed in an exasperated tone. "And you've made me forget why I came around this early in the first place. You've seen what happened to the girl two doors down?"

"An Te-si."

"Whatever her name, she managed to incur his highness's displeasure."

"To her everlasting regret, long after her scars are healed. She had visions of becoming his Royal Consort."

"Doesn't every concubine?"

"Not this one."

So-leng got up from his stool, stretched and, going to

the vanity, studied his face in the glass, blinking his watery, red-rimmed eyes, pulling his lower lids down with the tips of his fingers and sticking out his heavily coated tongue. "All the same, your name could go down on the jade tablet tonight; or tomorrow night, soon. If you don't want to be brought back half dead, you'll be careful what you do and what you say to him. He's vicious, sadistic, conscienceless, a drunkard, an opium addict. Think of all the mean things men can be and do and he's had a fling at every one—at *eighteen*. Can you imagine what he'll be in five years? God help China the day he ascends the Dragon Throne."

"I doubt if he'll write my name down. I can't believe he'd lower himself to sleep with a *wàigworén*."

"I can. He'd enjoy hurting you more than any Chinese or Manchu. He seems to have inherited his hatred for foreigners from his aunt. So be prepared for the worst. Two months ago he lost his temper and strangled a concubine, a girl just about your age, a pathetic little innocent thing. You can be grateful you're experienced."

"I'm not proud of it."

"I didn't imply that you should be. At any rate, Li-Lien-ying very cleverly hushed up the murder. But it's not the first time blood's been spilt. And last night won't be the last."

"Why doesn't Susie put a stop to it? She must know what goes on."

"Tz'u Hsi is deaf and blind to his faults. She indulges and pampers him, brags incessantly about him, fancies him a god-warrior. So when you're summoned, and you will be, see that you're extremely careful. Whatever he commands, do it willingly, eagerly, throw yourself into his play, like a pheasant* looking to double her fee. If, for example, he lies down on his back and commands you to sit on him and put his jade stem into your jade

---

* Common patois for a prostitute.

doorway, he'll insist you use your hands as levers and spin like a top. When you start, he'll want you to go faster and faster until you're dizzy and your jade doorway feels as if it's ripping open. Ignore the discomfort, squeal with delight, convince him you are in heaven, that the pleasure his skinny little jade stem is giving you is driving you insane with joy. Anything you can do to stimulate his manhood, to inflate his ego, to make him feel lordly and superhuman will ingratiate you with him." He nodded toward the bed. "And insure you climb back into your bed instead of being helped into it by a doctor."

"But if I do as you suggest and he likes me, he'll want me back."

So-leng shrugged. "Better to be inconvenienced and put upon than beaten to a pulp."

They went out for fresh air. They walked near the Well of the Pearl Concubine, sitting under what had become their favorite thuya tree on their favorite bench. The story of her capture, the vicious abuse aboard ship and the ensuing weeks in white slavery in Chefoo had touched his heart. But the growing bond between them seemed to be based on something more than two people with misery in common who merely felt sorry for each other. Both nurtured strong feelings of defiance, he with his continuing effort to hold his effeminacy in check purely as a matter of pride, she keeping the embers of hope alive among the ashes of her deepening discouragement. It was becoming an alliance of two captive hearts, each one willingly supporting the other in time of need for encouragement.

At noon she saw him to the West Flowery Gate across the moat and watched him lose himself in the teeming crowds of the Imperial City. It was less than two miles through the streets of the Imperial City, the Tatar City and into the Chinese City to the house of Kuo-cheng. By sundown, So-leng would be back. All she could do till then was bide her time and pray that the note would bring about the desired results.

Oddly, now that the wheel was beginning to turn, the senselessness of threatening Kuo-cheng seemed to rise up and present itself like a pillar of mist assuming human shape. Now that she thought about it, she would have been better off accepting So-leng's advice at the outset. Even if, by some incredible twist of fate, Kuo-cheng was to take her threat seriously, she could hardly expect him to thrust his hand into the fire, leap into action and attempt to move the mountain. More likely, he would pack up, run away and hide. If forcing her into concubinacy jeopardized instead of assured his button—brass gilt, smooth red coral or any one of the six others between—he need only think up another way to go about getting it; and put her out of his mind forever.

So-leng returned before sunset with news that surprised her. She could, he announced, abandon any ideas she might have that Kuo-cheng would become afflicted with a change of heart and decide to help her. He was, it seemed, in no position to help anybody. According to his neighbor, he had been murdered in the street, his purse taken, his body left in the gutter.

"A black lantern was hanging at his door," said So-leng, handing her back her note.

She crumpled it. "Then I'll find another way to get out," she said resolutely. "Out of the Forbidden City and out of China."

"You do and you'll be the first concubine in history," he said. "And to make things easier, with that skin, that face and hair, you'll stand out like a pigeon indoors. Deirdre, use your head; you haven't a chance!"

"Oh, but I have; that I'll always have. If I can get to the Marco Polo Bridge with a hundred taels bribe money, I can make it down the river to the coast. I'll need a disguise."

"If you're caught, they'll execute you. Any attempt to leave this earthly paradise of ours by anybody is a slap in Tz'u Hsi's face, a monumental insult to her hospitality. Tz'u An might not care, but Tz'u Hsi wouldn't stand for it, nor would the Chief Eunuch; with her blessing, he'd make an example of you. The whole city would turn out for your execution."

"I don't care how risky it is; I'm leaving. And nothing you say can change my mind." She thought a moment, then brightened. "I know what I'll do: I'll ask for an audience with both empresses. I'll tell them the truth."

"You little *sòhjái,** you haven't heard a word I've said."

"I've heard every word. I'm sick of talking. If you won't help me, if you're afraid to, I'll do it alone!"

"Deirdre, don't be angry with me. You know very well I'll help if I can. But you might as well try to float the White Pagoda; there isn't a chance in ten thousand you'll make it."

There was a knock at the inner door: It was Li-Sing, in tears. Sobbing loudly, she fell into Deirdre's arms. "She's going to die! She's going to die!"

"Nonsense," said Deirdre.

"It's true. When you were out, the doctor went away shaking his head. He was with her all morning. She doesn't wake up, and he can't seem to make her."

Deirdre and So-leng exchanged glances.

"Maybe she's lapsed into coma," So-leng said gravely. "If she has a head injury . . ."

"She's going to die!" repeated Li-Sing, and began wailing.

"Quiet down, girl!" snapped So-leng. "All your caterwauling isn't going to help any."

The front door burst open, slamming against the wall and setting the satin-covered stool to jiggling. Framed

* "Fool."

in the doorway, the scarlet rug rolled up over his shoulder, his evil eyes riveted upon Deirdre, stood the Chief Eunuch.

"Out, both of you!" He pushed Li-Sing through the open door into her apartment, slamming it after her, and turned to order So-leng out, but he was already gone.

XIII

He had no eyebrows, only a faint blue arc where each one should have been. His skin showed a strange gray-blue cast, like the color of the inside of a mussel shell. His teeth were rotted brown, but most loathsome of all was the vicious glare he fastened upon her.

"His serene highness Prince Pao-chu has inscribed your name on the jade tablet. Stand still!"

Dropping the rug from his shoulder, he began unbuttoning the collar of her dress, pulling at it impatiently in his haste to disrobe her. A button came loose, falling to the floor, rolling across it and coming to rest. Within moments she was standing naked before him, trembling slightly, a finger of cold tracing its way down her spine. Gooseflesh raised itself and her throat felt suddenly dry. He touched her breasts clumsily, one, then the other, sliding his fingers down her stomach to her vagina, caressing it, moving around her hip and rubbing her buttocks. His touch was as clammy as a corpse, sending chill after chill down her back, but she steeled herself to keep from shivering and gritted her teeth, avoiding his sick eyes, staring past him at the door.

"Your skin is like a pearl," he hissed, "white with the faint glow of pink. How is it you, a barbarian, come to be a royal concubine?" He spit at her feet. "Answer me, slut!"

"It was the will of my master, the scholar Kuo-cheng."

"The will of your master . . . Foreign sow, it was the

102

will of the Daughter of Heaven!" He glared. "Sight of
you disgusts me, but I did not write your name on the
jade tablet." Leaving her standing, he went to the vanity
and opened her kohl, dipping his little finger into it and
applying it first to one eyelid, then the other. He turned
back to her. "Tell me, is it true your priests use magic
to charm converts and drive them mad so that they
smash their ancestral tablets and violate shrines?"

"I—"

"Of course it's true. And we have proof that they
stretch the anuses of infant orphans to prepare them for
sodomy. Don't deny it! You Christians are spies and
slanderers, maggots on the living body of China. Your
Jesus is the Pig Incarnate, a licentious beast. Of all the
wives and daughters of the high officials of your country of Judea, not a single one failed to fall prey to his
lust. But when he schemed to usurp the thone, he was
caught and his crimes made known. They bound him
upon a cross and fastened him to it with red-hot nails.
He grunted, assumed the form of a pig and died. It's
true, isn't it? Isn't it? Say it is!"

"It is."

"You admit it!"

Unrolling the rug with the toe of his slipper, he gestured her to lie down in it. When he rolled her up, she
thought at first that she would smother, gasping to catch
her breath. But when he lifted the rug to his shoulder,
it gaped slightly, permitting her to breathe easier.

He walked for an interminable time, the point of his
bony shoulder jabbing into her stomach. She could see
and hear nothing, but presently he began climbing steps
and she assumed that they had reached the palace. The
muffled sound of first one door, then another opening
and closing reached her ears. Then a third door opened
—and closed. He lowered her from his shoulder and
unrolled the rug, snapping it open, sending her tumbling
across the floor against the closed door.

"Over on your stomach!" he hissed.

She complied, feeling the warmth of the heated parquet floor hard against her breasts, stomach and upper legs. She lowered her cheek to the floor, her eyes closed. Directly behind her, she could hear him open the door and slip out, closing it. Then she heard mumbled conversation and giggling, the voices of two men, one decidedly more corvine than the other. Whether it was the prince or his companion who sounded like a crow, she could not guess. And she was afraid to lift her head to look.

She drew in her breath. There was a strange odor in the room, as if the stench of vomit had been disguised with perfume. The prince and whoever was in the bed with him paid no attention to her. Time pushed forward. They went on laughing and talking in low tones; then the unmistakable sounds of sex play reached her hearing. It was followed by more laughter, the wailing of a *hu-chin** being bowed, a tune begun and abruptly stopped.

"Là an chùhng!" ** The command seemed to come from miles away, so deep was the rectangularly shaped room. Her eyes still directed at the uncovered floor, she fought down the urge to leap to her feet, run forward and beat the two of them with her fists. Instead, clenching her jaw, she crawled forward. Reaching the foot of the bed, a tangle of serpents writhing in relief across the full width of the frame end, she raised herself on her palms and pulled herself up onto the bed.

They sat grinning at her. Squatting in the lotus position was Prince Pao-chu, recognizable by his imperial-yellow jacket buttoned to the throat. He was naked from the waist down, his skin as pale as porcelain, slightly built, with bony shoulders as narrow as a slen-

* A small two-stringed fiddle.
** Literally, "Crawl, worm."

der young girl's. Effeminate-looking, his face small, the homely features bunched together wanting nourishment to fill them out and imbue him with robustness, he looked more like a half-starved peasant than the son of the Son of Heaven, lineal heir to the Dragon Throne.

His companion, completely naked, sat taller, healthier in appearance, but strange-looking, distressingly ugly, a younger version, at first glance, of the late Kuo-cheng, although not bald. Still, the mottled skin of his cheeks and the forward thrust of his lower front teeth ganged together tusklike against his thin lip reminded her of Kuo-cheng. Between the two of them, lying on a satin pillow displaying a mass of gaily colored peacock feathers, was a pipe, its long stem fashioned of cane and blackened with use. Its turned mouthpiece was made of bullock horn, and the bowl end of the stem was encased in copper strikingly inlaid with silver. A round copper socket roughly three inches in diameter was located midway down the silverwork. As she looked on, the prince's companion carried a clay bowl resembling a squashed turnip, with a pinhead puncture on its upper side, to the pipe from the nightstand. Upon the nightstand a spirit lamp burned brightly. Continuing to grin at her, both men lay down on their sides facing each other. Picking up a dipper lying alongside the lamp, the prince's guest placed the sharp end of it into a shallow saucer and picked up a drop of gumlike opium. Holding it over the flame, he turned it slowly. Gradually the drug lost its darkness, becoming whitish, softening, swelling, bubbling and sputtering. Just as the flame was about to reduce it to vapor, he carried the needle to the surface of the pipe bowl, tipped the bowl over the flame and handed the pipe to the prince. Pao-chu took the stem between his lips and inhaled deeply. This he did a second time and a third before the opium was consumed.

The procedure was repeated, the prince filling his

lungs with the smoke of a second drop. Then his guest smoked. Deirdre watched in silence, speedily becoming bored with the disgusting spectacle, as well as with the pretense on the part of both that she wasn't even in the room.

She looked about. The walls were hung with magnificent tapestries depicting a panoramic view of ladies preparing newly woven silk, black-capped, ruby-throated parakeets perched in dogwood trees in the royal aviary, a *na-po**—a vast tented encampment, characteristic of the reigns of the Khitan and Mongol emperors, showing domesticated water buffalo, Tatar warriors astride their ponies, and women at cooking fires. Two large antique lanterns of gauze and paper and horn and diaphanous gum, gloriously colored, provided illumination. They hung in opposite corners and cast a yellow gleam down the walls on either side of them, lending a golden sheen to the woven scenes.

"You smoke," said the prince's guest, whom Pao-chu called Heng-chi. Deirdre recognized the name: He was the son of Prince Kung's half-brother, with little royal blood distinguishing his veins but all the power and influence close association to the throne ensured. Prince Kung she had seen in Peking, a small, ferociously serious-looking man, aged well past his 50 years in appearance; the most imperious man she had ever seen. He was reputedly brilliant, China's greatest statesman, and curiously tolerant of foreigners. And this common-looking creature thrusting the pipe under her nose was his nephew.

"Smoke," he repeated. The prince stared at her, ignoring her nakedness, intent upon the challenge of the moment. She could imagine the consequences of declining, visions of An Te-si beaten and bloodied forming themselves with annoying vividness. She dare not refuse.

* "Felt city."

Hopefully, the two of them were enjoying themselves so much they would selfishly hog most of the opium remaining in the saucer, forcing her to smoke now and then for their amusement, but not enough to sicken or intoxicate her.

Heng-chi giggled; his was the high voice. He sat up, catching a drop of the insidious drug on the end of the needle, turning it over the flame, roasting it, quickly conveying it to the pipe and all but jamming the mouthpiece into her mouth.

"Suck! Suck!" burst the prince, clapping his hands together gleefully like a small child.

She inhaled, choking as the sickly sweet smoke was drawn down her throat into her lungs. It burned slightly, and she stiffened her jaw against reacting. Her eyes watered, dimming sight of them, and the smoke that failed to reach her lungs filtered lazily out of her nose. It too burned, grating the raw flesh inside her nostrils.

She was wrong in wishfully persuading herself that they were enjoying their pursuit of dreams too much to waste the precious treaclelike substance on a mere concubine. They made her smoke pipeful after pipeful until the room swam, the tapestries revolving around her, the scenes losing their detail and clarity, the colors escaping them, becoming astonishingly vivid—crimsons and purples, yellows and blues and greens shooting into her closed eyes like arrows from every direction. She felt herself go limp and her body begin to float, the bedclothes dropping from under her, the soft woolly comfort of the air in the room wrapping itself about her. And her subconscious captured her imagination. The colored arrows altered shape, gradually forming into swaths that curved and sharpened at their ends like scimitars. She envisioned her body floating, her breasts and stomach distending absurdly, her limbs growing longer to twice, three times their length, becoming as limp as serpents. She began to stretch in every direc-

tion, her neck elongating like a swan's, her arms and
legs intertwining, knotting, gradually forming an un-
identifiable mass that pulsed and pushed forth, glistening droplets of blood from her pores, until the mass was
floating in a pool of blood.

There was no feeling of any sort, only the continuing
sensation of being buoyed on nothingness. Then her
distorted body vanished, leaving empty space as bright
as the sun, becoming more and more intense, stabbing
her eyes, setting them broiling in their sockets. The pain
was instantaneous and excruciating.

Suddenly the colors returned, resuming their assault,
and a clanging sound steadily becoming louder began
accompanying their every pulsation.

She was vaguely aware of hands touching her, fingers
exploring her body, fondling, intruding into her pri-
vates, and cold, clammy flesh touching her mouth, finding its way between her buttocks. Low voices, indistinct,
distant. She wanted to cry out but was unable to. Nor
could she move to protect herself from the hands and
flesh invading her. Now a new sensation presented itself: consciousness of an immense serpent discovering
her, crawling across her stomach, over her breasts and
face, coiling about her, its thick, muscular length wind-
ing, slipping under her legs, up the valley of her thighs,
its loathsome head dragging its great weight around her
breasts and down across the small of her back, turning
her spine to ice. It thrashed about, locking her in its
curves from head to foot and slowly tightening. The
colors and the clanging persisted, attacking her from
all sides until, like a door closing and locking, all
trespass upon her defenseless body ceased.

She slept fitfully, awakening to find the prince gone
and Heng-chi standing over her, his crooked teeth
bared in a smile. He had covered her and now climbed
into bed beside her, his warm body touching her full

length. She tried to speak but discovered that her mouth
was as dry as old cotton. She could not recall ever
being so thirsty; it was as if the roof of her mouth and
her throat were preparing to shatter from dryness. Gulping for air, she eased over on her side away from him.

"Now, now," he whispered, "don't turn away." She
felt his hand on her arm. He ran it down over her
breasts, gently caressing her vagina and first one thigh,
then the other. "We must be affectionate to each other.
We musn't disappoint his highness."

He threw back the covers. Continuing to explore
and fondle her with his free hand, he explained that
while she had been sleeping off the effects of the opium,
Pao-chu had declared that since he, Heng-chi, had complimented her breasts and her hair, the prince had
generously offered her to him as a permanent gift. She
only half listened, her mind preoccupied with the dis-
couraging thought that one master was as bad as
another, regardless of rank. The effects of the drug
lingered, and her brain seemed to function in visual
spasms, as if the pictures in her imagination were photographs clicking into view one after another instead of
in continuous motion.

Pulling her gently down on her back, he eased her
thighs apart and mounted her, thrusting his member
between. He was awkward and inexperienced, fumbling
about clumsily, but surprisingly gentle in spite of his
haste. She felt him enter, and through sheer force of
will born of experience, she shuttered her mind against
the sensation, ignoring it. He began his rhythmic movements, and presently, in the midst of the act, with her
mind detached, carried aloft on a welcome cloud of
total indifference, she heard a strange cackling filtering
down from overhead. She moved her head to one side,
out of line with his face bobbing above as he drove to
climax. High up on the wall above the tapestry depicting the women flailing the silk fibers, drawing out the

threads and ironing the finished cloth, she saw a slit the size of a hearth brick cut out just below the ceiling. Twinkling dark eyes stared down through it, amused eyes, familiar eyes she had last seen through a haze of opium smoke at the head of the bed in which she lay.

XIV

She awoke the next morning in her own bed, her head splitting, her mouth and throat even drier than she recalled them being in the bed in the palace room. Throwing back the covers, she sat up. Instantly a wave of dizziness set her head to spinning. She inhaled the jasmine-scented air deeply, drawing it to the bottom of her lungs, driving away the sensation and with it part of the pain infesting her brain. She examined her body; there were no bruises, no swellings, no sign of blood. Other than being forced to smoke the insidious opium and submitting to Heng-chi—she could not remember how many times—she had evidently suffered no lasting effects from her night in the prince's bed.

Heng-chi's words came back to her: The prince had given her to him as a gift. But whatever his reason, Heng-chi had not seen fit to keep her. Or perhaps, like a toy consigned by a child to a toy box to be taken out periodically, played with, used, even abused and returned, she had been returned to this toy box of an apartment to sit and await his pleasure.

Swinging her legs over the side of the bed, she tried to rise, but the dizziness returned and she sat back down. Securing her temples to her head with both hands, she got up slowly, made her way to the wash basin and splashed cold water against her face. Then, going to the inner door, she knocked and opened it on Li-Sing's apartment.

The chubby, smiling girl was seated at her vanity, brushing her hair. Outside her window, squads of maids could be seen trooping toward the building. Seeing

Deirdre in her mirror, Li-Sing turned, beaming happily. "You're all right."

"Never mind me; how is An Te-si? Better?"

She nodded. "The doctor came back last night and awakened her with a saucer of ammonia under her nose. I fed her broth and some bits of chicken. She's going to be fine."

"Until the next time."

Li-Sing looked uncharacteristically grim. "The prince won't summon her again, not after she displeased him so, will he?"

"He will if he's in the mood to abuse someone. Poor An Te-si; she had such high hopes. She must be very disillusioned."

Li-Sing shook her head and, rising from her bench, came to the door. The outer doors to each apartment opened at the same time and in trooped their maids, chattering as usual, ignoring the two of them in favor of the latest gossip, the previous night in Prince Pao-chu's room. Deirdre sighed inwardly; the whole affair hadn't been disgusting enough, now it had to be tattled from one end of the city to the other. She ignored them, their lowered voices, their staring, their tittering behind their hands.

"She has to be disillusioned," she continued to Li-Sing.

"Not at all. I talked to her when I was feeding her. She can't wait to get better and to be summoned again. She insists she's not going to make the same mistake twice. She has her heart set on becoming a Royal Consort, you know."

"I know. She's a fool, the biggest I've ever seen." Deirdre paused, turning from the door, glaring at her maids huddled in a corner gossiping furiously. "Shut up, all of you! Get out!"

"But we must tidy up and care for your loveliness," began one, a hurt look wrinkling her dullard's features, her fat lower lip protruding in a pout.

"Out!" She herded them onto the veranda, slamming the door after the last one.

"You seem very nervous this morning," commented Li-Sing. She searched Deirdre's eyes. "Was it bad?"

"It was revolting." She did not feel up to explaining. "If you're curious, ask your maids. I'm sure they've heard every juicy detail." She caught herself. "I'm sorry, Li-Sing, I shouldn't take my frustrations out on you." She sat down on her vanity bench, her back to her mirror, the heel of her left hand going to her forehead. "I seem to be getting to the end of my rope. I don't know how much longer I can take this. I can't stop myself thinking about my mother and father and home. That's the worst part of it, being a million miles away from them, they not knowing where I am, whether I'm alive or dead. I'm going to crack; I can feel it coming. It's strange . . ."

"What?"

"I could never understand how people who weren't ill or wounded could pine away and die. I do now. Let me ask you something: What do you think would happen if I asked for an audience with the empresses and told them I wanted to go home? I mean a simple request to leave, to go back to my own country."

Li-Sing placed a comforting arm around her shoulders. "You can't ask directly. You'd have to talk to So-leng. And he would have to approach the Chief Eunuch."

"That simpering animal, the way he browbeat me . . ."

"If So-leng catches Li-Lien-ying in the right mood, he'll convey your request to the Empress Tz'u Hsi."

Deirdre shook her head sadly. "Li wouldn't lift a finger for me; he despises me." The dreariness flooding her heart rose in a wave engulfing her, swamping her thoughts. Her eyes brimmed with tears, and she began sobbing softly. Li-Sing took a hankie out of the sleeve of her robe and patted Deirdre's eyes and cheeks, consoling her.

Getting control of herself, Deirdre straightened her back, sniffed and steadied her voice. "I'm sorry, dear."

"It's all right, Deirdre."

"I'm not going to let it get to me; I refuse to. I've been through too much to go to pieces just because I have to spend a few weeks in here."

"A few weeks? We're here for the rest of our lives."

"Speak for yourself."

So-leng appeared at the window, waving greeting. Li-Sing let him in, excused herself and returned to her own apartment.

So-leng looked about. "Where are your maids?"

"I sent them packing. I don't need any of them."

"Good; I shall do your hair and help you dress and . . ." He sobered suddenly, remembering that she had little reason to be happy and eager for light conversation this morning. "I heard about last night," he said solemnly.

"All the gory details, I'm sure."

He sighed and sat on the stool by the door, his slender hands capping his knees. Then he reached inside his jacket and brought out a small square of rice paper. "Deirdre, I'm afraid I have some rather disturbing news."

"What news *isn't* disturbing around this god-awful place?"

"About your playmate."

"Heng-chi? He surprised me. He was very gentle; you could even say considerate. Would you believe I haven't a bruise on me?"

"It's possible he's diseased."

She lifted her glance and stared at him.

He nodded gravely. "Smallpox." Unfolding the small square of paper, he revealed a loathsome scab identical to the one given her by the doctor at her physical examination, which she had disposed of.

Her reaction to sight of it was a look of pure revulsion.

"You must place it in one of your nostrils."

"No thank you."

"You *must;* it will protect you. Smallpox can be fatal. Spring is coming; the weather will be getting warmer. If you don't prevent it, you can catch it as easily as a cold. From what I've heard, you'll be seeing a lot of Heng-chi."

"Who says he has smallpox?"

"It is suspected."

"If that were so, why would the prince allow him in his bed? It doesn't make sense."

"It is the prince who doesn't make sense. He does exactly as he pleases. Why shouldn't he? He's a prince, immune to mortal afflictions and illnesses." He proferred the scab. "Place it in your nostril, please, Deirdre. Don't think about it, just do it. Pretend it's a stone. Once it's in there, you'll forget all about it. You won't feel it; you won't even know it's there."

She made no effort to conceal her exasperation but did as he asked, taking care to hold the scab in the paper to avoid touching it with her fingertips.

"Good girl."

"What I should have is an inoculation, a needle."

"The doctors in the Forbidden City do not give needles. One other thing: It is known for certain that Heng-chi has had the Canton ulcer." *

"Oh, God!"

"I said 'had.' He's supposedly completely cured."

"I'll bet!"

He reached inside his jacket a second time, bringing out a small vial half filled with pale-brown liquid. "Keep a close watch on your skin. If you see any eruption, no matter how slight, you must begin drinking six cups of tea a day, every day, with four drops of this decoction in each cup."

"What is it?"

* Syphillis.

"The liquified root of *pung-fu-lin*.* While you're treating yourself, you must abstain from wine, vinegar, oil and any aromatic condiments. Do you understand?"

"Does this stuff work?"

"Hopefully. If it doesn't, there's a much more drastic method of treatment: mercurial pills. If it becomes necessary, I'll get some for you."

"What could be so drastic about pills?"

"Not the taking, the aftereffects. They are made from saltpeter, sulphur and mercury and are extremely powerful. They can cause violent vomiting and purging and agonizing pain in the bowels."

"How delightful."

"If you take this medicine faithfully, you may nip it in the bud and never need resort to the pills."

"Maybe I'll be lucky; maybe Heng-chi won't want me back. I let him use me because I had no choice, but he has to have noticed how unenthusiastic I was. I lay there like a lump."

So-leng shook his head. "No, he's telling everyone how delightful you were; he may even be falling in love with you."

"That's crazy."

"Is it? Perhaps, but don't be surprised if he petitions their highnesses."

"For what?"

"Permission to marry you."

"Oh, God!"

* "Peony."

XV

The fallow cotton fields swept by, endless stretches rendered dreary-looking by a dour and threatening sky. The click of the rails had long ago become as boring as raindrops rattling a tin gutter to Lisa, who was sitting in the middle of the car and staring with unseeing eyes at the gray land soon to be seized and stimulated, aroused and arrayed by spring. She had changed from the Baltimore & Ohio to the Southern Railroad in Washington four days earlier and since that time had been subjected to the widely touted but somewhat Spartan comforts of one of the new Pullman cars through Virginia, into Tennessee, across the northern tier of Alabama to Corinth, Mississippi. There she had changed to a day coach. The conductor had advised her that they would now be heading gulfward to New Orleans, more than 400 miles away.

The car was distinguished by twin lines of plush seats, a high clerestory roof with six shiny brass kerosene lamps, a stove and cramped little necessary at the front end. The unanticipated slowdowns and delays between Baltimore and Corinth had rendered the schedule useless and kept every stationmaster along the way busy erasing and rechalking his schedule annunciator from dawn till darkness. Lisa mentally calculated that by the time the train chugged into the terminal in New Orleans, she would have spent more than nine days ignoring the jouncing, staring out soot-stained windows, listening to raucous whistles, downing cold sandwiches and broiling-hot watery soup, and studying her fellow passengers getting on and off at every stop.

117

To her regret, the seats were reversible. A gangling, mule-faced man fully 6' 6", wearing a Stetson sombrero hat, box mackintosh coat and oil-grain plow boots half the size of her portmanteau had boarded at Corinth, taken one look at her, reversed his seat diagonally across from her own and was now sitting grinning at her. Periodically his hand went to the thatch of blond hair growing wild across his upper lip. Whenever her eyes inadvertently met his, his hand would desert his mustache and rise to the brim of his hat in greeting.

As he continued undressing her with his stare, she continued doing her best to ignore him, sending her thoughts back over the preceding days, the hastily scribbled note to Ross, packing her bag, gathering almost $600 in traveling money, rushing to the bank with the same two letters of credit she had carried with her on her journey to Singapore more than a year before, confirming that both letters were still usable and catching the first train to New York.

Ross would be furious with her, absolutely livid! She envisioned him reading the letter, angrily tearing it to bits and stomping up and down in the library, his favorite pacing ground, fuming and cursing while Thursby rushed to pack his bag and Enos Pryne brought up Caesar, his favorite and fastest horse, to rush him to the station. Every move he made, every phase of his pursuit could be easily conjectured; he would follow her down the identical route—to Washington, diagonally through the south to Corinth, down to New Orleans. Staying ahead of him, however, even the two hours she'd gained at the start would, with luck, enable her to reach her destination, hurry to the docks and book passage for Vera Cruz on the first ship out, the filthiest, smelliest scow imaginable, if necessary; anything that floated on which to get away before he caught up.

Although weary of train travel and absolutely dying for a first-rate hot meal, she was surprised at how well she felt. Not a single bad dream or hallucination had she had lying in her berth, dozing and sleeping. Boarding the New York-bound train had been, in retrospect, a turning point. Doing so had plucked her out of the doldrum shadows into the sunlight, enabling her to shed the shackles of frustration and discouragement welded onto her by the interminable delay in returning to the Orient.

Now that she thought about it, she hadn't felt this fit since shortly before the *Sea Urchin* had arrived at Fremantle, on the west coast of Australia. She and Ross had gone ashore to dine, and to learn of the insurrection that had erupted in Batavia during their absence.

She smoothed her black Berlin gloves, ran both hands over her lap, erasing the wrinkles of her blazer suit skirt, and checked in the window the angle of her fancy rough-straw bonnet, its plume finished with a large rosette of dotted net and trimmed on the left side with three loops of net and fancy straw braid. A darling helmet, she thought, in which to march into the fray.

She conceded to her conscience that it had been a deceitful thing to do to Ross. But she was fed up arguing about it, the two of them going round in circles over how much longer before she might leave, how she felt, Alex Craven's and Dr. Cairns's approval. One simply had to take the bull by the horns when the bull thundered by, or be prepared to sit and wait for another that might never show up.

On the other hand, she wasn't deluding herself. She realized that she wasn't completely cured; at any time her condition could flare up. If and when the monster reappeared, she would simply have to take it on and bully it into submission.

She would be her own doctor, healing herself with faith in herself and her mission. The job was one that she alone could bring to successful conclusion; that very knowledge would serve, as it was already serving, to spur complete recovery.

Deirdre: In spite of the nightmare and its horrifying aftermath, she was alive; that much Lisa's intuition confirmed. The indissoluble link between them remained intact. She refused to dwell on her daughter's plight, however; imagining the worst would only encourage despair. One bright light of optimism displayed itself in all its glory. Everyone but Jacobus Franeker had insisted that it was impossible to rescue a prisoner from the penal colony on Macquarie Island. It had never been done and never would be: The weather conditions were much too brutal, the colony itself too well guarded, the icy waters a natural barrier that no sane person would test. And even should they reach shore, finding one individual out of 200 was out of the question, impossible.

But with Franeker's help, she had done it. The *Sea Urchin* had anchored off the island, they had gone ashore, reconnoitered, established the location of the work gang Ross had been assigned to, returned to the ship, formulated a daring rescue plan and successfully carried it out. There had been no such word as "impossible" in the vocabulary of that mission.

The two letters of credit in her purse would provide her with all the money she needed to buy all the help she needed, bribe all the officials she needed to get her to Deirdre and the two of them out of China and back to Blackwood—and banish the ogre "impossible" to the realm of the pessimists who sincerely believed there was such a creature.

I am coming, my baby, I am coming.

She reached into her bag and brought out a pocket atlas of the world, which she had bought between trains in Baltimore and which she had been studying off and on ever since. From Providence to Gibraltar was . . .

"Excuse me, is this seat taken?" She looked up. Mule-face was staring down at her, his eyes boring into hers.

"It's sure 'nough a long jaunt to New Orleans. A body can git mighty lonesome settin' and starin' out the window. They're so dirty. Ah swear, when they build these cars they must install dirty windows. Ah never have seen a clean one. The name's Coley Hollis. You don't mind if Ah join you."

Without waiting for her answer, he lifted her portmanteau off the seat beside her, placed it under the seat and sat, bringing down with him the fetid odor of stale whiskey and staler tobacco. It was close in the car, and the addition of his odors to the air she was breathing was something less than welcome. Still, it was public transportation, and unless he made a pest of himself, she had little choice but to put up with him, smells and all. She glanced up and down the car: At least 30 seats were empty.

"Coley Hollis, that's me. Ah buy and sell hossflesh in Chalybeate. Ah didn't catch your name."

She turned back to watching the barren landscape slide by, the clouds overhead stuffed with rain, swollen to bursting with it.

"It wouldn't be Lucille? Lucille was my sainted mother's name. Lucille Crossett. Her family is quite well known in Chalybeate." Unbuttoning his coat, he reached inside and pulled out a half-filled pint of Montgomery Supreme Whiskey, uncorking and proferring it. "Care to join me?"

"No thank you."

"Oh, you got a voice. You got a name, too?" She glared at him as he swigged, recorked his bottle and restored it to his pocket. "Ah, that is good for what ails a body."

"Excuse me." She stood up, picked up her bag and started by him.

"Hey, where you goin'?"

"I'm changing my seat."

"Here now, don't go runnin' off just as we're about to get acquainted."

She took another seat and immediately he dropped down alongside her, grinning broadly. "We got to get to know each other. You're some looker, you know? Ah always was partial to red hair. You know what they say: Fire up top, fire down below."

Again his hand went inside his coat, this time bringing out a half-chewed plug of Battle Ax. He bit off a piece and began grinding away at it noisily.

She got up again, moving forward, and was about to take a third seat when he all but bowled her over rushing to join her. She glanced out the window. The train had started up a grade and was slowing perceptibly. Setting her portmanteau on the empty seat, she walked to the end door. She was about to open it when his hand flashed by her arm and opened it for her.

Out on the platform, she spun about, scowling frostily. "Will you please stop pestering me!"

"Pesterin'? Me?" Astonishment widened his ugly face, then a surly look replaced his surprise; he was insulted. "You got to be joshin'." He brought his hand down on her shoulder, caressing it. "Ah just want to be friends. Nothin' wrong with that."

Shaking him off, she stepped back, going into her handbag and bringing out a two-shot derringer. It had lain loaded in the drawer to the cabriole table for years. She wasn't even sure it would fire. But its introduction into the conversation had the desired effect.

Paling and gulping, he backed against the lazy-tongs gate separating the front end of the car from the tender. "Hey, what you got there?"

"What does it look like?" The train was continuing to slow as it approached the top of the grade. She brought one foot down hard on the trap release, the steel plate lifting slowly to reveal the steps. "Get off."

"Hey, are you serious? Ah got to git to New Orleans!"

"Not on this train." She waved the gun menacingly. But it was no longer the derringer he was looking at; it was her eyes. Swallowing, he backed down the steps, dropping onto the gravel bed, letting go of the hand grips, as the locomotive gained the summit and started down, quickly picking up speed. She leaned out and saw him standing on the slope of the bed, shaking his fist as the baggage car swept by him.

The sun, as drained of color as Coley Hollis's cheeks at sight of the gun, was well down the sky by the time the train pulled into the terminal. Carrying her own bag, she got off, pushed through the crowd clogging the ramp ascending into the station proper, made her way through the station and hailed a buggy for hire, the first in a long line drawn up to the curb by the front doors.

"Take me to the docks, please."

The driver was a gnarled little knot of a man with snapping blue eyes brightening his leathery face. "Which docks would that be, ma'am?"

"I'm going to Mexico, Vera Cruz."

The man was about to respond when a familiar voice interrupted: "That's all right, driver. The lady won't be needing your services."

She groaned and turned. There stood Ross trying his utmost not to smile in triumph but failing in the attempt. Taking her bag from her and gripping her by the elbow, he steered her back under the marquee shadowing the main entrance to the station.

She glared pitchforks at him. "How did you get here? What line did you take? How could you—"

"Darling, I've been waiting almost two whole days for you."

"It's not possible!"

He raised his hand. "Word of honor. You came down from Corinth?"

She nodded grimly.

"You came through Chattanooga?"

"Yes!"

He winked and laughed. "The long way . . ."

"What are you talking about?"

"I got to Chattanooga, got off and took the express down to Atlanta, then to Montgomery, where the tracks end. I hired a horse, changed to a fresh one in Darlington, changed again in Bigbee, crossed over into Mississippi, changed a third time in Wiggins, in Stone County, and here I am. Actually, it's only about three hundred fifty miles if you stick to the main roads. A spirited ride, though, I must say." He winced, tapped his backside and grinned.

"Of all the deceitful . . ."

"You look exhausted."

"I've never felt better."

"Liar!"

Their voices rose, gaining the attention of the line of cabmen awaiting fares, and passersby crowding the sidewalk. Ignoring one and all, they stood scowling each other down, exchanging accusations.

"Don't waste your breath. I'm on my way to Vera Cruz, and nothing you can do or say can stop me."

"Don't bet your last dollar on that. To get to Vera Cruz, you'll need a ship; only no ship will take you."

"Nonsense!"

"I mean it, darling. Don't bother going all the way over to the docks and buttonholing captains. Any man who sails out of here with you on board and has any idea of returning here had best be prepared to hand over his master's certificate to the Port Master. The word is out."

"That's ridiculous. Your head must be saddlesore, as well as your—"

Bringing out an envelope, he held it before her eyes. "I have here a statement attesting to your physical and mental condition sworn to and signed by Alex and Cairns. It's very simple, Lisa: You're in no shape to travel to Mexico, Vera Cruz or anyplace else. By now, thanks to your taking the scenic route down here, every captain in port knows all about the redhead from Providence. One thing more: I've arranged for a private detective to take you home, a Mr. Goff. He's full of funny stories; you'll enjoy his company. Alex has agreed to move into the house and divide his time between you and his other patients. Oh, yes, he'll be using the study as his office. As for me, I'm on my way to Singapore—"

"Not without me you're not!"

"Without you."

"No!"

"Yes!"

This exchange being carried on at the top of their lungs drew the attention of a passing policeman, who pushed through the crowd of gawkers gathered about them. Pushing back his helmet, he folded his arms, shifting his eyes back and forth from one to the other, a melancholy expression molding his fat features.

"Is this fella bothering you, lady?"

"He certainly is; he's making a public nuisance of himself!"

"Officer, I'm the lady's husband."

"I've never seen him before in my life!"

"Look in her bag. You'll see her identification, something or other. She's Mrs. Ross Dandridge. I'm her *husband,* I tell you."

From the look on the policeman's face, settling domestic quarrels, budding or raging, in public or in private, was patently not his forte. "Listen," he entreated, "why don't you two just take this away to some nice, quiet place? Settle matters in a nice, quiet way." Turning to the crowd, he lifted his arms and his nightstick. "All right, folks, the show's over. Go about your business."

"I'm hungry," Lisa said icily.

"I'll take you to a nice restaurant."

"Not to sit and argue while we're eating."

"All right, all right, all right, we'll discuss it like two intelligent, grown-up human beings."

"That, darling, will be the day!"

XVI

They made verbal war loudly, spiritedly, relentlessly and continuously six blocks up the street to Marceau's Delta Steak House. Marceau's proved to be a dimly lit, immaculate-looking and delightfully intimate restaurant virtually patronless at such an odd hour, midway between lunch and dinner. They were shown to a corner table by a nervous-looking waiter, who, seeing the electricity passing back and forth between their eyes as they caught their breaths for the next go-round, discreetly backed away as soon as he seated them.

"I'll go back with your Mr. Goff," said Lisa with affected sweetness, in consideration of two elderly ladies sitting nearby sipping tea, "but you'd better warn him that the first chance I get to lose him, he's lost. I'll head straight for the nearest port. Even if I go all the way back, I can leave Providence for Gibraltar, to Port Said, down the Suez Canal."

"Don't be imbecilic; the Suez Canal is barely started."

"That's how much you know; it's almost finished. It probably will be by the time I get there."

"And if it isn't, what'll you do? Ride a camel over what's left to be dug?"

"I've compared routes, Mr. Know-it-all: It's nearly seven hundred miles shorter heading eastward down the canal through the Indian Ocean."

"I'm impressed. I'm also sick of talking about it. You're not going anywhere but home!"

"Those two ladies are staring. Would you kindly lower your voice?"

"Lower your *own*," he whispered, seething.

"Would you care to order?" The waiter, as timorous as he was nervous, loomed above them, pad and pencil ready.

"In a few minutes," said Ross.

"Yes, sir."

She studied the menu, talking into it. "I'll make a bargain with you, darling. Do you have a dime?" He sighed and produced a dime. She picked it up. "This should settle matters once and for all. Heads *I* go, tails the *two of us* go."

"Lisa . . ."

"Very well, forget the coin. Simply choose one or the other. As for me, one detective, fifty detectives, I refuse to go home. I refuse to sit by the fire watching the clock, waiting for the mail—like waiting for the jury to tell you whether you hang or go free. I've come this far; I'm going on, all the way. And, darling"—she paused, leaning forward, her eyes burning into his—"I give you my solemn word, if you so much as lift your little finger to try and stop me, I shall march into the nearest court and divorce you. *That*, Ross, is a promise. Now you will order my dinner, please: double lamb chops, a boiled potato, broccoli, salad with roquefort dressing and coffee."

"You're on a strict diet!"

"I've been off it for nine days. I already told you, I've never felt better, except I'm famished."

"You're incorrigible!"

"Order."

"I love you!"

He leaned across the table, his hands to her cheeks, kissing her warmly, affectionately. The two elderly ladies gasped, tsked, well-I-nevered, and finished their tea, smiling broadly.

BOOK TWO
JOURNEY TO DESPAIR

I

It is, unfortunately, a securely established fact that life in what appears to be its most difficult and intolerable phase cannot only fail to improve but worsen. Soleng's words proved prophetic. Within the week, he brought Deirdre information that caused her to sink down upon her bed and bury her face in her hands.

"You are to be summoned by the Empress Tz'u Hsi to be examined and judged as to your qualifications for marriage to Heng-chi."

"No!"

He sat beside her, his homely face grim with sympathy. It was too lovely a morning for such gloomy news, a day that gave promise of continuing a sequence of days unseasonably bright and balmy for early April. In the wake of the discouragingly long winter, the sun seemed determined to rush spring onto the stage in atonement for the overly long absence of welcome weather. The dogwoods were in bud, as were the tiny and tall rhododendrons. The gingko trees were sprouting their familiar fan-shaped leaves, and the thuya and wutung were coming to life. Also displaying their colors about the grounds were the first azaleas and fat, round peonies.

"Let's walk to the Well of the Pearl Concubine," suggested So-leng.

"No."

"Please; you need the fresh air. It's beautiful out. The ducks are gathering on the River of Golden Water, the pheasants are back, and the little bamboo partridges are strutting about like General Sung. I saw three finches, little red and brown bunches of feathers flitting about the fountain, playing."

She shrugged and got up from the edge of the bed. He wiped the tear stains from her cheeks with the hem of his cuff.

They sat under the thuya tree, Deirdre's doldrums gathered about her like weighty robes. "I haven't even seen him since that night," she mused aloud. "I was sure he'd forgotten me completely. She can't make me marry him, can she?"

"I'm afraid Tz'u Hsi can make anyone do anything."

"But I don't love him! I'd never dream of marrying him. He's disgusting."

"Love is the least of marriage in China, Deirdre, even in all the millions of matches the empresses never even hear about. The most important thing is convenience. Will the marriage 'improve' the families."

"What can I do for his family? I'm a *wàigworén,* the oddity, the freak of the Imperial Court." She began heaping together all the negatives, the illogicality and awkwardness of such a match. Her tone gradually took on defiance, as if, having recovered from the shock of the news, she was girding her meager defenses in preparation for the action to come. "If I'm to be summoned, I'll tell her the truth, what I was, how I come to be here. She'll never permit him to marry a prostitute, not if his father is as important as you say."

"You're rationalizing. Don't; self-delusion is no protection. Tz'u Hsi won't attach any disgrace to that business in Chefoo. When she came here, she herself was a concubine of the fifth rank, as low as you are. If she hadn't been selected, if instead she had lived out her life in Peking, she probably would have become a prostitute."

"I don't believe that."

"It's true. Her family lived in obscurity."

"Her father was a Manchu, a bannerman."

"Yes, but he was disgraced, cashiered from the army

for deserting his post in the rebellion. He had no relatives or friends in high places. They say she hated her family."

"Because of him?"

"Because they paid no attention to her. Her parents doted on her sisters."

"If she was so insignificant, how did she get to be a concubine, even fifth rank?"

"She's a Manchu. Ever since the law of 1661, all young Manchu girls are eligible for service in the Forbidden City as either servants or concubines."

"She's come a long way."

"With luck, timing and the morals of an alley cat. Still, if I were you, I would think twice before telling her your background. You could be poking into a hornet's nest; you could be badly stung."

"What could be worse than having to marry Hengchi, with his smallpox, his Canton ulcer, his filthy opium?"

"One thing could be worse." So-leng drew his index finger across his throat. He studied her with pity in his eyes. "Marry him and you'll live outside the Forbidden City in the Imperial City. His father is a very important man, an assistant to his brother—"

"Prince Kung, the most powerful minister in all of China; I know. I don't care about any of that."

"You should; you might be able to turn it to your advantage. Once you're outside these walls, you may find escape easier, at least not completely impossible."

She pressed her fist against her mouth, sighing mournfully. "Dear God, I want to leave this place, this country. I want to go home. I want to wake up in my own bed, in my very own room in Blackwood. I want to be Deirdre Dandridge again, not somebody's plaything. I want all this to end; I want my life back. Is that so demanding, so unreasonable? I should think they'd be glad to get rid of me!"

"Sh, keep your voice down." He was right to caution

her; maids and eunuchs in pairs and groups were strolling about the area and standing admiring the crystalline beauty of the fountain, dazzlingly bright under the blazing sun. "We've been through all that. Unfortunately, your presence eases the annoying irritation of her majesty's inferiority complex."

"That silly-looking, conceited thing; what inferiority complex—"

"Regarding the French and the English—and the Americans. And what you do for her, you do for the entire court, particularly Li-Lien-ying." He paused and smiled wearily. "Sometimes I think the thing he does best for her is to exaggerate her dislikes and fears, make them seem more important to her than they actually are, the way you told me he carried on about Jesus Christ and Christian priests and ministers the night he came to take you to the prince. The trouble is, she listens to him. What you say may or may not upset her, but however you phrase it, you can be sure he'll jump on it and blow it up all out of proportion."

"He hates me. You should have seen his eyes when he was carrying on."

"I've seen his eyes. If you remember that night, I didn't exactly linger when he ordered me out."

She drew a hand down his cheek and smiled. "I'm sorry to be such a grouch. I know you're trying to help me make the best of things. I'm grateful; you know I am."

"All I ask is that you keep your head; don't go to pieces. Be patient; one day you'll get out."

She searched his eyes. "You don't really believe that, So-leng, but thank you, anyway."

The imperial summons arrived four days later; both she and Heng-chi were ordered to the Hall of Supreme Harmony, situated in the heart of the Forbidden City. They were escorted by the Chief Eunuch through seven interior gates linked by red walls, low galleries that served as waiting rooms, lesser two-storied halls and corner pavilions all forming a closed perimeter under the undulating roof-lines.

The throne room itself was 100 feet deep, 110 feet across and 200 feet wide. Its walls were three feet thick, and each lacquered pillar supporting the roof was the trunk of a single giant oak tree. The interior decoration was designed to coincide with the proper conception of the Five Colors in harmonious order with the Five Elements, the Five Spheres and the Five Directions. The paving in the courtyard was black; the marble terrace white; the walls of the building red; the gleaming roof yellow. The fifth and last color was the blue of the sky above. Adding accents were small designs of deeper blue, green, white and gold, painted on the crossbeams and ornamental flanges of the 12 pillars of the open porch. Also in evidence were gilt dragon handles and door hinges, while long gilt chains hung from the top of the ridge as protection against lightning.

Entering the royal presence, the Chief Eunuch ordered both Deirdre and Heng-chi down on their knees in the kowtow. Three times they knelt, touching their foreheads to the floor nine times. Completing the obeisance, Deirdre rose, her eyes taking in the surroundings and drawn to the two thrones. Flanked by their ladies-in-waiting, Tz'u Hsi-Duan Yo-Kong Yee-Joan Yu Ghwong Chung-Sho Goong-Chin Shen-Tsung She, the diminutive interloper Empress Dowager, and Tz'u An, Empress Dowager by marriage to the recently deceased Emperor Hsien-feng, were seated side by side under twin scones overflowing with peacock feathers. The scones were attached to a 12-foot-high screen depicting peacocks in a lovely garden. On either side of the thrones were teakwood stands occupied by brass plates piled with pyramids of apples. And all about were small tables displaying magnificent Ming three-color enamelware; Sung porcelains—vases, ewers and bulb bowls; goblets of brass and gold, urns and jars and beautiful gold and vermilion screens.

Tz'u An wore Dragon Robes of State and a sable hat studded with pearls, while "Old Buddha," as the eunuchs called Tz'u Hsi behind her back, was attired in a bamboo-leaf-embroidered robe. She also wore a number of jewels, including a cape made of 3,500 pearls of perfect shape and color and a single pearl the size of a hen's egg suspended from the top button of her robe.

As Deirdre expected, Tz'u Hsi took immediate command of the audience, Tz'u An deferring to her more aggressive ruling partner with a casual gesture of surrender. Both empresses appeared inordinately curious over Deirdre, staring at her as if, she mused, she had two heads. Tz'u Hsi gestured her forward.

"Closer, child."

"Let us see your hair," burst Tz'u An. "We want to feel it." Deirdre bowed her head and shuffled forward in the accepted manner. Tz'u An fingered her hair. "It's like spun silk; it *is* silk."

"It is not!" exclaimed Tz'u Hsi in the voice of an adult correcting an ignorant child. Reacting with a hurt look, Tz'u An pulled her hand back. It amused Deirdre to see that neither empress paid the slightest attention to Heng-chi, who continued to stand in place four paces behind her, with Li-Lien-ying behind him. "What is your name, child?" asked Tz'u Hsi.

"Deirdre Dandridge, Your Majesty."

"Louder; speak up!" exclaimed the Chief Eunuch.

"Be still, Li, we hear her perfectly. You are English."

"American."

"Indeed. Interesting. Do you know that you are the first American we have ever seen?"

"Do all Americans have red hair?" inquired Tz'u An.

"Of course not," snapped Tz'u Hsi. She pursed her mouth and shook her head gravely. "Unhappily, we do not feel generous toward foreigners. Perhaps you have heard that. You should know that our antipathy is not without cause. So you may understand why we feel as we do, perhaps we should explain." The cold eyes as dark as the heart of a storm cloud appeared to lose their coldness as she hastened to explain. Looking at Tz'u Hsi and listening, Deirdre began getting the impression that the empress was unnecessarily self-conscious about the matter and felt some strange sense of obligation to pour it all out.

"China's experience with the foreign devils began when the star of the Ming Dynasty was at its height. A fleet of white-sailed ships came up the Canton River from the country of Portugal. Their commander requested the privilege of mercantile trade. It is written that he was a charming man, princely in manner. The Canton viceroy was very impressed; he reported him favorably to the throne. Emperor Wu Tsung used the vermilion pencil to reply. He acceded to the commander's request and gave permission to trade; he invited the commander to Peking. He was given a royal escort to the court, where he was welcomed as an honored guest.

"The white-sailed ships were filled with green and black teas and silks, embroideries, porcelains, ivories, jute, kaolin, all sorts of products. The ships sailed back to Portugal. The Portuguese paid generously for the first shiploads. The commander secured permission for several hundred of his countrymen to settle in our beautiful southern cities, Foochow and Ningpo.

Months passed. The commander's brother arrived with many ships and thousands of armed men. They pirated our storehouses and our temples. They behaved like wild animals. One rashly slit open the wedding chair of a daughter of the House of Chu at Ningpo. It was clear to the emperor that he had opened the door to disaster. To rid our country of this pestilence, we were forced to rise up and massacre them all.

"Near the end of the Ming Dynasty, when the people

were in rebellion, Western ships again sailed up the Canton River. They bombarded our Tiger Forts and landed soldiers. They had with them a charter from the king of England, Charles. They desired to establish a trading post outside the walls of Canton. We had no choice but to permit it, since we had no gunboats with which to drive them away. All our precepts were against military power. The emperor issued edicts restraining these brazen intruders. It was some decades before the uncultured savages from England and later from France discovered that we had no great military power behind our edicts. They could therefore wander into the country whenever they pleased, to force their Christianity and their poisonous opium upon us.

"All this and much more, scores of true stories of a similar sordid nature are recorded in the books in the Halls of Literary Glory. We Chinese have a much longer history than other peoples in this world. For forty-six centuries we have recorded our history, the triumphs and the disasters.

"Over the past two hundred years, we have had nothing but woeful experiences with the foreign devils. We trusted them, we welcomed them, extending the right hand of friendship, only to be betrayed.

"I tell you this so that you will know that our feelings toward foreigners are justified. It is wisely written that the child burned hesitates to test his hand in the flame." She smiled, brightening her eyes, elevating her jowls, arcing the lines of her forehead upward, but taking care to keep her lips tightly sealed. "Now," she continued, "let us talk of matters more pleasant." She gestured Heng-chi forward, and bowing his head, he came up alongside Deirdre. "You two young people wish to be married."

This matter-of-fact assumption, eight simple words joined, lifted the lid on the cauldron of Deirdre's boiling emotions.

"No!" she shouted, tears bursting into her eyes, dimming sight of the two empresses. "No! No! No! I won't marry him! I want to go home, to my mother and daddy. Let me go home. Please, please, Your Majesty, I beg you!" Sobbing loudly, eliciting gasps from the ladies-in-waiting looking on, she sank to her knees. "Home, I just want to go home," she shrilled, the tears cascading down her cheeks, descending, striking the polished wooden floor. "I'm so terribly, terribly homesick. I want to go home."

Li-Lien-ying had rushed forward, but Tz'u Hsi gestured, staying him. "Leave her alone." Rising from her throne, she descended the two steps, gently lifting Deirdre up by her shoulders, cupping her jaw in one hand. "There, there, you musn't cry."

"Please let me go home."

"If that is what you wish, then go you shall." She turned to the Chief Eunuch. "The audience is ended; show them out."

II

The *Sea Cloud* had been designed for trading between California and China, but her appointments and accommodations for passengers were as elegantly comfortable as could be found on any first-class European packet ship. The six state-rooms were situated adjacent the ship's officers' quarters under the poop deck. All six boasted identical interiors, oak and rosewood paneling set off with arches and enameled cornices decorated with exquisite carving. Even the edges of the beams were carved and picked out in gold.

From bowsprit to taffrail, the vessel was an eye-engaging expression of man's challenge to the temperamental blue waters of the world. Great expectations had been held for her when she was christened and sent screeching down the ways in 1851, 16 years earlier. But ill fortune, inefficient handling, too frequent changes in ownership to develop "pride at the helm" combined to relegate her to the fleet of also-rans in the century-old contest to cut the Pacific crossing time to less than 33 days. The *Sea Cloud* had nevertheless seen uninterrupted, if undistinguished, duty between the west-coast ports of the United States and Mexico and the Far East. Her main-deck paintwork was a dazzling white with blue waterways. Stanchions, hanging knees, ledges and the lower squares of the beams displayed their natural color under gleaming coats of varnish, while the waterways of the lower deck were painted bluish-gray. Her graceful hull was black with a single slender gold band that terminated at the bow, which supported the figurehead of a gilded eagle. Her mainmast was two and a half feet in diameter

140

and, with the topmast and skysail poles, measured 193 feet from heel to truck. And full fitting of sails comprised well over 10,000 square yards of cotton canvas.

Her home port was San Francisco, but as the Dandridges' all-too-rare good fortune would have it, she was scheduled to come up the coast from Managua, Nicaragua, where she had taken on a load of cotton and coffee, and would be stopping off at San Marcos to add lumber before heading across the Pacific to Singapore. The *Sea Cloud* had been built for Garvey and Haymes in New York by W. H. Webb, Dandridge Shipbuilding's fiercest, ablest and most successful competitor in the spirited race to sow the seas with clippers during the middle years of the century. Their competition, however, in no way lessened the respect the principals of the two firms held for one another. And these feelings were in large measure shared by those who purchased their respective ships.

Before departing New Orleans for Vera Cruz, Ross had wired Tom Overstreet in Providence to sound out owners up and down the Atlantic Coast, seeking accommodations on any Orient-bound vessel, hopefully one heading for Singapore. Information had come back that the *Sea Cloud* was scheduled to arrive in San Marcos in six days. Accommodations would be awaiting Mr. and Mrs. Dandridge if they managed to reach Vera Cruz and cross the nearly 250-mile-wide neck of land comprised of the Mexican Plateau and the Sierra Madre del Sur in time. The 1,300-mile journey by bark from New Orleans to Vera Cruz consumed more than three days, their ship averaging a brisk 16 knots per hour. By the time they had reached port, a coach had been engaged and they had set out for San Marcos, the allotted time had shrunk to barely 70 hours. By changing teams every 75 miles, ignoring the ceaseless jouncing and bouncing and the onslaught of brick-red dust raised by the horses' hooves, which penetrated the isinglass win-

dows of the coach, they had managed to reach their
destination 12 hours before sailing time.

Now they stood together at the rail as the *Sea Cloud*
tacked, beating up to windward, swinging about to
catch its power from the other quarter. They looked
overhead as she bore off a trifle, standing away slightly
from the wind's eye and gradually picking up speed.
The command " 'Bout ship!" was heard and the helm
put down to leeward. The sails flapped and thundered as
they trapped the wind from the opposite quarter; the
yards of the mainmast were braced, the fore-topsail remaining across the wind, helping the ship fall off toward
the open sea.

It was an extraordinary sight in any weather, this
taming and pressing into service of the wind god, and
this weather was perfect for running at 22 knots. The
world was arrayed in blue and gold, white and silver,
the air crisp, the sky cloudless, the sea heaving its many
backs, white lash marks slicing across them, spume freed
by the wind and rising.

Lisa was grateful for the day. She was feeling poorly;
the journey overland from Vera Cruz had been much
more physically demanding and exhausting than either
the train trip down to New Orleans or the run across
the gulf. As it had been before, it was becoming again
more and more of an effort for her to concentrate, to
consciously stave off confusion and those annoying periods when her usually reliable memory deserted her.
Uppermost in her mind was the thought that she must
not let Ross suspect that she had slipped back from the
point of recovery achieved in New Orleans and temporarily sustained thereafter. It was with the greatest
reluctance that he had surrendered to her fiat; now she
must not let him down. Or herself.

The sea proved a tonic, the abundant fresh air strong
medicine for all the several ills that merged like the
strands of a rope to tug her down into melancholy.

There was, they had been informed by Captain Mac-Gregor, a doctor on board—of sorts, she had decided upon being introduced to him. Dr. Horace Seely impressed both her and Ross as a cut below either Alex Craven's or Howard Cairns's standards. Seely was in his early 60s, a garrulous man, a good-natured extrovert, but curiously lax about his personal appearance, looking, whatever the hour, as if he'd just gotten out of bed. Lisa noted too that his hands trembled in the act of lifting his rum to his lips, and murmured thanks to the stars that her condition could in no way demand surgery from him.

"This has to be the luckiest break we've ever had!" exclaimed Ross, standing beside her at the rail one afternoon two days out and hugging her to him with one arm. "From San Marcos straight to Singapore, with, that is, just a slight bend through the Philippines and around Borneo." Singapore coming to mind turned him serious for the moment. "Though I still wonder about heading there instead of Batavia."

"Darling, the only man in the world who can help us is Wo Sin, and he's not in Batavia."

"You seem very certain he'll want to help."

"He will. Wait till you meet him."

"Lisa, the man is a criminal, probably the biggest underworld figure in the entire peninsula; the sort who's as dependable as the wind and only if it means a nice, fat profit. What makes you think he'll even remember you, let alone offer to help?"

She patiently marshaled her reasons for putting her trust in Wo Sin. The year before, when she and Deirdre had arrived in Singapore in pursuit of Ross, only to find themselves forced to stand helplessly by and see him sentenced to penal servitude, she had subsequently tried to hire a ship to rescue him. She was turned down by a dozen captains, who wanted no part of the Gates of Hell—the entrance to Macquarie Harbor—and the fierce weather afflicting the area. No amount could induce anyone to attempt the mission, until Jacobus Franeker agreed to take her there aboard the *Sea Urchin*.

Prior to that, shortly before Franeker came to her hotel room and introduced himself, another captain, one who had declined her offer, suggested she contact Wo Sin. She had managed to meet with him, and he had listened to her story. He had been warmly sympathetic but explained that he would be unable to become involved. The fact that a British justice had sentenced Ross, and a British ship had taken him to a British penal colony, put the affair beyond Wo Sin's self-defined jurisdiction. He had pointed out that the British authorities and the Chinese underworld in Singapore scrupulously observed an unwritten code of ethics in respect to one another. The British dealt with their own problems in their own ways, the Chinese in theirs. Neither interfered with the other's intragroupal affairs.

However, Wo Sin had sent her away with the promise that should she ever need his help in any matter in which the English were not involved, she should not hesitate to call upon him.

"You actually trust him?" asked Ross.

"I do."

"Woman's intuition?"

"That and some small ability for judging character. Even if I had doubts, I'd go to him, because I can't see as we have any choice."

"There's your friend Captain Franeker. Two of his grandchildren were kidnaped along with Deirdre. He has a lot more at stake in this business than Mr. Big."

"Perhaps, but Jacobus isn't Chinese, nor can he pull strings the way Wo Sin can. You watch: He'll do what Evan Brockway and the whole U.S. State Department in Washington couldn't—get us into the country."

"If China is where she is. We can't even be sure of that."

"My, but we're in a pessimistic mood today."

"It's not pessimism; I'm being realistic. We can't get our hopes up too high with nothing tangible to support them."

"Hope doesn't need tangible support, darling; all it needs is voluntary encouragement."

"I wonder how much he'll try and bleed us for."

"I doubt very much if he'll want money, Ross."

"Don't be too sure. And as long as you're hoping, cross your fingers he's still alive. It's been more than a year since you've seen him. Men in his line aren't exactly noted for their longevity. I just wish . . ." He shook his head and stared out over the sea at a lone sea gull skimming a lacy edge of spume from the top of a wave, floating easily with the wind on its boomerang wings.

"What do you wish?"

"That we could go through legitimate channels."

"We tried; it didn't work."

He kissed her cheek and made love with his eyes. "You look exhausted. How do you feel?"

"Fine."

"You ought to lie down until dinner. Two hours' nap could do wonders for you."

"You think so, doctor?"

"Don't you?"

Captain MacGregor approached, touching the bill of his cap in greeting. He was a swarthy man of medium height, with an unkempt mustache that reminded Lisa of the one on the pest on the train coming down from Corinth. Like Coley Hollis's, it flourished but, from its condition, obviously merited little serious attention when the captain got out of bed and prepared his face for the day. He smoked crooked, rootlike cheroots with abandon, pulling the life out of the one presently plugging the corner of his mouth as if every draw was sheer rapture. With him was a tall, strikingly handsome man, prematurely white hair wisping forth from under the lining of his cap, his ice-blue eyes appraising her, a smile playing about his mouth, threatening to take possession of it.

"And what do ye think of the style in which we hondle her, Mr. Dondridge, sor?" asked Captain MacGregor pleasantly, his accent more Denbigh Welsh than Scottish, Lisa thought. "Do ye approve?"

"We're only passengers, captain, not critics or spies for the owners," said Ross, smiling.

"Your criticism is most welcome, sor." MacGregor turned to the man beside him. "Mr. Dondridge is *the* Mr. Dondridge, Mr. Burnette." The captain stiffened comically, self-consciously. "Do forgive me my bod monnors, Mr. and Mrs. Dondridge. May I present the first mate, Mr. Clay Burnette."

Nods, mumbled greetings, handshakes. "Are you enjoying the voyage so far?" asked Burnette.

Lisa nodded. "Very much so."

"We'll be raising the Revilla Gigedos off the starboard bow shortly," said MacGregor. "Oogly-looking rocks. There's an extinct volcano on Socorro." Looking upward, he considered the sky. "We've a sponking breeze. At this rate we'll be in the China Seas in less than forty days." Again he touched the bill of his cap. "A pleasure to have ye aboard, modom, sor." He smiled at Lisa and winked. "Begging yer pardon, but do I detect a British occent, modom?"

She laughed. "The remnants of one. I've been an American for seventeen years."

"Where in England did ye come from, may I osk?"

"Mansfield."

"In Nottingham."

"Yes."

"You'll want to meet Mr. Kirby, the sailmaker," interposed Burnette. "He's from Sutton."

Lisa gasped. "Is he really? Why, that's only a few miles from Mansfield."

"He speaks of Monsfield," said the captain. "When

ye get a chance, why not look in on him in his cobin?"

"I shall."

"He's British to the core," continued MacGregor. "Ond I soospect a wee bit homesick. Ye two should have lots to bandy aboot. We shall see ye ot dinner, sor, modom. Pleasant voyage."

They walked off.

"Nice fellow," commented Ross.

"He is, although I'm not too impressed with his choice of first officer."

"Burnette? What's the matter with him? He didn't say two words."

"He didn't have to; it was the way he stared at me."

Ross laughed. "The man knows beauty when he sees it. You ought to be flattered."

"I'm not. It's not funny, darling. I know his sort. Tall, good-looking, the type who turns little girls' hearts upside down and knows it. As vain as a peacock full tail. I don't like his eyes, the way he fastens them on you and holds them there."

"You're imagining."

"I'm not."

"All right, you're not. Now, what about that nap?"

"I suppose." He kissed her on the cheek and started her toward the state-room. Within a stride of the door, she stopped and, tilting her head, catching the lowering sun in the fiery waves of her hair, eyed him suspiciously.

"What?"

"I almost forgot. That letter you waved at me in front of the train station in New Orleans: That was all a great lie, wasn't it? Alex and Howard Cairns never wrote any statement."

"Oh, but they did."

"Cross your heart?"

"Hope to die."

"Where is it now? Let me see it."

"I . . . threw it away."

"Ah-hah! Faker, fraud!"

"Darling, they gave me a letter; I mean I asked for it. They signed it and—"

"You threw it away."

"Why keep it? It's useless now."

"You actually went to the Port Master with it?"

"I . . ."

"You didn't go to the Port Master."

"I was going to."

"So you buffaloed me, you deceitful thing!"

"Not at all. I had every intention of approaching him and of alerting all the captains. I didn't have time. Lisa, stop scratching, for goodness' sake. Everything I tried or was going to try was for your own good."

She grinned and patted his cheek. "My thoughtful Ananias."

She lay atop the bed fully clothed, dozing, unleashing her thoughts, letting them wheel ahead like autumn leaves before the breeze. Wo Sin was their towering hope. Captain China, his hands bright with blood, perhaps, but his eye as honest as Stephen's, the Apostles' first choice. Evan Brockway had tried his best, but if he'd accomplished anything, it was to prove that there would be no getting into China through the front door, fittingly announced and welcomed. It would have to be sneak in, snatch and grab and sneak out again. Thank the Lord Ross was by her side; he was bright, clever and resourceful, gifted with the nerve of a hold-up man. Between the two of them they could pull it off. Luck, bribery, threats—whatever was needed would be brought into play.

She gazed at the copper lamp swinging easily above her, letting it mesmerize her, leaden her eyelids, draw them together. She slept without dreaming, recouping her strength. How long she was asleep she had no way of judging, but when she awoke she saw that he had come into the room and was seated on the wicker stool at the foot of the bed, poring over a chart. Looking up, he smiled.

"Welcome back. Do you know you were sleeping with a smile on your face? You must have had pleasant dreams for a change."

"No dreams at all."

"Good." He glanced at his watch. "We've got about twenty minutes till dinner. Hungry?"

"Famished."

"Even better." He brought the chart to the bed, laying it across her outstretched legs as she sat up. With his finger he traced a line from San Marcos to the Revilla Gigedo Islands, tapping them. "From here to the Marshall Islands is fifty-five hundred miles. With any luck at all, we can make it in eighteen days, maybe less. That's well over halfway."

She wasn't listening, instead staring at him. Her hand went to his cheek, traveling down it, framing his mouth with the corner between her outstretched fingers and thumb.

"Give me this."

The chart slipped off her legs, falling to the floor with a crackling sound as he turned to kiss her. His mouth was warm, yielding. His arm slipped about her and began undoing the buttons of her dress, freeing them one by one. They undressed each other, slipping beneath the cool sheet, their naked bodies touching, sending a thrill coursing through her. Again and again he kissed her, each time clinging to her mouth longer, fueling the fires of her passion. She could feel his member stiffening against her thigh, throbbing, sending tremors of excitement and delicious anticipation driving through her body like a flight of arrows loosed and piercing all over, finding nerve ends, setting them tingling.

Now his right hand slipped between her thighs, seeking, finding, caressing. She moaned softly and he quickened the movement of his hand, his fingers exploring. On and on he played, arousing her, setting her to twisting and thrusting sensuously, her body begging to be joined to his.

"Now, Ross, now . . ."

He eased his weight over her, spreading her thighs, his member, like steel, slipping slowly forward. Again she moaned as a clove-pink cloud immense and beautiful spread itself to the limits of her mind. Larger and larger it became, forcing, filling, exploding, sending showers of flowers outward in every direction, obscuring the blue of the heavens in a riot of colors.

And she possessed him, engorging him, quenching the insatiable thirst of her desire with the flowing wine of his own.

III

Shortly after sundown the wind slackened and the sea settled itself like the great kraken of Norwegian sea lore, the crablike mythical monster whose back was as broad as the Labrador shelf. Dinner in the small, modestly appointed but immaculate dining room was a quiet affair, clicking and tinkling interspersed with low-voiced conversation. Second Mate Gatenbee was on duty, and only Burnette, the captain and Dr. Seely shared with Lisa and Ross the cook's best efforts and the conversation. The beef stew was gamy but delicious, the pudding that followed somewhat chalky-tasting and the coffee too bitter to delude even the most insensitive taste buds. By his own admission, the captain's taste buds had been dulled so long by continuous exposure to his precious cheroots that he was incapable of differentiating between sweet and tart.

Lisa did not enjoy the meal, not because the dessert and coffee failed to measure up but because Burnette disturbed her; he stared so. She could well imagine what was going on in his mind, as could any woman. Unlike Coley Hollis, he didn't descend to disrobing her with his eyes. Rather, she got the impression that he was silently offering himself to her, striving to convey all that she was missing by not tumbling into bed with him. It wasn't anything he said—not so much as a single suggestive phrase wedged its way into the conversation —it was what *she* felt. And she was not imagining. She could almost put his thoughts into words—words that, if uttered and heard by Ross, would have prompted him to erase Mr. Burnette's smile with a badly broken jaw.

Still, she thought, as she sipped her coffee, intending to quit at the halfway mark of the cup, nothing was to be gained by communicating her suspicions to Ross. Better she stay clear of Mr. Burnette, no simple matter aboard ship.

Good weather continued to favor the *Sea Cloud*'s advance toward the Orient, the wind working hard at bellying her canvas, her bow plowing the dark, restless water at a steady 18 knots. The days passed and the nights, and Lisa sensed that she was steadily improving. She felt stronger, more vigorous upon arising, markedly less fatigued at day's end, and her thoughts came in orderly fashion, no longer contradicting one another, jumbling and demanding conscious effort on her part to clarify her thinking.

She avoided Mr. Burnette as best she could; for his part, he did not go out of his way to pass her. Still, now and then their paths crossed, and when he greeted her and smiled, his eyes carried the same brazen advice she had read in them earlier. They would nod and speak and continue on their separate ways, but his smirk and the uncomfortable sensation it aroused in her breast invariably seemed to linger.

One afternoon, with time on her hands and Ross with the captain at the wheel discussing clippers, lamenting their passing and condemning the grimy, soulless steamships that progress had chosen to replace them, she made her way down the aft companionway toward Josiah Kirby's cabin. She went there daily, enjoying their nostalgic conversations regarding Mansfield and Sutton and England, Dover to Berwick-upon-Tweed. Turning the corner, coming within three doors of Kirby's cabin, she sighted Burnette walking toward her. He removed his cap, waved greeting and ran his hand through his hair affectedly, as if to draw her attention to its handsomeness.

"Hello, Mr. Burnette."

"Mrs. Dandridge. Lovely weather we're having."

"Yes."

They eased slowly by each other, her generous breasts rubbing against his shirt in spite of her effort to keep from doing so.

"Narrow going," he said, smirking.

She did not respond, avoiding his eyes. Wedged against her, he suddenly stopped; but she continued on, leaving him standing awkwardly, resisting the urge to glance back over her shoulder to see his reaction. Coming up to Kirby's door, she knocked.

"Yes?"

"Mrs. Dandridge, Josiah."

He opened the door, releasing the fragrant odors of hemp and tar into the companionway. His cabin was filled with sails, new and used, torn and mended. Behind a bench fixed to the wall beside a salt-skinned porthole was a wooden rack that held a cloth sack, filled with palms for seaming and roping, fashioned of hide lined with leather, each palm fixed with a plate having chambers to catch the head of the needle in the manner of an ordinary thimble on the end of a seamstress's finger. Various-sized needles, from six-inch heavy-duty ones to small seaming needles, hung from the rack. Fids,* splicing, serving and stretching knives, sail hooks, bobbins for twine and sundry small articles were also in evidence. But it was the canvas, spread and folded, hanging and carelessly dumped in heaps, that dominated the interior.

Kirby was a little man, but his forearms and hands in particular suggested considerable strength. A livid scar, a shade between purple and black, ran from under his right ear, down his cheek and across his chin. His nose, as substantial and doughy-looking as a mushroom, knobbed the center of his happy face. He hailed her and offered her the end of his bench to sit upon.

* A pin of hard wood or iron, tapering to a point, used to open the strands of a rope in splicing, to stretch eyes, etc.

"That's a lovely dress, I must say. Shantung silk, isn't it?"

She laughed. "I doubt Filene's in Boston has ever heard of Shantung silk. But, all the same, I'm glad you like it. I like Sligo green and these funny little flower buttons. What are you working on today?"

"The spanker Mr. Burnette just brought it in. It's old and overworked and got itself whipped ripped in last night little blow. See here . . . ." Hauling yards and yards of canvas up from the pile at his feet, he displayed a rip fully four feet long. "She'll need lining."

Selecting a rectangular piece of cloth, he stretched the tear across his knees laying the piece upon it. Then, selecting a needle he strung it and began sewing.

"Don't you ever get sick of sewing?" she asked.

"Only the first thirty years," he said, his eyes brightening impishly. "Now I'm used to it. It's the privacy I like."

"Why don't you work up on deck? It's a lovely day."

"Too much trouble hauling the work topside and bringing it back down. Sometimes I take a little job up. Did you see Mr. Burnette leaving?"

"I passed him in the companionway."

"Handsome devil, ain't he?"

"I suppose."

"Quite the ladies' man, they say. Bachelor. A girl in every port- -at least one. You've made a big impression on him."

"Have I?"

"He sings your praises. But anyone as beautiful as you has to be used to compliments."

"I'm getting beyond the age of deserving—"

"How old are you?"

"How old do you think?"

He paused in his stitching, cocked his head and appraised her. "Thirty? Thirty-one?"

"Thirty-seven."

"I don't believe it! You look a green girl, you do."

"Thank you. All the same, I'm getting close to forty."

"Don't crab. I'm close to seventy. Funny about Mr. Burnette."

"What's funny?"

"He's a bloody Adonis, but his brother looks more like a Bombay chimp than a man. Ugly as a deadly sin."

"I didn't know he had a brother."

"You never would if you went by looks alone. Able Seaman Wilson Burnette. Myself, I've small use for either of 'em. Don't trust 'em. Though you shouldn't worry about handsome, not with that strapping chap you're married to."

"I don't worry about Mr. Burnette, Josiah."

"Well, he is a charmer. They say he gets a big kick out of turning females' heads. Best be on your guard."

"You sound like my father."

"I'm old enough to be." He stitched, snapped his needle, muttered something unrepeatable, causing her to hold back a laugh, and took down another needle.

"Talking about Mansfield and Sutton as we've been, satisfy a nosy old man and tell me how a Mansfielder comes to be bride to a Providence Dandridge?"

"Ross came to Europe on the Grand Tour. We met in London; I was there visiting relatives. He went on to the Continent but quit the tour soon after and came back to London. By then I'd gone home to Mansfield. He followed me, asked me to marry him and—"

"Here you are. Most o' the young dandies that went over on the Grand Tour back then went home with paintings and statues and the like. I wonder what his folks said when he came waltzing in with you."

"They were a little surprised."

They chatted for two hours, as usual, mostly about Nottingham, Mansfield and Sutton, the fairs, the farming, the people and the beautiful countryside—until homesickness began tugging at her heart, a yearning to lift her feet and fly away home just to refresh her mind's-eye view of the old place. At length she got up from the bench, examined Kirby's work, pronounced it equivalent in skill and finesse to that of Queen Victoria's favorite seamstress and said good-by.

She found Ross on deck staring down into the black water rolling above the plimsol line, a pained expression on his face. Seeing her, he brightened.

"What's the matter, darling?" she asked.

"Nothing."

"You were practically grimacing."

"Was I?"

"Don't you feel well?"

"My stomach. It must be that fish soup we had for lunch. It was awfully greasy, wasn't it?"

"No more so than usual." She laughed. "This isn't the *Great Eastern,* Ross. Let's go see Dr. Seely; he'll have something for indigestion."

The doctor was in his room reading Sterns's *Anatomy,* his hair mussed, his tie askew. His cabin reeked of rum, a corked, half-filled bottle of it sliding slowly down the wall rack as the ship heaved gently to leeward. Lisa was surprised at the smallness of the cabin. Apart from his bunk and a single round-backed wooden chair, there was only the washbasin, a disreputable-looking high-boy all scars and gouges, and a metal locker fastened, as was the highboy, to the wall.

Seely buttoned his collar and straightened his tie as they entered. "What seems to be the trouble?"

Ross explained, dropping into the chair and bending forward in an effort to ease his discomfort.

"Take off your coat, loosen your trousers and pull up your shirt."

The patient's stomach exposed, Seely placed the tips of the fingers of one hand against it and tapped with his other hand, moving slowly about the surface. "Tell me when it hurts."

Ross suppressed a wince. "There."

"Mmmm, it's as hard as a rock."

"It's nothing serious," said Lisa hopefully.

"That's hard to say. Do you feel nauseous?"

Ross nodded.

Rising, the doctor opened his locker and took out his bag, snapping it open. Getting out his thermometer, he dipped it in the water pitcher, wiped it on his shirt and inserted it in Ross's mouth. "Any constipation?"

Again Ross nodded.

Seely called Lisa's attention to the area causing the pain, the lower right portion of the abdomen. "Appendix," he said quietly.

"You think he has appendicitis?"

"I can't say for certain yet." He turned to Ross. "It could be a kidney, your gall bladder, liver, the large bowel, anything in that general area." His voice was beginning to take on a questioning, rather helpless tone. "I can't see inside. Do you feel any cramps?"

Ross nodded.

Seely placed the flat of his hand against the upper, then the lower abdomen. "Here and here?"

Again Ross nodded. The color was beginning to drain from his cheeks. Suddenly he pulled the thermometer from his mouth, bolted to his feet and, cupping one hand to his mouth, rushed to the basin and began to vomit. Lisa stood behind him, patting his back.

Seely took the thermometer from his hand and read it: "Ninety-nine point two. Rinse out your mouth and lie down."

"The cramps seem to be getting worse," said Ross. He lay down on the doctor's bed.

Seely folded a napkin, soaked it in the pitcher and laid it across Ross's forehead.

Ross's fingertips went to the lower-right area of his abdomen. "It's beginning to feel like it's on fire."

Seely said nothing. Fumbling in his locker, he brought out a ponderously large book and began leafing through it. Finding what he was looking for, he read briefly, then closed the book and returned it to the shelf. "Let him stay here," he said to Lisa. "Perhaps nap a little."

"I'll stay with him," she said.

"That won't be necessary." He glanced at Ross. "Do you think you can sleep?"

"I'll do my best."

"I'd rather not give you anything. The idea is to keep peristalsis to a minimum. I think I'm going to have to operate."

Lisa blanched. "Then it *is* appendicitis."

"The symptoms are classic and he's got them all. Problem is, they're also the symptoms of practically every other stomach ailment."

"So you won't know for sure unless you operate," said Lisa.

"I wouldn't go that far. But putting it off could be dangerous, as bad as avoiding it altogether. When the appendix is inflamed, infected, filled with pus or gangrenous, due to impairment of the blood supply coming into it, it can enlarge to eight or ten times normal size. If it should burst, peritonitis would set in." He consulted his watch. "It's just past four. I think we ought to begin making the necessary preparations. We can set up one of the empty state-rooms as an operating room. Let's try for nine o'clock."

"You really must operate, is that it?" asked Lisa evenly, pondering the situation.

Seely nodded. "There's nothing to worry about; I've cut for appendix dozens of times. It's not a particularly difficult operation."

"But dangerous."

"Any surgery entails risk. We are, after all, making an opening where nature never planned one. Still, your husband here appears to be robust."

"I'm not feeling very robust," commented Ross grimly. "Do you mind if I go back to my own cabin and lie down?"

"I'd really rather you stay put." Seely walked Lisa

to the door. "Tell Captain MacGregor, if you will. I have everything we'll be needing here except two things: belts to hold him securely to the bed, in the event the ship decides to start rolling heavily in the middle of things, and there's a one-burner lamp stove in the second mate's quarters."

"To boil the instruments."

"Yes. Get things started, will you? I want to stay here with him." Turning, he glanced out the porthole. The horizon line eased gently upward to the right, then sank as easily. "Let's hope the sea stays calm."

IV

A state-room had been converted into an operating room. Ross lay unstrapped on the bed, sweating and forcing a smile, gripping her hand and sneaking a glance now and then at the lamp overhead slowly swinging, indicating a sea calmer than it had been earlier. In the hour since dinner the barometer had dropped slightly, but whatever heavy weather was in the offing seemed to be holding its bluster and fury in check until later that night.

The second mate's little stove had been brought in and the fire lit, and now the shallow water in the basin holding Seely's instruments was bubbling merrily. A copy of Wycliff's *Surgery* lay closed upon the nightstand. and an array of bottles and cans lined the rack customarily reserved for liquor above the sideboard. On top of the sideboard itself were clean towels and napkins.

Captain MacGregor was present, sitting in vest and shirt sleeves, lauding the good weather, his all-too-obvious contribution to morale. Mr. Burnette had only just ducked out the door to fetch Dr. Seely.

"If this wind holds to the Marshalls and into the China Sea, the old girl'll bust the record to smithereens," observed the captain expansively.

To Lisa, he seemed nervous, his eyes darting about the room, his fingers restlessly tapping his kneecaps. He went on about the weather, but something other than wind velocity and direction concerned Lisa. "Tell me, captain, what is a doctor doing aboard a cargo clipper?"

160

"We have six state-rooms, modom. We generally have a full complement of possengers. Had we sailed from Son Froncisco, we would have this time. And we've a thirty-four-mon crew."

"Still, it isn't customary, is it?" she asked, pressing for the explanation he appeared reluctant to give her.

"The *Sea Cloud*'s not the first cargo ship to have her own sawbones."

"She's not complaining," said Ross. "It's just her feminine curiosity."

Burnette came in. "He's on his way," he said to the captain. He glanced at Lisa and looked away, a somewhat embarrassed expression on his face. "He wants to start the chloroform."

"Is something the matter?" asked Lisa. "He's not drunk!"

"No, no, he's just had a tot or two to help him relax," responded Burnette.

"More like cork courage," said Lisa dryly, and went back to the captain and the response he seemed to be evading. "It just seems strange that with competent doctors in such short supply practically everywhere, he should be riding about the world on this ship."

Captain MacGregor sighed and lit a cheroot, sending a single large cloud of smoke lampward. "His sister is married to one of the owners. The family decided it was best for him to go to sea."

"For his health?"

"More or less."

She placed a cone of gauze over Ross's nose and mouth. Burnette took down the can of chloroform, unscrewing the top, and she tipped it over the cone. "Breathe deeply, darling."

"Here we go," said Ross. "See you in an hour."

She allowed a few drops to fall. Time crawled sluggishly by. The real reason for Dr. Seely's permanent presence on board the *Sea Cloud* slipped into the realm of insignificance in her mind. Whatever had brought him aboard and kept him there, Ross was stuck with him, she reflected, looking down at him sleeping, breathing easily. Seely gave the impression of competency, at least in examining and diagnosing, and seemed confident of his ability to perform the operation. She did wish he wasn't quite so fond of rum. Since leaving San Marcos, she couldn't recall seeing him free of the odor of it a single time, though even at breakfast she couldn't say she'd ever seen him drunk.

The door opened. He stood gripping the frame, supporting himself. His tongue was no thicker than usual when he mumbled greeting. He was not drunk, but he'd obviously had his "tot or two." "Are we all set?"

"He's just dropped off, doctor," she said. "Shouldn't we wait until he gets into deeper sleep?"

"A couple of minutes ought to do it. It'll give us time to check things out. Now, you'll be assisting me, Mrs. Dandridge, if you're sure you feel up to it."

"I do."

"Does the sight of blood upset you?"

"I'll be all right. I worked with a doctor some years ago."

"You were a nurse?"

"No, although I did everything a nurse does."

"You assisted during surgery?"

"Yes."

"Excellent."

Going to the sideboard, he knelt alongside it and lifted a curious-looking device resembling a coffeepot, with a small wheel attached to one side and valves at the top, out of a tall wooden box. "This is something I picked up in Edinburgh last year—a device for administering carbolic spray to keep the incision free of infection. It works very simply: Aim it and turn the wheel slowly; air pressure releases the spray. I'd like you to work it, captain."

Captain MacGregor stumped out his cheroot, got up from his chair and tested the sprayer.

"Mr. Burnette," continued the doctor, "you'll be our anesthetist. When we need more chloroform, you'll administer it. Stand by his head and don't move. A few drops at a time only, understand?" Burnette nodded. "Nurse Dandridge, you will assist." He gestured her to the stove in the corner and the basin, describing the eight different instruments lying in it—tenotomy knives, retractors, forceps, clamps. Then he handed her a pair of rubber gloves, putting on a second pair himself.

"Mr. Burnette, will you open the book on the nightstand to page four seventy-one and lay it on the bed alongside his left leg?" Seely smiled at Lisa. "There's a detailed step-by-step description of the operation, pictures and all."

"Didn't you say you'd performed it many times?"

"So I have, but it's been some time. It's just to play absolutely safe. He's your husband, nurse; we can't be too safe."

Drawing the sheet back, he revealed Ross's naked body. The area of incision had been swabbed with Merthiolate, a sickly-looking yellow. A heavier application designated the precise point of incision with a two-inch line.

"You're certain you'll be up to watching this, Mrs. Dandridge?"

"Quite."

"I'm sure you are."

"May we get on with it?"

"The small tenotomy knife, if you please. Be ready with a clamp."

Breathing deeply, she grit her teeth and, turning to the basin, picked out the forceps and with it the knife, handing it to him. Then she picked out a clamp, laying it on the towel Burnette had placed alongside the open volume.

"More chloroform, Mr. Burnette," said the doctor quietly. "Two or three drops." The mate obliged. Ross was now in a deep sleep, his brawny chest rising and falling rhythmically. "Mrs. Dandridge, lay all the clamps on the towel, if you please. Captain, be ready with the spray. Take care not too much; it's an acid and can play hob with healthy tissue. Here we go."

Bending over Ross, Seely raised the knife and brought it down to the designated spot, touching it, depressing the skin slightly, but not cutting. His fingers relaxed, cradling the knife in the groove at the base of his thumb. He sucked in his breath, his narrow shoulders rising and sagging, and began again, raising the knife and bringing it down. Again he stopped and relaxed just at the point of cutting in.

Lisa glared. "Doctor!"

"Ready with the sprayer, captain," said Seely, ignoring her. A third time he started—and stopped before incising. The knife tumbled from his hand, clattering lightly on the floor.

"I can't, I can't . . ."

Lisa's eyes blazed. The words erupted from her in a half-scream. "What do you mean? Cut!"

Seely hung his head, mumbling, letting it out in an unbroken string: "I can't, it's too hard, too dangerous, you don't understand, none of you, it could be all bound up inside him, the intestinal loops, dangerous, it could be stuck to an abscess wall, I can't, I just can't."

"For God's sake, mon!" burst MacGregor. "Do it!"

"If you don't, he'll die!" shrilled Lisa.

"You said yourself—peritonitis. Do it!" MacGregor glared.

"I can't." He held his gloved hands upward; they were stiff and trembling visibly. He shook his head, avoiding their eyes, dropping his hands to his sides and backing slowly away from the bed. Then his hands went to his face, covering it. He began to sob. "I'm afraid . . . afraid . . . it's been so long . . . too long . . . I can't . . . I can't." Jerking open the door, he stumbled out, slamming it behind him.

Burnette swallowed hard and stared. "What now?"

"Captain," began Lisa, holding down the hysteria building in her.

MacGregor bit his lower lip, holding it tightly with his teeth, his eyes flooding with fear. "Not me. I don't know how. I've pulled teeth, yes, I've set broken legs ond arms, but I've never cut. I'd botch it for fair; I'd kill him."

Ross moved slightly.

"Chloroform!" exclaimed Lisa. "What about you, Mr. Burnette?"

Burnette applied two drops to the gauze cone and lowered his eyes sheepishly. "I'd make a mess, too. I wouldn't know what to do."

"It's in the book, man, step by step. I'll read you through it. We'll all help. We have all we need to work with, and the book. If he isn't operated on, he could die!"

"I do it, I'll probably kill him!" blurted Burnette.

Striding to the door, Lisa wrenched it open. "Burnette, go get him. Bring him back, if you have to carry him. We'll make him operate!"

"He won't do it," said MacGregor, shaking his head. "I ought to have told ye before. The mon has lost his nerve. I doot he's operated in years."

"You fool; why didn't you tell me before? *Why?*"

"I osked him, put it to him directly. He swore to me he could do it. My right hand to God on it. I never would have—"

"He was on the staff at Cook County Hospital in Chicago," said Burnette, interrupting. "He was very good, but there was some trouble."

"Drinking?" Lisa said.

"We don't know," said MacGregor. "He never did explain. We never osked. But when the hospital discharged him, his brother-in-law osked us to take him on."

Her attentiveness to his explanation lapsed as she

knelt and picked up the tenotomy knife, then dropped it back into the basin of boiling water.

"What are we going to do?" asked Burnette in an anxious tone. "We can't just stand here gabbing, letting him lie there."

Snatching up the book, Lisa handed it to Burnette. "The second paragraph down: Read aloud."

"But what—"

"Just do it! Captain, you'll take care of both the chloroform and the spray."

"Ye can't operate!" exclaimed MacGregor. "Ye're no surgeon."

"I don't claim to be. But it appears we don't have one available, do we?"

"It's too dangerous," said Burnette. "One slip and—"

"I'm aware of that, Mr. Burnette. What do you take me for, a moron?"

Burnette proferred the book. "There're diagrams here; they show the steps."

"Stand aside; give me room. And bring the basin with the instruments over here. No, set the nightstand here alongside me and put the basin on it. Do it!"

Burnette started to say something, changed his mind and did as ordered.

"Be prepared for the worst, gentlemen. I may be sick, I may faint, but I'm damned if I'll stand here doing nothing. Captain . . ."

"Yes?"

"Soak a towel in cold water and wipe my face with it when I tell you."

"Yes . . . yes."

"Burnette, ready a clamp."

Picking up the knife, she held it over the spot, took a deep breath between teeth so tightly clenched they hurt, steadied one hand with the other firmly around the wrist and started it down.

"Dear God in heaven, help me. . . ."

And went in.

V

Deirdre could scarcely restrain herself from shouting with joy. She walked with Li-Sing in the West Flower Garden near the palace kitchens and the barracks. Spring flowers--azaleas, early peonies and lilies of the valley--displayed their all-too-brief beauty, and wild geese soared honking over the city in a perfect *V*, heading north. The sun was bright and deliciously warm and beautiful and the swallows had returned, fluttering and swooping gracefully through the plum and cherry trees.

"She said it, Li-Sing. I couldn't believe my ears. I almost pinched myself right there in front of them. You ought to have seen Heng-chi. His jaw dropped so, I thought it would rip the skin. I actually felt sorry for him, I did but I was so happy I couldn't."

Li-Sing's round face beamed. "So it seems Old Buddha isn't as hardhearted as everybody makes her out to be. When will you be leaving? How? By boat down the Hun?"

Deirdre stopped short and laughed. "Silly, we didn't get into details. Who cares how I leave? If they make me, I'll lily-walk to Tientsin." Balling her toes, she imitated the painful lily-walk of the bound-footed women of the leisured classes. "I'm going home! Home! Home!"

"I shall miss you, Deirdre."

"I'll miss you, and So-leng. He's such a melancholy man. Oh, but I want to see my mother and daddy so much. I'm dying to see them. I think my heart will burst!" She yelled loudly, scattering the sparrows, sending them flapping away from the branches overhead.

167

"Sh," cautioned Li-Sing. "Everyone's looking."

"Let them! Let them stare to their hearts' content." Running forward, she confronted two emaciated eunuchs walking hand in hand. They gaped at her. "I'm going home, do you hear? Home to America. She said so, she told me straight out!"

"Deirdre . . ." It was So-leng coming across the tennis courts, waving to catch her eye. Up he came, breathing hard.

"I've been looking all over for you."

"So-leng, did you hear? I'm going home! She's letting me."

He cast about, spotting a bench and hurrying her and Li-Sing to it.

"What's bothering you?" asked Deirdre, feigning petulance. "You're nervous as a frightened cat."

"We must talk."

"You didn't hear me."

"I know; you think you're going home."

"I *am*. She said—" The feeling building to detonation within her was the coziest, most satisfying sensation she had ever felt. She could walk on air, she thought, without weight on her shoulders, with her heart as light as a feather borne by the breeze. Hands high overhead, she spun about, cheering and laughing deliriously.

"Sit down!" snapped So-leng.

"What's bothering him?" Deirdre asked Li-Sing, frowning absurdly, then smiling.

So-leng pulled her down upon the bench. "Deirdre, be still a moment, and brace yourself. It's not going to happen."

"What?"

He took her hands and held them in his lap. "You're not going home, dear—at any rate, not with her blessing."

"That's ridiculous! You don't know what you're talking about. You weren't even there. I *heard* her."

"I don't care what you heard! Settle down, get hold of yourself, think! Yes, she said you could leave."

"I can!"

"You can't. They can't let you; they'd be idiots to. As soon as you got home, you'd tell your parents everything—the slave ship, Chefoo and Madam Ching, Kuocheng, the opium, the prince and Heng-chi, the Chief Eunuch . . . Deirdre, you could start a fire that could burn down the Forbidden City. You could disgrace the empresses, embarrass them frightfully—all their ministers, the whole government. Don't you understand? They can't possibly let you leave; you know too much. They've treated you like dirt—"

"I wouldn't say anything."

"Not even to your mother and father? Not much. Do you know you could cause a war? It's true; all by yourself. Incidents are what wars are made of, Deirdre."

"She said—"

"It doesn't matter what she said. Li-Lien-ying talked her into changing her mind five minutes after your audience was over."

"You know that? He told you?"

"Common sense tells me, as it should tell you."

Deirdre searched his eyes; then her gaze shifted to Li-Sing. The plump little concubine's smile had given way to a sober look, and her lower lip pressed hard against her upper lip quivered slightly as she nodded.

"I don't believe either of you! She said—"

"Deirdre," interrupted So-leng wearily, "you must believe me. I'm not throwing cold water on your hopes just to hurt you. I wouldn't be so cruel. It's simply the way it is, the way it has to be. Tz'u Hsi makes decisions, and if they're not right, if they're not in the best interests of the government, her advisors persuade her to change them."

"Li-Lien-ying's no advisor."

"He's her unofficial chief advisor."

Deirdre shot to her feet.

So-leng stared, aghast. "What are you doing?"

"Take me to him; I want to talk to him."

"What earthly good will that do?"

"I want to hear it from him. This is all your suspicions, the two of you. I mean, you think he's changed her mind, but you're only guessing; you don't know."

"I know. because I know her—and him," said So-leng quietly. "You know him, too. He is her self-appointed protector. She accepts that, encourages it. She can say anything she pleases, make all the promises in the world but she doesn't have to keep a single one. I mean, if she breaks her word, who is there to question her? You? Me? Li-Sing here?"

Deirdre sank down upon the bench, suddenly close to tears. "I don't believe it."

"Because you don't want to, naturally."

"It's not fair."

"What is fair for us?"

"It's not. It's mean; it's a terrible thing to do. How can you give somebody something they want so dearly, then snatch it back?"

"It would have been better if she hadn't said anything," remarked Li-Sing.

Deirdre bristled. "I want to talk to her."

So-leng shook his head. "You know you can't. You'd have to go through him. You know what he'd say. There's no point to it. He's changed her mind and that's the end of it."

"Take me to him; I want to talk to him."

"If you insist. At that, I imagine he's expecting you."

At the rear of the Halls of Martial Grace stood the long, narrow office buildings of the Imperial Household, curiously plain, undistinguished-looking structures roofed with yellow tiles architecturally consistent with the beautiful buildings surrounding them.

They were unable to get past the two imposing-looking eunuchs guarding the door to the complex at the rear of which the Chief Eunuch's office was located, but one of the guards consented to take a message to him. Twenty minutes later he returned with Li-Lien-ying's secretary, a eunuch who resembled a seven-year-old boy in the throes of premature senility.

"The Chief Eunuch is busy and will not be able to speak with you today," he croaked, drawing himself up to his full five feet and fixing them with a disdainful expression.

"Would you please ask him a question for me?" asked Deirdre.

"What question?"

"I would like to know when I am to leave to go home."

"You are the *wàigworén*."

"Yes."

"I can answer your question. The answer is good news. You will not be leaving after all. That is the empress's wish. Good day."

Spinning on his heel, he glided through the open door, one of the guards closing it after him. The other, who had gone to fetch him, commented with a shrug.

So-leng glanced at her, obviously anticipating tears. But crying was the furthest thing from Deirdre's mind. She was instead becoming angry, rapidly furious, seeth-ing, tightening her jaw muscles, clenching her small fists.

"It's a blessing in disguise, Deirdre," he said, taking hold of her arm as they walked away. "Had they let you go, you wouldn't have gotten fifty feet out the gate be-fore one of the guards would be after you. He'd murder you as soon as you got into the crowd in the Imperial City."

"I don't care about guards or gates or walls or moats; I'm leaving," she muttered. "There's got to be a way, and I mean to find it. I'll marry him."

"They'll drag you kicking and screaming to the temple, I know."

"Not at all. I'll marry him willingly, if he'll still have me. I'll be as cooperative as can be. I'll smile, I'll bow and scrape, I'll be as sweet as honey. I'll live with him, he'll give me money for the house, for clothes, I'll hoard it until I get two hundred taels, then good-by. I'll find a clever disguise, even if I have to shave my head. I'll bribe my way down the Hun to Tientsin, to the coast and away." She stopped walking and stared at him frigidly. "Watch me."

A thrush flew by them, stretching its little wings, soaring easily upward over the west wall of the Forbidden City and out into the world.

VI

Heng-chi seemed not in the least upset by Deirdre's outburst in the presence of Li-Lien-ying, the empresses and the ladies-in-waiting. Not even her announcement that she would not marry him disconcerted him. Eight days later, on an afternoon that saw all of Peking and the pine-packed plain surrounding it deluged with rain, Deirdre Allworth Dandridge, concubine fifth rank, the imperial *wàigworén,* was dressed by her maids in a white satin brocade gown embroidered with hollyhocks and the Chinese character *"Shou"* * and trimmed with gold braid; her hair was heaped high on her head, held in place with jade pins and laced with strings of tiny pearls, and she was carried in a sedan chair through the Gate of Spiritual Valor across the moat through the outer gate into the Imperial City to the Ti-an Men temple to be married.

So-leng was not present. But Li-Sing, An Te-si, now completely recovered from her first encounter with the prince, and three other concubines accompanied her as matron of honor and maids to the bride respectively. Buddha in bronze, decidedly more corpulent than the Empress Tz'u Hsi, but no less inscrutable-looking than she, gazed sightlessly down at the bride from behind the altar. Upon the altar were two enormous vases filled with pink and white dogwood, two baby white pine trees, candles, cakes and plates and bowls of fresh fruit, incense bowls and the groom's family's memorial tablets. In evidence as well was an asperge bowl and a

* "Long life."

173

rosary. Wooden blocks, an incense bowl, incense box and brushes, an ink stone and documents and paper occupied a smaller side altar.

Heng-chi's father, a tall man who successfully dignified an otherwise unprepossessing appearance with a stern look and a military bearing, Heng-chi's mother, two sisters and numerous aunts and uncles, including Prince Kung and his wife, were grouped at the right just inside the temple door.

The first drum sounded, and the celebrant's assistant lit the candles and the incense sticks. At the sound of the second drum, the guests were led to their seats. At the sound of the third drum, the best man led the groom to his chair, positioned at right angles to the front altar, and Li-Sing led Deirdre to a chair opposite him.

He smiled, and she returned the smile. He looked ill, she thought, as if he needed respite from his favorite pipe and a nourishing meal in its stead. A bell was rung and the celebrant entered, a bald and beardless elderly priest who might have passed for a eunuch, so effeminate-looking did he appear. He took his place on the bowing mat. The best man gave the order to proceed. The celebrant knelt and led everyone in bowing three times to Buddha. Then, handed a book by his assistant, he read aloud:

" 'We worship the Great Lord Shakyamuni Buddha, Kōsō Jōyō Daishi, Taisō Jōsai Daishi and all the Three Treasures in all directions and in the three periods of time. Here there are an excellent man and woman who are marrying each other, since their relationship has been consummated and prepared from ages past. Because of this they now stand before the Lord and beg to attain his benefits. They are praying deeply to the Three Treasures and to all the Buddhas for their protection. I am going to permit them to live together in pleasure and in pain, in happiness and in unhappiness, until a ripe old age, and to work for the benefit of both themselves and others and to offer the merits thereof to all creatures. I pray that the True Light of the Lord may shine on their excellent minds, thus purifying both their bodies and their minds.' "

The ceremony continued, Deirdre and Heng-chi holding the rosary in turn and reciting from the book at the direction of the celebrant. The contract was made and signed and sealed by the family. It was then examined by the celebrant, censed, signed and sealed. The sermon was read, the guests congratulated the bride and groom, the celebrant returned to the bowing mat and recited:

> *"We live in the world as if in the sky,*
> *Just as the lotus blossom is not wetted by the water*
> *   that surrounds it*
> *The mind is immaculate and beyond the dust*
> *Let us bow to the Highest Lord."*

In unison everyone present recited:

> *"I vow to save others endlessly,*
> *I vow to cease from desire for eternity,*
> *I vow to study the Dharma forever,*
> *I vow to perfect Buddhism in all lives and in all*
> *   worlds."*

The ceremony ended, the celebrant left the temple. The bride and groom followed, and the guests.

VII

Lisa awoke, bolting into consciousness, snatching up her watch from the bedside stand and confirming, to her chagrin, that she had slept nearly 11 hours. Her mind roused hurtled back to the night before: Dr. Seely's dereliction, the captain and Burnette's refusal to substitute for him, their willingness, in spite of their apologies, to let Ross lie untouched until his appendix burst.

The tenotomy knife in her hand . . . The first freshet of blood had been the worst. Her stomach had roiled with nausea, so that she had had to steel herself to keep from vomiting. The dizziness, the room beginning to revolve, the weakness in her knees, her body swaying . . . Fighting all of it off, going on, barking commands to MacGregor and Burnette, the two of them scurrying about like frightened schoolboys imprisoned in proximity to a bullying principal.

Locating the appendix, the repulsive-looking fat worm attached to the large intestine, bringing it up through the wound, tying it off at the base, slicing it laterally, removing it. Cleaning up, the carbolic spray, closing layer after layer. Nine stitches, fighting to keep her hands from trembling, MacGregor wiping her forehead and face with a towel. Thank God for the diagrams in the book and the clamps, gripping, securing. Without them, he would have bled to death. As it was, there was blood all over the place by the time the last stitch was drawn through.

Ross! Good God! Leaping out of the bed, she flew through the door, passing two deckhands, who gaped with astonishment at the sight of her nightgown, her flaming hair loose and flying like bunched banners in a gale, her breasts bouncing. Dashing into the room next door, she found him sitting up, grinning broadly.

"Good afternoon, Mrs. Dandridge." He spread his hands. "Look at who's back from the dead."

Throwing her arms around him, she smothered him with kisses. "Ross, my darling, darling, darling. . . ."

"Easy—my stitches."

She freed him from her embrace. "Let me see."

Pulling the sheet down, he displayed his incision. "Neat as a pin. Your friend, Dr. Seely, is good. He should be Chief of Staff at Roger Williams Hospital." She started to say something but held it back, letting him run on. "He's much too skillful to be buried aboard this tub. And you, did you play nurse?"

She nodded. It made sense: Let him think Seely had operated; he'd be more optimistic regarding his recovery. If she were to explode the truth in his face, convince him that it was she who had separated him from his appendix, clamped him, stayed his blood, cleaned up and closed and stitched him up like a Christmas goose, the shock might trigger a relapse. As it was, he looked a bit pale from loss of blood.

"Did you stand by through the whole thing?" he went on.

"Where else would I be?"

"Amazing."

"What's so amazing about that?"

"I would have thought at the first sight of blood you'd tumble in a dead faint."

"Why? Because I'm a woman?"

"Because—"

"*Of course* because I'm a woman. Two drops and milady swoons. That's nature's way—of course, which is the reason men give birth."

He laughed, but a trifle self-consciously. "Seriously, what did you do? Tell me."

"Seriously, I fainted. How do you feel?"

"Sore and tremendous and hungry as a grizzly."

She got up from the side of the bed and, opening the door, called to a man swabbing the deck. "Would you please find the cabin boy and tell him to come here?"

"Yes, ma'am." His eyes reflected mild shock at the sight of her standing before him in her nightgown.

She gasped. "Oh!" Concealing her décolletage with hands crossed, she kneed the door shut with a bang.

Ross laughed uproariously, then winced. "Ouch! Don't make me laugh."

She slipped into his robe, and moments later, when the cabin boy knocked at the door, she asked him to fetch a large bowl of soup.

"A steak!" snapped Ross. "Smothered with roast potatoes the size of your thumb."

"Soup," said Lisa.

The boy stared, his handsome brown eyes as guileless as a fawn's as they shifted from one to the other and back.

"Pay no attention to him; he's delirious," she said. "Soup."

"Yes, ma'am."

According to the section in Wycliff's *Surgery* devoted to postoperative treatment, the patient was to be confined to bed for two days. And to remove any temptation that might delay the healing process or risk disturbing his stitches, Lisa announced that she would move into the state-room next door. Ross's protests were leonine-loud and emphatic. She appeased him with a kiss and a pat on the back of his hand.

Following his first feeding, she gave him a sponge bath, and they talked for a time until he became drowsy and acceded to her order that he nap. She went in search of Captain MacGregor. He was in his quarters, poring over charts with Mr. Burnette and the second mate. The cabin ceiling was so low she was instinctively inclined to stoop; the paneled walls were busy with charts and framed photographs and drawings of ships, and the room crammed to the corners with the stale odor of cheroot smoke. At the sight of her, both men put on sheepish looks and exchanged glances.

"Captain, Mr. Burnette, forgive me for interrupting; I just wanted to tell you that he's awake, he's eaten and he appears to be doing very well."

"No thanks to either of us," said the captain curtly.

"On the contrary, had it not been for you two, things probably wouldn't have turned out as well as they have."

"I take my hat off to ye, Mrs. Dondridge. It took an ongel of mercy to deliver him from death's door."

"You're a very brave woman," added Burnette quietly, the familiar and nettlesome look creeping into his eyes.

She half laughed. "I assure you I felt anything but brave." She remembered what she wanted to tell them. "Ross assumes that Dr. Seely operated on him. I didn't tell him anything about what happened. I'd rather he didn't find out."

"Ye'd give Seely the credit ofter the way he bocked down on ye?"

"That's not important now. What I'd like most is to put last night behind all of us." She turned toward the port. A fat, fluffy cloud hovering just above the horizon created the illusion it was wiping the glass. "I've been thinking about Dr. Seely. I was very upset with him, but not now. More than anything, I pity him. After all, he has to go on living with last night."

"As do the two of us," said MacGregor. There was an awkward pause. The captain stabbed the chart spread in front of them repeatedly with his pencil, as if to blame it for his uncomfortableness.

"You're busy," she said. "I'll leave you to your work."

"We'll drop by to see Mr. Dondridge later, if ye don't mind."

"He'll be happy to see you both, I'm sure."

She went out on deck. The wind, so consistently favorable virtually all the way from San Marcos to this point, some 600 miles west of the Revilla Gigedo Islands, had evidently tired, hying itself off to some remote place to recoup its strength. The sails sagged at their masts, partially bellied only by a breeze so gentle as to be incapable of whitening the waves. She stood at the rail near the brace blocks, drinking the air deeply. Burnette came out of the cabin and approached her, his face betraying the deflation of his vanity.

"I just want to say I'm sorry about last night— sincerely."

"There's no need to apologize."

"If it had been my mother or my wife, I think I would have been able to . . . you know. But I didn't dare. I mean, if something had gone wrong, you'd have hated me."

"Mr. Burnette . . ."

"I wouldn't want you to hate me, you understand. You're too fine; I respect you a great deal, more than I can put into words." His hand touched her forearm; she drew it away.

"Please."

"Sorry." He touched his cap in salute and walked off.

She resisted the urge to look after him, instead turning her eyes up the deck toward the bow. A small, dark figure was bent over the rail—Dr. Seely, staring down at the water, his conscience punishing him brutally, she surmised; a man struggling with and losing badly to the devil's shame and humiliation.

She approached him. At the sound of her heels on the deck, he looked up, his cheeks flushing. He was very drunk and even more disheveled-looking than usual, as if he'd slept in his clothes and neglected to wash and shave, rather than force himself to look at his own face in the glass. He glanced about as if seeking a hole to hurl himself down into.

"May we talk?"

"I'm sorry," he said thickly, "you must excuse me; I'm just on my way down below." He did not move. The unpleasant odor of stale rum hung in the air, defying the breeze.

"Please, I must talk to you." She took firm hold of his arm.

He avoided her eyes, staring at the deck. "I couldn't, I just couldn't. I know you don't understand, but . . ." He gestured pathetically, trying to add something.

"Of course I understand. You're only human." It seemed the wrong thing to say, words jammed too quickly into a breach in the conversation, calculated to show her tolerance but instead reminding him of how ineffectual, how wanting, how cowardly he had been.

"Doctors aren't supposed to be human, Mrs. Dandridge. People see us as ten feet tall, superhuman creatures imbued with the power to rescue them from the jaws. If we fail, we fail; but God forbid we don't try."

Suddenly, as though something had clicked in his brain, he frowned and straightened up, his hand finding the knot of his necktie, adjusting it. He pulled his chin back and straightened his shoulders, a glimmer of self-assurance brightening his eyes.

"I was a good doctor, a very good doctor."

"I'm sure you were."

"But I was. At Cook County I was assistant chief. I operated in the theater for the students and the internes many times . . . many times. You can ask anyone. Young men idolized me. An appendix operation is the simplest thing in the world, usually: in, locate, tie, snip, clean and close. Easy as darning a sock. If you want to see a complicated operation, you should see tetralogy of Fallot--blue baby. *There's* surgery. Brilliantly conceived. Transposing and reimplanting the great blood vessels of the heart, diverting the blood so that it flows back into the lungs for reoxygenation. Extremely serious and delicate work. The resurrection of the cardiac cripple!" Up went his hand triumphantly.

He staggered and his hand shot out, grabbing the rail to keep from falling. His eyes met hers. His self-assured look faded, leaving a blankness that touched her heart.

"You'll excuse me," he said, "I'm on call: pneumo-nectomy." He walked off, waving.

VIII

The wind became whimsical, arriving, building round-
ness and tautness into the canvas, testing Josiah Kirby's
stitching. sending the *Sea Cloud* scudding over the blue
world of the mid-Pacific, then suddenly in seconds
gathering its gusts and whirling away, the ship slowing,
all but groaning to a complete stop.

Ross's recovery was surprisingly speedy. As for Lisa,
her unexpected sojourn into surgery and the aftermath
when she devoted all her waking hours to her patient,
although physically tiring, did her more good than
harm. So Ross observed.

In the early evening of his fourth day out of bed, the
wind waxed belligerent, rousing the sea, setting the
decks awash and the *Sea Cloud* to wallowing. The light
topsails were furled, then canvas further reduced down
to and including the lower topgallants, flying jib, middle
topsail and crossjack. The mainsail was shortened, the
wind force increased to ten, and the vessel ran swiftly
before it, drawing Singapore ever closer to the bowsprit.
Lisa had been below decks chatting with Josiah Kirby
and was on her way back to the state-room when she
came upon Mr. Burnette at the foot of the companionway stairs. At sight of him, the suspicion sneaked across
her mind that he had been standing topside and, upon
recognizing. in spite of wind and wash, the distinctive
clicking of her heels against the wooden floor, had
timed his descent to meet her. Reaching the bottom, he
was starting forward when they met.

"Mrs. Dandridge . . ."

"Good evening, Mr. Burnette."

He shook his head. "We're a pair, you and I, as formal as a funeral. Let's let our hair down, shall we? I'm Clay, you're . . ."

"Mrs. Dandridge."

She stepped to one side to pass him, but he moved and blocked her way, his dripping oilskins pressing against her. Close to him, the evil in his eyes quickened her heart.

"Mr. Burnette . . ."

"God in heaven but you're beautiful. Come, in here . . ."

Before she realized what he was doing, he had seized her arm, gripping it so hard that pain was instantaneous, and opened the door alongside them. In seconds she was inside, the door slammed and locked.

"What do you think you're *doing?*"

She knew exactly what he was about to do. Pulling free, she started to scream, but his hand covered her mouth, stifling the sound in her throat.

"Don't do that, Lisa. Just relax. I won't hurt you; I promise. I'm going to take my hand away, but you're not to scream, understand? Not a sound, or I'll have to hurt you. You'll hurt yourself. You'll fall down the stairs head first and crack your skull. 'Death was instantaneous,' as they say in the penny dreadfuls. You're not going to scream, are you?"

She shook her head.

"Good girl."

He removed his hand from her mouth, speedily divested himself of his southwester and oil skins and lit the lamp hanging from a hook beside the door. Light flooded the little room, revealing sacks and stores in barrels and crates. She flew to the door, grabbing the latch, but he gripped her wrists and pulled her away.

"I'll say it once," she murmured, seething. "Touch me, and my husband will kill you. If you know what's

good for you, you'll unlock that door and let me walk
out. We'll forget this ever happened. Open it!"

He grinned expansively, his eyelids closing to slits.
"Relax; you're going to enjoy it." Unbuckling his belt,
he whipped it out of the loops, slapping it loudly against
the wall. 'Hear that? That's just to show you nobody
can outside. The bulkhead's six inches thick, and the
wind's getting louder by the minute."

"You must be insane."

"If I am, you're the one that's made me. Three weeks
looking at you, drooling over you, clenching my teeth
till they ache. Your skin like a baby's, pink and perfect,
your breasts, your hips and what's between 'em. I'm
going to give you a man, Mrs. Dandridge. You'll love
it; you'll beg for more and more and more."

"You pig! You dare touch me . . ."

He laughed, then his face clouded, the tip of his
tongue running across his upper lip. Tearing off his
neckerchief, he held the ends, whipping it into a slender
roll, knotting it in the center and gagging her, the knot
forcing itself between her teeth. He was perspiring now,
his cheeks reddening as his lust came to a boil in his
loins and rushed upward, flooding his body and his
brain. Seizing her by her bodice, he pushed her down on
the sacks. She screamed soundlessly, again and again,
wrenching and wriggling to free herself; but he was
down upon her, pinning her arms, then bringing them
around under her heaving breasts, clamping both wrists
together with one hand, exposing his throbbing member
with the other. Reaching beneath her skirt, he pulled
away her underclothing, exposing her trembling thighs.
He lowered his head to kiss the throbbing swell of her
breasts, his tongue lashing the firmly erect nipples. Her
heart quickened, thundering against her ribs as she
struggled, writhing to free herself. It was useless. His
eyes blazing with lust, his tongue tasting the air lascivi-
ously, the sweat pouring off him, an animal growl es-

caping his throat, he entered her. She screamed without sound and, summoning all her remaining strength, thrust her thighs to the side to dislodge him, but could not. He moved inside her, stabbing, driving deeper and deeper. . . .

IX

Three times he raped her, three times his body crushing hers, pinning her in place against the pile of sacks. He was an animal, with no thought of gentleness, no thought of anything but to satisfy his lust as quickly as possible, a crazed beast in the guise of a man. The hideous guttural sounds, his evil laughter, his wanton brutality all but reduced her helpless body to a pulp. The little room dimmed, the barrels and crates gradually losing their solidity as her tortured brain yielded to unconsciousness.

He meant to murder her to cover up his crime; she was certain of it. The accident he'd mentioned; when he was done with her, when his lust was satisfied, he would stage it.

Now he was standing over her, staring down, a look of malevolent triumph twisting his handsome features. He stood with his feet spread to take the steady roll of the ship. The roar of the wind, the waves sweeping over the deck seemed to reach her ears from 100 miles away.

In ravaging her, he had ripped away her blouse, exposing both breasts. Now his huge hands seized them, mauling them roughly, then his hot, dripping mouth was down upon them, his tongue lapping, lips sucking, gorging himself. His face buried in her breasts, the back of his head bobbing slightly under her gaze, she glanced about. Her wrists were free of his hand now, but to attack him would only invite his wrath, his vicious and terrible strength. If there was something she could use as a weapon, something within reach she could snatch up and slam down upon his head . . . But there was nothing.

Suddenly she spied it, shoved between two sacks alongside her left shoulder, its round end barely visible. She had seen many like it hanging in Josiah Kirby's rack—an iron fid, used, she conjectured, to loosen knots in the tops of sacks. Her left hand inched toward it, but halfway there she stopped abruptly, drawing back as he raised his head, revealing his loathsome wet mouth and leering repulsively at her.

"We're going to do it again. You're getting me hard; you're magnificent!"

Down went his head. Her hand shot out, her fingertips closing on the head of the fid, gripping it, easing it out. Its point caught the light and gleamed momentarily as she lifted it, clenching it so tightly her hand shook, and drove the point with every ounce of strength she could muster straight into his ear.

His howl of agony slammed against the wall of the room. Blood spurted from his ear, drenching her fist still clutching the fid. He rolled off her. She leaped to her feet and, standing over him, brought her heel down on his face, pounding again and again, his nose, his cheeks, his mouth.

He lay lifeless as she stared down at him, his mouth gaping ludicrously, blood seeping out of one corner. Shock, like a wave hurtling over the deck, overwhelmed her. She cried out, a pitiful whining sound. In a daze she groped for the door latch, found it, swung it upward and pulled open the door. Stumbling out, fighting the roll of the ship and threatening unconsciousness, she pulled herself up the steps onto the deck. Spray ripped from the crest of a wave slapped her face, chasing the giddiness threatening to engulf her. Lurching down the deck, she reached the state-room door and tried to open it, but it was locked. Pounding with both fists, she cried out: "Ross! Ross!"

He opened the door, his eyes saucering at the sight of her. "Lisa, good God, look at you!"

"He . . . *raped* me." She fell into his arms.

He carried her to the bed, laying her lightly upon it, sitting on the edge, brushing the sweat-matted hair from her eyes. "Who did this?"

"Burnette," she murmured between sobs.

"I'll kill the bastard!" He shot to his feet. "Where—"

"Down the afterdeck stairs. Ross . . ."

With her last remaining strength, she lifted her hand and grabbed hold of his sleeve, but he pulled free, jerked open the door, rushed out and down the deck toward the stern, the anger rising in his breast clutching his throat like a hand of steel.

"The filthy bastard!"

Seizing the hand grip at the top of the stairs, he hurtled down. The door at the left was open, men milling about. He shouldered through their midst, sighted the mate lying on the floor unconscious and dove at him, choking him, tilting his hands upward, his thumbs pressing hard against the soft flesh under the jaw, tightening in an effort to snap his windpipe. But strong hands seized Ross's shoulders, pulling, breaking his grip.

"You'll kill the blighter!" exclaimed a voice behind him.

It took two men on each arm to hold him back while Josiah Kirby wedged himself between him and the prostrate Burnette. Kirby laid his hands flat against Ross's chest. His voice was calm, his expression solicitous: "Easy, Mr. Dandridge, he's already hurt bad."

"He raped my wife! I'll kill the son of a bitch!"

A loud gasp in unison; glances exchanged, muttered comment.

"Best take him out of here," said Kirby to the men holding Ross.

"I'll kill him, I'll kill him, I'll kill him!"

X

Continuing to roar, Ross was brought back to the state-room. Sight of Lisa lying on the bed, her breasts partially exposed, calmed him considerably. He rushed to her, embracing her, comforting her. The men who had brought him back withdrew, closing the door. Gently he undressed her, cutting away her blouse with scissors. Then he helped her into her robe, leaving it untied and open and bathing her face and breasts and the lower portions of her body.

And throughout his ministrations, in spite of his soothing words, his consoling kisses, she continued whimpering and trembling, her eyes wide and staring like those of a frightened animal. Over and over she repeated his name, now and then throwing herself into his arms, hiding in his embrace for protection. By the time he was done bathing her and had gotten her under the covers and reasonably relaxed, his anger had reduced itself to muttering and whispered threats.

Fear rapidly replaced his ire, the phantom of worry rising to confront him. She was obviously in shock, her face distressingly pale, the trembling persisting, her skin drenched with sweat and her pulse unnaturally rapid. He eased the pillow out from under her head, permitting her to lie flat, and placed a second blanket over the covers to keep her as warm as possible. Then he called out the door to the first man passing to get Dr. Seely.

Captain MacGregor arrived before the doctor, his face ashen, his movements nervous and self-conscious.

By this time Lisa had fallen asleep, her cheeks still pale, her breathing rapid.

"Is she very bod off, Mr. Dondridge?"

"She's in shock. I've sent for the doctor."

MacGregor slumped into a chair, producing a wooden match from his breast pocket, fishing for a cheroot, failing to find one and absentmindedly dropping the unlit match to the rug, unable to tear his eyes from her.

"Seely'll be a few minutes; he's tending to Burnette."

"He'll be smart if he lets the bastard die. It'll save me killing him."

"Please, sor, that sort of talk does nobody ony good. The fid pierced his eardrum! He'll be deaf in thot ear. And what she did to his face . . ."

"What do I care about him? What do you?"

"I know; I'm sorry. This is terrible, terrible." He closed his eyes and shook his head.

"I promise you, captain, he'll hang for this. Whether or not you realize it, this is worse than rape alone. She was on the mend from a severe case of acute melancholia, making splendid progress, thanks to concentrating all her thoughts, all her energies on this mission of ours, all but completely recovered. Now this; it's got to set her back, back to the hideous nightmares, the hallucinations, insomnia, fever, all of it.

"Look at her; she's fighting the monsters right now. She's suffered the tortures of the damned. If she doesn't come out of this, if she doesn't recover a hundred percent, I'll cut what's left of his handsome face off his head. I'll hang him from the yardarm before we sight the Marshalls!"

Before MacGregor could respond, a knock came at the door. Dr. Seely entered, carrying his bag. Ignoring them, moving quickly to the bed, he examined her. Then he placed her left arm outside the coverlet, prepared an injection and administered it. "It'll help her sleep more comfortably."

"Will she be all right?" asked Ross.

"I would say so. I see no physical injury."

"It's not physical injury that worries me, doctor."

"Sleep's the best thing for her, and forgetting, banishing it from her mind as speedily as possible—something neither of us can do for her."

MacGregor got up. "Mr. Dondridge, sor, I've given orders to remove Burnette to his quarters, where he's to be confined oonder guard. The second mate will assume his duties ond responsibilities. When we get back to Son Froncisco, Burnette will be honded over to the authorities. I give ye my sacred ond solemn word on it, sor. And I will pray that yer poor wife will recover. Onything ye need to make her more comfortable ond speed her return to good health, feel free to request. Dr. Seely?"

"Yes?"

"She's in your hands. God guide them."

Lisa slept and dozed on and off for nearly two full days. During brief times of wakefulness she was fed broth and tea. Her condition improved, and she was soon able to sit up in bed and talk for extended periods without tiring. But when the horizon captured the sun, and night blanketed the sea, liberating the stars and the full moon following the ship, back came the fear and anxiety to shackle her, causing her to start at the slightest unexpected sound, to shudder when invisible fingers crept up her spine and fall into Ross's arms, clutching him tightly, begging his protection.

It was, she knew, a fear spawned in darkness and nurtured by dreadful memory conceived to thwart her conscious determination to recover, to return to and reclaim normalcy—a fear she knew she must either subdue or be slave to for the rest of her life. And so she fought it, as she had fought the phantoms of melancholia, the tethers of disappointment and despair and hopelessness that sought to pull her down as she climbed out of the depths toward the sunlight.

By week's end, six days and nights removed from the hour of Burnette's vicious attack, the tide of battle gave indication of turning in her favor. She no longer dreaded the onset of darkness, nor shrank and shuddered at the slightest unexpected sound. As effective as Dr. Seely's dreamless sleep jabbed into her vein and circulating through her body was Ross's patience and gentleness. He rarely left her side, and when at length she felt sufficiently fit to dress and venture out on deck for the fresh air the doctor insisted she have, Ross stayed by her, his arm about her waist, his hand warming hers, his cheek pressed lovingly against her own.

On Sunday afternoon, shortly after the noon meal, Captain MacGregor summoned them to his quarters. Dr. Seely was present and Gatenbee, the second, now first, mate.

"Mrs. Dondridge, I've osked ye to join us, but only if ye feel oop to it. Should what we have to do begin to exhaust ye, we'll call a halt then ond there ond continue it onother time ogreeable to ye."

"I'm all right, thank you, captain. What is it you want?"

Three large volumes occupied a corner of his worktable. He tapped them. "I've consulted my law books, ond the procedures in a crime of this nature in respect to the occused ond the victim are clearly stated. Os ye know, Mr. Burnette has been confined to quarters onder guard, to remain there oontil the ship anchors in Son Froncisco. He will then be turned over to the authorities.

"However, since ye yerselves will not be returning to Son Froncisco, ot least not until yer work is completed, the law clearly specifies that ye must write oot and swear to a deposition describing the incident in detail, his actions and yer own. I realize this is no pleasant thing I'm osking ye to do, but it will be odmissible os evidence ot his trial, making yer own oppearance unnecessary."

"That's good news."

"When ye can, would ye kindly write it oll doon? Two witnesses to it are required. Mr. Dondridge, ye, I'm afraid, are not eligible. I myself ond the first mate here or Dr. Seely will be happy to witness for ye."

"Very well."

"There are a few other details. As ye know, Mr. Burnette's brother is a crewman aboard this ship. I don't know if either of ye have made his occuaintance, but from here on into port, I would advise ye to steer clear of him."

"You think he might cause trouble?" asked Ross.

"No, but blood being thicker thon water, who con predict? Able Seaman Burnette hos a clean record here on the *Sea Cloud*. No drunkenness, no fighting, exemplary deportment, octually. But his fondness ond odmiration for Clay are well known, ond he may consider his brother's confinement os overly severe punishment— I mean even before the trial is held."

"I think you're being overly lenient, captain," observed Ross airily. "If I were you, I'd shackle him to the rudder bar in the bowels of the ship with a bucket of warm water and a loaf of bread."

"Mr. Dondridge, if we had a brig aboard, bars ond a Pittsburgh lock, you con be sure he'd be in it. Os it is, he's restricted to his quarters twenty-three hours a day ond allowed one hour a day on deck. Even a criminal hos need for fresh air."

"We'll give his brother—"

"Wilson."

"—a wide berth," continued Ross.

The captain turned the conversation to Singapore, reiterating his best wishes for their success but voicing his view on the wisdom of a white woman traveling about the Orient, even in the company of her husband.

"Mrs. Dandridge will be staying with the American

consul in Singapore," said Ross. He glanced at Lisa seated beside him and smiled. "We've made an agreement, she and I."

"Mr. Dandridge twisted my arm behind my back, captain. He agreed to let me tag along only if I promise to stay put in Singapore, while he does the searching."

"On intelligent decision. Ye'll be safe with the American consul."

"And worrying sick every waking minute, wondering what he's getting himself into."

They went for a stroll on deck, Captain MacGregor, the doctor and the second mate, a young and eager Vermonter who confessed to having run away to sea at 14. Now 22, he had signed on with Captain MacGregor and, finding the Sea Cloud very much "my kind of ship," planned to stay with her.

The group stood at the bow, watching it carve the onyx skin of the sea, the bowsprit pointing the way to the Marshalls dead ahead and soon to be rising through the gray-green mist shrouding the horizon. Ross and Lisa excused themselves and went back to the stateroom, she to begin preparing the statement. They were scarcely through the door when a knock was heard and a voice called from outside. Ross opened the door. From Josiah Kirby's description of him, Lisa recognized Wilson Burnette. Twisting his cap between his hands, his dark eyes flashed nervously out of his ugly, simian features.

"Mr. Dandridge?"

"Yes?"

"Able Seaman Burnette. May I come in? I have to talk to you, sir."

"I'm sorry; we'd just be wasting each other's time."

Lisa avoided the man's stare, busying herself smoothing the bedspread.

"If you don't want me in, can you come out, sir? Just out here on deck . . ."

"Let him in," said Lisa.

"Lisa!"

Burnette came in apologizing, profuse in his gratitude. "It's really you, sir, I want to talk to."

"I'll leave," said Lisa. "I feel a headache coming on."

"Lie down," said Ross.

"No. I'll go find Dr. Seely and get some powders."
Before he could object further, she was out the door.

"Sit down, why don't you." Ross stared grimly at
Burnette.

"It's about my brother, Clay."

"I'm afraid there's nothing I—"

"It's a terrible thing he did to your missus, sir—
unforgivable. I gave him holy hell. I was so mad I came
near beating his brains out. Told him he was a disgrace,
ought to be ashamed of himself."

"What is it you want from me?"

"Well, when we get home and Captain Mac turns
him over to the law, it's going to go heavy hard with
him. The judge'll throw the book."

"I say he deserves everything he gets."

"You're right, everything. The trouble is . . ." He
hesitated, shifting his feet awkwardly and continuing to
punish his cap.

"Well?"

"I'll be honest with you; no point in not being."

"Go on."

"It's happened before."

Ross stared. "Has it, now."

"In New York last year. The judge suspended sentence. The girl was a prostitute; that's why, I guess.
Anyhow, he went easy. Still, it's on Clay's record. And
this on top of it could—"

"Put him away for the rest of his life, right?"

Wilson nodded.

"And you think that's going a bit too far."

"It's not for me to say, sir. The thing is, you don't
know him like I do. He's really a good boy. He is.

Wouldn't harm a flea. He just gets wild sometimes with women. He's handsome, he was . . . Women come around like flies when you're handsome. That white hair of his . . . He has all the women he wants. It makes it hard."

"I don't follow you."

"He's spoiled. When a fellow gets all that attention, well, when he spots a beauty and she won't even give him the time of day, it what you might say 'frustrates' him."

"Does it? The poor man; you're getting me all welled up with sympathy."

He let the sarcasm pass. "The thing is . . ."

"What is the 'thing'? Tell me."

"Well, sir, if you and your missus were to speak to the judge, or even just sent a letter . . ."

"I'm sorry, Mr. Burnette, you're wasting your breath. Your brother nearly killed my wife."

"But he didn't. He'd never do such a thing. He just goes overboard."

"The point is, the whole business is out of our hands."

"But it's not, don't you see? You could drop the charge. You could. I'm appealing to you, sir, to your good heart. It'd be the Christian thing to do, wouldn't it? You know the old saying, 'To err is human—' "

"I'm sorry."

"You could do it. I've talked to Clay. He feels terrible; he wants to apologize, if she'll let him."

"Amazing."

"Sir?"

"You're making it sound as if he'd stepped on her toe. Look, *I* apologize for being flippant before. I know this is embarrassing for you. You're as innocent of wrongdoing as either of us. You're only doing what any brother would do. I can appreciate that, but there's nothing we can do for him."

"You mean there's nothing you *want* to do." The

words came out flat and hard. The air of desperation was vanished. His plea had failed and he knew it.

"There's no point in dragging out this discussion," said Ross, "is there?"

"I guess not, if that's the way you feel. Good day."

"Good day."

XI

Lisa was touched by Dr. Seely's zealous, almost relentless concern for her. He looked in on her morning and afternoon every day, to some degree reclaiming the respect he had lost in everyone's eyes on the night of the operation.

She wrote out her deposition describing Burnette's attack and her retaliation. It was witnessed and locked in the captain's safe against the day the *Sea Cloud* docked in San Francisco.

The emotional scars healed and faded. With the day drawing nearer when she and Ross would be embarking on the search for Deirdre, she made a conscious effort to avoid cluttering her thoughts with depressing recollections. Wilson Burnette approached her, catching her alone on deck one morning. He poured out his plea, and when she politely but firmly told him the matter was closed, he became demanding, insisting that "everybody was entitled to forgiveness." His disappointment got the better of his common sense, and had not Captain MacGregor happened by, the confrontation would have turned ugly. To her astonishment, the man seemed genuinely upset over her reluctance to let his brother apologize.

She made no mention of the incident to Ross, nor did the captain, although he issued a stern warning to Wilson to keep away from the passengers.

She stood at the rail one night after dinner with Ross by her side, gazing out over the water streaked with silver, silently contemplating its beauty and thanking God for Ross, his consideration, devotion and love over the course of the year that had elapsed since Deirdre's abduction. Surely it had been the cruelest, most depressing period in her entire life, and without his presence and support, without all that he gave her, she knew in her heart she never would have pulled through.

"Two weeks to port," he said. "Past the Marshalls we ride the south equatorial current, and with the northeast trade winds coming down, there's no cause to worry about any prolonged calms."

"If anyone had told me the day the *Sea Urchin* left Singapore harbor I'd be going back there, I would have laughed in his face."

"I was discussing it with MacGregor this afternoon. He's as worried as I am over this business of your going ashore alone to contact Wo Sin. You're going to be begging trouble, Lisa. I should be with you."

She shook her head. "It's too risky. The British authorities have your name and your description on file, probably even your picture. If the police were to recognize you walking down the street, they'd arrest you on the spot. And there'd be nothing either of us could do to keep them from shipping you back to Macquarie Harbor."

"I disagree. It's been a whole year; they've probably forgotten all about me."

"Possibly, but why take the chance? I'll go ashore; you stay on board."

"The *Sea Cloud* will be in port only four days, just long enough to unload and take on new cargo."

"Plenty of time for me to meet with Wo Sin and arrange for a ship to take us north, once he puts us on the right track."

"You make it sound so cut and dried."

"We've got money; we've got Wo Sin. Any obstacles in our path, we'll blow them out of the way."

"Spoken like an artillery officer."

"Is there any other way to look at it? The war starts the day we reach port. Us against—"

"The Chinese Empire."

"If it comes to that, yes." Touching his cheek, she turned his face to her. "Whatever happens from now on, one thing is sure: I have no intention of going home without her, even if we never see Blackwood again."

"You mean it, don't you."

"I do."

"You know something, darling? I love you, but there are times when you scare me a little—like now. I'm glad I'm on your side. I pity the empress; she doesn't know what she's in for."

He pecked her affectionately, enjoyed it, embraced her and kissed her, ardently, hungrily.

She pulled back and appraised the passion smoldering in his eyes. "Take me to bed, Mr. Dandridge."

"Darling . . ."

"Take me to bed, my husband."

The aftermath of their lovemaking was always the same for Lisa, a time to lie in his arms indolently basking in the glow of contentment, an interlude that had never been less than beautiful, from the first time to now. In all the glorious years together, all the intimate hours experiencing each other, feeling his member moving inside her, his tongue swollen by lust dueling hers, his touch, his heart beating frantically against her naked breast, the yearning to at once possess and belong never ceased. This magnificent man, this immortal creature whose love fire ignited and consumed her, whose devotion filled her being to overflowing, whose love swept her beyond the stars, must never let her go, never release her from his mind. For his unfailing strength was the source of her own, her tenacity of purpose, her unflinching resolve to challenge and conquer the future rooted in the rapture they shared.

And with this thought, she snuggled closer to lose herself in the universe of his eyes.

She no longer engaged nightmares, no longer struggled to raise insurmountable walls against the dragons of hallucination, no longer envisioned Deirdre being ravaged by the faceless animals who had stolen her. Nor did she see Burnette's lascivious leer as he lowered his body to rape her. The obliteration of all these hateful monsters of the mind was Ross's doing as much as her own—his caring and kindness, his love driving them away.

She was sleeping unaided by Dr. Seely's needles, awaking rested, no longer weak-limbed, having to force herself to get out of bed.

Wilson Burnette had evidently accepted their refusal to drop the charges against his brother. When he passed them on deck, he pretended not to recognize them, for which Ross expressed appreciation. As he put it, he had no desire to be pressed to the point of physically shutting the man up; Wilson, after all, had done nothing to either of them.

One morning, as the ship was passing through the Marshall Islands east of the Carolinas, Bikini atoll, the nearest land, barely rising above the horizon, thrusting its scattered coconut palms toward the sun, Ross and Lisa were standing at the stern rail when the cabin boy came up to them.

"Excuse me, Mr. Dandridge: Captain MacGregor would like a word with you in his cabin."

"What is it?"

"He didn't say, sir. But he's there now waiting for you."

"I'll go for a stroll," said Lisa. "It's such a lovely morning. See what he wants and hurry back."

Ross found MacGregor alone in his cabin. The captain wore the look of a man overburdened with cares. When he spoke, Ross detected a vague trace of annoyance in his tone. Before him on the table, lying atop a chart, was a white envelope, the flap unsealed. Out of it he took three papers, squaring them together and setting them before him.

"I'm ofraid I have some distressing news, Mr. Dondridge. Would ye please read this?"

"What is it?"

"A deposition."

"Not Burnette?"

MacGregor nodded.

"You mean a confession, don't you?"

"Read it."

On the evening of April 29, 1867, I was on my duty tour, making rounds, and came down the aft stairs. Coming up the companionway from midships, I noticed one of our passengers, Mrs. Dandridge. She greeted me by name and I returned her greeting. I then moved to one side to let her pass, pressing my back against the wall. She started by, but in doing so, to my surprise and embarrassment, deliberately rubbed her body against mine. She then stopped short, noticing that the door to galley stores behind her was ajar. She took hold of my hand and urged me to go with her into the room. I refused. She then placed the flat of my hand against one of her breasts and rolled the tip of her tongue over her lip in a most seductive manner. The next thing I knew, we were inside galley stores. She closed and latched the door and bade me light the lamp hanging by the door. When I did, I saw that she had dropped down upon a pile of rice and flour sacks and was removing her underclothing. I remonstrated with her, but she pretended not to hear me and continued undressing. Her actions were so unexpected and I so shocked and amazed, I stood staring like a fool instead of leaving. She lifted her skirt, exposing herself, and made a lewd remark, to wit: "This is for you, Clay darling, come, take me. I want to feel you in me." I hasten to add that our ship had been at sea almost continuously since February 5, nearly three months. In all that time I had not even seen a woman. Mrs. Dandridge and her husband had boarded in San Marcos, and from the first time she saw me, she repeatedly looked at me in a suggestive manner, smiling, winking and rolling the tip of her tongue across her upper lip— even running one hand down her breast. She was clever about this forwardness, never letting her husband see what she was about when he was close by. I confess to being a fool, but she aroused me. Not content with removing her underthings and exposing herself to me, she then unfastened her blouse in a most licentious manner, revealing her naked breasts, cupping them, rubbing them and pushing them together. She is a beautiful and voluptuous woman, and, admittedly, so taken was I by her displays and her persuasive words, I was unable to control myself. She then proceeded to unbuckle my belt and, reaching inside my trousers, began fondling me. She continued making suggestive comments as she played with me. She then proceeded to lie back and draw me down on top of her. She disported herself in a most unseemly manner as to suggest that she had not been made love to for a long time. When we were finished, she insisted I immediately make love to her a second time. I refused. She persisted, and fondled me in such a shameless manner as to arouse me again. And once more she pulled me down on top of her. But realizing what I was about, I continued to refuse. She insisted, her voice and her manner becoming more and more savage. When she saw that I only wanted to leave her, she became furious. She repeatedly insisted that I didn't think she was good enough, that she had failed me, words to that effect. I could see that she was becoming extremely frustrated and confused and losing all control. I knew then that I had to get away from her, that I never should have given in to her in the first place

*and to remain with her would only make matters
worse. I tried to explain this, the disastrous consequences for us both if we should be found out,
the fact that she was a married woman. I tried my
utmost to calm her down, but she wouldn't listen.
When she began to curse me loudly, I covered her
mouth, realizing that should anyone passing by outside hear her and find us, I would be the one who
would have to answer for it. Then she lost control
completely and began pounding me in the face with
her fists. She was like a wild demon. She was on
top of me now, holding me down, despite the fact
that I am twice her size and weight. I have never
seen a human being so furious. I could not believe
my eyes. My heart went out to her. I was pushing
her off when she suddenly seized a fid stuck among
the sacks next to the door wall. She stabbed me in
the ear. It felt as if my head would split with the
pain. The blood gushed out and I quickly lost consciousness. The next thing I knew, I woke up in
great pain from my ear and wounds inflicted on my
face when she stomped upon it, this according to
my shipmates. They were leaning over me. She had
vanished. I swear under God, as a churchgoing
Christian, that this is exactly what happened on the
date and at the time specified above."*

His signature and those of two witnesses, including
his brother, appeared at the bottom alongside the previous day's date.

"It's a pack of lies from beginning to end," said Ross
evenly, fighting so hard to control his temper his hands
shook. He flung the papers down upon the table and
got up from his chair.

"Whether it is or not—," began MacGregor.

"What do you mean, 'whether it is or not'?"

"Calm doon, Mr. Dondridge. Kindly don't cross-
examine me. Ye're not a lawyer; I'm not a witness."

Ross slumped down into the chair. "I apologize."

"You have every reason to be oopset."

"The man is a lying son of a bitch! His brother couldn't get me to drop the charge, so he's resorting to this. He's drowning; he's grasping at straws."

"Oonder the law, it's his right."

" 'Right'? What rights does a rapist have? We can thank God he didn't beat her to death!"

"A murderer, a child molester, whatever the crime, regardless of how heinous, the mon still hos rights. Mrs. Dondridge gives the court her version; he hos the right to rebut her. He osked to borrow my law books; I could not refuse him. It does create a problem for ye ond Mrs. Dondridge. Since he's come oop with this, she'll doot-less have to appear ot the trial in person to refute his claims of seduction."

"That's impossible and you know it! When this ship reaches Singapore, we're getting off. We may not get back to San Francisco for two years."

"That's for ye to decide. It's yer case. I'm only telling ye this in yer own best interests." Reaching into the envelope, the captain drew out a single sheet of paper. "I'll not trouble ye to read this, but it's a statement he got from two hands who claim that on the morning following the night ye were operated on, they saw Mrs. Dondridge run oot of one of the state-rooms in her nightgown"—his eyes went to the paper—"disporting herself in a most revealing fashion."

"She'd overslept; she was running in to see me! She was curious to see if I was alive or dead," he added sarcastically. "Captain, what in hell does that have to do with Burnette's raping her?"

"You're osking the wrong man, sor. I'm not the judge. There's one other thing.

"I'm sure there is. Let's have it all out."

"Burnette plans to sue yer wife."

"You're not *serious*."

"*He* appears to be. He's osking two-hoondredthousand dollars in domages, citing permanent loss of hearing in his left ear ond permanent disfigurement."

"This is the most ridiculous goddamned nonsense I have ever heard!"

"Mr. Dondridge, I'm only telling ye these things to keep ye abreast of what he's oop to. How ye propose to deal with the situation is entirely oop to ye. If I may make a suggestion, I would discuss it with Mrs. Dondridge . . ."

"Forget that. In less than three weeks she's succeeded in wiping the worst of it out of her mind; I'm not about to refresh her memory."

"Os ye wish."

"Exactly. Is this all the good news?" He didn't wait for MacGregor's response. "Then good morning, captain."

Out on deck he cursed loudly, slamming both hands down on the railing. Lisa was at the bow. She came running down to him.

"What's the matter, darling?"

"Nothing."

"What did he want?"

"Nothing important."

"Nothing?"

"That's what I said."

"You should see yourself; you look ready to explode into a million pieces. What is it, Ross?"

"Let's go back up to the bow."

"I'm not going to stand here repeating myself. Are you going to tell me, or do I go in and ask him?"

He sighed and simmered down and kissed her forehead, holding her close affectionately. "It's really nothing to worry about." He told her about the statement only, discounting its relevance as he did so, relegating it to the realm of absurdity. His ploy misfired; she became furious.

"The lying pig! The disgusting animal!" Pulling away, she swung about.

"Where are you going?"

"To read it."

"Why bother?"

"I want to!"

Bursting into MacGregor's cabin without knocking, without even so much as a "good morning," she shoved her hand under his nose. "Give it to me; I want to read it."

He complied. Ross drifted in, exchanging glances with MacGregor, each of them eyeing the ceiling. She read silently, her expression unchanging. When she had finished, she laid the papers down upon the table.

"Captain, I would like you to send a man down to his quarters and bring him up here."

"Mrs. Dondridge . . ."

"Do it. We can settle this right here and now. We'll need Dr. Seely, too."

"Lisa, what are you doing?"

"Darling, you arrange the chairs behind the table—one on either side of you, captain. Mr. Burnette will sit on your right, Dr. Seely on your left. Humor me, please, both of you. I promise this won't take more than ten minutes."

XII

Mr. Burnette's face had healed, but his mirror would remind him of the night of April 29 for the rest of his life. Sitting alongside the captain, when Lisa addressed him, he turned his head to the right to enable him to hear with his left ear.

"I've read your statement, Mr. Burnette," she said calmly.

"I've read yours, Mrs. Dandridge. One of us is lying."

"So it appears."

"I guess it's up to a judge and jury to decide which." His glance drifted to the porthole. "It should be quite a spectacle."

So that was his game, she mused: threaten to put on a performance the tabloid newspapers would make merry with, dip his brush in the bile of fabrication and smear her up and down. In the end he'd lose, of course. But how could she win? His suddenly all-too-obvious strategy made his three pages of nonsense prose nothing more than a club with which to bully her into dropping the charge.

"We shall see. Shall we proceed?"

Burnette smirked and gestured with exaggerated magnanimity.

"According to your version of what happened, I met you in the companionway and enticed you into the galley storeroom, actually led you in by the hand. Correct me if I'm wrong, but throughout your whole statement you say you never laid a hand on me."

"What I wrote I swore to, I stand by."

"Dr. Seely, back in our state-room you examined me, is that right?"

"I did."

"I was asleep. What did you do for me?"

"I gave you a needle to help you sleep more comfortably."

"A needle in my . . ."

"Left forearm."

"And did you happen to notice the condition of my wrist?"

"It was badly bruised. Both were."

"But you never laid a hand on me, Mr. Burnette."

"I defended myself. I may have grabbed your wrists only to keep you from scratching my eyes out." His fingertips went to his cheek. "Look at my face, lady, a good look!"

"Dr. Seely, you saw my breasts."

"They were bruised."

"Did I attack you with my breasts, Mr. Burnette?"

"Well . . ."

"I stuck you in the ear with a fid."

He pretended not to hear, turning his head, pushing his left ear toward her. She repeated herself.

"I'm totally deaf in my right ear. I'll never hear again, right, doctor?"

"Right."

"You misunderstood, Mr. Burnette. I don't deny I stabbed you in the ear. But you claim I attacked you. I say I was defending myself with the first thing I could lay my hands on. You were on top of me—"

"No, no, I was underneath. You pushed me down. I tried to wrestle free."

"Ah, that's the point, the crux of this whole matter. Captain MacGregor, doctor, please pay close attention to this. Mr. Burnette, if, as you claim, you were under me and I picked up the fid from . . ." Picking up the page describing that phase of the incident, she indicated the passage and handed the paper to MacGregor. "Captain . . ."

He read: " 'I was pushing her off when she suddenly seized a fid stuck among the sacks next to the door wall. She stobbed me in the ear.' "

"Which ear, Mr. Burnette?"

"My right ear, of course."

"Hold it," interrupted the captain. "If ye were on the bottom, mister, ond she was on top ond she reached in the direction of the door for the fid ond stobbed ye, it wouldn't be yer right ear; it would be yer left." He swung his hands about, pantomiming the act.

"*That,* Mr. Burnette, is my point," said Lisa quietly.

Burnette's eyes darted to the captain, then to the doctor. "She must have switched it to her other hand," he blurted. "She did, I remember now."

"Ye didn't say so here," said MacGregor, rattling the three pages. He began rereading the passage.

Burnette cut him off with a snarl. "All right! I made a mistake."

"A very big mistake," said the captain. "Big enough to make all o' this soospect." He tossed the pages down. "Mr. Dondridge, sor, the mon outside the door. Would ye osk him to come in, please, to escort the prisoner back to his quarters?"

"Thank you, captain," said Lisa, standing. "Dr. Seely, Mr. Burnette . . ." She turned to follow Ross out. The last thing she heard in the room was the unmistakable sound of paper being crumpled.

XIII

Slipping through the Philippines and putting North Borneo on its larboard beam, the *Sea Cloud* entered the South China Sea. Altering course to the southwest, two days later saw Natoena Eilanden emerge from the placid green water, placing Singapore less than 200 miles distant.

Wilson Burnette, meanwhile, recognized the necessity to resume his campaign to dissuade Ross from filing the charge through Captain MacGregor. Time was growing ominously short. He twice appeared at the door of the state-room, the second time all but falling to his knees to plead for his brother. Lisa felt sorry for him, caught, as he was, in the middle of the situation and plainly embarrassed. But Ross refused to discuss it. He and Lisa did talk about it as they prepared to retire shortly after Wilson's latest unannounced visit.

"I feel sorry for him, too," said Ross as he pulled off first one boot, then the other. "Still he seems to think all we want is to get even."

"Isn't that at least part of it?"

"Not to me. All I want is to make sure his brother's taken out of circulation for a while. He might change his ways. As I see it, there's a girl walking around somewhere singled out by fate to be his third victim. The bastard's lust needs a chance to cool off. You know damned well if he had attacked you on land, where he could have gotten away, he wouldn't have hesitated to kill you."

"I can't argue that. The look in his eyes . . . Howard Cairns would have a field day with him on his couch."

Ross pulled her down onto his lap and kissed her. "Tomorrow we'll be in Singapore. You can put Burnette, his brother, this ship, the whole trip behind you. We have so much to do."

"Which has to be done as quickly as possible. God only knows where she is and what they're doing to her. If we can spare her one day of it . . ."

"We promised ourselves we wouldn't dwell on that, remember?" He kissed her eyes. "You look tired. How do you feel?"

"Like I look." She stifled a yawn and smiled. "Tenterhooks are always exhausting."

"Patience."

They went to bed and made love and later she dozed in his arms, determinedly slowing her racing mind. All the memories, good and bad, of Singapore when last she had seen it lined up in chronological order. Closing her eyes, she visualized a familiar face, Mr. Justice Sir Reginald Lowell, in his judicial cap and robes, gavel in hand. The courtroom was filled to overflowing, the curious onlookers flailing the sultry air with their fans, the steady swishing sound underscoring his brittle voice:

"In the view of this court, your contention that your fellow seaman, Cyril Alfred Deering, was wholly responsible for the crime of which you are accused is without merit or foundation. I therefore have no recourse but to find you guilty as charged of the crime of opium smuggling. I sentence you to seven years' hard labor at Macquarie Harbor."

Down came his gavel, the hammer of doom, striking her heart. Lisa stirred as if the blow were real.

"Darling, what is it?"

"Nothing, just nerves."

"Try to sleep. Tomorrow's too big a day to take on tired."

The *Sea Cloud* entered the Singapore Strait an hour before dawn, passing between Johore, at the southernmost end of the Malay Peninsula, and the islands of the Riouw Archipelago. They were up and dressed and at the starboard rail forward when dawn arrived swathing the murky water, lightening the mist shrouding the city with a faint gamboge glow, like some eerie illumination run up a fissure from hell. The waterfront was clogged with vessels, clipper ships lording it over the area, the tops of their masts seemingly pinning down the under-belly of the mist blanket. Interspersed among them were grimy merchantmen from every port in Europe and Asia, mat-roofed sampans, square-sailed junks, ladder-masted Bugi ships, shallow-draft tongkangs, *prahus,* pinnaces, koleks, bunder boats, dinghies and dugouts so closely jammed together that one could walk from vessel to vessel without fear of falling into the water.

The *Sea Cloud* slipped behind the mole into the Telok Ayer Basin, wedging her slender hull into a berth to the shouting of deckhands and the whip song of hawsers flung and made fast fore and aft. The mist gradually dissipating over the warehouses and freight depots revealed the city—the atap-thatched shacks of the poor, brick shops, orange-roofed stone buildings, domed temples and spired churches. In spite of the early hour, the docks were alive with activity, ill-clad Malays, Indians, Burmese, Thais, Japanese and hundreds of Chinese scurrying about. As Lisa and Ross stood under the ratlines watching, the lights of the city continued to go out, lending the scene a sepulchral atmosphere from Johore Strait down to the mole.

Captain MacGregor joined them, his manifest board in hand. "I wouldn't be in a roosh to disembark to go looking for yer friend," he cautioned Lisa. "Give the sun on hour to burn away the gray. By then the pick-pockets ond opium oddicts ond other vermin will be off duty mostly. Not thot thot'll turn the place into onother Vatican City, boot with what ye have to do, modom, ond where ye have to go, ye'll be a sight safer."

"I don't like this at all," said Ross. "I'll be on pins

and needles until you get back. Why not take a couple of men with you?"

"I don't need anybody, Ross."

"Can you remember how to get there?"

"Of course. It's a twenty-minute walk from the Equitorial Hotel to Chinatown, to Songkok Alley."

"Ye're not plonning to walk it," said MacGregor. "For God's sake, ot least take a gharry."

"I will. I won't have any trouble finding it, darling. I've seen the building a hundred times in my mind's eye these past few months."

"Ye ought to take a policeman with ye," remarked MacGregor.

"To the house of Wo Sin? You're joking; that would be like walking a cat into a dog pound. No, I've got to go by myself." She turned from the rail, shifting her glance from one to the other. Their concern was evident in their faces, and she was touched by it. "Stop worrying, you two; I'll be fine. The only thing that's bothering me is what do we do with you, darling, if he's out of town or I'm not able to reach him straightaway for some other reason? If we have to sit and wait for more than four days, where will it be safe for you?"

MacGregor pointed past the south end of the mole. "Out on one of the islands."

"No, that's still British jurisdiction," she said. "Maybe we should hire the ship we'll be using for the next leg today, right away. You'd be safe on board."

"My God!" exclaimed Ross. "You'd think I was an ax murderer with ten thousand pounds on my head and every police in the straits out looking."

"I have a thought," said MacGregor. "I think we should continue this discussion over breakfast. I'm hungry os a shark."

XIV

She waved up to them from the bottom of the gangplank, blew Ross a kiss and patted her bag to make
doubly sure her loaded derringer was in it. Walking to
the street past workers stripped to their waists glistening
with sweat and pausing to gape at her, she hailed a
gharry. She ordered the driver to take her straight to
Beach Road and down it to Bencoolen Street, located
on the right bank of the Rochore River. Off they rattled
at a brisk pace, and almost before she knew it, the
Bencoolen Street sign was rushing up to meet her.

Here was a vast congestion of shop houses originally
built with one room open to the street for business and
a second in the rear, where the shopkeepers and their
families lived. Now every shop had added one or two
stories, which in turn had been subdivided into cramped
little cubicles to accommodate dozens of residents.

The fronts of the buildings displayed garish patterns
of acanthus leaves and mock Corinthian pillars and
were color-washed in brilliant blues, greens and pinks.

She stopped her driver at the head of Songkok Alley.
Getting out, she paid him and off he drove, leaving her
standing staring at the forbidding-looking teakwood
door at the opposite end of the alley. She trembled as
recollection of what had befallen her on her previous
visit reared up in her mind like a cobra lifting its head
from its coil. The now-blinding sun drenched the city
in the soft yellow of orpiment, and the air was redolent
of the sweet odor of temple flowers, their lofty trees
rising in the cramped little backyard of the building.
But within, she remembered, the odor would be lilac,

216

striking her nostrils in a powerful wave as soon as the door was opened.

Once again she heard the soft clap of a drape being raised and lowered as the guide who had brought her from the Equitorial Hotel had led her blindfolded into a room. When he had removed her blindfold, the first sight to meet her eyes had been that of myriad candles sputtering, throwing eerie shadows over the bare walls and ceiling. Fear, like a trap closing, had seized her and she shrank back. Lying about on worn pallets spread across the rough-hewn plank floor were a dozen half-naked coolies. Even as she screamed, half turning to flee, she was grabbed from behind and thrown down. And they had come at her, pushing and shoving to be the first to assault her, their lust firing their eyes. She had never told Ross what the coolies had done to her, how she had passed out later, to awaken in a bed in Wo Sin's house. He had introduced himself, telling her that the man who had brought her to him had had his eyes gouged out in punishment for his infamous conduct, that all the coolies who had attacked her had been harshly dealt with. He had apologized profusely, insisting that he had never received her message asking to speak with him.

She had believed him. He had been very kind and considerate, very forthright.

But that was then, and now she stood staring at the door, imagining the powerful scent of lilac on the other side of it. Steeling herself, she shuddered away thoughts of the candle-lit room and the horror to which she had been subjected. Finding a pencil in her bag and a receipt, she wrote a note on the back of it, pressing it and a shilling into the hand of the first passerby, a distressingly emaciated and wrinkled old coolie shouldering a yoke supporting two buckets of water.

"Give it to Wo Sin, in the rear of that house . . . Wo Sin."

The man nodded agreeably, recognizing the name.

Divesting himself of his burden, he padded swiftly down to the door, knocking, turning and grinning at her, holding the note high as he waited for the door to open. It did. He spoke to the person, he or she staying back in the shadows, handed over the note and came back, gesturing her to go up to the door.

She did so, her heart rising in her breast and thumping too loudly. Taking a deep breath, she knocked. The door whined open a second time.

"Wo Sin!" Her sigh of relief was so pronounced and so obvious, it brought a smile to his face.

"Mrs. Dandridge! What a wonderful surprise! Come in, come in!"

A pretty, almond-eyed Chinese girl in a red and gold *cheongsam,* her jet-black hair securely bound atop her head, served them tea and a platter of fruit—mandarin oranges, carambolas, soursops and papayas—in a room resplendent with sandalwood and bamboo furniture and dozens of satin pillows. Wo Sin had not changed a hair in the year since last she had seen him. If anything, he appeared younger, trim and vigorous-looking in his pristine white cotton suit, his hair neatly parted, his fingernails manicured, his mustache snipped and brushed to perfection. Had she not known him, she would have taken him for a bank president rather than Captain China of the Sing Yops, the bloodthirstiest and most powerful underworld gang in Malaysia.

"I was delighted and relieved to hear that you were able to rescue your husband from the penal colony in Macquarie Harbor."

"You heard?"

"Everyone in Singapore knows about your exploits." He laughed. "They call you the 'Iron Lady.' Somebody even wrote a song about you."

"The 'Iron Lady'? That's not very flattering."

"It was an incredible accomplishment. Such determination." He raised his cup. "I salute you."

"Thank you."

"You're blushing."

She laughed and he joined her. Then she sobered. "Your time is valuable, I know, so I'd best get straight to the point. As you've probably already guessed, I'm here to ask a favor."

"One I owe you."

"No, Wo Sin, you don't owe me a thing."

"In conscience I do. Be that as it may, I would consider it a privilege to come to the aid of the Iron Lady."

"You're the only one in the world who can help us." She explained, and he listened without interrupting, his broad brow crinkled, his lips shrunken into a tight little pink bud.

"Ironic," he said when she was finished. "You left her in Batavia because it was safer than Singapore. Alas, where is there that is safe in the Orient?" He rose from his chair, setting his empty cup on the tray and standing at the window, looking out at the temple trees in the yard, their delicate white petals swirling about their mustard-colored centers like bent pinwheels. "This is a chronicle of horror you tell me."

"Do you think we'd be chasing a wild goose?"

He turned and smiled. "Surely you haven't come all this distance to stop short and let doubt overtake you. No, I would assume that she is alive. A most reasonable assumption. Corpses are of no value to anyone. One other thing is very much in your favor: the fact that she so closely resembles you, her skin, her eyes, especially her red hair. Such looks would catch everybody's eye. People would remember such a person. There can't be more than half a dozen girls who look like her in all of the East."

"She must be in China; the slave ship was Chinese."

His smile contracted into a look of concern. "We can't be sure. They took her to sell, to where there's a buyer for human chattel."

"Not in China?"

"Not necessarily. She could be anywhere, from Sumatra to Hokkaido, in Japan, to Mongolia."

"But aren't there slave markets?"

"Not anymore. Nowadays they're usually sold right off the ship."

"Then it'll take us a hundred years. It's hopeless!"

"Now, now, now, that doesn't sound like the Iron Lady who stormed the Gates of Hell. Be patient; I will send out feelers. I have many friends, and there are many others who would be eager to do me a good turn. If she's in the Orient or near it, we can find out where."

" 'If.' I've been living with that word for over a year." She sighed and smiled grimly. "But you *will* help us. If we can find out where she's being held, that's all we'd need to know. We'd be most grateful if you can just get us on the right track."

"You mean you'd deny me the satisfaction of being in on the final victory, seeing the three of you reunited?"

"It's going to be risky."

"Extremely so, I'm afraid. And you must be prepared to pay exorbitant bribes. There are doors out here only money can open." He paused and sat and refilled both their cups. "But the dangerous aspect is the one thing that worries me. Must you yourself be directly involved?"

"Definitely. I haven't come all this way to sit by the fire in Singapore and wait, although my husband would be happy if I did."

"Mmmmm. Well, after what you accomplished at Macquarie Harbor, I'd be the last one to attempt to talk you out of it." Clapping his hands, he beamed brightly. "Enough chit-chat; we must get down to business. How long is your ship going to be in port?"

"Four days."

"Not long enough. I'll need at least a week to send out feelers and get the answers we'll need to plan strategy. You must take rooms at the Equitorial Hotel, where you stayed last time."

"I can, but I can't bring my husband ashore. I was thinking of hiring the ship we'll be needing and living on board until we leave."

"That's possible. Leave it to me. I'll arrange passage for your party on the cleanest merchantman I can find. It'll be slower than sail but safer in the event of heavy seas. You can be thankful you're three months in advance of the typhoon season, which makes one thing less to worry about."

"You said 'your party.' "

"I myself can't go with you—too many commitments —but I have an associate, a French national who speaks Cantonese, Manchu, a half-dozen dialects. Very capable, handy with weapons. You'll appreciate his protection. Forgive me, I'm getting ahead of myself. We must first determine where your daughter is. This will be the hardest part for you. I want you to go back to your ship and wait for word from me. As I say, it could take a week, possibly less, if we're lucky. But we'll find her, and you and your husband will be reunited with her. You have my word on it."

XV

Chiding her for coming to Songkok Alley alone, Wo Sin insisted she return to the *Sea Cloud* in the company of one of his men. Heading out of Chinatown past the hawkers' stalls lining both sides of the street, goods of every conceivable type and description laid out for sale on cloths in front of them, she warmed her face in the sun and her heart in the certainty that the first strategic moves were about to be made. Wo Sin had enlisted and taken up the banner of the cause. She couldn't wait to tell Ross the good news.

"Faster, faster!"

The driver slapped his horse's flanks with the reins, sending him clopping hurriedly across Victoria Street and Bridge Road down to Beach Road, careening around a corner to the right, heading in the direction of the Telok Ayer Basin. Carriages, gharries, rickshaws and trishaws passed them and on all sides great masses of people, predominently Chinese—women, cone-hatted or bareheaded, *Samsui* laboring women, wealthy ladies clad in high-collared, slit-skirted *cheongsams*, men in all sorts of attire, from blouses and jackets and traditional silk shirts to smartly tailored business suits. There were turbaned Sikhs; Punjabis and Chettyars from Madras; Malayan men in *bajus** and ill-fitting trousers; Malayan women in colorful, close-fitting jackets and long batik skirts. There were Thais, saffron-robed, Japanese, Russians, Eurasians, British civilians and pith-helmeted soldiers; but the Chinese—transplanted

* Loose, collarless jackets.

222

Cantonese, Teochews, Fukienese, Hainanese and Hak-kas—outnumbered all the other nationalities combined.

Ahead of the gharry the golden-roofed Thien Hok Keng temple rose above Telok Ayer Street, its eaves upturned in the traditional manner. Turning into Telok Ayer, they passed a funeral cortege, the coffin riding a cart and decorated in garish colors in determined challenge to the sadness of the occasion. Shading the deceased was a painted canopy surmounted by a stork, indicating that the corpse was a woman's. The mourners preceded the coffin, riding in carts. They wore roughly made hoods fashioned of unbleached calico, and between them and the coffin cart walked professional mourners dressed all in white, energetically beating drums and clanging cymbals to frighten away the evil spirits congregating along the route to the cemetery.

When they came in sight of the docks, Lisa stopped the driver and got out. Walking back the way she had come earlier, under the gloriously bright sun, she greeted the workers, who touched the brims of their straw hats in response. She greeted the world. She felt as if her feet were scarcely touching the wooden walkway, as if her spirits had lifted her just high enough to prevent her toes from reaching it. The gulls and terns circling overhead, shrieking insolently, looked like angels. She could have burst into song she felt so lifted, so jubilant, so marvelous.

Hurrying her steps, she came to the foot of the gangplank. To her surprise, there was nobody at the rail, nor was a single hand aloft. At first glance, it appeared that the ship had been completely abandoned. Up the gangplank she raced. There was no one on deck. Strange, she thought; she had expected him to be hovering over the bowsprit, peering out from under his hand, anxiously awaiting her return. She ran to the state-room and knocked loudly.

"Ross! It's me, darling; open the door!"

No response. She jiggled the handle. The door was unlocked. She pushed it open. Empty.

Back up the deck she ran, her heart suddenly beating wildly. Something was wrong, something terrible. . . .

"Ross! Ross!"

She came to the forward companionway stairs, swinging around to start down, stopping short. The murmur of many voices came drifting up. She hurried down. Men crowded in and around the doorway to the infirmary and inside. Those outside stared at her.

"Ross!"

They gave way, letting her pass. Inside, the odor of ammonia struck her nostrils; officers and men stood about with stricken looks on their faces; a body lay on a table. MacGregor was holding up the end of a sheet. At sight of her, he dropped it, covering the face of the corpse.

"Mrs. Dondridge, stay back."

She ignored him. "My husband; where is my husband?"

Reaching out, she was about to pull back the sheet end when MacGregor grabbed her wrist, stopping her.

"No!"

She broke free, jerking back the sheet.

It was Ross. He was dead.

XVI

She sat slumped in a chair across from Dr. Seely and MacGregor in the captain's cabin, her fingertips against her forehead, her elbow on the chair arm supporting her. The Veronal given her by Seely still fuzzied her mind and left a bitter taste in her mouth. MacGregor was rambling on in halting tones, floundering in the mire of explanation. Ross's face, his cheeks and lips drained of color, his eyes sealed in death, filled her mind. Coming upon him lying there, confirming the suspicion speedily rooting itself in her brain, she had fainted, strong arms catching her before she hit the floor.

MacGregor's voice sounded as if it were coming from the other end of the ship. "It hoppened shortly ofter ye left. Wilson Burnette went to see him. They began talking ond then, occording to one of the men walking by the state-room, they started to argue. Mr. Dondridge lost his temper. He hit him in the jaw. Burnette pulled a knife."

The air about her seemed clammy, damp and as cold as the tomb, and the room was becoming a single enormous block of ice enclosing her in its center, collapsing her body, squeezing her heart in the rack of her ribs.

"He stabbed your husband in the stomach," continued the doctor. "The worst possible place. By the time I got there, he was dead."

"Burnette dove over the stern," said the captain. "He swam off toward the mole. Two men went ofter him, boot he got away over the mole ond in among all the ships onchored there. If the oondertow hasn't gotten him, a sea snake will."

Seely got up, coming around the table, touching her shoulder. "You should get back into bed."

"No."

"But . . ."

"Please. Let's get this over with."

"There's no way I can put into words how sorry we both are," said MacGregor. "I hold myself responsible."

"You're not, not in the least; you didn't send Burnette to the room."

"What can we do for you, Mrs. Dandridge?" asked Seely, folding his arms, leaning against the table, looking down at her.

"I don't see as there's anything anyone can do, thank you. You're both very kind."

"Ye'll be returning to Son Froncisco, of course," said MacGregor.

"No."

Seely gasped. "Surely you're not going on."

"I must."

"That would be most unwise," said MacGregor. "A lone woman wandering about this part of the world . . ."

"I won't be wandering, and I won't be alone." She raised her eyes to MacGregor's. "What are we to do about my husband's body?"

"Whatever ye wish, we'll do. There's the old Christian cemetery on Fort Canning. It's a lovely spot. The gravestones are set into the walls."

"No, I'm afraid the British authorities would take a dim view of an escaped convict being buried among their heroic predecessors."

"Would you consider burial at sea?" asked Seely.

"Not here, so far from Blackwood, from where he belongs, where he deserves to be."

"That would be a long trek back," said the captain solemnly. "I wouldn't troost the transportation from

Son Francisco overlond all the way to Rhode Island."
She glanced at Seely. He nodded agreement.

"The sea is the sea," he said, "even unfamiliar waters.
For a man who built so many splendid ships, whose life
was dedicated to such a distinguished enterprise, it does
seem fitting. Of course, it's for you to decide."

"Perhaps you're right," she said quietly. "I'll have to
think about it. I feel a bit fuzzy. Maybe I'd better lie
down after all."

The ceiling lamp hung motionless, catching slender
bands of sunlight reflecting off the varnished mahogany
railing outside. She lay staring at the lamp, unwilling to
close her eyes, unable to invite the darkness and with it
certain resurrection of all the monsters buried in her
subconscious.

He was dead, gone, leaving her with a heart overflowing with love for him—love now with no other
heart to go to, to join. The book of rules demanded that
she accept his death. Was not death, after all, the only
permissible discontinuation of life? Accept it, yes, she
would have to; but not now, not right away. No stoical,
tight-lipped, tear-locked capitulation, please. Better to
fly in the face of it, claw and scratch and scream at the
fates for their callous unfairness. That much he de-
served. And was she not entitled to the semblance of
satisfaction it would stir in her breast?

Accept his death, yes, and pick up the pieces of her
life and go on. She would—in spite of a heart that
threatened rebellion, stubborn refusal. She placed her
hand against her heart, drawing the thumping into her
palm, the repetitious denial of the undeniable.

No, no, no, no, no. . . .

Then, sighing, she let her hand fall free across the
empty place at her side.

BOOK THREE
THE EYES OF THE DRAGON

I

Ten centuries before the birth of Christ, Homer wrote in *The Odyssey* of a party given by King Menelaus in Sparta upon the visit of Ulysses's son, Telemachus:

Then Helen, daughter of Zeus, turned to new thoughts. Presently she cast a drug, nepenthes, into the wine whereof they drank, a drug to lull all pain and anger, and bring forgetfulness of every sorrow. Whoso should drink a draught thereof, when it is mingled in the bowl, on that day he would let no tear fall down his cheeks, not though his mother and his father died, not though men slew his brother or dear son with the sword before his face, and his own eyes beheld it. Medicines of such virtue and so helpful had the daughter of Zeus, which Polydamna, the wife of Thon, had given her, a woman of Egypt, where earth the grain-giver yields herbs in greatest plenty, many that are healing in the cup and many baneful.

Nepenthes was opium; no other substance grown in the world produces such a response to its ingestion. Opium antedates history. The *cultivated* poppy, *Papaver somniferum,* is an annual. The seeds sown germinate quickly in warmth and sufficient moisture. Within two months the plants can reach a height of two feet. The leaves are a light greenish-blue. Buds six inches long appear on the ends of the stems. They hang their heads, as if the plant were withering or as if in shame, knowing that their life juices can be the cause of such wretched misery for so many humans.

231

Inside the head the flower develops; the flaccid stem becomes rigid and erect. Over the course of a single night, the grayish-green covering drops off, segment by segment, revealing the flower. It is crumpled like paper balled in the hand, but the morning sun infuses it with life and it spreads its petals.

Soon the petals fall. Relieved of its delicate finery, the seedpod swells to the size of a hen's egg. When it is scratched, a sticky white juice exudes. Coagulating quickly, it turns brownish, becoming a gummy mass. Crude opium. During ten days of its brief life, *Papaver somniferum* manufactures this extraordinarily complex chemical; on the eleventh day it destroys it.

But ten days is time enough to steal the juice of this innocent, uncomplicated-looking plant born of a minute black seed.

In the house of Heng-chi on Ti-an men Hsi-ta-chieh Street, in the shadow of the White Dagoba in the Imperial City, Deirdre, the *wàigworén,* wife of the young master, lay on a stripped bed beside her husband. The room was small but tastefully furnished; colored lanterns hung from the ceiling, their soft light bathing a couch, two bamboo chairs and a low table fashioned of squares of polished teak joined at angles. Richly embroidered damasks hung from the four walls, the floor was colorfully carpeted, and on a sandalwood corner table a large bowl was heaped high with almonds and watermelon seeds. On a pillow on one of the two chairs stretched a frosty gray-pink Siamese cat, its footpads mauve, its blue eyes alert and staring.

Between husband and wife upon the bed was a rectangular board and upon it an oil lamp, its feeble flame flickering, casting slender shadows up the walls and across the ceiling, challenging the bands of light thrown from the open tops of the lamps. Holding the bowl of the pipe over the chimney of the oil lamp, Heng-chi drew deeply, his nostrils collapsing, the air rushing the fumes into his lungs. Retaining them for a short time, he then exhaled, sending slender ribbons of smoke upward into the pattern of lights and shadows.

He offered the pipe to her. She smoked, unhesitatingly, drawn to it as an iron needle is drawn to a lodestone. It was, after all, her fourth meeting with opium. Her introduction to its seductive enchantments had come in the prince's bedchamber, where it had been forced upon her. The second time had been here in this bed. She had resisted, stubbornly declining, pushing the pipe from her, but the insidious fumes of the smoke exhaled by Heng-chi had permeated the air in the closed room and invaded her nostrils. Other than to leave the room, there was no way she could avoid the fumes. He would not permit her to go; she had persisted in her refusal to smoke, but at length had given in to his wheedling and coaxing.

The colors and images and sounds had come rushing into her brain bringing forgetfulness, beautiful, welcome indifference to him beside her, to her surroundings, to her melancholy plight, to China and everything Chinese. She was blissfully disinterested in caring, wholly unconcerned over her paradisical bondage, disinterested in all things save the sensations of the moment. It was as if body and mind she had slipped into a giant envelope of insouciance. Sealed inside it, her senses put out to play, to revel in the willful abandonment of discipline and responsibility for her actions.

That she was becoming enslaved to the drug troubled her not in the least, now that the pipe was in her mouth and she was filling her lungs with the smoke. The colors assaulting her like the soft thrashing of feathers, the bells and cymbals clanging soundlessly, were awesomely beautiful; for sheer magnificence, no Elysium, no playground of the gods conceived by the poet could rival the sights filling her inner eye. There was no loathsome serpent this time, nor had there been after the first experience. No discomfort, no pain, none of the guilt that had triggered them. There was only the spectrum revealed, colors passing through an unseen prism, dispersing, red, orange, yellow, green, blue, indigo, violet . . . twisting, knotting, loosening, dissolving, reappearing, enmeshing her body, infusing it with luscious warmth and comfort, transporting her out of it, multiplying her, posing her in a score of positions.

Languor possessed her; she felt as if her bones and other solid anatomical parts were melting, and upon her mind's screen a cup appeared. Her several bodies hovered over it, pouring their liquified flesh into it. The bodies vanished; the cup was filled three quarters, then tilted itself, pouring its contents into a slender fissure in a lime-green stone. As the last drops fell inside, the fissure closed, the stone sealing perfectly, so that not even the line of juncture could be seen. Then the stone melted into a puddle, bubbling gently, as a mineral pool bubbles, small domes erupting from its surface, enlarging, popping.

The scene tilted, the puddle running off a shelf into a pile of broken glass, bits and shards catching a blinding white light from an unseen source, the glass gathering itself together in a tight mass to form a ewer in the shape of a woman: herself. It filled to the top, the ewer vanishing, leaving her standing naked, arms raised and waving. Out of the grayness surrounding, the colors returned, flashing at her from all sides, from overhead and under her feet, placing her in the center of a sphere fashioned of color bands resembling a sea urchin.

She had been the wife of Heng-chi for seven days and nights, only three devoted to his use of her and the pipe. On the other four nights he had left the house, going into the Chinese City to the Flower and Willow lanes of the brothels, where, according to the gossip of the maids, in the company of the prince, he drank and smoked opium while enjoying and even becoming involved in the wild orgies of the transvestites and prostitutes. Learning of this, Deirdre began taking So-leng's prescribed dosage of the brown liquid he had given her as a defense against the Canton ulcer. Heng-chi's dissipation was already beginning to erode his health. Lying in bed at night, he coughed almost continuously, a grating, wracking sound. Hardly the curious and concerned wife, she did not ask him where he went and what he did in the city on the nights he was absent; she did not care. Her only concern was escape, how best to disguise herself and find her way to the Marco Polo Bridge with at least 200 taels in her pocket.

In the week since their wedding, she had already saved 34 taels, sneaking one and two at a time out of monies he gave her for household expenses and for her personal shopping.

There appeared to be an endless supply of money flowing through his hands. He did not work. He had neither schooling nor training in any trade. He was not gifted in any of the arts. He shunned reading and writing as if they were infectious diseases, although he enjoyed music played by others and expressed a fondness for the theater, amused in particular by puppet shows and female and transvestite dancers.

Her major obstacle to escape did not appear to be money. At the rate she was hoarding it, in six weeks she would have all she would need. Her problem was privacy. She was not permitted outside the wall surrounding the house and garden without an escort, usually her two incredibly dense personal maids, who she had already dubbed "Stupid" and "Moreso," and a eunuch, a mean-eyed, shiftless, middle-aged castrate named Yao, whose loyalty to his young master he consistently exhibited and announced in terms impossible to be misunderstood. The three accompanied Deirdre everywhere. It was clear that her outburst at the audience with the two empresses was still fresh in Heng-chi's mind.

She was now outside the walls of the Forbidden City, but these of the Imperial City and of the Tatar City surrounding them continued to present formidable obstacles. All the gates of both the Imperial City and the Tatar City, as well as of the Chinese City, adjacent to the latter, were closed and locked at sundown. Fifteen minutes before closing time, an iron gong was beaten outside each guardroom. This "death knell to hope" impressed itself indelibly upon Deirdre's mind. Commencing slowly, the tempo was gradually increased to create a continuous resonant bonging. As the vibrations died down, the guards inside the gate tunnels shouted for another five minutes. Finally, the heavy portals were swung closed and bolted with huge wooden beams. And as night came on, the various quarters of all the cities were blocked off from one another by gates across the main thoroughfares.

Escape, it appeared, would have to be by day. When the sun rose and the clepsydra* in the guardhouse reached the time prescribed by law, all gates were opened with a noisy confusion of ceremony. The watchmen, beating a loud cadence with their bamboo clappers, directed the straining gate crews. The gates open, the ordinary traffic of the cities was allowed to pass in and out.

On the morning of the ninth day, following a night during which Heng-chi remained at home, sleeping in his own bed with his pipe and his wife, Deirdre broached a subject close to her heart. They were seated at breakfast eating *yin sze chuan*,** nibbling at dates and other fruits and sipping quantities of jasmine tea. A big and decidedly scruffy-looking Christmas-colored parrot swayed on his perch in a brass cage suspended

* Water clock.
** Buns stuffed with thin noodles.

from the ceiling in one corner of the room. The open windows looked out upon the sun-favored garden, troops of peonies and gardenias, roses, lilies and camellias overlorded by peach and gingko trees, rhododendron and square-stemmed Fukien bamboo. All surrounded a miniature pond filled with lotus and water lilies.

Heng-chi looked ill, she thought, his cheeks pale and drawn, his lips as colorless as glass. He did not cough during the day; it was as if his body somehow restored itself during the absence of darkness, although his appetite was consistently poor.

"I thought I might go shopping this morning," she said offhandedly. "Would you like to come along?"

He shook his head. "I must go to the Forbidden City."

"The prince?"

He nodded. "He has a business venture of some sort in mind, in which he hopes to interest me."

She almost laughed in his face. His summons was by imperial command; and any "business venture" that Pao-chu had in mind was certain to interest Heng-chi, if he knew what was good for him. He was, she had come to decide, not a bad sort, not a bully, not overbearing, neither cruel nor malicious. Neglectful, yes, but for that she was grateful. His worst faults were his moral weaknesses, his partiality for the company of depraved and degenerate people, his toady's respect for the prince, who had nothing about him worthy of anyone's respect, his addiction, his dedicated laziness, encouraged by his father and Pao-chu, and the fact that he had all the money he needed without lifting a finger to earn it.

"May So-leng come to live with us?" she blurted, yielding to impulse and crossing the fingers of both hands under the table.

The parrot stopped exploring its chest feathers with

its beak and cocked its head absurdly, as if suddenly interested in the conversation.

"Who?" asked Heng-chi.

"My eunuch. He was very helpful when I was living in the apartments."

"What's the matter with Yao? He's helpful, isn't he?"

"Yes, but . . ."

"What?"

"He's not mine exclusively."

"That's a pity."

"I'm serious, my husband. Don't you think the wife of the prince's dearest friend should have a personal eunuch?"

He smiled. The compliment had gone into his ears straight to his vanity. He considered the matter. "What about Yao?"

"He's always busy in the kitchen; he has dozens of jobs. Besides, he's all thumbs doing my hair. He really has no flair for it. Nor does either of the maids."

"This . . ."

"So-leng. He's very talented, very bright and a good worker. Couldn't you ask the prince as a favor?"

"The prince doesn't concern himself with eunuchs." He laughed. "Not as to who is assigned to whom, at least. Other 'activities,' perhaps." He snickered suggestively. "I'll write a note and give it to one of the maids. She'll see that it gets to Li-Lien-ying."

To Deirdre's surprise and delight, the Chief Eunuch granted Heng-chi's request "for the services of So-leng." Perhaps, she thought, hearing the good news from the maid who had given the note to a gate guard, who in turn had taken it to the Chief Eunuch's secretary, Li-Lien-ying had completely forgotten that So-leng had been assigned to the despised *wàigworén*. Either that or he had no desire to stir up a possible fuss with the prince over something so inconsequential. One of Pao-chu's very good points was the fact that he had little fondness for Li-Lien-ying and his enviable proximity to Tz'u Hsi's ear.

The following day, So-leng appeared at the door of the house on Ti-an men Hsi-ta-chieh Street.

II

She never would have believed she could be so heartened by sight of anybody so depressingly glum-looking as So-leng. As usual, his face was as taut as a Tatar bowstring, his black eyes as suffused with sadness as she had ever seen them.

They strolled together in the garden, Yao staring critically at the newcomer from the kitchen window. His nose was obviously out of joint. Too bad, mused Deirdre gloatingly.

"You look tired," said So-leng. "Those shadows under your eyes . . ."

"Kohl." She forced a laugh, frightening a black-throated blue warbler in mid-song, sending him flapping nervously up to the top of a rhododendron tree, shaking the blossoms, setting them to nodding like pink-faced officials at their superior's speech.

"Of course. I take it married life isn't exactly agreeing with you."

"I'm better off here than back at the Forbidden City."

"Are you?" He plucked a rhododendron, smelling it, twirling it under first his nose, then hers. "Has anyone ever explained China's three obediences to you?"

" 'Obediences'?"

"In case it's missed your notice, women in China are distinctively inferior."

"Missed my notice? Are you serious?"

"Oh, there's nothing personal in it; it's all according to imperial plan."

"That makes it acceptable, of course."

"The Manchus have practiced it for centuries; naturally, the Chinese would be expected to imitate it. A woman is always subject to the men in her family —before marriage, to her father; during it, to her husband; in widowhood, to her son or, if she has no son, her father-in-law."

He went on to explain that polygamy was tolerated, secondary wives sometimes even provided by the first wife when she grew old. The sale of wives was practiced, although not recognized by law.

"But aren't wives of the upper classes supposed to be treated with respect?" she asked.

"Theoretically. Who can say what goes on behind closed doors?"

"I get next to no respect around here, not that it would help matters any. The bad part is they don't trust me."

"Would you expect him to trust you after your outburst in front of Old Buddha, with him standing there?" He was staring at her. "You do look dreadful, Deirdre."

"I'm all right."

He sat her down on a bench, behind a tree, out of sight of Yao. A gleam of understanding leaped into his eyes. "You've been smoking!"

She shrugged.

"My God, you admit it!"

"Please, spare me the lecture."

"You stupid fool! Do you have any idea what you're doing to yourself? That filthy stuff is pure poison. How many times have you smoked it?"

"Four."

He was aghast, groaning and shaking his head vigorously. "I don't believe it! I don't believe you could be that stupid!"

"It doesn't hurt me; there's no pain, no after-effects—"

"Be patient: You'll have 'aftereffects' you never

imagined possible! I know, everything's beautiful now, the colors, the images. Such freedom, your mind, your imagination running riot. Then comes the second stage, if you're not already into it. It gets a grip on you and all at once you no longer enjoy it; *it* enjoys you. It enslaves you. You begin to get weak; pains fill your gut. You barely eat or drink, and you can't even digest what you do take. Your arms and legs begin to ache so, you pray they'll drop off. And all your beautiful inner visions turn to nightmares. You're addicted."

"I'm not!"

"Idiot, you don't even know you are! You can't resist it, though, can you? He offers you the pipe and you can't snatch it away quickly enough. You bang your lips in the rush to get it into your mouth and suck and suck."

"You're wrong; it's not like that at all. The smoke fills the air in the room."

"So get out of the room."

"How?"

"Tell him you have to go pee. Tell him anything; just get out. He can't make you stay."

"He insists."

"He still can't physically make you; it's already got him by the throat. He's too weak to stop you from getting up and going. Deirdre, you can't let it do to you what it's done to him!"

"He's ill, all skin and bones. He coughs and coughs."

"And you're heading the same way. You fool with it long enough and addiction becomes the least of what it can do. It can drive you insane, kill you! You mustn't take even one more draw, not one! When the temptation is on you, resist. Use your willpower as you've never used it before. Do it or you're finished!" He glared, the chastising parent angered by the wayward child. "I promise you that as sure as there's a sun in the sky you'll lose all desire to escape, because leaving would separate you from your precious pipe and your beautiful fantasies, and that would never do."

"That's not true!"

"Not yet, but it will be."

"Let's stop talking about it."

"I'm sorry; you'll never stop me talking about it—not until you stop using it!"

"He'd never let me."

"Because he knows he can do what he pleases with you when your brain is filled with the fumes. And you don't care. You can't; you forget how to."

She studied the ground at her feet. "He can do what he pleases with me without the pipe."

"But it's not the same. It's so much easier, there's no resistance, you're eager to cooperate, you can't remember why you shouldn't. Why do you think they call it the drug of forgetfulness? He can do the vilest things imaginable to your body, he and Pao-chu. Watch: One of these nights he's going to drag you into the Flower and Willow lanes and introduce you to his private hell."

"How can I get away? He lets me go into the city, but always with two maids and Yao."

"I don't like Yao's looks. He reminds me of Li-Lien-ying."

"He's a simpering bootlicker."

"Perhaps you can talk Heng-chi into letting me go shopping with you in place of Yao."

"He'd never."

"I suppose not. How do you plan to get away?"

"How far is the Marco Polo Bridge? And how would I get there?"

"From here, thirty-five, forty li." *

"That far?"

"I'm afraid so. You would have to get to the Kuang-an Lu onto the Lu-kau-chi'iao Lu and straight on out to the bridge. So you get there; what then?"

* Three li to a mile.

"Bribe a boatman to take me aboard, somebody heading downriver, naturally."

"You'd need a disguise, though how in the world you'd disguise your face . . ."

"I have an idea; see what you think. There's a jewelry shop near the west gate. Between the counters there's a drape to a rear room, probably the storeroom. I know there's an alley in the back, so there has to be a door opening onto it. If I could get through that door, run down the alley to a waiting cart . . ."

"Hide in the cart and get through the gate."

"Then out of the Tatar City, through the gate before closing time. You could bribe a driver for me. All I'd need is a piece of canvas or even a blanket to hide under, and my disguise there waiting for me: pantaloons, a jacket with a hood of some sort to cover my hair; I'd tie it up. I could pretend I have a cold and hold a handkerchief over my face when I talk to the boatman to bribe him."

"It sounds terribly involved. Does he permit you out of the Imperial City into the Tatar City?"

"Not yet, but it doesn't matter. If I can hide in the cart . . ."

"What's the name of the shop?"

"Jade Abyss. I was planning to tell him that I want to buy a bracelet or something for his mother. Once inside the shop . . ."

"I could get a cart."

"You could go with me."

"I expect I could." He weighed the thought. "Why not? What is there here for me I won't find in Tientsin —or anyplace else? Besides, if you do get away, they'll know you had help. I'd be the first one they'd suspect. I'll do it, yes, purely for self-protection, you understand."

She threw her arms around his neck, kissing him

loudly on the cheek. "You'll do it because you want to help me; admit it. You are such a stiffneck!" She released her hold, becoming serious. "Do you think we have a chance?"

He shrugged. "Ask me when we're on the boat."

"If it doesn't work, we'll be finished. A wife running away from her husband has to be the worst humiliation there is for Heng-chi. He'd never forgive me."

"He'd do a lot worse than that. How much money have you saved?"

"Less than forty taels. I was planning on taking at least two hundred. We'll need more with two of us."

"I have money—plenty."

She clapped her hands delightedly. "We can go right away!"

"Sh, do you want the whole world to know?" He paused, corrugating his brow, plunging into thought.

"What?"

"It might be best to leave Saturday, when traffic in the streets in the Tatar City is as thick as mud. If we can get a head start, they'll never be able to follow us through the crowds. Once we're outside the gate, the worst will be over."

"Oh, So-leng, we can make it, can't we? Say it. How far is it down the river to Tientsin?"

"A little over two hundred li."

"If we leave late in the day, it'll be dark by the time we're on board and started."

"We won't want to linger in Tientsin. It's the first place your husband will think of when Yao and the maids come running back here with the good news. Perhaps it's best we get off halfway to Tientsin. We could head overland to Chung-wang to the south, then east to Ch'-i-k'ou. It will be a long ways."

"How long?"

"If we get off at Han-kou, twice as far."

"Oh, Lord."

"The thing is, Ch'-i-k'ou is a port. Once there, you're practically out of the country."

"Saturday—four days."

"Four days for you to stay clear of that filthy pipe."

"I will."

"You'd better."

III

That afternoon Heng-chi's father, Tung-chi, his mother and two sisters came to the house unannounced in the company of a stunted little grinning photographer, his bellows camera and tripod all but caving in his left shoulder. Momentous good fortune had befallen Tung-chi; he had been appointed by his brother, Prince Kung, to the Imperial Board of Punishments. In celebration, the day would be fixed in memory with enough photographs to fill an album. The family was posed and shot over and over again, the acrid stench of the flash powder filling the living room. In the garden, where dozens of additional photographs were exploded into being, the powder spread in a cloud and wafted upward into the defenseless rhododendrons. The photographer departed; the family stayed for tea and conversation. Deirdre felt as out of place as a man in a frock shop, but she fulfilled her duties as hostess with all the enthusiasm she could muster. Sight of her husband's family talking amiably, swapping gossip, displaying their warmth and affection for one another stirred dismal feelings of homesickness. Blackwood and her parents seemed far beyond the stars, as unreachable as immortality.

And the tears in her heart lingered long after her in-laws had departed.

Heng-chi braved it through the afternoon all smiles and graciousness, successfully concealing what appeared to Deirdre to be an attack of nervous exhaustion. She was right. No sooner were his father, mother and sisters out the door than he ordered Yao out of the

247

house to fetch the doctor and crawled into bed, pulling the covers up to his chin. He sweat pearls, his teeth chattering, his eyes glazed with fever. The doctor arrived, an ill-humored, older man given to whip-snap answers and a frigidity of manner that conveyed little optimism. He took one long look at his patient and concluded that the cause of the condition yet to be diagnosed was Heng-chi's outrageously run-down physical condition.

The doctor sat by the bed, squinting down the patient's throat, examining his eyes, tapping his scrawny chest and shaking his head pessimistically. He gave Deirdre a bottle of clear liquid, explaining that Heng-chi was to be given a spoonful of it four times daily. They talked outside the closed door, Heng-chi audible through it alternately coughing and cursing his misfortune.

"Is it pneumonia?" asked Deirdre.

"I wish," said the doctor. "Pneumonia's bad enough. This is much worse. I'm afraid he has galloping consumption." He showed a tongue depressor caked with yellow sputum. "See for yourself; he's bringing up bits of rotted tissue."

She turned from the loathsome sight. "It's that bad?"

"It's very bad."

"There's nothing you can do to relieve it?"

"It's too advanced. He'll die."

IV

Heng-chi died promptly at twelve noon two days later, gasping for breath, unable to get enough of it into his beleaguered lungs, falling unconscious with an ominous rattling sound, struggling to hang on for a brief time, then giving it up, his cheek falling against the pillow, the trace of a contented smile lifting his firmly sealed lips.

She covered his face and left the room to find So-leng. Instead she came upon Yao, in the living room, fastidiously arranging freshly picked peonies in a vase.

"He's dead," she said quietly.

"No! Oh, dear . . ." He began wailing loudly, wringing his hands, then slapping them against his temples as if to pound the information out of his brain before it had time to accept it. "My poor master, my poor master . . ."

"Oh, shut up!"

He did so abruptly, with the look of a frequently beaten dog. "What are we to do?"

"Go and tell his father. I must see about the funeral arrangements. Where is So-leng?"

"In the garden; where else?" Yao's dislike of So-leng and disapproval of his presence appeared to increase daily. He made no effort to conceal how very hurt he was at being shunted aside in favor of a new hairdresser for the mistress. He was preparing to leave when a knock rattled the door. It was Tung-chi.

"Good day, mistress," he said, baring his yellow teeth in a leer intended to be a smile. She had come to loathe the sight of it. It was the furthest thing imaginable from

a warm and friendly look, and he seemed to reserve it
for her eyes only.

She told him the news. To her mild surprise, he did
not take it hard. On the contrary, for a split second, as
his understanding grasped her words, she was sure she
saw a faint glimmer of triumph creep into his eyes.

"Dr. Weng came to my house last night. He said it
did not look promising."

He was lying. The doctor had minced no words with
her; why do so with his patient's father? What this
leerer was telling her, she thought, was that he had been
apprised and yet had neglected to come around until
now—as if to give death sufficient time to arrive, stake
its claim and depart, leaving the corpse. It said something about the relationship between father and son.
Again her eyes met his. Perhaps it wasn't triumph she
had seen, after all, but only the look of the lecher en-
visioning a most promising future.

V

Plans for the projected visit to the Jade Abyss jewelry shop had to be put aside in favor of the funeral. The sudden widow who admitted to herself to feeling nothing at all like a widow, no shock, no bereavement, had discussed the necessary arrangements with her father-in-law. Later that afternoon Heng-chi's remains were to be removed to be prepared for burial.

Deirdre knew that once Tung-chi began spreading the news, the relatives would be descending upon the house like locusts upon a grain field. Two things had to be accomplished before the invasion got under way. No sooner were her father-in-law and his leer out the door than she rushed into the bedroom, found the opium pipe and Heng-chi's modest supply of smokable extract and carried them out into the garden. Breaking the pipe in two over a stone, she buried the pieces and the opium while So-leng looked on approvingly.

He smoothed the dirt covering the hole with his shoe. "His timing was dreadful," he said. "Today was the day I was going to arrange for the cart for Saturday."

His attempt at wry humor went unnoticed by Deirdre. "What'll happen to me now, I wonder?" she asked.

"Nothing right away. You'll go on living here, the grieving widow . . ."

" 'Grieving'?"

"Outwardly."

"Inwardly so relieved I could shout it from the housetops."

"I wouldn't if I were you."

"You're not thinking; this makes it all as easy as pie.

251

Don't you see, we can go out to the Jade Abyss Monday. Nothing's really changed, just pushed up two days."

"I suppose."

She took him by the hand, swinging him about to face her. His customarily glum look appeared glummer than usual. "What's bothering you?"

"His father. The way you say he undresses you with his eyes, the disgusting old goat."

"I'm not afraid of him."

"You ought to be."

"He wouldn't do anything so soon; he couldn't, could he?"

"It would be indiscreet of him, to say the least. But dirty old men don't have much consideration for discretion. How old would you say he is—sixty?"

"At least."

"A terrible age, the time of life when men take the last serious stab at proving their virility."

"You're going overboard, old friend. Do you realize what you're saying? That he'd take his son's widow for a second wife." She laughed. "You and your obediences."

"I wasn't thinking of a second wife, more a mistress."

"He wouldn't dare, a man in his position?"

"Men in his position dare anything they please. That's what's so attractive about position. The higher the official, the more he gets away with."

"That's so, isn't it."

He nodded. "Simply because nobody has the courage to question him, he could pluck you out of this house and cache you away in an apartment someplace, two rooms, a stove, a bed and somebody to keep an eye on you."

"No thank you!"

"Tell him, not me. Where are they going to bury your husband? Which cemetery?"

"What's the difference?"

"Which?"

"Lien Ho, I think."

So-leng's face exploded in a grin. "That's near the T'ieh-lu-yüan Hospital."

"So?"

"Near the road to the Marco Polo Bridge, idiot!"

"You mean we get away at the funeral? How? There'll be mobs of people."

"Most of whom don't even know you. You'll be in black, a shawl over your head. You could veil your face with it like a Turk." He paused, looking about on the ground. Finding a small stick and kneeling, he began sketching a map. "If we staked a donkey and cart—"

"We don't need a donkey and cart. Too slow. We need two fast horses."

"I don't know how to ride a horse."

"I'll teach you; it's easy."

"As pie? Seriously, I could be waiting with them in the bushes. They grow very thick along here." He drew a line paralleling the Kuang-an Lu Road southwest of the cemetery. "And there are plenty of trees and bushes in and around the cemetery. All you'd have to do is slip away."

"But when?"

"At the grave, silly. The priest will be chanting; everyone will be busy praying for the soul of the deceased. Picture it: The whole ritual is being carried on, everyone in sort of a self-induced trance, nobody paying the slightest attention to the widow. It's perfect, Deirdre, much better than trying to get away down the alley in back of the shop. No crowds to fight, no gate to close before we reach it."

She threw her arms around him, hugging him tightly. "So-leng, I love you; you're the best friend I have—the only friend, really. You'll come with me home, all the way to Providence."

"Nonsense! What would your father and mother think, you walking in with a castrate by your side? You might as well show up with the plague."

"You're coming!"

The cat broke out of the bushes and padded toward the door, ignoring them.

"Look who's been spying on us," said So-leng.

"It's settled. You will too come with me. I wouldn't have the heart to leave you behind in this terrible country."

He laughed. "*My* country, dear girl. Now, one thing you really must do: Get that happy look off your face and keep it off. You're a widow in shock—maybe not in shock, but desolate. Go into the kitchen and steal some glycerin. When you're with the family and during the funeral, rub it in the corners of your eyes and it will make you tear. You must look properly wretched and forlorn."

VI

The day of the funeral dawned bleak and sunless, promising miserable weather. Fat black clouds padded the heavens, and by ten in the morning it was already raining heavily. The cortege started from the funeral house of Chao-yüan in San-Li-ho. Deirdre rode with her husband's family in a lorry pulled by two horses behind a platoon of professional mourners energetically beating out their traditional cacophony calculated to scare off any curious evil spirits along the way. Heng-chi's corpse in its coffin rode on a lorry painted a wild splash of all the colors of the rainbow, excepting imperial yellow. The silken drape thrown over the coffin bore the likeness of a dragonlike lion, announcing that the sleeper within was a man. Nearly a hundred members of the family and friends followed on foot, their umbrellas, like those of everyone else, angled forward against the thrashing downpour. The rain pounded against the umbrellas, setting up a sound like a thousand drums rolling in unison on a parade ground, all but drowning out the efforts of the professional mourners. To assist them in their task, a piece of red paper had been placed under the lid of the coffin, the lucky Chinese color, it too designed to ward off evil spirits.

The cortege wound its way noisily through the city streets, drawing the stares of the curious, many of them recognizing Tung-chi on the front seat of the family lorry. People splashed into the street to seize hold of the tow ropes attached to the bonnet of the coffin, temporarily halting the procession for a symbolic "pulling of the coffin."

255

The rain reduced the narrow streets to quagmires, the lorries lurching along, jolting their occupants, including Heng-chi, stretched out in his lodgings for eternity. It occurred to Deirdre that he must be bouncing about inside like a dead silkworm in its cocoon. The progress of the procession was agonizingly slow. The rain continued to batter them in sheets, the wind arriving and brazenly reversing those umbrellas under which it was able to steal.

On and on they plodded; on and on the professional mourners banged their drums and clanged their cymbals. Outside the gate the T'ieh-lu-yüan Hospital rose like a feudal castle against the gray background of the rolling hills. Somewhere beyond, straight down the road, the Marco Polo Bridge waited, joining the banks of the Hun, attracting a jumble of rafts and barges and boats, with the commander of one destined to be enriched by a generous bribe before nightfall.

They came within sight of the cemetery, situated on the long slope of a hill, a multitude of white pines scattered in and around it. The cortege entered the open gate and ascended the slope to the grave site, those paying their respects reassembling themselves in a semicircle about it. The coffin was carried up to the side of the grave and set down.

The priest was preparing to commence when, to Deirdre's chagrin, Tung-chi deserted his wife and daughters, making his way up to her side, slipping under her umbrella, grasping the handle, holding it for the two of them. Everyone bowed his head in prayer. He began whispering to her:

"I've never had a chance to say it, but I compliment you, mistress. My son's taste is most admirable. Alas, I can see that you are in no mood for compliments. It's plain that Heng-chi's death has crushed your heart. A pity; he was so young, so full of life. Still, he mistreated his body in such a shameless fashion. I warned him repeatedly as to the inescapable consequences of such

arrant dissolution. The body, after all, is a one-time
gift. Mistreat it and it collapses; then where are you, eh?
Myself, I take excellent care of my body. I am in superb
condition. I exercise morning and night. I am particularly fond of running in place. I have not an ounce of
fat on me; all muscle, hard as a stone. The doctor tells
me I have the body of a man half my age. Look around
you at some of these men, pudgy, jowly, they don't even
know how to breathe properly. There's not one among
them in such superb condition as I. I have the body of a
man half my age, and the soul—and best of all, the
desires, the needs. You understand."

He droned on, and after the priest had finished, while
the coffin was lowered, the mud shoveled in and the
traditional lanterns on sticks brought up to be placed
upon the mound, he stayed with her, sharing her umbrella. She glanced about the cemetery. Her heart sank.
She prayed for a knife to stick in his ribs to silence
him. Directly behind her, less than 30 feet away, was a
grove of pines enclosing a thicket of wild berry bushes.
The crowd dispersing, loosening the tight knot gathered
about the grave, brought the trees even closer, tantaliz-
ingly close. Slipping to the edge of the crowd, she could
easily back into them and vanish—and turn and run
for her life. But he stuck with her, one hand on the
umbrella, the other on her arm, continuing to seize
upon and apply crudely inverted logic to his lust:

"You're alone now, poor child—alone with a broken
heart. You have my most profound sympathy. It can be
a harsh world for a woman alone, especially one as
young and inexperienced as you. Ten days married,
such a brief time, such a tragedy. Still, nothing is so
tragic that it blocks out good fortune entirely. You have
much to be thankful for. You are one of us, a member
of our family, one of the most respected families in all
of Peking. Being a member of the Imperial Board of
Punishments is very prestigious. Yes, in spite of your
heartache, there is much from which you may derive

comfort. When we get back to the house, we must sit down and have a long talk about your future."

He chucked her playfully under the chin. The touch of his fingers, rendered clammy and cold by the weather, was repulsive to her. It was all she could do to keep from pushing his hand away and recoiling in disgust.

"Make no mistake; I am not one to shirk my responsibilities. And you, my dear child, are my principal one. I intend to take very good care of you. You will want for nothing."

She wasn't listening. Her thoughts had fled the cemetery and the storm, returning to the garden and the broken and buried pipe of forgetfulness.

VII

A week had dragged by, a struggle of seven days of misery made more so by the stifling heat that crept in through the windows of Lisa's room on the third floor of the Equitorial Hotel and into her body, stagnating her energies, leaving her limp with exhaustion. The air refused to move, hanging over the city, an invisible inverted bowl. So insufferably hot and dry was it, it almost burned the lungs to breathe.

Ross had been buried at sea out beyond St. John's Island, south of the mole—a simple ceremony witnessed by everyone on board, hats between hands, heads bowed; a few words from Captain MacGregor, "Heavenly Father, we commit thy servant, Ross Richard Dandridge"; the plank lifted, the tightly wrapped body sliding down it into the green water, taking with it her heart. She had jammed her fist against her mouth to keep from crying out, and the instant the water closed over the body, she felt herself seized by a soul-grinding bitterness. What was this life, this rudderless drifting between the womb and the end, but a senseless, self-destructive struggle, with no hope of victory? What was hope itself; why must it be so fragile? Why was despair so tenacious, so capable of withstanding one's best efforts to dislodge it? For a man like Ross Dandridge to die so ignominiously, to give up his life to a knife in the hand of a nonentity like Wilson Burnette . . . Good men, giants in the crowd, capable and fine men died of old age in bed, their loved ones at hand, the crossover comfortable and serene. To die as Ross had died, when he had died, on the start mark of the

mission of their lives, was outrageously wrong. It was
like killing Michelangelo just as he was about to lift his
brush to the chapel ceiling for the first stroke; like
killing Christ at the onset as he arrived in Jordan to
baptize John. It was infamous, this death in this place
at this time. It flew in the face of all decency, all justice
and fairness. Now he would never see his daughter, the
daughter he had not seen in nearly 16 years; never see
her beauty, the great green depths of her eyes, the
radiance of her smile; never hear her voice, her laugh;
never kiss her cheek or touch her hand or walk with
her and share the loveliness of a morning in spring. All
that was in her inherited from him, those things that
blood bound her to him, that could not help but swell
his fatherly pride when his eyes were upon her would
never be his to enjoy.

Lisa had given in and agreed to burial at sea, rationalizing that it was the best that could be done for him
out here so far removed from Blackwood. Seely's contention had proved convincing, that the sea was the sea
anywhere in the world, that he who had given so much
to it, challenging and conquering it, had earned the
right to make it his final resting place. Still, she wished
with all her heart that he could have been interred in the
family vault, to lie with his father and grandfather. The
three Dandridge men: Weren't they, after all, really one
—inseparable in vision, in purpose, in dedication and
now in death?

His death had killed her, or so she had thought at
first as she lay on the bed in the cabin, staring at the
ceiling through a diaphanous veil of unshed tears. He
was dead, so love was dead; that had to be. Therefore,
she was also. Never again would she kiss him, never feel
his arms around her, his body one with hers, his words
of love, his eyes gleaming with love and the glorious
feeling of being drawn into them, drowning in them.
To think, those beautiful eyes were now closed forever.

Seven days had come, taken their toll upon her

strength and gone. Now she stood at the window fanning herself listlessly with her hanky, looking down at the squalid little yard below and the golden shower tree struggling for survival, its roots fighting to stretch themselves in the clay the monsoons created where soil ought to have been. The trunk was bent grotesquely, almost back into itself in a double curve, and the branches twisting skyward resembled the tortured limbs of a paralytic. And yet, for all its ugliness, its gold was lovely, huge clusters of bright yellow blossoms reaching for the sun.

She turned from the window. Deirdre waited. Any day, now, Wo Sin would get back to her with word—a vessel, captain and crew hired—and off they'd go. Waiting was tiresome; doing nothing, depressing. Had she something to keep her busy, it wouldn't have been nearly so bad. But, apart from eating, struggling with insomnia and sitting reading newspapers, either in the room or downstairs in the lobby, there was little to keep her mind occupied and free of thoughts of Ross. Following his burial, after the initial wave of bitter resentment had passed, she had taken herself in hand, looking forward to the immediate future and the obligations ahead.

But two days later the *Sea Cloud,* her holds bulging with rice and silks and ginger, had weighed anchor and headed home for San Francisco. Standing on the dock, Lisa had watched it shrink into a small black mass the size of her thumb, clear St. John's Island and head for distant Borneo. Its departure had taken with it much of her resolve, for now she was alone—no MacGregor or Seely to chat with, no companionship whatsoever, no friendly, well-intentioned encouragement—alone and waiting, waiting, waiting. . . .

She tried not to think about Wilson Burnette's escaping and now roaming about somewhere free as any flying thing, as conscienceless as a puff adder. He would not have stayed in Singapore; nor could he return to

San Francisco. To show up at his brother's trial would be much too risky. No, like Clementine in the song, Wilson Burnette was now "lost and gone forever."

She changed into a pink blouse with bolero front and a lavender skirt to go downstairs. She was pinning on her silver and amethyst brooch when there was a knock at the door.

"Who's there?"

"Paul Gerard, Madame Dandridge." A French accent as musical as tinkling bells. "Wo Sin sent me. We have news of your daughter."

She flew to the door. He was tall and deeply tanned, his blue eyes flashing warmly, his elegant mustache balanced across his upper lip in perfect conformity with the upward curve of his smile. He was dressed in a cheap cotton suit, a horizontally striped red and white shirt revealing itself between his lapels. He doffed his cap.

"Good afternoon."

"Come in, come in. Sit, please. What have you heard?"

"She is alive."

"Praise God! She's all right? She's well?"

"That we don't know. It would seem so. Do you mind if I smoke?"

"No, please go on. Tell me everything, the good and the bad."

He extracted an abused-looking cigarette from his breast pocket, a match from his lower pocket, snapped it across the sole of his boot and lit up, holding the cigarette between the tips of his thumb and forefinger and puffing as gently and self-consciously as a schoolgirl introducing herself to tobacco.

"She is in Peking," he said.

"China; I knew it! A brothel?"

"No. Our informant tells us that she is married."

"You're not serious!"

"So it seems."

"She's only sixteen!"

"Nevertheless . . ."

"How far to Peking?"

"Not down to the corner." He considered his answer for a moment, resting his cigarette hand on one knee, crinkling his chin and tilting his face from one side to the other comically. "Maybe thirteen hundred miles, mostly by sea, naturally."

"When do we leave? I can pack in ten minutes. Do you have a ship?"

"Wait, wait, wait, one at a time. We can leave tomorrow morning. Wo Sin has arranged passage for us on a boat."

"Ship."

"Whatever. It is a steamer. It burns coal; it will be filthy."

"Who cares!" She brightened. "We must sit down with Wo Sin and make plans."

Paul resumed puffing. "That is already done. Wo Sin is very thorough. Four of his men will be coming along —your bodyguard, Your Majesty." He grinned and winked. "I'm sure he's told you that foreigners, we French and Americans, are not exactly welcomed with open arms up there. We are to meet with a contact in Tientsin. From there we will head north to Peking." He paused and sobered. "Forgive me, madame, Wo Sin sends his most heartfelt condolences on the unfortunate death of your husband. And please allow me to add my own."

"You heard—"

"*He* hears everything. If you had a thousand ears listening, you too would hear everything."

"I appreciate your sympathy. You mention a contact in Tientsin."

He began fumbling in his jacket, finding a crumpled piece of paper in his inside breast pocket. Smoothing it out, he read: " 'Travis Collier, managing director of the British Board of Trade in Tientsin.' We will meet with

Mr. Collier. Mr. Collier will put us in contact with Mr. So-and-so, Mr. So-and-so with Mr. So-forth, on and on until we locate her. Unfortunately, it may take time and it's certain to be expensive."

"I'm prepared to pay bribes, very large bribes."

"Not to Collier. The British are very honorable about such matters. Not so much as a threepenny bit for doing one's Christian duty, pip pip. Just don't give them a chest of opium to peddle. That, you understand, is business. So much for the stout fellows." He slapped both knees, sending the ash from his cigarette to the carpet, where it extinguished itself. "Now, what can I do to help you get ready?"

"Nothing, thank you. What can I do to help you? May we go see the ship?"

He made a face. "What for, madame? It is only plates and steam and soot and disgusting stenches."

"Then may we go see Wo Sin?"

"If you wish. Come, we'll catch a gharry at the corner."

VIII

Wo Sin stood at his favorite window, talking over the timid tinkling of the wind chimes. Paul Gerard had brought her to the house in Songkok Alley, then gone back out to see to the arms they would be taking with them. Lisa sat with her cup and saucer on her knees, listening.

"Lean on Paul; he's a good man. He won't hesitate to risk his life in a cause such as this one."

"Let's hope it won't come to that." There was a weighty pause. She reached into her bag and withdrew a sealed envelope.

"This letter is addressed to my daughter."

"I don't understand."

"If anything should happen to me, and Paul or one of the others gets through, finds her and brings her back, I want her to have this. I spent most of the past two days writing it. It's mostly about her father and what happened, and instructions to help her straighten things out when she gets home."

He accepted the letter, laying it on the table between them. "As you wish. But this is very unlike you; you're no pessimist."

"Sometimes I think that's what's been causing me so much difficulty. It's true, I've never been a pessimist, never really acknowledged there was need for such a thing. But, of course, there is; what better cushion to soften the blow of disappointment?"

"Is this the Iron Lady I'm hearing?" Coming around the table, he took her hands in his, helping her to her feet. "You must keep faith, Lisa, the same faith you brought with you into this house last time you came, that marvelous determination of yours. Your tragedy, as devastating as it is, has nothing to do with this. You must start out with optimism. You'll have a lot of help this time, all along the way. Travis Collier is only the beginning. Wait and see: It won't turn out nearly as hard as Macquarie Harbor, what with Mother Nature and precedent and most of the gods against you."

"I disagree. In a way, Macquarie Harbor's got to be easier. At least we knew exactly where Ross was. We had only to determine which logging crew they had assigned him to. We were able to go straight to him." She paused, picking up her cup and saucer and sipping the last of her tea. "We're going to have to turn a whole city upside down to find her."

"Perhaps not. Perhaps you'll be led right to the front door of the house she's living in and be able to get her out without spilling a single drop of anybody's blood."

"Hopefully."

The pretty, almond-eyed Chinese girl appeared, lifting the beaded curtain.

"Excuse me, sir, Mr. Gerard is back."

"Show him in."

Paul came in puffing proudly on a cigarette, smirking, the cat that had sneaked the cream. "All set; beautifully set." He balled his fingertips and bussed them loudly. "Six Spencer repeating rifles—seven-shot, the very latest invention in guncraft," he added, turning to Lisa, obviously gauging the weight of the impression on her.

"Spencers, yes; we used them at Macquarie Harbor. They were very effective against the guards' old-fashioned Austrian muzzle-loaders."

Paul's face sagged into a hurt look.

"You won't be able to take rifles along when you enter the country, will you?" inquired Wo Sin.

"Aha, you underestimate Lieutenant Gerard. I have

also secured a coffin. We will be escorting the body of a Mr. Spencer home to Peking. Besides the rifles, there will be room for a few grenades and half a dozen fire bombs."

Wo Sin's reaction was a jaundiced look. "Are you planning to rescue the girl or are you going to overthrow the government?"

" 'Be prepared' is my motto. Of course, we'll be mainly relying on small arms." He produced a .32-caliber Beretta from his inside jacket pocket, hefting it. "Ten rounds, very accurate. It weighs only nineteen ounces." He proferred it to Lisa. "Feel of it."

She showed him her derringer. "Two rounds, not very accurate, eleven ounces."

He laughed. "A cowboy-lady popgun. Amusing."

"Put away the guns, please," said Wo Sin. "They make me nervous. Paul, why don't you take Mrs. Dandridge over to the Empire Docks, introduce her to Captain Fedde and let her get a look at the *Nautilus*."

"Fedde, ugh . . ."

"Lieutenant Gerard is not one of Captain Fedde's biggest admirers."

"I don't like Denmarkers," said Paul. "They are solid teak between the ears, they have big mouths and big feet, they have bad manners, they spit their fish bones back into their plate . . ."

"All right." Wo Sin cut him off, waving both hands. "Lisa," he said, covering her hands with his own and smiling benignly, "I'm afraid this has to be good-by. I am leaving in one hour for Kuala Terengganu on business, so I will be unable to see you off in the morning. I wish you Godspeed, and depend upon it, we will be doing everything we can at this end to facilitate your search. If matters work out as I hope, you and your daughter will be seeing each other within days after you reach Tientsin. Paul, keep your head, old friend. Don't take your eyes off the lady; don't let her get more than twenty feet away from you at any time. Keep your gun and your famous Gallic temper in your pocket until you really need them. And the two of you—correction, the three of you—see that you get back here as speedily as you can."

IX

The Empire Docks were crawling with coolies, a score of them with their scrawny backs doubled over under the weight of sooty burlap sacks crammed with coal. The holding bands taut about their brows threatened to pull their heads off their necks with the weight as one by one they filed aboard the little vessel, dumped their loads and made their way back along the narrow gangplank to the yard pile. Their ceaseless jabbering filled the air like a flock of squabbling jays, but the line never slowed, and the 60-foot coal hatch—stretching from the cabins located abaft midships to the bow—filled rapidly, almost up to the level of the deck.

Captain Ove Fedde's *Nautilus* was not an impressive-looking ship. At first sight of it Lisa felt her heart sink, until she remembered that they weren't about to cross the Pacific or take it into the turbulent seas surrounding the Gates of Hell. According to Captain MacGregor, the waters of the South China Sea, through the Taiwan Strait into the East China Sea and the Yellow Sea to the north of it, were lakelike before and after the typhoon season. Also, the fact that it would essentially be a coastal run minimized the danger of the usual storms and the heavy seas they precipitated. If necessary, they could run into port, lay to and wait for the weather to change.

The *Nautilus* was painted a funereal black from bow to stern, barely 150 feet separating the two. Even the cabin and hollow iron mizzenmast, which had been converted into a boiler when her rigging had been dismantled, were black. Her power derived from two compact engines, each 35 nhp geared to a single shaft. According to her master, she had been built in 1840 and put into service as a mail and passenger packet between Copenhagen and Göteborg, up and down the Kattegat Strait. It had been no easy run in the winter, and her hull, although painted a half-dozen times since her glory days, showed much of the punishment inflicted by the Kattegat ice. She carried 650 tons, and in calm seas her twin engines were capable of driving her at 18 knots an hour. Her captain touted her as the most powerful ship for her size in the entire Orient, able to haul any paddle-wheeler half again her size across the line in a stern-to-stern tug of war.

Paul Gerard had exaggerated: The *Nautilus* was plates and steam and as homely as a coal scow, but she was not overly sooty and not nearly as odoriferous as he had described her. Nevertheless, it was no *Sea Cloud;* there was nothing of majesty or dignity about her, no stunning white sails rising to steal the four winds, no gleaming mahogany deck railing to lean upon and watch the waves and the miles roll by, no decks varnished dazzlingly bright under the sun or elegantly appointed state-rooms. Lisa's cabin offered little other than privacy. Her bed was the bottom of a double bunk. Nailed to the floor was a crudely made table. A straight-backed chair was fixed in the same manner, and there was a kerosene lamp. She left her portmanteau open on the upper bunk and her clothes hanging about on nails to stretch out the wrinkles.

In Captain Ove Fedde, she saw much less than Paul to dislike. Meeting him, hearing his voice, she was reminded of Jacobus Franeker, the master of the *Sea Urchin,* which had taken her to Macquarie Harbor and safely back to Batavia. Like Franeker, Ove Fedde was white-haired and white-bearded, although everything else visible appeared to be gray—his eyes, his unhealthy complexion, even his two silver front teeth, which flashed between his lips like the stern lights of a bunder boat whenever he smiled. The mild thunder of his voice, the pleasant singsong of his perfect English seemed ill-suited to his unhealthy appearance. At that, it was only his face, or what she could see of it, that looked unhealthy. His broad shoulders were separated by a massive chest, and his huge hands appeared capable of straightening and stretching horseshoes.

For some reason, possibly a pride-inspired desire to retaliate, the captain behaved very coolly toward Paul. The conversations between the two that she overheard were terse and absurdly formal. They exchanged no pleasantries, no idle comments regarding the weather. It was speak when spoken to only.

They were to be at sea a minimum of four days, from Singapore to Pei-t'ang at the mouth of the Chi-yün Ho, the point closest to Tientsin. Tientsin was situated some 70 miles inland at the junction of the Pei and Hun rivers. On such a small vessel, over such a length of time, it would obviously be difficult for Paul and the captain to avoid each other completely. She could only hope that their antipathy would not lead to words and worse.

X

The *Nautilus* did not take the gently rolling waters of the South China Sea as easily as the *Sea Cloud* took those of the mid-Pacific, in spite of a full load of coal. But, as Captain Fedde's pride was to be home for Lisa, Paul Gerard and their four companions for only four days, she resolved to ignore the continuous shifting from side to side and slept with a square board jammed into the side of her bunk against the possibility of tumbling out of it while fast asleep.

Thankfully, sleep was one thing the ship's rolling encouraged. Lisa needed all she could get. Since Ross's death she had been plagued by insomnia, rarely putting together as much as two hours' slumber. Sleeping poorly was not the worst of it, though; it was the return of all the old ogres, the specter of Deirdre in chains, ravaged and humiliated, taunted beyond endurance, and her pitiful cries for help, the way she reached out pleading, her feeble struggling against her assailants, their jubilation at her misery. The whole vivid panorama of cruelty and debasement sickened Lisa's heart so, even when she awoke she had little energy or enthusiasm for anything except to stand at the rail and urge the ship on to greater speed.

Everyone but those crew members on duty ate in the forward cabin. It doubled as a workroom for Captain Fedde. The cook was a grinning, curly-haired Dubliner, whose gift for interesting conversation and sense of humor far outstripped his galley skills. It was he, Mr. Jerome Walter Sean Clancy II, who solved for Lisa the

272

minor mystery of Captain Fedde's dislike for Paul Gerard.

"The skipper's wife run away with a frog," declared Clancy early in the afternoon on their second day out. They stood at the rail, the coast of Annam* vaguely visible through a pea-green mist off the port beam. "Twelve years ago. Which is why he come to the Far East. He figured there'd be much less chance o' running into any Frenchies out here." He pointed toward the land. "Them in Annam stick pretty much to home, so it's a rare day when he bumps into one, let alone ships with one. And he'd rather sign on a gibbering idiot than a Frenchie any day."

"Does Paul know about his wife?"

"Not unless he was the one run away with her."

"Well, whatever you do, don't tell him. The last thing we need is the two of them at each other's throats."

"Your friend Paul wouldn't want Ove at his throat, I guarantee you. I seen him take on four Lascars at once in a bar in Hong Kong. Broke 'em into little pieces, he did. I think he's the strongest man I've ever seen. And when he's drunk . . ." Clancy paused, crossed himself and flattened his palms against each other to pray.

"Sh . . ." she cautioned.

Paul was coming toward them. Clancy nodded greeting, excused himself and headed for the galley. Paul looked after him. *"Mon Dieu,* what swill that man concocts!"

"Stay with the bread and tea," she said. "Don't touch the meat, his soups or his puddings."

"How are you taking this tumble roll?"

"All right. You?"

"Magnifique! I've been sick to my stomach ever since we left the dock. These four days are like four months."

She looked past him, her eyes drawn to a dark shape in the distance off the stern. "What's that?"

* Shortly to become French Indochina.

"A ship, what else?"

"The stern is very high." She squinted under her hand. "It's carrying lugsails."

"Then it's a junk."

"It's following us. I thought I saw it before lunchtime; then the mist carried between us, blotting it out. It's closer now."

"It's got to be at least four or five miles back."

"It doesn't matter; the wind is up."

Captain Fedde emerged from the aft companionway with one of his men. They carried lamps. Lisa called to him, and when he approached, she pointed at the junk.

"Pirates," he said quietly. "Thomas . . ."

"Sir?" The little man alongside him stiffened his narrow shoulders in attention.

"Tell the boys to pour on the coal. We've got a fair lead; let's see if we can outrun 'em to Hainan . . . Lingshui. They won't dare chase us into port."

"Lingshui's a long haul, sir."

"Do as you're told, man!"

"Yes, sir."

Off he ran; but before he turned away, Lisa saw the same worried expression seize his features as that in possession of the captain's.

The *Nautilus* increased her speed to 18 knots, the cylinders pounding away, setting the stern deck to vibrating and loosening soot from the ship's seams, black powder rising fore and aft. The propeller churned the water mightily, sending up a welter of foam. But, with her sails bowed round as barrels, the junk continued to gain on them. By nightfall barely a mile separated the two vessels.

Paul accosted Captain Fedde shortly before the dinner bell. The captain had brought a small wooden chest up from his cabin, placing it in the open coal hold at a spot where the pile had been depleted, well out of sight except to one standing directly over the hold. Lisa looked on and sighed as Paul leaned over and began waggling a finger under the captain's chin.

"I say we get all the arms up on deck and prepare to beat 'em off."

"I hear you say it." Fedde pulled himself up out of the hold, dusting his hands. The two of them stood eye to eye.

"I'm not trying to be funny."

"Gerard, I am the master of this ship. I will handle this situation as I see fit. I do not need any landlubber mercenary's advice on how to deal with pirates."

"We have a lady on board. I'm responsible for her safety."

"I'm not?"

"I say everything up on deck and prepare for the worst. Our group has rifles, fire bombs, grenades, small arms. I'll go see to bringing them up."

"Stay where you are! I don't want so much as a toy pistol out here for that mangy sea scum to spot. That's all the excuse they'll need to start shooting."

"They won't see; it's getting dark."

"Yes, and the moon's out, if you'll take the trouble to lift your head and look."

"Fedde . . ."

"*Captain* Fedde, *Mr.* Frog."

"Why, you stupid squarehead!"

Paul grabbed the captain's lapels. Just as speedily, Fedde seized both his wrists. The Dane's gray face was rapidly reddening, his jaw jutting forward, his words shooting from his mouth like darts from a blowgun.

"That's enough!" snapped Lisa, attempting to shove between the two to separate them. "Let go, both of you." There was a long and apprehensive moment before they relaxed their grips and released each other. Fedde muttered something under his breath. Out shot Paul's hand, pushing against the bigger man's chest. Fedde knocked it away. They began pushing and shoving; Lisa yelled at first one, then the other. It was useless. They despised each other; it had been simmering below the surface since their first meeting. That sooner or later it would erupt was inevitable.

As Lisa looked on in dismay, Paul drove his fist straight into the bigger man's brisket, driving him back a step, clearing space between them so that they could swing freely. Fedde reacted with a loud grunt, but before Paul could follow up his advantage, the captain retaliated, a left, a right, catching Paul in the side of the head and under the heart. Bellowing, he doubled over, coming up from his crouch both arms pumping like pistons, finding Fedde's belly with one, two, three, four pile-driving punches, all but lifting the captain off the deck. Now they stood toe to toe smashing at each other, trading insults and curses as they pounded away. Lisa yelled at them to stop, but they were oblivious of anyone or anything, wholly intent on beating each other to a pulp. The men began gathering to watch, enjoying the show immensely, rooting for the captain. With a sledge-like blow to the temple, Paul dropped Fedde to his knees, diving on him, wrestling him flat to the deck. The captain battled back, catching him under the chin with his forearm, squeezing, choking him.

Lisa stopped yelling, whirled about and, spying a wash bucket 20 feet up the way, ran to it, snatched up its rope in one hand and, with the other, tossed the bucket over the side. Hurriedly hauling it up full, she rushed back to the tangle of arms and legs and torsos and hurled the water.

It was ice cold. Roaring and sputtering, they disentangled themselves and staggered to their feet, dripping and gasping for breath.

"I said enough!" shrilled Lisa. Slamming the empty bucket to the deck, she grabbed Paul, pushing him back against the rail. He had a two-inch cut across his jaw, one cheek was puffed up and his left eye was rapidly closing. "You ought to be ashamed of yourselves! Two bad little boys in the school yard!"

"I'll break him in two!"

"Shut up!"

Fedde came over to them. His face appeared fairly well mauled, and one ear was as red as a rose. "No arms on deck!" he growled. "None!"

Wrenched back to the threat of the moment, all eyes turned to the junk speedily closing the gap, coming up to less than 100 yards off the starboard stern.

"She's going to pass us!" yelled a man.

"She's going to fire across our bow," said Fedde between clenched teeth. "Okay, all hands go about your duties."

"Go about . . ." Paul glared in mingled shock and disbelief. "Are you crazy?"

"You, mister, get below if you know what's good for you." Fedde softened his tone. "Mrs. Dandridge, would you please do likewise and take him along?"

"What are you going to do, captain?"

"Mrs. Dandridge, the idea is for nobody on this vessel to get hurt; that's first priority."

"Yes, but—"

"No buts, please. Get below."

Lisa complied but only partially, taking Paul by the arm and walking with him to the forward companionway, slipping inside, out of sight.

By now the junk had come up alongside the *Nautilus,* the pirates gathered on deck grinning insolently, waving their rifles and sabers and shouting at them. An ancient fourpounder could be seen lashed to a platform on the forward deck. Two men were bent over it. Captain Fedde was behind the companionway, out of Lisa's sight, but she could hear his voice above the babble of the men dispersing:

"Half speed. The second she fires, run the white flag up the stack line."

"Did you hear that?" groaned Paul. "Of all the craven—"

"Be still. And from now on, do as he says. He *is* the captain. We're only passengers."

"I don't give a damn! I'm not about to give up and take a knife to the throat when they board us."

"Paul, simmer down. You're lucky he hasn't thrown you in irons."

"I'd like to see him try, the stupid squarehead!"

He poked his head up, she with him. Captain Fedde was back down in the coal hold, hunched over out of sight of anyone at the port rail of the junk. He was the picture of relaxation, a large green cigar stuffed in his mouth. As they looked on, he lit it and began puffing contentedly.

"What is he up to?" asked Paul.

"Sh."

The junk edged slowly forward until her stern reached a line parallel to the bow of the *Nautilus*. Looking on by the ghostly light of the moon, Lisa and Paul could see the gunner ignite his fuse. Seconds later a loud explosion split the night and a shell came whistling across the bow, plunging into the black water some distance away.

"Full stop and surrender!" shouted a voice, and the chant was taken up by a dozen pirates, continuing to wave their weapons menacingly. "Surrender, surrender, surrender!"

The oncoming junk was now less than 50 feet away, turning sharply to port, ostensibly heading into the *Nautilus*'s bow to force her in the same direction.

"Speed one quarter!" snapped Fedde. "Up the flag."

The white flag climbed speedily up the smokestack, fluttering lightly from it, a solitary white spot against the blended blackness of the stack and the night.

Paul began cursing volubly. "Damned gutless squarehead!" he snarled.

"Full stop!" bellowed Fedde. He was bending over the small chest, lifting the lid, reaching inside for something. The jubilant pirates crowding the rail of the junk closing in on them continued jeering victoriously. Two men raised their rifles and shot at the white flag, a bullet striking the top of the smokestack with a loud pinging sound. Fedde straightened up. Back over his shoulder came his right arm, in his hand sticks of dynamite bound tightly together. A single short fuse sputtered, touched off by the captain's cigar. Into the air the dynamite rose, describing a wide arc, heading unerringly for the oncoming junk. Down went Fedde flat on his face in the coal.

The dynamite landed, a tremendous explosion, ear-splitting, a huge red ball flaring up midships, raising men with it like wood chips propelled into the air by an ax. The little vessel split cleanly in two, her bow and stern rising, her splintered masts crossing each other like lances in a joist as the center collapsed. Limbs and heads and broken bodies crashed downward onto the divided deck and into the water. Those landing on the ship slid down into the chasm created by its raised ends. To the accompaniment of a chorus of agonizing screams, the junk began to sink, the sea drawing the two halves down, down.

Gaping thunderstruck, Lisa counted only four survivors. They floundered about helplessly in the water, struggling to swim clear of the undertow actuated by the sinking, without success. Down went the hull halves in concentric circles, sucking all four men with them, down the splintered masts and spars, the sails, ripped and rent, circling, spinning faster and faster. Down, down to the bottom.

Seconds passed. The whirling vortex spent itself, the ominous rushing sound faded, the sea settled in a silence so utterly awesome that a chill raced up Lisa's spine. Then a muffled rumbling sound was heard and the sea erupted, hurling up the wreckage of the ship—and the corpses of her crew.

"My God," said Paul in a tone that was filled with wonderment.

"I think," said Lisa quietly, "you owe Captain Fedde an apology."

"He took a big chance. What if it had fallen short?"

"An apology."

"What if he overthrew?"

"Paul . . ."

Fedde had gotten up out of the coal hold, dusting his hands, moving to the rail, raising one foot to the lower bar, casually resting his elbow on his upraised knee, puffing on his cigar and studying the moon with the most satisfied look Lisa had ever seen on a human face.

XI

The *Nautilus* gained the Taiwan Strait and continued northward into the East China Sea past Ningpo and Shanghai to port and the Ryukyu Islands to starboard.

To Lisa, Paul Gerard appeared drained of all enmity for Captain Ove Fedde. His antipathy appeared to have been supplanted by a combination of awe and grudging admiration. No longer did he refer to the master of the *Nautilus* as a stupid squarehead. For his part, Fedde accepted his former antagonist's change of attitude most graciously. Jettisoned from his own vocabulary was the word "frog," "Mr. Gerard" taking its place. Neither man threw his arm around the other's shoulder in the fashion of old school chums, but neither did they indulge their mutual predilection for sniping and glaring at each other.

Captain Fedde was just saying that the Gulf of Chihli, the last body of water they would be traversing just beyond the Yellow Sea, was only an hour distant, when dinner came to a merciful conclusion with buckets of tea and a mountainous plate of freshly baked nut cookies that proved as hard as hatch covers. Lisa toyed with one, finished a fourth cup of tea, said good night to all and retired to her room. Sitting at the little table, she read for a while, Corbin's *History of China,* lent her by the captain. Presently her eyes grew tired and she closed the book. She undressed and prepared for bed.

Lying in the bunk, she considered what had transpired over the past few weeks, the astonishing velocity of events, enjoyable, exciting and dreadful, the voyage so far and what they could reasonably expect once they reached their destination.

It was impossible to plan strategy past their meeting with Travis Collier in Tientsin. His information would dictate their next move. Wo Sin's words came back to her: "If matters work out, you and your daughter should be seeing each other within days after you reach Tientsin."

God willing, she thought. Her mind fled the future to return to the past. It was strange. Losing Ross had crushed her, in quite the same way losing Deirdre in Batavia had—the same shock, the same nagging torture, the same useless second-guessing. Batavia had broken the back of her endurance, plunging her into the abyss. Oddly, the shock and aftershock of Ross's death failed to duplicate the condition. Perhaps the mission pending—now in her hands entirely—prevented it. Perhaps some mysterious force was obligingly holding off relapse until she and Deirdre were reunited, stiffening her resolve, propping her up until the conclusion. A favor from the Lord? Was it possible? Could it be that when one had suffered so for so long, a sort of balance was automatically brought into play, good fortune arriving in quantity measure for measure?

Not that she could will Ross out of mind and heart, out of her dreams and memories. All the same, it was as if his death, as bitter as the blow had been, as grievous, as painful, had become a sort of goad to prod her onward, helping her keep her feet and her faith when they faltered and keeping the cup of her confidence in Wo Sin full to the brim.

At that, there was no way she could let Ross down, let alone herself and Deirdre. With Paul's and everyone else's help, it was go forth and find her and bring her home; pick up the fragments of their shattered lives and piece them together; resume the beautiful relationship that had rooted and blossomed before the heavens had crashed down upon their heads.

I'm coming, my darling. Be patient; have faith. Don't give in to hopelessness. Believe in me, darling, and in yourself. The day is coming, the hour, the moment. Our hands joined, the smiles through the tears, hearts beating wildly, stumbling words . . . I love you, Deirdre. I love you, I love you. I'm coming, my darling. Soon, soon . . .

And with this vow, the steel of her steadfastness softened and her heart turned over in her breast. Tears started, all the tears her grief could contain gushing forth, streaming down her face, drenching her pillow.

She sobbed and sobbed, yielding up her wretchedness, discharging it from her heart, and sleep came, slowly enveloping her mind, stealing through it, gently closing the gates against intruding dreams.

Sleep.

XII

Pei-táng appeared on the horizon on the afternoon of the fourth day, a sprawling assemblage of wooden buildings interrupting the horizon under an evil-looking sky, its color almost jasper green. The *Nautilus* entered the harbor, easing into her berth with three times her length for maneuvering room. She was by far the largest vessel in sight. A half-dozen junks of the type sent to the bottom by Captain Fedde's unerring toss and scores of sampans trafficked the water. Sea birds by the hundreds winged about in quest of nourishment or perched atop the rotting pilings, squawking at one another and at the coolies scurrying about the area. The coolies' slouch Lisa had seen in Singapore was here duplicated to perfection, back bent under the combined weights of poverty, consciousness of inferiority and whatever burden was being toted, the ever-present straw hat designed to keep the wearer from shriveling up like a slice of frying bacon under the broiling summer sun, and the naked, sweat-lathered upper body.

She paid Captain Fedde. Farewells were exchanged, the coffin unloaded with their baggage, and down the gangplank they filed to the wharf. Paul went immediately to find transportation, the decision having been reached earlier to purchase a wagon outright. Lisa and her four Chinese bodyguards—all of whom had suddenly begun acting nervously, standing about muttering to one another in low tones, their eyes darting about— stood at the end of the wharf, waiting for Paul to return. Glancing down, she watched the dirty black water lapping against the pilings. Here she was, she thought, standing in China, suddenly just as apprehensive over what lay in store as the four men grouped close by. Thank the Lord for Paul and the contents of the coffin. She hoped that things would never come to such a pass that it would be necessary to resort to weapons, but knowing they were at hand was a comfort, particularly when little else outside of the prospect of meeting with Travis Collier nurtured the same feeling.

They waited and waited, turtle-backed sampans coming and going, the majority of them fishing the waters of the harbor. The sun slowly sank, firing the western sky. It was preparing to set when Paul came back, driving up all smiles, perched high on the seat of a dilapidated-looking farm wagon drawn by two of the most sorrowful and underfed-looking mules Lisa had ever seen. The wagon was loaded and off they drove between two rows of disreputable-looking houses and shops, none taller than two stories. Although posted as a street, the way they were traveling more closely resembled a stream bottom, with ruts and gullies and holes and endless mire. It stretched westward into the setting sun toward Tientsin, some 30 miles away.

Lisa shared the driver's seat with Paul, while the four Chinese sat on the coffin, placed parallel to the seat, babbling excitedly at the sights. Lisa's understanding of Chinese was slight, but even a deaf person could recognize that the four men had little that was complimentary to say about the inhabitants and the conditions in Pei-t'ang. The people walking the wooden sidewalks and picking their way carefully across the rain-rutted thoroughfare were a sorry-looking lot, their cheap clothing ill-fitting and drab in appearance, their posture and carriage listless, their faces uniformly betraying the relentless exhaustion that poverty and hopelessness so effectively combine to produce, in the eyes, in the glum set of the mouth, in the tendency to look down instead of straight ahead.

Beyond the last of the houses at the edge of the little town, the land appeared as flat as the palm of her hand in every direction. According to Paul, they were on the edge of a vast alluvial plain that extended from well above Peking, to the north, all the way down to the sea.

They drove slowly, sparing the mules. Their hooves slapped softly, squishing the mud, the wagon groaning and rattling, threatening to collapse into kindling with every turn of the wheels. Huddled on the coffin, the four Chinese dozed against one another. The sun burned its way through the horizon, flooding the plain with pink fire, taking with it a measure of the stifling heat that had punished them since early morning. Small farms devoted to corn, kaoliang, winter wheat and soybeans were scattered about the landscape. These were the principal crops in this part of the country, according to Ling Wu, the only one of the four Chinese able to understand English and speak it, relying on a vocabulary of fewer than 50 words. Perceiving his chance to shine, he stood up behind the seat, hanging onto it with one hand to keep from falling and waving the other over the area:

"Kaoliang. Good for eat. Good for house."

"What exactly is it?" Lisa asked Paul.

"Sorghum, I think." He sputtered in Chinese to Ling Wu, who nodded so eagerly she feared his neck would snap.

"That's it," said Paul. "They use it for cereal, thatching, fodder, even brushes and brooms."

"Are all the roads in China as bad as this?" she asked, eyeing the deep ditches on either side.

"We're in the midst of the rainy season," said Paul. "It's like this most of the summer." He paused and glanced at the sky. "It's getting dark; you'd better get ready."

"For what?"

He grinned. "Your first bribe is coming up. The gates into Tientsin close at sundown; they do in every city. We'll either have to pay to get in, or sleep outside in this lovely wagon until they open at sunup."

"I'll pay, thank you."

"Maybe just the two of us should go in. We can leave Ling Wu and the others to guard the coffin. If we try to take it inside, the guard may insist on opening it—you know, anything to flex the muscles of authority and break the monotony."

"Is transporting munitions against the law?"

"Transporting anything in most any country that might be useful to the people inspecting . . ."

"Is illegal."

He nodded. "On-the-spot legislation. Still, it makes no sense wasting bribe money to get that box into the city when we'll be bringing it right back out again sometime tomorrow."

"You're optimistic about all this, aren't you?"

"In my line, Madame Dandridge, optimism is the first thing you pack when you get ready to go to work. There's no need to be otherwise with Wo Sin behind us."

"He's a big man, isn't he?"

"None bigger."

"How long have you been with him?"

"Seven years, since before the end of the Taiping Rebellion. Do you know any Chinese history?"

"Not much, although I did manage quite a bit of Captain Fedde's history book. It helped pass the time between your squabbles with him."

"One squabble. Anyway, Wo Sin was involved in the Taiping Rebellion."

"Here in China?"

"No, pulling strings from Singapore. I don't think he's been back to China in twenty-five years."

"What about the rebellion?"

"It was started by a man named Hung Hsiu-ch'üan, a schoolteacher and later a Hakka leader. He collected a number of followers in Kwangtung and Kwangsi. He claimed he was called by God to convert the people from the worship of idols. This all happened about twenty years ago, around 1848. They took up arms and tried to overthrow the government. Hsien-feng was emperor back then. As things turned out, the rebels were never very successful, but they had a remarkable instinct for survival. They did manage to take Nanking and held it for ten years. It wasn't that they were so well organized or anything; it was that the imperial government was in its usual shambles.

"Eventually they were put down, chiefly by a government force led by an American, Frederick Ward, and later by an English major, Charles Gordon."

"Chinese Gordon. I've heard of him."

"The whole long-drawn-out mess cost millions of lives and wasted some of China's finest provinces, besides practically bankrupting the imperial treasury."

"How exactly did Wo Sin figure in it?"

"Mostly raising money for the rebels. In '61, Hsienfeng, the Lord of Ten Thousand Years, mounted the fairy chariot and returned to the nine sources. He was thirty years old. That's when Wo Sin really got involved. He despised the court. To him the empresses and the princes, everybody with any power were and still are nothing but parasites feeding off the people. He's right. Tz'u Hsi is a bitch, stupid, spoiled, selfserving, as autocratic as Genghis Khan. Somebody would be doing this country a big favor if they put a bullet through her head. Wo Sin would love that. At one time he offered fifty thousand British pounds to anyone who would assassinate her."

"Any takers?"

Paul shook his head. "She lives mostly in the Forbidden City, with occasional trips to the Summer Palace. She's very heavily guarded. To attempt to assassinate her would be certain suicide. Besides, even for a fanatic willing to sacrifice his own life trying, there are too many walls within walls."

"Which is what we'll be up against," she said soberly.

He patted her hand. "Every wall ever built has a gate. It's like Wo Sin said: We'll probably get your daughter out without having to shed a single drop of anybody's blood."

"I appreciate your optimism, even if I do have a hard time believing it."

The outline of a wall that looked to be almost a mile long began to clarify its dimensions directly ahead. Tientsin. As Paul had told her, like all other walled Chinese cities, the gates were locked and conscientiously guarded until sunrise. Such precautions were a lingering relic of earlier, considerably more dangerous times, when the Mongols rode and bandits roamed the countryside in far greater numbers than at the present time.

As they drew nearer, the open country began to be laced with canals and irrigation channels and revealed numerous marshes and placid-looking lagoons reflecting the soft light of the full moon. The only approaches to Tientsin, the second most important, and by far the wealthiest, city in northern China, were by causeways, four of them running from the four points of the compass straight across the wetlands to each of four gates.

Within 100 yards of the east gate, Paul stopped the mules, helped her down and issued instructions to the dozing bodyguards. Securing their bags, Paul patting the pistol shoved into his belt inside his shirt, they started toward the gate. Lights shone feebly through the gloom, the watchman dutifully walking his post, swinging his lantern. To Lisa, it resembled a yellow firefly nervously rocking back and forth, unable to decide on direction.

His lantern was down, his musket at parade rest

as they came up to him. Lisa gave him money, and without a single word passing between them, he opened the gate door and ushered them inside.

The city was ablaze with lantern lights. The streets appeared in somewhat better condition than those of Pei-t'ang and the road that had brought them to the causeway, for obvious reasons. Here the traffic was much heavier. Few people seemed to be walking on the sidewalks; the streets, however, were packed with them. Paul inquired directions to the British Board of Trade office and had to ask four different people before anyone had even heard of the place. It turned out to be located on the corner of Nan-ma Lu and Tung-ma Lu streets. Paul wrote it down. They then found the nearest hotel and took rooms for the night.

XIII

The apartment was lavishly furnished in gilded wood furniture, low tables cluttered with sculpture—T'ang horses in bronze, stone heads, an exquisitely carved crouching musician executed in marble—and dozens of painted-glass and porcelain vases. Deirdre sat at breakfast, alone, her eyes fixed upon the bud vase containing a single lonesome tiger lily drooping its head dejectedly, personifying her own state of mind. She could never remember feeling quite so depressed, so utterly defeated, hope routed, optimism destroyed. The bubble had burst so suddenly, the end arriving, this new life thrust upon her, just the thought of how she had been whisked from one cage to another in a matter of hours encouraging her to groan inwardly.

Yao hovered over her, her breakfast tray in hand, his homely face contorted in a smile of triumph at the sight of her misery.

"Missus not hungry?"

It was the first of the day's five meals—little sugared cakes, a bowl of soup with herbs in it, *ping** and tea.

Her appetite had abandoned her. Yao's presence, his contemptuous eyes, his endless gliding about the rooms all day long, the absurd efforts of Stupid and Moreso to appear busy, and *his* unannounced arrival come nightfall dissipated all desire for food.

The apartment in which Tung-chi had imprisoned his new mistress was situated within two Imperial City blocks of his dead son's house. It was luxurious, six

* Crisp-fried pancakes.

large rooms all newly furnished, no cat, no parrot for companionship, nor a garden, but everything else, including a small balcony outside the master bedroom, where, each passing day, she was spending more and more time looking down upon the crowds five stories below and debating whether or not to leap to her death.

Lately she thought about death constantly, as both the most practical and most desirable way out. Any method of self-destruction would be painful. But what, after all, was physical discomfort compared with the unremitting agony of her life? This most recent setback, the situation into which her devoted father-in-law had forced her, was much more than a psychological defeat; it was entombment in despair. Tung-chi was not Heng-chi. He did not ignore her, he did not frequent the Flower and Willow lanes by night, nor did he submit to the seductive charms of the pipe and poppy; he was much too health-conscious. He was also a creature of schedule. His day's work at the Board of Punishments ended at five o'clock. Home he would go to his adoring, if aging, wife and his dull and homely daughters. He would dine, discuss the events of the day for precisely one hour, bid his family good night and repair to his mistress's apartment. Promptly at ten o'clock, having satisfied his sexual urgings, he would leave Deirdre and return home for the night. The only interruption in this routine were his thrice-weekly visits to his son's grave to pay his respects.

Deirdre hated him. She had never realized how immense her capacity for hatred could actually be until he had come into her life. She hated him and the life of servitude into which he had forced her with a remorseless passion. As early as her second day in her new cage, she had made up her mind that hate was the only constraint she required to stay her from leaping to her death. Why elect suicide and therewith banish any chance for vengeance, however remote?

He would pay with his life for what he was doing to her, for what all of them had done to her, from the slavers down the long line to the heartless hierarchy of the Forbidden City! But it was in him, in Tung-chi, that all the cruelty, the callous debasement, the pain and suffering that had befallen her since Batavia seemed to crystallize. He was the evil incarnate, the source and soul of her misery.

She thought about So-leng, wondering where he could have gotten to. She pictured him waiting impatiently at their rendezvous with the horses, waiting and waiting in the rain until the day gave way to darkness. Knowing Tung-chi's fondness for her, perhaps So-leng, having since learned what had happened, had decided to remain out of the picture, concluding that there was no place for him in her father-in-law's plans for her. Nevertheless, she couldn't believe that he had given up on her. They had grown so close; he'd been so helpful. He'd risked everything to help her. Had they made it to the Marco Polo Bridge and been caught there or somewhere downriver, he would have paid dearly, and he knew it.

She hesitated to mention So-leng to Tung-chi. Her late husband had been too preoccupied with nightly carousing and his other interests to care one way or the other whether So-leng came into the household. But Yao had been practically up in arms at his arrival. Only the fact that the young master had taken ill and died so speedily had prevented him from an attempt to rid the house of his rival. She could safely assume that now that So-leng was gone, Yao would do everything in his power to forestall his return. Besides, there was little need for a second eunuch in six rooms, not with two maids sharing the work.

She could ask Tung-chi; the worst he could do

would be to say no. If only she knew where So-leng
was. If only she could go looking for him, assuming
he hadn't returned to the Forbidden City, or deserted
Peking altogether.

Tung-chi did not forbid her to leave the apartment.
She was free to go anywhere she pleased within the
confines of the Imperial City, but not alone. Wherever
she went, Yao padded along three steps behind, watching her like a goshawk stalking a mouse lemur.

It had been nine days since the funeral, eight since
Tung-chi had "honored" her by installing her in the
apartment. Time passed sluggishly. Without a garden
to wander in, work in and enjoy, life was becoming increasingly boring. When the sun went down over the
west wall, burning the top of it to the corners, the
evening's ritual was begun. She disrobed, bathed,
assisted by the two maids, powdered and perfumed
her body with essence of jasmine, his favorite perfume,
and put on the robe he had given her in observance of,
as he put it, "the commencement of their incomparably
beautiful friendship."

The robe was silk decorated with sequin thrushes
perched on slender branches. It buttoned up the side
like a *cheongsam*. Unlike a *cheongsam,* it was completely transparent. He adored it. She was tempted to
rip it to shreds, but she had yet to see him lose his
temper and was in no hurry to test its severity.

Their nightly get-togethers had become ceremonial.
His instructions were punctiliously specific. She was to
bathe, powder and perfume herself, attire herself in
her thrush robe and sit at the end of the bed awaiting
his arrival. He would walk through the doorway,
through the outer rooms into the bedroom, shutting
and locking the door. They would greet each other
formally, master and mistress. He would disrobe before her, plunge himself into a waiting tub of cold

water, lather his body with soap, rinse himself, dry
himself and begin exercising. For fifteen minutes they
would talk; rather, he would declaim upon his triumphs of the day, the stupidity of his fellows on the
Board of Punishments, the state of politics in the
capital and current events of interest to him. She would
listen discreetly, stifling yawns, now and then mur-
muring a brief response to a question. While he
talked, he exercised, executing deep knee bends, squat
jumps, hip, back, arm and leg stretches and his favorite, running in place. And so went one night after
another.

At the moment, thinking about it while out on the
balcony watching the crowd pass below, her eyes were
drawn to a kite vendor displaying his wares designed
as different species of fish. Suddenly, just as she was
turning away from the railing, she started, gaping.

So-leng! He actually saw her first. Moving out of
the crowd to the far side of the street in front of a
poultry shop, he smiled up at her, waving both hands
and shouting something. But the rumble of traffic, the
crowd and the racket raised by the dozens of hawkers
lining the sidewalks in front of the shops made it impossible for her to hear him. Nor could he understand
what she said, as loudly as she shouted. Her outburst
brought Yao running into the bedroom, gaping inquisitively. She shut the balcony doors in his face.

So-leng threaded his way through the crowd to the
near side.

"Where have you been?" she yelled.

He read her lips and shrugged, holding his hands
out, smiling sheepishly.

"Come up, hurry!" She gestured. He nodded understanding. Moments later he was at the front door. Yao
answered it, his features freezing in a frown. Brushing
by him, she seized So-leng's hand:

"Into the bedroom, come . . ."

"Missus," began Yao, "the master does not allow visitors."

"Oh, shut up and mind your own business!" She practically pulled So-leng into the room, slamming and locking the door. "My God, what happened to you? Where have you been?"

"Nothing happened; I simply lost you. I went back to the house. It was locked up, everybody vanished. I went to Tung-chi's house, but nobody seemed to know where you'd gotten to."

"Keep your voice down," she cautioned in a hushed tone. "I'm sure Yao's outside with his ear glued to the door. Let's go out onto the balcony." She closed both doors behind them. "Tell me everything."

"You first," he said.

"I couldn't get away from Tung-chi at the cemetery."

"That I guessed." He jerked his thumb at the doors, the room on the other side of them. "Very nice, I must say. You've come up in the world."

"You're not funny." She shuddered. "He's a dirty old man, So-leng, with a new toy. I've got to get out of this hellhole. The Jade Abyss . . . Can you get a cart and donkey or horse, anything, by tomorrow noon?"

"That's pretty short notice."

"Bribe somebody, can't you?" She threw open the doors and, striding to the nearest table, snatched up one of the T'ang horses, thrusting it at him. "Pawn this if you have to!"

"Money's not the problem; you're the problem. You don't show up when you're supposed to. 'Not funny,' I know." He drew her back out onto the balcony. "My poor, poor Deirdre."

"Oh, damn!"

"What?"

"The Jade Abyss. I can't get out of the Imperial City; he won't let me."

"That's bad."

"When I go out shopping or just to stretch my legs and get a little air, Yao goes along. He sticks to me like glue, just like before. If I tried to get away from him, he'd scream for every policeman in sight."

"What about your maids?"

She shook her head. "Just Yao goes."

"That's good."

"What's good about it?"

"I can take care of one a lot easier than three."

"You mean knock him over the head?"

"With pleasure. He and I have what you might call a classical dislike for each other."

"He's jealous of you. Don't feel bad; he's not overly fond of me, either."

"Thinking about this, it's getting more and more complicated."

"Why?"

"I can't be in two places at once. I can't stand at the end of the alley in back of the Jade Abyss minding the cart and be back here in the Imperial City knocking him over the head so you can get through the gate into the Tatar City."

"If I can get out of the Imperial City, we won't need the Jade Abyss."

"If he kicks up a fuss, you may get through the first gate, but by the time you get to the second . . . I just don't know. It's harder than before."

"Isn't there someplace you can get rid of him without raising a big fuss?"

So-leng thought a moment. "Do you know the street of the silversmiths?"

"No."

"It's close by the west gate." He gave her directions.

"One of the shopkeepers is a friend of mine. If I asked him, he'd let me hide in his storeroom. You could come in with Yao, ask for something that's obviously not on display. The owner would say it's in the back and ask you to come back with him. They always do, you know, when they're alone with only one customer. They lock the door to keep thieves from running in. Yao would come with you, of course."

"You could hide behind a crate or something." She beamed, then sobered.

"What's the matter?" he asked.

"Yao. He's got to know we're in here cooking something up. When I ask to go out tomorrow, you watch: He'll smile that infuriating smile of his and proceed to make a great mess of things."

"How? Make you stay home? How can he?"

"He's certain to tell Tung-chi you came here, and tell him he suspects something is up."

"Does Yao know you want to leave?"

"I don't know if he does or not. If he's got a brain in his head, he suspects it. We'll have to play safe and assume he does. I have an idea."

"What?"

"Instead of tomorrow, we'll leave three days from now."

"I'd rather. It'll give me more time to set things up, get the cart and everything."

"It'll give me time to ask Tung-chi if you can move in."

"Two eunuchs in this place?"

"It's worth a try. Can you come back tomorrow? By then I'll know."

"If he turns me down, what then?"

"You show up in front of the poultry shop across the street at noon tomorrow. We'll signal each other. If I hold my thumb up, that means Tung-chi's given his permission."

"And if he doesn't?"

"I'll hold it down, naturally, then up if I can go out shopping. But to keep Yao from suspecting anything, we'll have to do it at least twice."

"Do what twice?"

"I'll go out tomorrow and not go near your friend, the silversmith's, then go again two days later. We'll catch Yao with his suspicions down."

So-leng nodded approvingly. "I'll try to get the horses I took back last week. They're marvelous animals and reputedly very fast."

"The faster the better. You'd better go now."

Yao glared So-leng out, shutting the door and reiterating his warning that the master did not permit visitors.

"Make sure you tell him, Yao. Whatever you do, don't tarnish your image by showing me any charity."

That evening she dined alone on three-plant soup and fish with lotus flowers, picking at her food, as usual. Tung-chi arrived, and the customary ceremony had progressed to the running-in-place phase when he abruptly began expounding on his favorite subject:

"Look at me: I'm sixty years old—as hard as a schoolboy. Perfect muscular coordination, amazing lung power, the endurance of a Gobi stallion! You should see my associates on the board. They're either as fat as pigs, like Chung-li, the one-eyed one, or starvelings, like Pi-Lee-yung, forty pounds underweight, exhausted by two in the afternoon, no more energy than a fledgling fresh out of the shell. A disgrace to the empresses, that's what they are!

"I ask you, what is man's most precious possession? Money? Jewels? Rank? Never, nothing of the kind. It is his body, mistress, his muscles, his strength. Why do you imagine I am such a frisky colt in bed? Condition; good health; vigor that comes from rigid discipline. One two, one two, one two . . .

"You should exercise, mistress. Your body is magnificent, but only because it's just attained maturity. Given ten years, if you don't exercise, if you don't eat properly, get sufficient rest, sunshine and fresh air, you'll begin to fall apart."

He stopped running, clapping his hands and yowling like a stricken dog. "What am I saying? What am I doing? I completely forgot: I have news for you, momentous news!" He tossed his hands high. "You're moving."

"What?"

"Moving. Are you hard of hearing?"

"Where?" Her heart quickened.

"Where do you think? Guess."

"I have no idea."

"Guess, guess; I love guessing games."

She turned away, unable to stand the sight of him posing naked before her, puffing, his sweaty chest heaving and falling.

"Shame on you; you have no fun in you. Be sporting, why don't you? You're moving to the Forbidden City."

"No!"

His face clouded. "What? Do you hear yourself? Has your brain stopped working? I said the Forbidden City."

"I heard!"

"The empresses have invited me to stay for one month, maybe longer, a special assignment—work, work, work—and you're coming along."

"Must I?"

"You must."

"When?"

"Tomorrow morning. We'll have a lovely apartment, much nicer than this. More servants for you, perhaps a second eunuch to help Yao. We'll be able to be together all night long, every night." He laughed; then he stopped abruptly, staring at her. "What is this, mistress; why the long face? You disappoint me. You have no enthusiasm for any of my good news. I know: You want to go home. Well, we can't possibly allow that, can we?"

"You could, if you had one ounce of decency in you. You can do anything you like."

"But why would I like to do that? Would you if you were me?"

God how she hated him—his leer, his snide tone that cut to the heart, his disgusting vanity! She would give anything for the courage to sneak into the kitchen, steal a knife, hide it in the bedclothes and, when he came at her, jam it into his throat up to the hilt! She could envision his blood spurting all over the place, his eyes bulging, the roar, the gagging.

And what would it accomplish? Within the hour she'd be in a cell, within a week hustled out into the prison yard in the company of a dozen others convicted of high crimes, made to listen to the reading of the imperial decree, bowing and acknowledging the justice of her punishment, thereby absolving the officials and anyone else of blame; and, given over to the tender mercies of the Devil's Hand, compelled to kneel on the ground, her head held down by a cord, the great sword rising, the bloodcurdling shout of the executioner and one flashing downward stroke.

To trade her life for his would be pointless and stupid. But the temptation was oh so strong! His voice cut into her thoughts.

"This is your home, mistress. In here . . ." He threw one arm around her, hugging her close to him, kissing her loudly on the cheek, enjoying it and finding her mouth with his. "Home, home, home. Into bed, mistress. Hurry, hurry. Look at me: A little exercise, two kisses and I'm ready for you. You must be ready for me!"

Again he yowled and pushed her lightly down on top of the bed. She closed her eyes and fled his presence—the apartment, the city, the country—and began to cry, without a tear, without a sound.

XIV

Early in the morning, following Tung-chi's shocking disclosure, he had seen to moving the maids, Yao and his mistress to an apartment in the Residential Palaces across from the Great Theater. There were eight rooms, including a spacious bedchamber boasting a k'ang bed, constructed, as usual, of brick, a six-inch-legged table set at the foot of it, porcelain, teak, ebony, marble and glass figures and vases and urns, and a nameless Sung artist's silk tapestries depicting scenes in and about the Han Palace nearly 2,000 years earlier. Deirdre's new surroundings displayed a dignity decidedly lacking in the modern appointments of the six-room apartment in the Imperial City. However, she took little notice of the differences between the two. Her thoughts were otherwise engaged, and even as Tung-chi bid her good-by in the middle of the morning to go to take up his new duties at the offices of the Imperial Household near the South Garden, she was busy contriving an escape strategy—her second in two days, she mused ruefully.

Her window afforded full view of the Great Theater, its unseen rear wall flush against the East Wall of the Forbidden City. Everyone inside and outside the city knew of the Empress Tz'u Hsi's positive passion for the theater. On the first and 15th of every month, traveling troupes were admitted by the guards at the Meridian Gate and conducted to the theater, affectionately nicknamed the "Hall of Joyous Sounds." The stage was built on three superimposed levels fitted with

303

complex machinery and supplied with an enormous collection of props.

The play to be performed was always selected by the empress beforehand. She preferred the classics, in particular the Buddhist legends, most of which, it was claimed, she knew by heart.

Princes, high-ranking eunuchs and many officials also attended, sitting in the pit, while the two empresses and their ladies-in-waiting in their boxes sat watching from behind a curtain of imperial-yellow gauze. In summer they would sip bamboo-leaf juice; in winter, hot tea. In any season they would crack nuts, nibble and gossip throughout the performance. Below the stage and facing the imperial boxes stood the musicians, tooting their gloomy-sounding pipes and flageolets, beating drums, scraping away on two-stringed fiddles, picking the Chinese guitar and moaning into the double flute. The music sounded distressingly weird, particularly to ears unaccustomed to the intricately arranged dissonant chords. The plots of the plays were based upon histories or well-known legends, some poignant, some comic, others epic, even bawdy. A library of no less than 365 standard dramas and episodes in the hundreds depicted innumerable villainous tyrants usurping the throne, concubines and their royal masters trapped in soul-wrenching intrigues, heartless mothers bent on ruining their sons' lives and murdering their daughters-in-law.

The performances per se were highly stylized: Actors carrying black flags personified evil spirits; fireworks announced the appearance of evil demons; a piece of white paper covering an actor's face and chest transformed him into a ghost. All the roles were played by eunuchs. They swayed gracefully on platform boots with little shoes attached in imitation of lily-feet, or costumed themselves elegantly, painting their faces or donning masks.

The actors completed their performance late in the

afternoon and left the Forbidden City en route through the Imperial City to the Tatar City and their next engagement that evening. To advertise their presence and encourage attendance, they often marched through the streets in full costume, painted faces, elaborate mustaches and beards, or masks.

In three days it would be the 15th of the month. The troupe expected would arrive sometime around the noon hour and begin performing. Tung-chi would be at work. Deirdre need have no concern that Yao would follow her about the grounds. Walled in as they were, she was at liberty to go wherever she pleased and do whatever she pleased until five in the evening, when her lord and master finished work and returned to the apartment.

If she could slip backstage during the performance, she could dress up in the first costume she found, steal a wig and mask and leave with the troupe. When they got within walking distance of the west gate of the Tatar City, she could break away, buy or steal a horse and head straight for the bridge. All that was necessary would be to beat sundown, for if they closed the gates, she would have to spend the night inside the Tatar City, giving Tung-chi sufficient time to alert the guards and scatter the police in search of her. Even in disguise, since she certainly couldn't continue wearing her mask once she'd deserted the troupe, with her luck she would be found and brought back—and given her first opportunity to see Tung-chi's temper in action.

She left the apartment to go to Li-Sing's, a few minutes away. Sight of the building stirred recent memories. Here she was, back to square one. She found Li-Sing seated at her vanity, humming happily to herself as she fussed with kohl, painstakingly converting her eyelids into absurd-looking black smears.

"Deirdre!"

They threw their arms around each other, hugging, babbling excitedly. Deirdre finally managed to calm her friend down. She explained about Heng-chi's death and her captivity at the hands of his father, as well as what had brought her back to the Forbidden City.

"What have you been up to, dear?"

Li-Sing pouted. "If you're wondering if I've made the jade tablet, forget it. The prince doesn't know I'm alive. He doesn't know most of us are. He has his five or six favorites; he spends all his time with them. The rest of us sit around and stand around, eat and sleep and gossip. What a boring, boring life!"

"What about An Te-si?"

"She's still waiting for her second chance." Li-Sing tittered, moving to the door, opening it wide to the sight of a snow-white pigeon strutting about impudently. She began fanning the air with her hand in a fruitless effort to steer it into the room. "God it's hot!" she exclaimed. "I'm burning up. It hasn't rained for more than a week."

"Not since the funeral. Tell me, is An Te-si still devouring *The Art of the Bedchamber?*"

"Of course. She claims she knows it by heart. The silly thing recites long passages." She drew herself up taller, posing, imitating An Te-si. " 'The Black Cicada Clings: The woman lies on her stomach and opens her legs wide. The man bends his knees and stays between her thighs. Holding her shoulders with his hands, he pushes his jade stem into her jade doorway from the rear. The Goat Faces the Tree—' "

"Please . . ."

"She's ridiculous."

"She'll probably end up the Royal Consort."

"Never; she's not clever enough." Li-Sing sobered. "I've been thinking and thinking about you. It's only been a couple of weeks since we've seen each other, but it seems like months."

"Years to me, so much has happened."

"You still want to leave in the worst way, don't you. I can see it in your eyes."

" 'Escape' is the word." Deirdre sat with her on the edge of the bed. "Is she in?" she whispered, nodding at the inner door leading to An Te-si's apartment.

"No."

Deirdre poured out her plan. Li-Sing listened, nodding politely, but nothing resembling enthusiasm for the idea appeared on her round face.

"Then I can sneak away from the troupe in the Tatar City—"

"Deirdre."

"What?"

"It'll never work. It can't."

"It can!"

"It can't, because it depends upon the troupe—"

"Obviously."

"Please, listen to me. There won't be any troupe, not for two months at least. They're rebuilding and redecorating inside the House of Joyous Sounds. When they're done, the empress plans to bring in a troupe to live there permanently and perform plays every day, not just on the first and the fifteenth. They won't leave the Forbidden City to perform in the Imperial City or anywhere else."

Her words were like a knife in Deirdre's heart, plunged in and turned and thrust deeper with every new bit of information.

"Who says so?" she asked in a defeated tone.

"Everybody knows about it."

"Then that ends that. Damn!"

Rising from the bed, she moved to the wall alongside the front door, leaning her forehead against it, continuing in a subdued voice: "I give up, I really do."

"You mustn't. I told you I've been thinking. I have an idea."

"What?"

"There's one sure way you can get out of the Forbidden City, even out of Peking, slow but sure: You could take vows."

"You mean religious vows?"

Li-Sing nodded. "Buddhist. They have nuns."

"I didn't know that. Still, I couldn't, Li-Sing. You forget, I'm no longer a virgin. Sometimes I feel as if I never was."

"It doesn't matter. I had a friend, a girl I lived next door to. She got married and her husband died. She took it terribly hard. She became a nun; she's still one, in P'ei-hsien in Kiangsu Province."

"But I'm not Chinese or Manchu."

"They don't care what you are as long as you're willing to make a commitment."

"What do they do besides pray, look properly glum and take a vow of chastity?" She groaned. "God, what a hideous joke!"

"They work. They beg for the poor and tend to the sick. Deirdre, think about it: Getting out of a nunnery has to be easy compared with Peking. The only thing is, you've got to be terribly sincere."

"Who could help me?"

"The prince."

"Pao-chu? He never would."

"He might; he was Heng-chi's best friend. Whatever you do, don't go to the Chief Eunuch; he'll pull the rug out from under you. He's the meanest, most sadistic thing I've ever seen."

"You should meet Tung-chi." She thought a moment. "You really think it's possible?"

"It's worth trying. What can you lose?"

"You're right about that. What's one more disappointment after all that's happened?"

Li-Sing slipped one arm around her shoulder comfortingly. "Let me find out everything I can, so if you do decide to try, you'll do it correctly."

"I've got to try; I've got to do something. If I stay here much longer, I'll kill myself."

"Don't say that! Don't even think it."

"Me a nun." She laughed bitterly.

"It'll mean a lot of studying and memorizing whole big chunks of the canon, you know, the scriptures, and praying morning, noon and night."

"How long will it take? Ages, I'll bet. I'd have to go through a trial period."

"Yes."

"Oh, Li-Sing, when will this all end? When?"

"It's certain to get you out of Peking."

"Mmmmm."

Why, she pondered, was her every effort at escape destined to either die aborning or threaten to be too difficult or outrageously complicated to even warrant serious consideration? The whole world seemed to be conspiring against her.

"Have you seen So-leng?" Li-Sing asked.

Deirdre filled her in on what had happened. "I don't suppose I'll ever see him again now."

Li-Sing shook her head. "This is so unlike you, to be so gloomy."

"There's very little left to pick me up, dear."

"I'll talk to some of the girls and ask about the procedures. There must be one with a sister who took holy orders. I'll come and see you tonight."

"Not tonight, not any night. Tung-chi isn't interested in socializing after dark. I'll come tomorrow morning. We can meet by the Well of the Pearl Concubine at ten, after he's gone to work." She sighed. "A nun, a *Buddhist* nun, no less. It's all so bizarre, so crazy—too crazy even for a bad dream."

She paused, kissed Li-Sing on the cheek, said good-by and left. Wandering about the grounds for a while, she happened by the building housing the offices of the Imperial Household. She stared upward at the top floor, where Tung-chi was working, and found herself wishing she might blow the whole building higher than the wall.

She returned to the apartment at noon to a pleasant surprise awaiting her: So-leng stood by the front door, beaming. On the ground beside him sat a large cloth bag.

"So-leng!" Running up to him, she threw her arms around him.

"Your friend Yao said you'd gone out. What an absolute donkey he is. If looks could kill . . . I've been waiting and waiting!" he snapped in mock impatience.

"How did you get here?"

"I live here, remember? At least I used to. And believe it or not, it looks as if I'm back to stay—with you."

"You're not serious!"

"When am I ever otherwise? I came around to the other apartment about ten this morning, found the birds flown, made inquiries, found out where he'd taken you, and here I am. Oh, yes, I went up to his new office, marched in as if I owned the place and had a little talk with him. He was very magnanimous. He's invited me to stay. Do you mind?"

"Do I *mind?*"

"We still have some unfinished business, you and I, something about some bridge?"

Picking up his sack, he walked with her to the nearest bench, under the spare branches of a gingko tree. The bright-green fan-shaped leaves stirred lazily as a breeze slipped over the wall by the palace kitchens and past them.

"What's in the bag?" she asked.

"My things and a present for you."

"What?"

"Patience; you'll see. Do you have any idea what he's doing up in that office all day?"

"Some sort of work for Susie's eyes only."

"A friend of mine told me. Your generous benefactor's interviewing people. He's a *jēngtán** for Tz'u Hsi, making up personal histories on everybody in the

* "Spy."

government—their private lives, their personal opinions of their imperial majesties, their thievery."

"I'm not surprised."

"He's determined to blackmail everybody in sight. He could end up the richest man in Peking."

"I couldn't care less. Still, a job like that suits his sort perfectly."

So-leng loosened the drawstring of the bag. "Look."

"A wig." She reached into the bag.

"Don't take it out." He glanced about. "A man's wig and farmers' clothes, wide-brimmed straw hat, linen work coat, pantaloons, boots . . ."

She poked about in the bag. "There's two of everything."

"Remember me?"

"Why farmers' clothes?"

"So we'll look like two hundred million other people; why else?"

"What about my face?"

He reached into the bag and brought out a jar. "You rub this cream on your face and the backs of your hands. It's made with peony seeds and goat's milk. It will give your skin a yellowish cast. It's shiny at first, but when it dries, yours will look like mine." He examined her eyes. I can make up your eyes so that they won't look so round. You'll need kohl to darken your eyebrows."

"You've got a plan, haven't you! Li-Sing had one."

"Oh?"

"What's yours?"

"What's hers?"

She explained it.

From beginning to end, he shook his head. "That could take you six months. Even then, there's no guarantee they'd accept you. All it really does is get you away from Tung-chi. But he'll find out where you are. My idea is ten times as good."

"Tell me."

"Keep your voice down." He tightened the sack-strings, knotting them securely. "You know the *godows?*" *

"Down by the River of Golden Water? Of course. But concubines aren't permitted down there; it's off limits."

"You no longer are a concubine." He searched about the ground at their feet, found a twig and, shifting his body, widening the distance between them on the bench, began sketching invisibly upon it.

"Here are the *godows.* Tomorrow is Tuesday. The farmers will be bringing in their wagons loaded with rice and vegetables, everything, coming in here through the West Flowery Gate, one driver to each wagon, which is all the guards allow. That way they can keep track of everybody coming in and going out."

"We can hide."

"Be still; we don't have to hide. Remember, eunuchs can go in and out any gate anytime between sunrise and sundown."

"A lot of good that does me."

"I'm going to show you what good it'll do you. All right, here comes Farmer Wo-cheng bringing in a load of rice, past the guards, across the River of Golden Water, over the Treasury Bridge and up to the *godows.* He starts unloading. I step up as he's working and begin talking about the weather. I casually offer him ten taels for a small favor. When he brings his last sack inside, adding it to the pile, instead of coming back out, he's to sneak around behind the pile where you're waiting. I'll give you at least ten minutes to change your clothes and put on your makeup. You come out, climb up on his wagon and join the line of empties heading on out."

"And you walk out."

"Right behind you, my disguise tucked under my

* "Storehouses."

arm. Outside, out of sight of the guards, you pick me up and we drive straight to Lo-ti Street to the stable. You'll stay there and wait, still in your disguise. I change into my farmer's outfit, stuff what I have on under the wagon seat, pick up a load of rice or beans or whatever, drive back through the West Flowery Gate and dump my load. Our friend the real driver comes out of hiding and drives his empty wagon back out. Changing back into my regular clothes, I walk out a second time."

"And meet me at the stable in Lo-ti Street."

"And away we go on fast horses, outside well before sundown, to the Marco Polo Bridge."

"It's perfect, marvelous, beautiful!"

"Sh."

"One thing, I've been thinking: Why the Marco Polo Bridge?"

"So we can get on a boat or raft, naturally."

"Why bother? It's too far out of the way and too slow. Once we get our horses, we could ride down to Tientsin, to anyplace."

He shook his head. "Too dangerous; too many bandits roaming about."

"So we ride at night. We'll be able to see their faces from a distance and avoid them."

"No good; we could accidentally ride right up to their guards. They'd rob and kill us in seconds."

"Why is it any safer on the river?"

"It is, that's all. There's nothing being shipped down they want, no money or jewels or lovely young women to rape and knife. What do they need with sacks of grain? No, the river may be slower, but it's much safer."

"Not if Tung-chi comes after us."

"We'll have to take that chance. If we get away early enough in the day, we can be almost to the coast by the time he gets home and finds you gone."

"We can, can't we!" She hugged him tightly. "I love you, So-leng."

"Don't be ridiculous!"

"I do!"

"Settle down. Let's be realistic. All this is much easier said than done. Bribing the driver is the big thing, talking him into playing along. Of course, there's not one of them who isn't as poor as Kang-t'su.* Still, I think it's a workable plan. I've gone over and over it."

"It's perfect. Why didn't we think of it weeks ago?"

"It wouldn't have worked weeks ago. For one thing, you were a concubine. You would have been chased away from the imperial *godows,* without a chance to get inside and change your clothes. Even now there's one pretty big condition: Whoever I bribe has to trust me. He'll be hiding inside, waiting for me to drive his precious wagon back in. If I don't show up, he's going to have to explain a few things. He could end up a lot worse off than losing a horse and wagon."

"You've got an honest face."

"If the first one I approach turns me down, and the second, by the time I do talk somebody into agreeing to do it, it may be spread all over the place. If the guards get wind of it . . ."

"Please, let's not talk about the dark side."

"We have to. We have to find all the flaws. However we work it, we'll be taking a chance. We need luck, timing, everything in our favor."

"Not really—just a driver who's willing to take a risk for a small fortune." She got up from the bench. "Come, let's go down to the *godows* and get the lay of the land."

"Let's not. We can find our way around there without any trouble. It's not complicated. What we should be doing is trying this outfit on you to see if you'll really fool anybody."

She picked up the bag. "We'll go back to the apart-

---

* A legendary beggar without arms or tongue who begged with his eyes.

ment. We can lock ourselves in the bedroom and keep Yao from sticking his nose in."

"I worry about him. If he finds out what we're up to, he'll run straight to Tung-chi."

"Nobody's going to find out anything!"

XV

Yao met them at the door, a look on his face that suggested he had just swallowed a persimmon. "Where have you been?" he asked Deirdre in a put-upon tone.

"To the moon. None of your business where I've been."

"You mustn't be rude. I was worried about you."

"I'm sure."

He glared balefully at So-leng. "You I thought we'd seen the last of."

"You thought wrong," said Deirdre. "He's back to stay."

"Is that so? I'm sure the master will have something to say about that!"

In a voice affecting exaggerated boredom, she calmly advised Yao that So-leng was coming into the household with Tung-chi's approval.

"Now, if you'll excuse us . . ."

They walked by him standing with his hand still on the inside knob of the door. Going into the bedroom, they locked the door.

"Whisper," cautioned Deirdre. "He'll be on the other side of the door straining to hear every word."

So-leng set the bag on the vanity bench and glanced at the door. "There's no keyhole; he can't see anything."

He helped her dress in the farmer's outfit, all but the straw hat. She pulled on the boots and began buttoning the linen coat up to her neck.

"Oh, dear," he said, "that'll never do."

"What's wrong?"

"Your breasts are much too full. You can see you're a woman a mile away."

She undid all but the two bottom buttons and sat on the edge of the bed. "Better?"

He nodded. "Keep it like that, loosely draped, both sides close as you can get them without buttoning."

"I'll be sitting all the time; that should help."

He tried the hat on her. She made a face in the mirror. "It's much too big."

"The bigger the better. We'll have to cut your hair, though. There's no way you can stuff all that under your wig."

She sighed. "If we must." She swiveled about on the bench, opened a drawer and brought out scissors.

"Not yet, for heaven's sake! What would your lord and master say? We'll do it first thing in the morning, right after he goes to work."

She removed the hat and fingered her hair, studying it in her mirror. "Good-by, good-by. Try your things on, why don't you?"

He widened the top of the bag with both hands and, turning it upside down, dumped its remaining contents on the bed. At once there was a violent hammering. The door burst open, the wood surrounding the bolt seat splintering loudly.

"I knew it! I knew it!" Yao stood framed by the doorway, glaring viciously, his beady eyes flashing like a snake's. Before either of them could utter a word, he came striding into the room, flinging an accusing finger at first Deirdre, then So-leng. "Ingrates! Rascals!"

"How dare you burst in here!" she shrilled.

"Yes, I dare! The master doesn't trust you. He never has. How right he is. And now"—he turned again on So-leng—"get out of this house and stay out! If I so much as see you hanging about the grounds, I'll kill you!"

Deirdre bristled. "Now, just a minute."

He glared venomously at her. "As for you, you're not going anywhere. I forbid you to set one foot—"

"Shut your stupid mouth and get out of here!" bellowed So-leng. He was standing between Deirdre and Yao. Confronting the older eunuch, he began pushing him boldly out the door.

"You dare lay hands on me, you filthy pig!" Yao lost all control, his anger exploding, his face scarlet, his eyes fairly bursting from their sockets. His hand went inside his blouse and he whipped out a dagger, pushing it straight into So-leng's stomach.

Deirdre screamed as, his jaw sagging, his eyes wide with amazement, So-leng slumped to his knees, the knife hilt protruding from his stomach, and toppled over.

Like a cat pouncing, Yao was down on the floor beside him, grinning satanically. "Good enough for you, pig. Pig!"

Blind with rage, Deirdre picked up the nearest heavy object, a stone vase, and brought it crashing down upon Yao's head. He groaned and toppled over. Blood spurted from his ear, describing a jagged crimson line diagonally down his cheek.

Pushing himself up on one elbow, So-leng stared at his attacker. "You've killed him."

Yao's eyes staring sightlessly sent a shiver down her back. No mistake; he was dead. Closing her eyes to the sight, she groped for the knife, finding the hilt, pulling it out. Blood followed, gushing up and subsiding, drenching So-leng's shirt and the rug. She dropped down beside him. "I'll get you up on the bed."

"No." He was staring past her, through the window at her back. "Great God, look!"

She turned and gasped. Huge clouds of billowing black smoke studded with sparks were pouring by the window.

"Go look out the door," he said.

"But you . . ."

"Go!"

He fell back, both hands pressing his wound, trying and failing to stanch the blood. She hesitated, then ran out of the room through the apartment to the front room. Through the double windows she could see the barracks and stables beyond the Well of the Pearl Concubine. Great tongues of flame sliced through the billowing smoke, leaping up the sides and fronts of the buildings. Horses had gotten loose and were staggering around. Eunuchs and servants and concubines ran about in confusion, screaming at the tops of their lungs. Deirdre glanced about the room. The two maids were nowhere to be seen. She ran back into the bedroom.

"The whole city's on fire!" To her amazement, his grimace of pain softened into a grin.

"Wonderful. This is your chance: Go; get out!"

"I can't. I can't leave you."

"I'm dying, can't you see? Don't you have eyes in your head?"

"So-leng . . ."

"There's nothing you can do. Go. All the gates will be open. Get out while you can. Hurry!"

Taking him in her arms, she hugged him tightly, her tears falling down upon his face. "I can't leave you."

"Go-o-o-o-o." The effort enfeebled his voice, the single word barely audible. She could feel his blood warm against her. Then he moaned and his body went slack. Loosening her hold, she gazed down into his eyes. They were glassy, and as she stared, her heart sinking in her breast, they began to roll slowly up into his head.

XVI

The flies buzzed aimlessly about the room, landing on the shellacked windowsills, inching about investigating, resuming flight, climbing to the stain- and crack-covered ceiling and circling back down. The morning sun rising over the distant mountains in the east sent its light through the open windows, painting the bare floor and filling the room with 130 degrees.

At least 130 degrees, mused Lisa, sitting alongside Paul Gerard in an uncomfortable wooden chair set in a line of similar ones against the wall. Opposite them was an inner office paneled four feet up from the floor, the wood giving way to glass badly in need of polishing. Through it three desks could be seen. Two men in shirt sleeves, collars unbuttoned, neckties loosened, the perspiration pouring down their pink faces, dampening their armpits in unsightly blotches, sat at the two smaller desks, writing laboriously. The unoccupied third desk was situated in respect to the other two so as to leave no doubt as to who was in charge. To the right of the inner office, a door led to the stairs that descended to the street. It was ajar, as if anticipating the arrival of the absentee.

Mr. Travis Collier was late. He had been due at the office at 8:30 sharp; the hands of the solid oak drop octagon clock on the wall across from the windows had passed that time nearly an hour and a half earlier. Lisa reached into her bag for her sodden hanky, unballed it, flattened it as best she could across her lap and began fanning herself with it. How anyone could work in this steam bath was a mystery to her.

The clerk inside seated closest to the interior door got up, his chair scraping the floor. He came out, grinning awkwardly. "I'm dreadfully sorry he's so late."

"It's not your fault," said Paul.

"He was due back last night."

"Yes."

"It's possible he slept late, although he would have sent a boy around to tell us. I really am sorry, what with your having had to wait five days already."

"Six," said Paul.

The clerk's pink face dipped in a nod. The heat of his brow appeared to be clouding his coquille spectacles. He removed them, wiping the lenses with his handkerchief. "He rarely goes away. Are you sure I can't help?"

"Thank you, no," said Lisa. "Our business is with Mr. Collier."

"May I get you a cup of tea?"

"No thank you."

Muffled footsteps sounded below.

"It's he," said the clerk.

A middle-aged man carrying a bulging briefcase came in. Encroaching upon a harried expression in defiance of the sultry weather was a full, fiery-red beard. His white cotton suit hung loosely from his spare frame. It appeared as if he'd been caught in a thundershower and it had dried on him. Divesting himself of his straw hat, he nodded at them and threw a quick look at the clock.

The clerk retreated, following him into the inner office, shutting the door behind them. Lisa and Paul looked on as they began a pantomime. The flies continued their explorations, the sun continued hurling its ferocious heat into the room, Paul shifted his hat from one knee to the other and sucked in his breath in exasperation.

"Pip pip and all that."

"Sh."

The clerk who had been so solicitous was explaining something or other. Collier went into a long response, waving both hands, shrugging his shoulders up to his ear-lobes, now and then sneaking a sidelong self-conscious glance at the two of them. Opening his briefcase, which he had thrown on his desk, he took out a sheaf of yellow pages, thumbing rapidly through them, quickly giving up the search and thrusting them at the other man.

Coming out, he greeted them: "I'm frightfully sorry. I've been running about like a headless chicken. Things are suddenly in upheaval. I wasn't looking for you till next week. This is all very embarrassing."

"It's perfectly all right," said Lisa. "May we talk?"

"By all means."

He led them into another room in use by an even larger contingent of flies and stiflingly close. He opened both windows, and a jumble of sounds—of chickens, pigs, people and creaking carts and wagons—came floating up from below. "Murderous, this heat. Worst bloody time of the year."

The room had been painted a sickly yellow. The walls, well webbed with cracks, were completely bare. The only furniture was a long mahogany conference table surrounded by an ill-matched assortment of chairs. He gestured them to sit.

"Wo Sin—," began Lisa.

Collier cut her off, smiling, begging her pardon, then surrendering his pleasant look to one so grim it startled her. "Before we begin, I'm afraid I must tell you some rather disturbing news."

"About my daughter?"

"Possibly. There's been a disastrous fire up in Peking, in the plesaunce they call the Forbidden City. A number of buildings have been destroyed. The latest I heard, last night in Ching-hai they just finished getting the worst of the blaze under control."

"Is she in the Forbidden City?"

"That's difficult to say with certainty."

"Dear God."

Paul covered her hand. "Easy. Have there been many casualties?" he asked Collier.

Collier nodded. "But see here, we musn't be pessimistic. It's possible she was nowhere near the fire."

"But she is in Peking?"

He nodded. "The thing of it is, this throws a bit of a damper on any plans we might have made."

"How so?" asked Paul.

"I had sent word up to our contact in the Chinese City, a Mr. Simon Atkins. Simon is acquainted with the late emperor's brother, Prince Kung, a very important man, important to their highnesses. He can be extremely valuable in any negotiating we get into. We're fortunate to have a line to him."

"Can he order her freed?" asked Lisa. "And can he or Atkins help her get down here?"

"That I wouldn't know. We have every hope."

"Mr. Collier, hope isn't enough at this stage." She stood up and began pacing. "If your friend Atkins can pinpoint exactly where she is, why can't we just—"

"Mrs. Dandridge, forgive me, but you really must allow me to explain, to clarify the ground rules. Whether we like it or not, we have to play the game according to the rules. I know how eager you must be to have it over and be reunited with her, but however we elect to approach matters, we must accept the fact that we have a discouragingly sticky situation facing us. This is not a chair I'm sitting on; it's a powder keg. We foreigners are here by the empress's sufferance, actually by Prince Kung's brother's sufferance, the chap who preceded Tz'u Hsi. Tientsin is what we call a treaty port, as are Hong Kong, Canton and various other cities, where foreign merchants are permitted to live and trade. Not necessarily actual ports, that is, on rivers or the sea . . ."

"Mr. Collier!"

"Be that as it may, I have just come back from Tai-so in the west. It appears that the lid is about to blow off the kettle. The French are preparing to annex three provinces of Lower Cochin, which will give them control of the entire Mekong Basin. I realize these are only strange names to you, but in point of fact they are flint and tinder to what is rapidly shaping up as an extremely volatile situation. The Empress Tz'u Hsi bloody well begrudges our presence, and she's managed to stir up the scholars, the military, the peasants, just about everybody, against us. It's deucedly lamentable, but that doesn't seem to faze our friends, the French.

Anyway, the upshot is that in the entire capital fewer than half a dozen foreigners are permitted to live and conduct trade, and they're there only because they can afford to pay the exorbitant bribes demanded by the authorities."

Rising, he placed his fists against the table and leaned toward her, his steel-gray eyes like opals in a face of dark stone. "Getting your daughter out of there at this time will be about as easy as abducting Tz'u Hsi."

"We'll get her out," said Lisa calmly.

"We'll try."

"We'll do a great deal better than try, believe me!"

"Hopefully. But, at the moment, that bloody fire has tied our hands."

"We can't let that hold us up."

"That's precisely what it's going to do. Things are in a great uproar up there. Until they settle down . . ."

"How long?" asked Paul.

Collier shrugged. "Three weeks, a month."

Lisa glared. "Ridiculous!"

"Mrs. Dandridge . . ."

"*Mr*. Collier: Mr. Gerard and I and our people have been sitting in this lovely town of yours waiting six days for you to come back. At long last here you are. Mind you, I'm not complaining—business is business—but now that you are back, you had better understand that I have no intention of sitting on my hands waiting three weeks to a month to start the ball rolling. If you can't help us, we'll simply have to go elsewhere. I appreciate the time you've spared us. I can see you're extremely busy. We'll make no further demands upon you."

"Suit yourself. I'm trying my best to tell you what you're going to be up against. Obviously you prefer a rosier picture."

"Now, now, now," said Paul in a conciliatory tone. "This is all wrong."

"It is. I'm sorry," said Lisa. "I apologize, Mr. Collier."

"There's no need."

"I insist. I know you want to help; you've offered to. I realize the situation is tenuous at best. Still, I must be stupid. I fail completely to see the connection between the fire and the French taking whatever it is they're taking and Mr. Atkins and Prince Kung's willingness or unwillingness to help."

"It's not Mr. Atkins or the prince; it's Old Buddha. The fire and the French will put her into the foulest mood imaginable. And in the eight years I've been here, she's had some frightfully foul ones. And the people read her inflammatory edicts and react accordingly. Moreover, if Prince Kung were to approach her now, she'd cut him off after the first two words—if, that is, he was fool enough to approach her. You had best believe he is not."

"You're saying that in three or four weeks she's going to be more cooperative?"

Collier shrugged. "If something else comes up, she could be a good deal less cooperative."

"What you're saying is, we could sit and wait for her mood to change and it probably never will."

"It's possible."

"Probable." She thought a moment, then extended her hand. Collier shook it. "I appreciate all you've done."

"I haven't done a blessed thing."

"You've clarified matters. You've been very helpful."

He tugged at his beard and studied her, a worried

look narrowing his eyes. "I wouldn't go off half cocked."

"We won't."

"But you do intend to take matters into your own hands."

"It appears we're going to have to."

"You realize you could make a bad situation worse."

"I pray that we won't."

He reached into his breast pocket and brought out a pencil and notebook. Scribbling briefly, he tore off the sheet and handed it to her. "Simon Atkins's address. It's L'ang Tien Street, the street of jewelers. You'll find Peking similar to Tientsin in that all the trades are bunched together in their own streets. I take it you're armed." She and Paul exchanged glances. "Be careful you don't get into a scuffle. You could get yourselves killed, which could make things difficult for all of us— as if they're not bad enough already."

"We have no intention of causing an international incident."

"People who cause international incidents rarely do so intentionally, Mrs. Dandridge. They always seem to develop as the result of something infuriatingly insignificant."

"What about the French taking the three provinces?"

He smiled. "There you have me."

They shook hands a second time.

"I'm sorry you can't wait. But, to be honest, I can't say I blame you. Good luck. Godspeed."

XVII

They stood outside the building under a straw awning, watching the crowds surging back and forth along Tung-ma Lu Street. Having arrived and settled over the land, spreading its stifling discomfort, the heat was rising in shimmering bands as if returning to its source to prepare for the next assault.

"Let's get something cool to drink," suggested Paul.

She nodded but did not move. "We've come all this way for this, to be stopped practically at the outskirts of Peking." She bristled. "Well, I don't care what's happening up there. I don't care about the French or Kung or Atkins or any of it; I'm going on."

"If we waited perhaps a week," said Paul, "we might get a clearer picture."

"I'm not waiting, not another hour!"

"If you say so."

She placed her hand against his arm, smiling thinly. "My good friend, this is all very wrong. I've no right to make demands. It's wrong for me to drag you along against your judgment."

"Who's dragging?"

"I am, not just you, but Ling Wu and the others."

"Nonsense. We're here because Wo Sin wants us to be. We volunteered."

"Now, *that* is nonsense. You know perfectly well you did nothing of the sort. She's my flesh and blood. Paul, I have to go on. But you and the others don't even know her; you've never even seen her. You heard Collier: It could turn out the wildest goose chase in history and the most dangerous."

"Madame, for the past twelve years I have been shot at, stabbed, blown up, have fallen into traps, been bitten by a krait and out of my head for six days, contracted malaria, beriberi, jail fever, spotted fever and black-water fever. I've been wounded so many times I've lost track of the places. I've got lead in my left leg and in both arms and a bayonet scar in my right thigh big enough to stripe your Old Glory. I have had sixty-two pieces of shot picked out of my backside, been declared officially dead from drowning, been captured by Sepoys at Nowabanghi, tried by a military court, sentenced to hang and escaped. I've been run over by a water buffalo and had my skull fractured by a Portuguese *gendarme* in Macao. A Lascar bit my left hand in a bar fight in Bandar Penggaram; it took eleven stitches to sew it up. I nearly died of blood poisoning, but I didn't. Do you know why?"

She smiled. "Tell me."

"Because I, Paul Phillipe François Léon Etienne Gerard, am immortal. I cannot die. I don't know how and I'm too stupid to learn. If I tried to commit suicide, I would fail."

"I'm being serious, Paul."

"No more so than I. If you are going to Peking, we are going to Peking, seriously."

She kissed him fondly on the cheek. "You are a very dear and brave man. Wo Sin is fortunate to have you for a friend. So am I."

"What about that drink?"

"Of course." They started up the street. "What about the rifles?"

"The boys buried the coffin outside the east wall. Pay no attention to Collier. We'll dig it up and take the whole shebang with us. It's stupid to tie one arm behind your back going into a fight."

"You think it'll come to that, don't you."

"Figure of speech. I really think we should take everything."

"You're the general."

"You, madame, are the general. We are your army."

They shared a small corner table in a restaurant that, if nothing else, offered relief from the blazing sun. The ceiling was lofty, and all the windows had been thrown open to lure inside whatever breezes happened by. They drank a bubbly soda water well chilled but, to Lisa, tasting slightly of disinfectant. She had lapsed into a somber mood. Whatever happened, she prayed that Deirdre would make it to freedom—and home. There was a chance; there was always a chance. With any luck at all . . .

"You're daydreaming," he said.

"I was. You've been busy these past few years, a full calendar. I take it you've killed a few men."

His tone in response was that of a bored clerk repeating a job applicant's address: "Thirty-eight."

"My goodness!"

"Every one self-defense, of course."

"Of course."

A lull settled between them. They sipped in silence.

"It tastes like medicine," he said at length.

"It does."

The room was crowded, the low rumble of conversation resembling the sound of distant cattle on the run.

"A pity Mr. Travis Collier turned out to be such a wet blanket," Paul said.

"I expected pessimism. You can't fault him for being honest. He's certainly sincerely concerned."

"Mostly about the powder keg he's sitting on."

"It looks bad, but it could be worse. Peking could be under siege."

He agreed and proceeded to shower her with optimism, citing all the things in favor of ultimate success: Atkins, the element of surprise, their portable arsenal, the pressure and influence that could be brought to bear through bribery. He was grasping at straws, but she let him ramble on, her thoughts outdistancing the present, neatly filing the future step by step.

They would finish their drinks, rejoin Ling Wu and the others, recover the coffin and start out, bother the heat. It was imperative they arrive in Peking before dark. She had to meet with Atkins as soon as possible. She needed his optimism regarding their chances fully as much as she needed her next breath.

She half listened to Paul, letting her thoughts drift to Deirdre and beyond Peking and the next few days to the future. Here she sat, 37 years old, a widow, dependent upon people she scarcely knew to help her bring about a miracle. And when all the heroics had been performed, when she and Deirdre were reunited, then what? Home to Blackwood, to a new life, without Ross. Together mother and daughter would share the house with his unseen presence. In every room, every moment she would feel him by her side, a comfort certain to lessen her loneliness. But sight of his portrait smiling down at her, silently reminding her that she would never again feel his arms, his kiss, would be all but unendurable. Oh, the wonder, the fire, the sublime satisfaction, the sunshine in her soul that was their marriage!

But for Deirdre life from now on would be so gray and empty. Darling Deirdre. Once they got home, they must swear a pact between them never to leave again. No more trains, no more ships, no more distant lands and alien strangers, no further alliances with dangers and disasters. To Boston for the day and back— travel enough for the rest of their lives.

They would live; they would try their utmost to make each other happy.

The golden times of the early years had been so precious and so few. As for Deirdre, all too soon she would grow up and meet a young man, fall in love, be married and have children, a handsome boy and a beautiful little girl.

Name the girl whatever you please, darling, but the boy, can he be Ross? Ross Richard. Ross in a little boy, dark, curly hair, dark eyes, that devil's grin, imperious challenge to the world—to her eyes, the look of the last of the gallants, mingled self-assurance and pride.

Grandmother would spoil her grandchildren outrageously: playthings, ponies, parties. They would grow up; she would grow old. Life would be as beautiful as memory could make it; and her heart would be forever full of him.

Paul finished his drink. "Ready?"

"Ready."

BOOK FOUR
BITTER TRIUMPH

I

For thousands of years the Chinese had used stone to build their bridges and walls, pagodas and tombs. But their buildings, from the hovels of the poor to the palaces of the emperors, had always been constructed of wood. Wood was a living, "breathing" material derived from the noble tree, God's longest surviving creation. Nevertheless, the imperial partiality for wood was not shared by the rulers of the Greeks, the Romans and other great nations, possibly because of wood's known vulnerability to fire.

Perceiving the inferno in the making out the front windows of the apartment, Deirdre had run back into the bedroom. There she had helped So-leng to die with dignity and finished disguising herself—cutting her hair, darkening her eyebrows with kohl, reshaping her eyes with makeup and applying the yellow cream to her skin.

By the time she was able to flee the apartment, the fire had eaten its way southward to the Hall of Imperial Peace and the Residential Palaces.

So-leng had been right. All four gates had been thrown open. While the eunuchs, servants and concubines inside were fleeing, imperial guards and soldiers were filling anything able to hold water in the moats and battling the blaze. Indescribable confusion resulted from the traffic surging in opposite directions, particularly at the Gate of Divine Military Genius and the gate outside it.

Once out of the apartment building, Deirdre captured one of the horses freed from the burning stables and wandering about unattended. Mounting, she galloped toward the West Flowery Gate, well to the south of the encroaching edge of the blaze. By now the northern quarter of the Forbidden City had been all but consumed, the flames borne by a light breeze slipping down from the Drum Tower beyond Coal Hill, spreading from the east wall to the west. The Hall of Imperial Peace, directly opposite the Gate of Divine Military Genius, went up like a paper lantern touched by a candle. Deprived of support, its curved roof collapsed, forcing the four blazing walls outward crashing down upon horses and people. The screams of the living and the dying vied with the ominous crackling of flames and the rumble of falling beams, roofs and walls. It was as if the entire city were a penny matchbox, the neatly aligned heads of the matches lying inside ignited and flaring up, the fire speedily spreading down the box.

Deirdre raced through the narrow space separating the Treasury Building from the Imperial Storehouses, crossed the little bridge, and, slapping her horse's neck with her right hand, sent it thundering to the left toward the West Flowery Gate and through. Heads turned, guards carrying buckets shouted, but she was across the moat and into the Imperial City in seconds. Skirting the lake stretching the full length of the city and beyond into the Tatar City, she headed south for the road leading to the cemetery. She would avoid the Marco Polo Bridge and ride down the plain between the Hun and Pei rivers, straight for Tientsin and the coast beyond.

The streets were mobbed with the curious coming toward her, attracted by the conflagration. She glanced over her shoulder. Thick black smoke climbed clear of the walls, billowing heavenward into the sun. Above the rumble of the crowd she could hear loud crashing as building after building collapsed. Even as she stared, the closely clustered buildings fueled the fire larger and larger, lifting the flames above the walls.

The horse was a sturdy little wild-maned mare, eager to run, stretching its legs as the crowd thinned. Directly ahead the Chinese Inner City Gate revealed itself. Beyond it lay freedom! She slowed the horse. Why race like a fleeing thief through the open gates and engage the guards' suspicions? And why exhaust the horse, with so many miles to go? Passing through the gates and out onto the Peking plain, she veered left, riding at an easy gait until the Hun River came into view, a sluggish, muddy wash snaking its way down from the mountains of the north. The plain drained poorly, sprawling marshes and large tracts of saline land sharing dominance. Here and there sandstone ridges uplifted themselves as if in anticipation of the sculptor's hammer and chisel and conversion into lion-dogs, imperial dragons and other creatures. Farmhouses shadowed by rickety-looking, unpainted barns could be seen, but the farms themselves were miles apart, deployed only where the land was capable of sustaining crops.

Peking grew smaller behind her as she drew within 100 yards of the river and began following it down. As the city shrank in size, it became increasingly darker in spite of the dazzling light of the early-afternoon sun bathing it. Smoke continued to pour from the Forbidden City, smudging the yellow sky, spreading, thinning, dissolving.

It was incredible; in less than 20 minutes she had fled one wall after another, one box after the other, the smallest to and through the largest, and was now at least five miles from her prison. He who does not hesitate is free, she mused. Free! Out and on her way to a ship, hopefully American or English. She wouldn't be choosy as to size or condition; anything capable of getting her across the Gulf of Chihli to Australia would serve. From there on to San Francisco should be easy.

Free! Unbelievable, astonishing and oh so beautiful! The gaining and savoring of freedom, the feeling suffusing her . . . The eraser swiping across the blackboard, wiping away the nightmare, reducing it to the realm of unpleasant memory, all thanks to So-leng. The poor man, poor, dear, good-hearted soul. In a way, he had given his life for her. She would never forget him, his glum face, his bitter outlook on life, his resentment against the fates that had used him so shabbily, his willingness to help the helpless *wàigworén*. She could count the ones who had cared and whom she could trust on the fingers of one hand—on two fingers: old gloomy and Li-Sing, dear little moon-face and her Buddhist nunnery.

The horse was lathering despite its measured pace. It obviously wasn't used to running under such a sun, and yet it seemed to revel in release from the crowded confines of the cities, the chance to fill its lungs and flee across the harsh and alien land.

The sun was halfway between its zenith and the horizon, which gave her about eight hours to reach the coast. Yet, now that she thought about it, would that be her best option? Did it make sense to rush to the docks and the dangers they presented? Despite her disguise, she was still a lone female, without friends or contacts or protection. She could be all too easily prevented from boarding ship, from even locating one that suited her needs. She could be robbed and raped and worse if the good luck riding with her suddenly reverted to bad. Now that distance had given her time to consider her situation, perhaps rushing pell-mell to the coast was all wrong. It would be safer and more sensible to ride into Tientsin and locate whatever Americans were working there, or British, or French, any nationality with shipping ties to a safe port. Once she had explained her predicament, they'd help her.

So it was settled: Tientsin it would be.

II

The coffin, buried in a grove of trees about a mile from the west causeway, was recovered, the mules fed and watered and the party started out. They were guided by a crudely drawn map given Paul by a helpful foreman overseeing a group of workers braving the brutal sun to repair a portion of the west causeway. Two miles north of the city the mules were stopped, the coffin opened and five of the Spencers taken out and loaded. Ling Wu and the others sat in the rear of the wagon, their weapons held between their knees, muzzles upward.

Paul let the mules walk at their own gait. Any effort to push them would have been useless in such heat. As he pointed out, they could be grateful that Peking lay only about 70 miles away.

The narrow road circled marshes and twisted around outcroppings. The landscape became drier, the mud ruts under the wheels surrendering clouds of thick yellow dust behind them that rose a mile in the air. They passed a farm lying west of them two miles distant, a shabby little house hugging the land like a tortoise, with a barn that looked as if the next stiff wind would collapse it. A sea of waxy white sorghum rose to the height of the eaves of the house, surrounding it on three sides. As Lisa watched it, the sorghum bent slowly in the gentle breeze, darkening in color, regained its upright posture and reached once more for the sun.

"There's one sure thing," said Paul after a lengthy silence broken only by the tired creaking of the wheels.

"There's nobody out in this heat who doesn't have to be."

"Do you think we'll make it to Peking before sundown?" she asked.

"It's hard to say. I know one thing: We don't want to be on this road or any other after dark." He brought out the map, holding it on his knee with the heel of his hand and indicating a cross approximately midway between the two cities. "Here's a town we might lay over: Wu-ch'ing."

"How big is it?"

"About the size of Pei-t'ang, I think. We should be there by the middle of the afternoon."

"But there'll still be daylight until eight-thirty or nine. That's plenty of time to get to Peking."

"Maybe not. Why take the chance?"

"Time, Paul; it's against us—every day we delay, every hour. I don't even know why we hung onto this broken-down wagon. We could have gotten horses back in Tientsin."

"If we had, we'd have had to leave the coffin."

"We could have brought the rifles along."

"Sure, but what if we had to hide them? We could bump into soldiers or the police."

"On horseback we could get there in a quarter the time. We could at least have gotten four horses to pull this wagon."

"That wouldn't make any difference. We couldn't go any faster than we are now, mules or horses. I don't know what's holding this thing together as it is."

"Couldn't you find anything better back in Pei-t'ang?"

"I suppose I could have, but I didn't, did I?" He was becoming resentful. She let the subject drop. "If you like, we can get horses up ahead in Wu-ch'ing," he added.

"Then we could make Peking before dark easily."

"Look."

He pointed directly ahead. A gully snaked across the road, as if an earthquake had separated the land. It was at least four feet wide, but as they came closer, she could see that it was only about two feet deep— just deep enough to jolt the wagon enough to shatter it. Pulling the mules to a halt a little ways from it, Paul helped her down. Leaving their rifles in the bed of the wagon, Ling Wu and the others climbed down. Paul walked the team to the edge and gingerly across. The front wheels followed, dipping, finding bottom and rolling easily up the other side. But when the rear wheels started through, the left one heaved to the side awkwardly, all but slipping free of the axle. Paul yelled at the mules and reined up, but a split second too late. One extra step forward and they pulled the axle free, the wheel falling, clattering to rest in the gully. Down the wagon bed slid the coffin, bumping to rest against the tailgate, the Chinese gaping wide-eyed in fear that the bombs would explode.

"Goddamn!" burst Paul. "You might know!"

Lisa bent to examine the spindle at the end of the axletree. "The peg is sheared off."

"It's rotten," said Paul. "You'd think they'd use iron to peg a wheel on." He glanced about, his eyes lighting upon the tailgate. Freeing one of its pegs, he tried it in the spindle hole. "Perfect fit." He handed it to her. "We'll lift up the corner and slip the wheel on. You drop it in. Careful of your fingers."

At Paul's direction, Ling Wu and the other three men raised the corner of the wagon. Paul then moved the team forward with a snap of the reins, lifting the wagon free. The men continued holding up the corner as he fitted the wheel over the spindle. Lisa was preparing to slide the peg through the hole when the rumble of hooves shook the ground like sudden thunder. Over a nearby rise, a band of wild-looking men appeared, yelling loudly, their swords flashing in the sunlight, their ancient muskets aimed and firing.

In seconds, before her horrified eyes, before Paul or any of the others could recover their weapons and bring them to bear, he, Ling Wu and the others were shot down. The bandit leader raced around the wagon, waving his sword and yelling above the fearsome din. She dropped to her knees in the gully, shocked speechless at the sight that followed, the bandits dismounting, running up to the corpses and hacking them to pieces. A sword whistled by her head, decapitating Paul. Blood spurted from the stump of his neck and his body twitched hideously. She screamed and fainted.

III

The huge round tent was made of white felt, lending it the appearance of a mammoth igloo. In spite of the large vents tied open in a circle around the base of its dome, the air inside was searing hot. She had regained consciousness, to discover herself lying on a clutter of pillows. In front of her sat a giant of a man, his complexion so brown as to be almost black. His rat-gray hair hung from his scalp in slender tails, and his face looked as if it had been smeared with grease. It was oddly shaped, almost wider than long, his piercing eyes peering out at her from the folds of flesh. From each earlobe a large copper ring suspended, stretching his lobes fully two inches. Gleaming across his upper chest was a necklace of gold coins, while girdled snugly about his waist was a red silk gown, its front stained with grease and ripped under the right arm.

He sat cross-legged, eating, thrusting first one hand, then the other into a cast-iron pot sitting by his right knee, bringing out chunks of meat and what looked to be the intestines of some animal. They were raw, a pinkish-white, and dripped oil. As she stared, he stretched and ripped a length in two, stuffing one handful into his toothless mouth and offering her the other. She shook her head, shuddering, turning her eyes from the grisly sight.

He called out and a man came in through the open flaps, his grin splitting his face, displaying twin rows of overly large and crooked yellow teeth. He began bowing, jerking up and down like a string puppet.

FIRE AND FLESH 345

The eater barked an order. Ducking out, the man returned immediately with a large leather jar, pushing it at her. It was half filled with a colorless liquid she assumed to be goat's milk. Again she shook her head, declining. He shrugged, set the jar to one side and backed out of the tent, letting both flaps fall.

Her heart raced, thumping against her rib cage as the other fastened his eyes on her and leered. Her thoughts flew back to Paul and the others, the five of them brutally murdered before her eyes. Paul, glib and charming, generous of heart and spirit, and immortal. *"It is impossible for me to die!"*

Dear God! It was all so sudden, so unexpected and so unspeakably horrible. Paul had reset the wheel; she was about to push in the peg to lock it on when they had burst upon them, screaming, waving their swords, shooting. The groans of the dying, the blood, the vicious hacking, Paul's head . . .

Uncrossing his ankles, the man-animal rose to his knees, set the pot well out of his way and got up, yawning and stretching. She gaped. The top of his head came within inches of the top of the tent, and even though he had been sitting on a wooden platform raised a foot off the ground, he stood easily six and a half feet tall. His shoulders were the widest she had ever seen, and when he raised his hands, his forearms resembled the trunks of small trees. He gestured her to rise. She hesitated just long enough to see the leer vanish and a look of irritation replace it. Wearily she got up, her heart continuing to pound, fear welling in her stomach in anticipation of what was to come. Approaching her, he began stroking her hair with his greasy fingers; then he seized her chin, pulling open her mouth, lowering his head, squinting, examining her teeth. Wrapping his arms around her, he lifted her lightly, bringing their mouths together. The stink of his breath nearly caused her to wretch as he crushed her lips in a brutal kiss, driving his tongue into her

mouth. She struggled to pull free, gagging, her stomach
rolling, cold sweat popping from her forehead in tiny
beads. She could feel the color draining from her
cheeks, and her knees felt as if they would give way
as he set her back down.

Now his hands moved down her body, fumbling
at her clothing. His foul breath came in gasps like
that of a jungle beast lusting for its mate. Struggling
feebly, she prayed for unconsciousness, but it was not
to be. Pushing her to her knees, he bent her backward, forcing her down on her back. She lay helpless
and trembling as one massive hand held her down by
the chest and the other pulled her underclothing free
of her thighs, exposing her. Closing her eyes, she
stiffened determinedly, locking her legs together. It
was useless. In an instant his great weight was down
upon her, one knee forcing her thighs apart. She
could feel the heat of his rapidly stiffening member
against the soft flesh. He entered her at once, ramming
his member full length, eliciting a scream of pain.

It was hideous, the tortures of the damned com-
pressed into minutes. She screamed and struggled as
his member grew enormous within her, filling her,
stretching her so, it felt as if she would rip. Sight of
his greasy face, the tiny flecks of the foam of his lust
emerging at the corners of his mouth, his eyes fired
with ravening hunger for her raised her cry to a pitiful wail. She began begging for mercy, but he was deaf
to her pleas. She was not human to him, merely an
elemental object upon which he might vent his over-
mastering lust. She attempted to reach around his
shoulders to get at his face, to pound it and drive it
from her sight, but she could not budge her arms. He
made no effort to stifle her screams; rather, it was as
if the sound of her voice was the spur to hurry his
driving and thrusting deep into her.

Drowning in despair, she had all but given up the

ghost when he stopped abruptly, withdrawing, freeing her, rising and standing over her, staring down triumphantly. Without a murmur he turned his back on her, dropped to his knees and resumed eating from the pot. With what little strength she had left, she turned on her side, crawling off the pillows onto the ground. Her brain caught fire; she felt as if her skull would shatter. Casting about, her eyes settled on her open portmanteau, its contents strewn about. Beyond it lay her handbag. He continued eating, his back to her. She crawled toward the bag. Stretching one hand out to it, she flicked it open.

To her horror, she heard him rise and approach her, his steps practically shaking the ground beneath her. He crouched, and she turned to find herself staring straight into the muzzle of the derringer. Chuckling, he cocked it, setting the muzzle firmly against her forehead. It was like ice. She gasped, and he roared laughter, pulling the weapon away, aiming it straight upward and firing both bullets. He then flung the gun to the other side of the tent, seized her and kissed her brutally, mauling her breasts as he did so, releasing her finally, letting her sink into a heap at his feet. Again he went back to eating, sprawling on his pillows, bracing himself on one elbow and cramming the meat into his mouth.

It occurred to her that she had been unconscious for much longer than she had first assumed upon awakening—for hours, for now the sky visible through the vents overhead was losing its dazzling brightness, softening into a pale azure. The tent continued to hold its heat, however, and she was dripping with perspiration and so exhausted she could barely keep her eyes open. But her mind was alert and racing, cataloging events, probing the future. With Paul, Ling Wu and the others dead and she herself prisoner of this vicious animal until he tired of abusing her, or until his "tender" ministrations broke her mind and body, it was clear that all was lost now, her hopes dashed, her faith in the rightness of her cause, the fairness of the gods, swept away in 60 seconds of carnage.

The horrifying reality of her plight become clear. She began to cry, tears dimming her sight, a sob filling her throat. To come so close to within a few hours' ride of Deirdre only to lose the game with the loss of the wheel seemed so contemptibly unfair. Had it never come loose, there would have been no need to stop, no need for Paul and the others to relax their vigilance and be caught off guard.

Had it never come loose . . .

The rectangles of sky overhead were darker now and two stars appeared, tiny fire-eyes discovering her, peering down appraisingly. Closing her eyes and folding her hands, she prayed, for deliverance, for one last chance to complete her journey and be reunited with Deirdre. To rescue her and bring her home: Was that, she mused, so much to ask for, so demanding of her? Was it so wrong for her to claim all that she had left in the world?

But, as the minutes dragged by, logic and reason stirred their bulks in their cage in her mind and awoke, to attack and rout her prayers. Who was there who even knew what had happened on the road, or where she was now? Not a living soul besides her tormentors. She was alone now, and not all the entreaties of all the angels in Christendom could alter that. The nearest helping hand was Travis Collier's. And wasn't it his advice she had spurned? When she and Paul had walked out of his conference room, he must have written the two of them off as headstrong fools not worth the smallest corner of his conscience. In his position, wouldn't she have done the same?

Her quest had failed, as the odds had warned it would. It was ended, done with here in this remote corner of nowhere. Even more marvelous, it promised to be the final entry in the ledger of her years. This hulking, heartless throwback to the Stone Age would use her until her last breath rattled from her throat, then drop her body in a ditch.

Leaving Deirdre to fight on alone.

IV

The bandits' hideout was situated in a small recess
in a stretch of rocky terrain that permitted the sentries
at their posts unobstructed view of anyone approaching from any direction. The leader of the 30-odd men
and four prostitutes, who were servants as well, was
called the *Lánsè Láng*.* Although Lisa did not understand a word any of them spoke, it was obvious that
he ruled the little band with an iron fist. Permitted
outside his tent, she could see that the bandits stole
only those valuables that could be easily carried—
mostly money and jewelry. They also collected weapons and ammunition, as well as horses healthier and
stronger than those they rode. Their horses, for the
most part, were sturdy little mares, creatures as wild-
looking as they themselves and as dirty and noxious-
smelling. Everyone, the Blue Wolf included, smoked
opium, the sickly-sweet odor wafting over the camp.
He had turned to his pipe after ravishing her a second
time, then pushing her outside to apparently do as
she pleased.

From in front of his tent she could see three of
the four sentries posted on the tallest rocks surrounding the camp. They sat silhouetted against the sky,
their knees pulled up to their chests, their muskets
balanced across their laps. The men were all dressed
in similar fashion, the uniform of the trade, she assumed; cotton shirts and trousers bagging absurdly,
ill-fitting, ostensibly stolen from their victims. These

* "Blue Wolf."

were fastened about their waists with a length of twine or rope. Most of the bandits, like their leader, were bareheaded and, like him also, wore jewelry of gold and precious stones.

The four camp followers wore filthy, ragged dresses and pounds of beads and bangles, giving them the appearance of gypsies. They ignored her, neither welcoming her nor showing resentment at her presence. Then one brought her a large wooden cup of hot soup. Lisa was famished, and it smelled delicious. She drank more than half of it before discovering a chunk of white meat lying in the bottom of the cup. It was raw liver. What sort of creature had contributed the organ to the pot, she couldn't imagine and didn't, her curiosity focusing instead upon how long the soup she had already swallowed would stay down. To her surprise, it managed to.

The sky was clear, a deep aquamarine in color and brilliant with stars. The moon shone gloriously, lighting up the plain for miles. The bandits appeared to be uncommonly careful with their fires, keeping them small to minimize smoke and surrounding them with packs and their own bodies to prevent the flames being seen by any chance passersby. Conversation was carried on in hushed tones; no laughing, no merrymaking. Plundering, wholesale murder, kidnaping and rape, all the talents of the hard-working professional brigand were subject to a rigid code of conduct, so it seemed. The Blue Wolf symbolized the Trinity in a red silk gown and Khalkha boots. His men were slavishly devoted to him; his judgment was beyond question, his word as much law as Attila the Hun's. Shooting off the derringer had not even brought the guard outside to the flap to satisfy his curiosity as to what was going on. The Blue Wolf might as well have been shooting at her rather than at the dome of his tent.

Noting the sentries on duty as she moved about the

camp, drawing stares from the men, she considered her chances of escape, and concluded that they were non-existent. She might steal a pony—all were tethered to a single rope stretching 40 feet between two stakes —but she would have had next to no chance of clearing the rocks before being sighted by a sentry and shot out of the saddle.

Would that be so terrible, to tumble to earth with two bullets in her spine? It would certainly be fast and relatively painless and eliminate any further abuse and suffering at the hands of the Lord High Brute. Her stay in his private felt-domed hell could drag on for weeks, even months. She could be ravaged and beaten and starved until her mind shattered and heart and will to go on gave out. Being shot while attempting escape began to look not only preferable but was a fairly enticing prospect.

She was continuing to weigh one fate against the other when his hand came down on her shoulder, spinning her around. Her heart sank as he pushed her, stumbling ahead of him, toward his tent and back inside. The odors of his body, his breath, the dregs in the pot and the opium mingled in a single nauseating stench. Her eyes teared and she choked as he pushed her down upon the pillows and, lifting the skirt of his gown, took hold of his member and began working it into stiffness.

She died inwardly, surrendering to anguish that wrenched her soul, sweeping over her, engulfing her, inbuing her with a feeling of no feeling, as if every drop of blood had been drained, every nerve cut off and deadened, every muscle, every fiber rendered insensible in anticipation of the agony and humiliation that were to come.

But come they did not. He was down on his knees, his huge member erect and throbbing, started forward, the head touching her thighs, when a shot stopped his grunting deep in his throat. There followed the rapid fire of many guns, loud screaming, horses neighing, galloping hooves. Before the clamor had even fully registered upon her weary brain, the tent began shaking. Her first thought was an earthquake, but then she heard loud slashing sounds. Turning her head where she lay, she could see knife blades cutting the tent wall. In rushed uniformed men yelling loudly, dropping their knives, bringing their guns to bear on the Blue Wolf.

He backed away from her on his knees, his eyes saucering panic. A rifle butt swung, smashing him full in the forehead. Roaring, he toppled over sideways, hammering the ground with his right temple. Two men stepped up on either side of him, planted the muzzles of their rifles flush against his eyes and calmly pulled the triggers.

The noise was deafening. Like a melon dropped from the roof of a building onto a stone pavement, the fragments of his skull burst outward in all directions. She was up on her knees now, her hands planted firmly against her ears, her fingers moving to cover her eyes. Two men helped her to her feet, one patting her gently on the back, the other addressing her quietly in Chinese, his tone consoling, comforting.

V

The room was barely long enough to accommodate the narrow wooden bed upon which she lay. The ceiling was low, so low she fleetingly imagined she could reach up from flat on her back and touch it easily. The walls were freshly painted, the odor lingering in the stuffy air. They were slate-colored, as somber and dreary-looking as a crypt. She eased her left foot to the floor, following with the other, raising herself to a sitting position on the edge of the bed. She felt weak but not dizzy, and surprisingly well rested and refreshed. The day was fading outside the window, the right side of the frame afire with a slice of the dying sun. She had been asleep close to 20 hours. Yawning, she stretched and stretched again, and thought about the domed tent, the Blue Wolf and the surprise attack of the soldiers. From their uniforms, she had assumed they were soldiers, but they had brought her here to a police station where all the men on duty were similarly garbed.

She was fully clothed. She dimly recalled snatching up her underthings, stuffing them into her bag hastily repacked, grabbing her handbag, discovering, as she expected, her money and personal effects missing but her letters of credit intact. She had emerged from the tent to the ghastly sight of all the bandits and their women lying about dead.

A knock rattled the door; she opened it to a smiling young police officer. His grasp of English proved tenuous at best, but he was so proud of it, and so enthusiastic over the opportunity to test it on her, he could scarcely contain himself.

"You feel fine yes."

"Fine, yes, thank you. I . . ."

"Me Lieutenant Sung."

"And I am Lisa Dandridge."

"English."

"American."

This seemed to surprise him, but he bridled his curiosity, at least for the moment.

"Bring washtub for missus water hot soap," he announced.

Saluting, he vanished down the hall, returning moments later with a large wooden tub, which he proceeded to fill with buckets of water, adding a boiling pot, bringing the temperature up to a comfortable tepidity. Locking the door, she undressed and bathed, discovering a number of angry-looking bruises on her arms and upper legs. They were sore to the touch, but she dismissed this discomfort and the dull aching between her thighs. She was too relieved at her timely and unexpected rescue to be bothered by such trifling inconveniences as discomfort, the unwelcome company of flies and her hunger. She finished bathing and dressed in her plain navy linen crash suit.

She was dying to find out everything about the raid, how close she was now to Peking and how soon she could be on her way. She would need an escort, of course, all the men who could be spared. Opening the door, she found a narrow hallway. At her feet sat a tray with a bowl of soup and what looked like fried beef. The soup was egg, spiced and slightly vinegary-tasting, but delicious. The beef was as tough as old leather. She ate every bit of both. Then she left the room, moving to the end of the hall and coming upon a large office painted the same dismal color as her bedroom and cluttered with cheap wooden furniture.

A door opposite was open, and through it she could see two rows of cramped little cells facing each other.

Seeing her, a policeman rose from his chair and closed the door to the cells. Then he motioned to her, inviting her to come in and readying a chair. Lieutenant Sung, who, now that she could compare him with his fellow officers, appeared to be barely out of his teens, joined her at once, coming from the opposite corner.

"You feel fine yes good. You tell how everything."

Suppressing a laugh, she smiled. "Gladly, but first would you mind telling me where I am? What is the name of this town?"

"Wu-Ch'ing. No town, city big."

She detailed the events of the previous day and night, taking care to delete the more grisly aspects of what had transpired in the Blue Wolf's tent. She then explained that she was on her way to Peking and had to get there as quickly as possible. He listened attentively and appeared to understand, but made no comment.

"Might I have an escort the rest of the way? Men to go with me?"

"Why you go?"

"I have urgent business in the Chinese City."

"What business?"

"It's personal."

"Yes yes personal."

"I can't tell you how grateful I am for all you've done for me, the bed, the bath, everything, but I really must leave right away."

"Must wait for chief."

She all but groaned aloud. "But why? I've already explained—"

He raised his hand, cutting her off. "You foreign. Must wait, law."

"Where is the chief?"

"In Tou-chang-chuang. Come back soon. In hour."

Red tape, she thought, as unavoidable here as it was anyplace else in the world. But, considering all that Wu-Ch'ing's finest had done for her, apart from saving her life, she decided against pressing him to let her leave at once. They entered the second hour continuing to test his English. She complimented him on it, asking him where he had picked it up.

He lowered his voice and his head, looking both ways and whispering, "Dr. Jason. Christian missionary."

"You're a Christian?"

His index finger flew to his lips. "No more. Christians bad, make much hell." In a low tone he struggled through misused tenses and distorted sentence structure, describing the current unrest in China. His views were not notably different from those of Travis Collier. The government blamed the English, French, Americans and Japanese for everything that was going wrong, economically, industrially, in trade, even the mediocre rice crop and the weather. One problem was rapidly leading to another, establishing an ever-lengthening chain of adversity. To make matters worse, the army was so busy keeping the foreigners in line that roving bandits, like those who had kidnaped her and murdered Paul and the others, were beginning to run amok. Responsibility for running them down fell to the local police, who, in turn, were becoming so involved in chasing about after them that local law and order was coming apart at its judicial seams. The people themselves—peasants, farmers, city workers, officials, the destitute, the wealthy and everyone between—were becoming restless, increasingly unhappy and impatient with the deteriorating state of things and the ineffectual rule of the empresses.

Collier's concern over the effects of the seizure by the French of the three provinces was echoed by the lieutenant. The Confucian scholars, the country's intellectual elite, uniformly loathed and despised all foreigners, their missionaries in particular. Matters were reaching the stage where the hatred of Europeans, Japanese and Americans, aggravated by isolated actions, such as that perpetrated by the French at Cochin, and encouraged by almost daily imperial edicts denouncing the presence of foreigners on sacred Chinese soil, was such that anyone whose eyes were round and whose skin lacked at least a tinge of "imperial" yellow found himself subject to rudeness, insults and worse.

"You no go Peking missus. You safe go other country. Back to docks port."

She stared at him steadily. "Are you advising me or ordering me?"

"You go you hurt. No police protect you. No friends."

She patiently explained that she had come all the way from the United States on a mission that could not possibly be jettisoned on the very brink of completion. As soon as her business in Peking was completed, she could leave China on the first ship. He understood, but his concern lingered, evident in his eyes and the lines bunching the center of his brow.

She returned the subject of conversation to the bandits. "Were they all killed?"

He nodded. "All."

"In less than sixty seconds, so it seemed."

He smiled, proudly, she decided, as if he himself had pulled every trigger, swung every sword.

The front door opened. In waddled a squat, sweating, flabby, multichinned man, a pistol holstered at his hip, a battered leather bag in one hand, a riding crop in the other in imitation of a caricaturist's impression of a British colonial officer. Every policeman present shot to his feet; down came the crop in acknowledgment. Down sat the men.

Passing by Lisa, the chief stopped short, his mouth sagging open, his porcine eyes, enlarged behind thick brass-framed glasses, catching her eyes. It was as if he were seeing a ghost. He appraised her to his satisfaction, then, nodding curtly, went into his office. Lieutenant Sung scurried after him in the fashion of all overly conscientious underlings.

Unbuckling his belt and hanging it from the coat tree stationed in the corner, the chief deposited himself in a chair barely large enough to accommodate his bulk and groaning resentfully as it did so. Lisa could hear them talking in low voices. Sung then came to the door and beckoned her to join them. The office was stuffy and filled with flies, the furniture badly in need of dusting, the floor of sweeping. A rat scratched in the wall behind the desk, and the flies quietly buzzed away what remained of the day.

The lieutenant set a chair for her across the desk from his chief, who, it was immediately evident, spoke no English. He began questioning her through the lieutenant.

"You come from . . ." began Sung.

"Tientsin."

"You go . . ."

"Peking. I already told you."

At this answer, the chief shook his head and repeated the same word over and over, which she took to be "no."

"Tell him it's so. That's it exactly, Tientsin to here to Peking."

"He say other way. You come from Peking, go south toward gulf."

"He's wrong. Tell him."

The chief let loose a barrage of syllables, his pudgy fist pounding the top of his desk in punctuation, visibly upsetting a circle of flies in the vicinity. He reached into his leather case and took out a manila envelope. It contained what appeared from the back to be a tintype photograph. He showed it to the lieutenant, who studied it, stared at her, studied it again and slowly shook his head, mystified.

Lisa fidgeted. She wasn't by nature overly enamored

of gameplaying, and being "it" in this one was becoming annoying. Visions of an armed escort to Peking began to fade. "What is all this? Would you mind explaining? What do you have there?"

The chief's response to all three questions was to rise from his chair, come around the desk, lean against the edge of it and busy himself comparing the face in the picture with her face at close range, while carrying on a running commentary. Then he lay the picture on the desk face up.

It was a family portrait taken in a garden filled with rhododendron trees, a Chinese family: father, mother, grown son and two grown daughters, all smiling happily. Standing next to the son, her expression as doleful as Lisa had ever seen it, was Deirdre.

"My God!" Snatching up the picture, she stared at it. "Where did you get this? Who gave it to you?"

The chief pulled it away from her, holding it up, indicating Deirdre and barking three words.

"Chief say face same you. You, missus."

"Don't be ridiculous; it's my daughter!"

The word translated for him, the chief broke into a grin, shaking his head.

Good Lord, she thought, he doesn't believe me; he really doesn't. He thinks it's me. "Lieutenant, tell him I said to look closely. She's much younger than I. She's not even half my age. Look yourself; look closely."

Sung shrugged and studied the picture, his face taking on a bewildered expression. Far from convincing him, she was only confusing him. At the same time, the self-satisfied grin on the chief's face was enough to tell her that his small and duty-bound mind was made up.

"Lieutenant, ask him where he got that picture."

Sung questioned his superior, was answered and explained. "Picture copies given all police chiefs, soldier captains by Tung-chi. Big official Peking, on

Board of Punishments." The chief cut in. "Chief say Tung-chi say you kill two eunuchs in Forbidden City and run away. You murderess. You be brought back to Forbidden City to be charged. You go before Board of Punishments."

VI

Shortly after Lisa and her party had departed Tientsin, a series of incidents took place that, on top of the rumored impending seizure of the three provinces by the French, served to prod the patience of the Chinese people to the breaking point.

Seven years earlier, the parties to the Treaty of Tientsin had mutually agreed to the quartering of both French and British troops in the city. For nearly three years the Chinese tolerated the presence of the invaders. Curiously, it was not the round eyes and fair skin of the soldiers of Louis Napoleon and Queen Victoria that outraged the people; it was their Christian religion, in particular their missionary priests' and ministers' tireless efforts to gain converts. To the Chinese, the Catholics and Protestants seemed to be in a contest to determine which faith could establish itself most solidly in Chung Kuo, the Middle Kingdom. In 1861, from Hunan to the south of Tientsin, a province historically noted for the rugged persistence of traditionalist philosophy, a deluge of propaganda poured forth. This substantially encouraged alliance of the three great Chinese religions—Taoism, Confucianism and Buddhism—against Christianity.

On the very morning that Lisa had set out for Peking, the news broke in Tientsin that nearly 40 Chinese orphan babies in the care of the nuns in the convent of the Sisters of St. Vincent de Paul had died, the presumed culprit typhoid fever—so the Mother Superior claimed. But the fact that she had elected to keep the tragedy secret for nearly three full days only fanned the fires of hatred and suspicion. Gruesome tales of witchcraft and black magic practiced on the helpless children quickly spread. Angry students assembled and marched to the cemetery, disinterring a number of infant bodies. It was these headstrong young men who spread the vicious and totally unfounded rumors of murder. In an effort to appease the mob, the Chinese magistrate and other officials decided to search the convent. This threatened invasion of sacred ground was thwarted by the Mother Superior, but only temporarily. One misunderstanding quickly led to another; by late afternoon the youthful gangs, encouraged by their elders and ignored by the sympathetic authorities, had begun wreaking vengeance upon the despised, bloody-handed *wàigworén*.

Riding at a steady gait, keeping the Hun River on her right, Deirdre had come within sight of the city without incident. Approaching the north gate, however, she intuitively sensed that all was not well within. Allowed to enter, she was surprised to see wild-eyed groups of young people surging through the streets, waving clubs and farm implements and carrying crude banners denouncing the French. The sidewalks were crowded, bystanders cheering the protestors on while uniformed policemen stood about, pretending indifference to the goings-on. Any establishment, any office, any sign or shop window indicating foreign ownership or control had already fallen to the mob. Store fronts were smashed and covered with mud, windows shattered, and in a few places bombs had been thrown, starting fires.

She rode about for half an hour, surveying the scene, eventually deciding to continue on to the coast. Unluckily, by the time she'd reached this decision, the sun had gone down and the gates closed for the night. Disguised as she was, she was not worried over her personal safety in the city, but seeking the help of any foreigners here now could be begging trouble.

Still, what alternative was there? And since she was stuck, at least until morning, what would be the harm in trying? She found her way to the corner of Nan-ma Lu and Tung-ma Lu streets, only to discover that the building housing the British Board of Trade had been blown up, the front corner of the first floor hanging precariously over the rubble of the ground floor, with glass and broken furniture, filing cabinets and fixtures liberally strewn about the area.

At once she set out for the only foreign consulate in the city, the French, getting this information and directions to the consulate from an elderly knife sharpener who was carrying on business as usual, oblivious of the increasing unrest around him. To Deirdre's relief, the consulate building was still standing. It proved to be a brick house two stories high, with barred windows and a ten-foot-high wrought-iron fence surrounding its little yard. A loud and angry crowd milled about the front gate, people shaking their fists and yelling imprecations. Inside the gate stood four French soldiers in their red and blue uniforms with white puttees, rifles at present arms, faces stony, but visible apprehension in their eyes. A rock was thrown; it struck the front door and bounced harmlessly away. One of the soldiers lowered his weapon as if to aim it, and those outside in his line of fire fell back. It was a tense situation, the fuse lit, the explosion imminent.

Tying her horse, Deirdre pushed through the mob up to the gate and, in English, asked to enter. The soldier shook his head mechanically, staring past her.

"Let me in, I say! At once, do you hear?"

The people around her gasped in surprise as she pulled off her black wig, revealing her sheared-short bright-red hair. The four soldiers gaped, and the one she had spoken to unfastened the chain, opening the gate a few inches, pulling her inside, slamming and locking it. She hurried up to the front door, a clod whizzing over her shoulder and bursting to pieces against it. The windows on either side of the door were broken. She rang the bell and pounded the door with both fists, cowering slightly as she did so, expecting more dirt or another stone.

"Let me in!"

Bolts were thrown, the lock clicked and the door opened a crack, disclosing a single frightened blue eye. She pushed inside, all but bowling over a pasty-faced and extremely nervous-looking clerk in vest and shirt sleeves.

"Who are you? What do you mean bursting in here?" He gaped incredulously, unable to connect her red hair with her clothing.

To aggravate his confusion, she promptly unbuttoned one blouse cuff and began wiping away her eye makeup and the yellow cream covering her face. "I wish to speak with the consul at once!"

The clerk had closed the door and thrown the upper and lower bolts. Turning on her with a jaundiced look, he shook his head. "Monsieur Chenier is in conference. He has left orders he is not to be disturbed."

"I'll wait."

"You may have a very long wait."

"So?"

He shrugged and gestured her into the front office, a musty little cubicle barely large enough to permit the presence of a small, exquisitely carved, flat-top teakwood desk, a wooden chair behind it and two Napoleon chairs upholstered in silk brocatelle.

"Sit down." He retreated behind his desk, which, she was quick to note, seemed to invest him with a self-confidence he notably lacked at the door. Picking up a pen, he dipped it in a stone inkwell and held it poised over a blank sheet of paper. "Your name, please?"

She was about to answer when something thumped against the topmost pane in the window at her left. The clerk sighed, went to it and pulled the portieres closed, plunging the little room into virtual darkness.

She gave him her name, told him that she had escaped from concubinage in Peking—which startled him so, he very nearly snapped his pen point—then announced that she wanted help in getting to the coast.

"How did you get down here?"

"Horseback."

"Where is your horse?"

"Tied outside."

"Pity. That's the last you'll ever see of it."

"What would you have me do—bring it in with me? I doubt if anyone'll steal it."

"In normal times perhaps not, but today . . ." Reminding himself of the situation flooded his face with fear. "Those damned babies, damned, damned babies!" He explained. "Then, about four o'clock, the roof fell in."

"What happened?"

"The Chinese announced they intended to search the convent. What they expected to find, God only knows. A torture rack? An iron mistress? They really are such absurd people!"

The Mother Superior had called Monsieur Chenier for help in preventing the search. Arming himself with two pistols and a sword, Chenier, the consulate chancellor, two attachés and two of the soldiers on duty outside had raced to the convent. Arriving, Chenier was confronted by Ch'ung-hou, a city father, a man of noble lineage and the Superintendent of Trade for the three northern ports.

"The fool insisted that His Excellency permit soldiers to search the convent."

"Is that so unreasonable?"

The clerk's eyebrows arced halfway up his forehead. " 'Unreasonable'? The convent of St. Vincent de Paul is sacred ground. No non-Catholic is permitted through the front door without the express permission of Mother Philomena."

"What happened?"

"Ch'ung kept insisting and they began arguing. Monsieur Chenier lost his temper. With all due respect, His Excellency is very short-fused. He brandished one of his pistols, Ch'ung-hou backed off, the main door was closed and locked, and Monsieur Chenier and our people started through the crowd to come back here. Unfortunately, the rabble pressed forward and refused to let them through. Monsieur Debarmy, the chancellor, tried to carve a passage with his sword."

"He what?"

"I'm telling you, the people refused to let them through. Somebody lost his head, some minor official. He got in the chancellor's way. It appeared to Monsieur Chenier that he was attacking the chancellor."

"Was he?"

"What a question! Who knows? At any rate, Monsieur Chenier discharged one of his pistols. The bullet accidentally hit a bystander. How the six of them got out of there alive is a miracle!"

"It's lucky they were so well armed," commented Deirdre dryly.

"They're upstairs now with some British gentlemen and French nationals, people come here for sanctuary. It's really more a council of war than a conference. That's what this will come to, war!"

"Nonsense."

"No nonsense, Miss Know-it-all. Listen to that crowd. The city's crawling with troublemakers. You've been out there; didn't you see?"

"It's only a handful stirring things up."

"Oh? It might interest you to know that that 'handful,' as you call them, have already set fire to the cathedral and the orphanage. At least a dozen nuns have been seized, stripped, mutilated and brutally murdered. Priests, foreigners, even Chinese converts have been caught and thrashed. If we get through this night alive, we'll be the luckiest people on earth!"

"It's really that bad?"

"It can't possibly get worse. And you want help to reach the coast? Little girl, we're *all* going to want help to reach the coast."

It was rapidly becoming a jumble to Deirdre. Monsieur Chenier, the distinguished, albeit headstrong, representative of the Third Republic had murdered a man on Chinese soil. And now the volcano had erupted.

"How long will he be in conference?"

"Who can say? Possibly until the building comes down around our ears. Luckily, we have managed to get word out to Singapore—that is, if the messenger reaches there. There are gunboats between Hong Kong and Swatow in the south."

"How long will it take for them to get here?"

"They say three days. If we can hold out till then, everything will come out all right. Prince Kung, Li Hung-chang and the rest of those ruffians up in Peking will get their comeuppance at the end of the French guns. Things will settle down quickly. The ringleaders will be severely dealt with, hanged and jailed. The imperial treasury will pay a fat indemnity for the murders at the convent and for damage to our property and that of the British. There'll be profuse apologies. Yes indeed, Old Buddha will be wearing red on her bilious yellow face for a long time to come, mark my words!"

Deirdre paid little attention to him. Her chances of getting to the coast and out of the country, even to nearby Korea, seemed to be fading by the hour. Her timing couldn't have been worse. The crowd continued rumbling outside; occasionally the muffled sound of glass shattering came from somewhere in the house, and darkness blotted out the gray line separating the closed portieres at the window.

She was hungry, achy from riding and tired, and all but overcome by the haunting specter of defeat. The fates seemed to have developed a fondness for treating her harshly. When would it all end? she wondered. Would it ever?

Footsteps sounded overhead, chairs scraping the floor, then a door opening and closing. The clerk stood up.

"They're coming down."

A number of solemn-looking men and women began filing past the open door, going into the large room across the foyer. One man, wearing a fiery red beard and a cotton suit that looked as if he had slept in it, walked by, glanced into the office, saw Deirdre, looked away, looked back and shook his head slowly in disbelief.

"You!" He came into the room, pointing at her. "You're—"

"Deirdre Dandridge."

"Of course. Uncanny resemblance, amazing! What on earth have you done to your hair?"

"Who . . . I don't understand. Have we met?"

Collier introduced himself. "You're wondering how I know you?" he inquired, smiling. "I know your mother."

Her heart leaped and she jumped to her feet.

Collier glanced at the clerk, who understood and withdrew, closing the door.

"You've seen her!"

He nodded. "She left here no more than six hours ago."

"With Daddy . . ."

"Uh, no, actually. I believe he's back in Singapore."

"Singapore? That doesn't make sense." She hesitated, waiting for an explanation.

He sighed wearily, shook his head, and his voice took on a sheepish tone. "Please sit down."

She complied.

Avoiding her eyes, he pretended to study the desk top.

"What is it?" she asked evenly.

"Forgive me, I'm not awfully clever at this sort of thing, obviously not clever enough to deceive you. I do tend to bumble."

"Something's happened to him!"

"There was trouble of some sort on board their ship shortly after they arrived in Singapore, so I was told. Your father was . . . was killed."

A great weight suddenly dropped down upon her, crushing her into herself, collapsing her.

"Dear God."

"I'm sorry."

Bowing her head, she began to cry softly. He brought out his handkerchief, giving it to her. She hid her face in it. "There, there . . ."

"You don't understand," she said quietly between sobs. "I haven't even seen him, not since I was a baby." Explaining, suddenly aware of the need to do so, seemed to help her get control of herself. "He had been sent to the penal colony in Tasmania. Mother left me behind in Batavia. The Franekers . . . There was terrible trouble, an uprising . . . Chinese pirates, slavers . . . He's dead—my daddy. No! He can't be! It's too awful!"

"Deirdre, listen to me: It was a bloody courageous thing you did escaping from Peking, riding all the way down here alone. That took spirit, backbone. You've been through hell."

"I don't understand."

"You've been through it; it's all behind you. Your courage got you through. Use that courage now, child. Draw on it, stiff upper lip, that's the girl." Gently he lifted her chin, taking the handkerchief from her and daubing her eyes. Then he restored it to her hand, closing her fingers over it. "There's still a few innings to go before match end. You've got to be strong; you've got to see it through, for her sake as well as yours."

She shook her head, sniffed, smiled weakly. "Mother left for Peking, you say?"

"Yes."

"You shouldn't have let her."

"There was no way I could stop her; a bloody regiment couldn't have."

"On horseback?"

"They had a wagon."

"What kind?"

He shrugged. "I never actually saw it. I believe a farm wagon of some sort, pulled by two mules."

"How many in her party?"

"I'm not altogether sure. I know there was a Frenchman, a mercenary of some sort, and some Chinese."

Deirdre rose slowly, her face suddenly ashen. "How many?"

"I told you, I'm not sure. Is it important?"

"I followed the Hun down all the way to Wu-ch'ing. I skirted the city and on the other side picked up the road. I'd been afraid to follow it till then. I saw a wagon, no mules, just the wagon itself broken down, bodies lying about. I didn't ride up close; I didn't see how many or what had actually happened. I was afraid. I circled wide and went on."

"Oh, my."

"Bandits!"

He nodded reluctantly, his eyes brimming sympathy. When he spoke, it was as if the effort inspired pain. He almost seemed to wince. He took her by the shoulders. "Sit, please. You'll be staying here. You'll be safe with us."

"She's dead, isn't she?"

"That's not so."

"It's true; you know it is. You think so; I see it in
your eyes."

"My dear child, whatever you see in my eyes is not
that. Let's be logical. You saw a wagon, yes, but
there are thousands, possibly millions like it. You didn't
see how many were lying on the ground. You certainly
didn't see her."

"I told you, I couldn't get close; I was afraid."

"Who wouldn't be? But even at a distance you
would have seen her, her dress, her hair as red as
ours . . ."

"I don't know."

"You didn't see her because she wasn't there!"

"She wasn't there because they took her away, the
bandits. They don't kill women, not until they're done
with them."

"My God, what a bloody pessimist you are!"

"I can't help what I feel."

"It wasn't her wagon; it couldn't be!"

She thought a moment, groping about for a straw
of optimism, finding one. "You're right about one
thing: There are scads and scads like it."

"Absolutely. Now, do kindly stop letting your emotions run away with your common sense. You're too
hard on yourself. Your mother is in Peking with a
friend of mine, one Simon Atkins. She's in no danger."

"Oh, but she is."

"Deirdre . . ."

"You took me for her at first glance. You did."

"You're a great deal younger."

"But you did think, if only for two seconds, that
I was she. Tung-chi will know she's my mother. And
once he gets his hands on her—"

"Tung-chi?"

She explained.

"My, my, that is a bit unsettling."

"It's like some stupid farce. She's coming up, I have
no way of knowing that, I come down . . . Oh, Mr.

Collier, you don't know that place; you can't imagine. It's a beautiful prison; that's the only way to describe it—lovely and ghastly at the same time."

"I've met your mother, young lady. She makes a bloody strong impression. I have every confidence, and so should you, that she'll be up to handling this Tung-chi—any and all Tung-chis. If he crosses wills with her, he'll wish he hadn't."

"You have no idea how ruthless he is. We've got to get her out of there, the quicker the better. The question is, how? What's the safest, surest way possible?"

This unexpected onset of determination, the question coldly voiced, brought him up short. "Well, now, I can't say I've the answer to that on the tip of my—"

"What about those soldiers outside? There must be a whole company in Tientsin."

"*They* are it, I'm afraid. And having pledged allegiance to Louis Napoleon, I doubt they're available for private forays. Perhaps something can be done through diplomatic channels."

"What?"

"Well . . ."

"Forget it. That would take a year and a day. It's beginning to look as though I'll have to go back up there myself."

"Oh, no!"

"You mentioned somebody called Atkins."

"I'm afraid this upheaval will more or less neutralize him." His glance, wandering about uneasily, met her eyes. She was almost glaring at him, silently accusing him of ineffectualness.

"I'm curious: How did my mother come to contact you?"

He told her about Wo Sin and the benefits from mutual cooperation between them over the years. "He's a positive genius at expediting things, snipping red tape."

"I know about Wo Sin. How do you communicate with him?"

"Messenger. It generally takes a week to ten days to get a question down and an answer or action on whatever it is back up here."

"That's much too long. In ten days she could be dead." She slumped dejectedly. "What are we going to do? What?"

"First off feed you, then see that you get a hot tub and some clean clothes. Then we'll put our heads together and come up with something workable."

"We'd better, and fast!"

VII

The chief was adamant. Lisa might as well have argued with the wind. Even using a magnifying glass, as she suggested, he persisted in identifying the solitary glum face in the photograph as hers. A positively ancient carriage, resplendent with well-worn peach-colored velvet upholstery, shiny brassware and glass bud vases fastened to the corners of the mud guard, was brought up to the front door. Giving up the game as useless, Lisa tied back her temper and politely requested pen, paper and an envelope. Lieutenant Sung obliged her, and under the curious stares of both officers, she scribbled a note to Travis Collier in Tientsin, detailing what had happened and apprising him that she would be in Peking until he heard further from her. The lieutenant promised that the letter would be delivered. She then left Wu-Ch'ing with her driver and two mounted escorts.

The trip was uneventful, even boring, but it did afford her opportunity to consider all the aspects of her situation, what she would have to do, what she would have to avoid doing. She missed Ross so enormously, his shoulder to lean on, his objectivity, always so valuable in counterbalancing her impulsiveness, his warm and wonderful presence, her dependable bulwark against the ogres loneliness and irresolution.

But Ross was not with her, would never be with her again, and whatever had to be done, she alone would have to do it—alone. She was the sole survivor in a rescue mission that had departed New Orleans with such boundless, blind expectations.

She had all but exhausted herself completely protesting to the chief of police and Lieutenant Sung. It was evident that both men's unwillingness to accept her explanation had nothing whatsoever to do with comparison of the two faces. Anyone three-quarters blind could see that they were mother and daughter. There were, she mused bitterly, none so blind as those who can see only their duty. Certainly the moment this Tung-chi laid eyes on her, he would see that she wasn't Deirdre, only the next-best choice and a most convenient hostage to ensure Deirdre's return. Not the biggest feather in the collective caps of the Wu-Ch'ing police, but a feather nonetheless.

As if she'd permit him to hold her hostage! As if she could do anything about it. At the moment, she was in no position to help herself, let alone Deirdre.

Less than four hours after leaving Wu-Ch'ing, she found herself in a small, dimly-lit room in the Palace of the Young Princes. Passing through gate after gate and arriving in the Forbidden City, her escort had turned her over to two soldiers, who had marched her into the room and were now stationed outside the locked door. The room was on the second floor. One of the guards had opened the balcony windows, and the delicate scent of the white jasmine growing in abundance below sweetened the odor of burnt wood carried on the breeze gliding over the east wall and gently billowing the curtains. Across the foot of the bed lay a transparent robe of silk designed with sequined outlines of thrushes perched on branches. Like the *cheongsam* worn by Wo Sin's pretty young Chinese companion, it buttoned up the side.

In spite of her reluctance to accommodate it, fear had settled in the pit of her stomach. Not fear of the Forbidden City or even of Tung-chi and his Board of Punishments. This fear was securely fastened to Lieutenant Sung's translation of his chief's disclosure that Deirdre had murdered two eunuchs. It was absurd, of course, nothing more than a spur-of-the-moment lie designed to lend priority to her capture and return and to minimize Tung-chi's loss of face.

But, at the moment, essentially, she herself was Deirdre and, if not answerable to the charges, certainly in no overly enviable position. She was continuing to weigh her situation when a key sounded and the door opened. She had been standing looking out over the balcony railing, her back to the door, and did not turn around immediately.

"Well, well . . ."

At his voice, she turned her head. His third "well" was delivered with a half-croaked ring of hollowness. Gaping at her, his face lowered itself feature by feature. Under different circumstances, she would have laughed out loud, but there was nothing amusing about the moment. She was at last face to face with her enemy.

"You're not—"

"I am her mother."

"You most certainly are," he hissed. "Incredible. Fascinating. You could be twins!"

"Where is she?"

"Ah, would that I knew. The authorities have been searching high and low. It puzzles me. Running off like this is so unlike her."

"Who wouldn't run off, charged with a double murder?" she said dryly.

He ignored this riposte, assuming an air of bewildered resentment. "She was happy, content. She wanted for nothing. All of a sudden, this gory spectacle and off she flies. I simply don't understand."

"I do. Obviously you mistreated her."

"Never! Not in a thousand years!" he exclaimed in a shocked tone. "What do you take me for? A barbarian? A savage?" He paused and smiled, sitting down on the edge of the bed. "I must ask you: Don't you think my English superb? I speak five languages fluently. I pride myself on my scholarship."

"We were talking about her!"

"She was married to my son, you know."

"Forced into it against her will, dragged kicking to the altar."

"Not at all. They loved each other. She adored poor Heng-chi. He died of a heart attack. Such a tragedy. He was the light of my life, that boy—handsome, brilliant, ambitious. Prince Pao-chu's closest friend. To be cut down in the prime of life . . . She was desolate, poor child, suddenly alone, not knowing where to turn. I felt so sorry for her. I did what any man in my position would have done: took her under my protection. I gave her a lovely home, servants—"

"How charitable."

"I denied her absolutely nothing."

Striding to the bed, she snatched up the transparent robe, holding it before him. "Not even this! You pig! You filthy animal! Dissipating your lust on a helpless child!" She flung the robe at him; it tumbled to his lap. "We have a term for your sort in America." Leaning over, she spit the words in his face: "We call you a dirty old man!"

Clenching his jaw and his fists, he rose slowly from the bed, the robe falling to the floor. "You're not in America; you're in China. In this country, women do not talk to men in such a manner. Women do not insult their betters. They do not dare."

"A pig, that's what you are! Don't tell me you didn't abuse her! Why so eager to get her back?"

"You're wrong, completely."

"She hasn't killed anybody and you know it!"

"What I know is that she brutally killed two eunuchs. Your dear daughter, madam, is a cold-blooded murderess."

"You're a liar!"

He sucked his breath in sharply. "For those three words alone, I could have you severely punished. I could make you wish you had never set foot in China!"

"You don't frighten me. Deirdre, perhaps; she's only sixteen, uninitiated when it comes to your sort, a defenseless innocent."

"Not so innocent anymore." He leered at her.

She slapped his face. The sound of contact was like a heavy belt striking metal. He drew back, his eyes wide in amazement, his hand starting toward his reddening cheek. Then he caught himself. The tone of snobbish vanity vanished, replaced by one of mounting anger.

"She'll try to get out of the country, but she'll be stopped. Copies of her picture are being distributed far and wide. We shall bring her back, depend upon it. And while we wait for word, you, madam, will be my guest."

"No thank you. I'm leaving. If you know what's good for you, you won't lift a finger to stop me."

"You're not going anywhere, not until she comes through that door."

"You're a bastard, do you know that? Does your 'superb' English vocabulary include the definition of 'bastard'?"

"Madam . . ."

"You'll pay for this with your skin, I promise you. I'll make you the laughingstock of the court. You'll remember the name Dandridge as long as you live!"

He moved to the balcony, looking out upon the night. "We had quite a fire here the other night, almost the entire northern third of the city. You probably saw the rebuilding going on when they brought you in. Our apartment was in a building that was one of those destroyed. The maids got out safely before the fire reached there. I myself had business outside the city that night. By the time I got back here, the building was leveled."

He turned to her. "I was crushed. I thought at first

she'd been burned to death, but we found only the
bodies of the two eunuchs in the rubble, charred almost beyond recognition."

"Killed in the fire."

"I'm sure that's what she wanted us to think. But
we examined both thoroughly. One had been stabbed
in the stomach; the other's skull was fractured. What
seems to tie the thing up in a neat package is the fact
that she was the only one here. Only she could have
done it. Oh, I know what you're thinking: self-defense." He shook his head. "You're forgetting, your
sex needs no defense against a poor eunuch." His
voice had softened perceptibly. Angling his head, he
studied her. "I'm sure you've heard it a thousand times,
but I can't resist telling you that you're an exception-
ally beautiful woman. I do wish you weren't so hostile
toward me. You really are misjudging me. I'm no
monster. I'm a gentle man. I did her no harm. She
was becoming very, very fond of me."

"Stop it! Just shut your filthy mouth and go away.
Leave me alone."

"Is that what you really want? Think about it.
I'm not the vindictive sort; your insults go in one ear
and out the other. Be reasonable. Meet me halfway.
We could strike a bargain, you and I. Are we not
both adults, mature, worldly? This is a serious matter
—murder always is—but I could straighten things out
easily. I have tremendous influence at court. My
brother is the famous Prince Kung, the most powerful
man in the country. One word from me and the entire
matter would be swept out with the ashes. When
Deirdre is returned—"

"Don't say it!"

"I beg your—"

"Her name. I don't want to hear it from your lips.
You make it an obscenity. *You're* an obscenity, a
disgusting, dirty old man, a pompous, loud-mouthed,
stupid, bungling glorified clerk, the sort that's helping

to keep this beloved country of yours five hundred years behind the rest of the world. You're ridiculous, pathetic. Get out of my sight. Out!"

He seemed to freeze in place. When he spoke, his lips barely moved. He was unaccustomed to being addressed in such a tone, and the chauvinist in him made it difficult for him to understand, let alone accept. He had never met a woman like her.

"I will leave," he said quietly, "but not because you wish me to. I go to pay my respects at the grave of my son. I shall return by midnight, at which time you will have readied yourself to receive me." He toed the robe on the floor. "I shall seduce you. I shall revel in your nakedness, your helplessness. If you are so foolish as to resist, I shall rape you. When you plead for mercy, I shall be deaf. Please, dear lady, please resist me."

He left, locking the door. She sank into the chair, her face in her hands. Tears did not come. She was too exhausted, too debilitated by defeat.

VIII

She had no idea how long she had been sitting unable to stir, with neither the desire nor the will to do so. Times beyond number back over the years she had arrayed her resources against formidable opposition. She had won, she had lost, but never had she given up. To throw down one's sword was nothing less than the act of a traitor, to one's courage, one's self-respect. Just as to accompany Death when he approached, beckoning, calling one to rise, without protest, with no reluctance, was the way of the coward.

But, examining her plight in the cold light of reason, stripped of her resources, imprisoned within walls within walls, she wondered what was left but to surrender? With Deirdre gone God in heaven only knew where—to freedom, to new captivity—what could she herself do now? Where could she turn? To whom?

If only Deirdre had known she was coming, if only they had had a prearranged rendezvous point far away from this loathsome place . . .

If only Wo Sin were within reach. He had the strength, the patience, the wherewithal to help. She herself had nothing left. Heart, mind and spirit, she was empty—and tired, aching weary, sick to death of the strain and suffering, the endless worry, the thorny path, calamity and adversity.

When she was seven or eight, living in Mansfield, a cousin had drowned. Her father had told her mother about it at the kitchen table, and she had overheard their conversation. He had seen it happen, reaching the pond too late to help. She could remember his mystified tone of voice describing it. The boy's strength had given out; he had stopped shouting for help, stopped struggling and turned over in the water, his eyes looking up at the sun directly overhead. And he was smiling "serenely," her father had said. This he didn't understand; nor had she at the time. She did now. The boy had fought to survive; he had exhausted his strength but, instead of going down fighting in the accepted fashion, had given up, and in so doing, in making his pact with fate, in capitulation to the inevitable, he had found peace.

The door burst open, so frightening her that she all but leaped out of the chair. Standing there was a man as tall and powerful-looking as the Blue Wolf. He was dressed in a black cotton jacket and trousers; his jacket buttons were undone, his sweating, hairless chest visible.

"Mrs. Dandridge!"

"I—"

"No time talk, go fast!"

He barged in. She backed away, her heart pounding. Behind him two others appeared, each carrying one of the guards posted outside the door. Both guards were unconscious. The men began binding and gagging them.

"Who are you?" she asked.

"Eng-chow, at your service." He grinned and bowed, snapping his fingers at one of his companions. The man opened a canvas sack slung over his shoulder and brought out a cloth bag with a drawcord top.

"You please to get in."

"But—"

"Hurry fast!"

Picking her up impatiently, he dropped her into the bag held open by the other man. "We friends of Wo Sin. We get you out of here."

"To Tientsin?"

"Tientsin. Sh, no make sound, even whisper. Trust us."

The bag was pulled up over her head, the cords drawn, and up onto his shoulder she went.

IX

The bag was stifling, so hot she feared she would faint, if she didn't suffocate first. Her breath dispersed against the cloth and came burning back in her face, and sweat burst from her forehead, racing down it, stinging her eyes with salt.

"I can't breathe," she whispered. "Loosen the top, please."

"No."

"A little?"

"Soon, when we're through the gates."

"How long?"

"Half an hour."

"I'll suffocate."

"When we get out of Chinese City, we open."

Twisting her neck awkwardly, she brought her mouth up to the small opening at the top of the bag, breathing in little pants. He carried her along effortlessly, his shoulder digging into her stomach, whatever dregs of dignity she had left rapidly draining away. She might as well have been a sack of dirty laundry. Still, to get away from that place, from Tungchi, from the walls and more walls, she would have cheerfully crawled on all fours.

Wo Sin. He reached everywhere, thank the gods. Beyond Travis Collier. No man of action he. Small wonder Wo Sin kept alternatives in reserve. Eng-chow was a eunuch, as were his friends—shadows for eyebrows, no facial hair, no hair on his chest showing between the sides of his open jacket. His voice reminded her of the crows and grackles at dawn in the hills surrounding Blackwood. How could such a manly sort as Wo Sin have any connection with palace eunuchs? Why ask? She should be grateful, rather than curious, that he did.

Dumped into an open cart, the gentle, restless clopping of hooves in place becoming audible, the telltale creaking of old wood . . . With an effort of strength that surprised her, she was able to wriggle and squirm and get both hands up to the hole to stretch it larger. It was small improvement. All she could see was blackness punctured by a scattered strewing of stars.

"What's in these bags?" she whispered hoarsely.

"Rotten millet."

"It smells."

"Rotten millet smells."

The three eunuchs climbed up; she heard the reins snap, and the cart lurched forward. It was to be a ride only slightly less uncomfortable than Eng-chow's shoulder; the sacks beneath her were as hard as concrete. One hand to her face, she pinched her nose against the musty stench. Closing her eyes, she tried to doze away the miles to and through the last gate into the suburbs, but Eng-chow's chatting with the guards at every gate and the city noises rendered sleep impossible.

After what seemed aeons, she saw his smiling face framed by the circle of the bag opening. He reached down and loosened the knot, pulling the top wide.

He chuckled. "Not bad, yes?"

"No complaints. It got me away from that place. I'm very grateful."

She glanced about, getting her bearings. Both sides of the road were lined with white pines, many reaching so high into the darkness they seemed to be touching the stars. The cart was moving along at a good pace now, although the road appeared to worsen the farther they distanced Peking. Through the trees she could see the city on the right, its walls blackened by night, lending it the forbidding aspect of an immense fortress of evil.

Slipping free of the bag, she sat on the topmost millet bag, elbows on knees, her chin in her hands. "I'm famished," she murmured.

"Hot food wait at bridge," said Eng-chow. "We all eat."

"Good. Tell me, how do you come to know Wo Sin when he's way down in Singapore?"

"Rebellion." The word seemed anathema to him, his grin giving way to a melancholy frown. "Wo Sin send arms help take Nanking. Two days' siege. Nanking Heavenly Capital Heavenly King Hung Hsiu-ch'uan."

"King?"

"Our king."

"That was a long time ago, wasn't it?"

"Fourteen years."

"You fought with the rebels?"

He nodded, recognizing the doubt in her eyes. "You think eunuch afraid shoot gun?"

"You misunderstand. I'm not questioning your courage, not tonight. I just don't understand. You fought against the government and now you serve the empresses."

"Serve Old Buddha, yes." He said something to the others and they laughed.

She studied his smirk, the devil in his eye. "You intend to assassinate her?"

"Wo Sin great man, honorable, love China, weep for China's . . ." He hesitated, unable to find the right word.

"Plight?"

"What is 'plight'?"

"A sorrowful state, misfortune."

"Plight, yes. If wise and just ruler sit on imperial throne, China no more sorrow, people not starve, provinces not break into pieces like stale bread."

Her interest seemed to warm him to his subject. He impressed her as somewhat of a visionary, a man heavily laden with hopes and ideals, those of his long-dead hero, the Heavenly King of Nanking. In Eng-chow's dark eyes glowed the fire of fanaticism, just enough to keep alive and active his enthusiasm for the aims of a cause long lost. It was the old story of social levels in conflict, a venal, heartless hierarchy of Tung-chis surrounding ignorant leadership resolutely oblivious to the needs of the suffering masses. And now the presence of foreigners in China was molding itself into a tool in Tz'u Hsi's hands, a device to divert the people's attention from their poverty and affliction.

Eng-chow snapped in Chinese to the man beside him just as the left front wheel found a ditch-deep rut, dropping Lisa off her sack and thumping against the side of the cart. Eng-chow unfolded the worn piece of paper the man gave him and showed it to her. It was a crude drawing of what appeared to be nuns filling a steaming pot with the bloody limbs and torsos of Chinese babies.

"I read you: 'The missionaries steal the heart, eyes and marrow of the dead infants to make medicines. Whoever drinks a glass of tea given by a foreign devil priest dies instantly, his brains bursting out of his skull. Infants are in great demand. Their throats are slit, their bodies torn apart and boiled to make soap. Their intestines are used to change pewter into silver and to make evil concoctions the foreign devil priests and nuns use as remedies.' Stupid nonsense, crazier and crazier, but the peasants believe it."

He insisted heatedly that Chinese converts, including two of his own cousins, were being murdered by the hundreds. The situation was worsening daily. "You are wise to leave China now, as quickly as you can."

"As quickly as I find my daughter or learn for certain that she's already left."

They arrived at the Marco Polo Bridge, spanning the banks of the Hun, its marble eminence the gathering point for dozens of small vessels, mostly sampans, rafts and barges. The place glowed with lanterns and torches, and the babbling that filled the air recalled the docks in Singapore and Pei-t'ang. Every craft was piled with the produce of the area: broad-tailed sheep, rabbits nibbling at greens, scrawny chickens crammed in crates, fat pigeons in wicker hampers, yellow-billed white geese, pigs, ducks. And vegetables—beetroot, celery, beans, lettuce, cabbage, bushels of hulled rice, corn and pyramids of eggs.

Eng-chow helped her down, and they approached a long, heavily loaded raft crewed by four men. Two others dressed like Eng-chow and his companions were placing a coffin aboard, setting it down at right angles to the rudder pole.

Braziers burned, and the cooking odors filling the air set her mouth to watering. Eng-chow removed the lid of a cauldron, releasing a great cloud of steam. Poking a pointed stick into the cauldron, he impaled two pieces of meat, offering her one and downing the other himself. It was hot but very tasty and chewable, and she swallowed it greedily.

"Delicious. What is it?"

"Steamed duck tongue."

She swallowed a second time, her mind assaulting her stomach with the prejudices of a lifetime against brains and testes and tongues and other bizarre delicacies.

"Duck—"

"Old Buddha eats many every day. You like soup?"

"What kind?" she asked warily.

"Chicken, good."

"Chicken meat or—"

"White meat."

"Fine, very good. Yes, I'll have some, thank you."

"And rice?"

"Yes."

"More steamed duck tongue?"

"No thank you."

As they talked, one of the other eunuchs got into a heated discussion with the owner of the raft. Eng-chow excused himself and joined the argument. The soup and rice were marvelous. She gorged herself shamefully. Within the past few minutes it had clouded over, the moon and stars blotted out behind a thick coverlet of blackness tinged with purple. Thunder rumbled in the east, the restless storm monster stirring, preparing to prowl the heavens. In the distance, back the way they had come, the lights of the cities rose over the walls, blending in a roseate glow. Almost two hours had passed since Eng-chow had broken into the room. By now Tung-chi would have returned to find her missing.

Eng-chow called to her, beckoning her aboard.

"Is something wrong?" she asked.

"No. Raftsman afraid coffin make evil magic."

"There's a body in it, isn't there?"

Winking, he took her by the arm, moving down the edge of the raft hawsered snugly to the bank. The top of the coffin was loose. Kneeling, he lifted it easily.

Tung-chi.

She gasped. "He's dead!"

"Look close."

"I'd really rather not."

"He sleep. Morphine." Eng-chow pinched his own neck lightly and laughed.

"What is he do— Why is he here?"

"Hostage."

Of course! What better hostage than the man who would follow them, with soldiers, with the police. Eng-chow tilted his head toward the two eunuchs already on board when they had driven up.

"Friends find him at son's grave."

"You think of everything."

"He wake up soon, maybe before Tou-chang-chuang. Will be very happy to see you again." He roared laughter, frightening the geese on the barge behind them, setting them to flapping noisily.

Weapons were broken out, old muskets—relics, she guessed, from the Taiping Rebellion. Sight of them brought to mind the Spencer rifles seized by the Blue Wolf's men in the massacre. The appearance of the rifles, the substance of the hate pamphlet, Tung-chi drugged and lying in the coffin and the threatening storm created a restless feeling in Lisa's mind, concern that the worst was yet to come. What lay ahead of them? she thought. What devils would crop up between here and Tientsin?

"You expect trouble?" she asked.

In his halting English, Eng-chow assured her that he expected nothing but preferred to be prepared against everything. The anchor lines were loosed, the raftsmen's poles driven to the muddy bottom of the river, the tops pushed down to their knees and the raft slipped soundlessly out into midstream, easing between a smaller raft and what looked to Lisa to be a junk stripped of its masts and sails.

Lightning crooked-lined the sky, bluing the landscape eerily. The thunder echoed approval. It was coming regularly now, rumbling belligerently, the swollen clouds overhead lowering. The rain began, gently pocking the surface of the water, tapping against the canvas-covered boxes and crates securely lashed in place and the unprotected coffin. Eng-chow found a woolen blanket, and she draped it over her head, but it was much too warm and she put it aside.

The rain needled the darkness at an angle, pelting

her cheeks. It was cool, even refreshing. The raft slid silently along, the Marco Polo Bridge and the craft swarming about it dropping farther and farther back until the lanterns merged into a single light that disappeared altogether as they rounded a bend. On and on they traveled, the poles puncturing the water with a soft, roiling sound. A stone bridge approached them, arching itself like a cat.

The current was carrying them now. The poles, their ends caked with thick black mud, lay at rest along the sides of the raft. Eng-chow moved to the rudder for another look at the hostage.

Tung-chi slept on, his face serene, the ends of his mouth turned slightly down as if, even in dreaming, his ego was at work feeding his incredible vanity.

Eng-chow contemplated him. "His sort will be death of China."

"Do you intend to kill him?" she asked.

"It would be like killing locust. One dead, two others take its place."

His tone lacked conviction. Tung-chi would be dead, she decided, within moments of their landing and her departure.

Time dragged on and on. The rain was falling harder now, drenching her uncovered hair and clothing, chilling her, causing her to shiver slightly. Ahead, lights bobbed in the darkness. One of the other eunuchs, sitting well forward, turned and called to Eng-chow.

"What is it?" asked Lisa.

"Trouble. Get down flat on stomach"—he indicated —"by coffin." He draped the blanket she had put aside over the coffin.

The owner of the raft was talking excitedly. He was frightened and upset with Eng-chow and his friends. The two men shouted at each other. The owner kept pointing at the coffin, pantomiming throwing it overboard. Eng-chow refused. By now, men in the drab brown uniforms of the imperial army could be clearly seen less than 50 yards ahead.

"Down!" snapped Eng-chow.

Lisa got down, pressing her cheek flat against the raft, biting her lower lip, her heart drumming her ribs. The coffin blocked her view of the soldiers; she inched forward. They were waving excitedly and shouting.

"They want to board us," hissed Eng-chow.

Rifle shots in quick succession sounded, and the raft owner yelled. The rudder man responded, steering toward the bank. The soldiers waded out and began climbing aboard. The raft, already overloaded, its waterline dangerously low, was unable to take the added weight. One corner dipped under, water rushing up, sloshing against the coffin, retreating, pulling the blanket loose. Lisa was on her feet now, hanging onto a crate rope to keep from being washed overboard. Two soldiers clumped by, ignoring her, coming up short at sight of the exposed coffin. Dropping on their backsides, they set their heels against it and pushed it overboard with a loud splash. Eng-chow yelled something, and the officer in charge turned on him angrily. The raft's owner, meanwhile, had taken to screaming at the top of his lungs. At least 20 men had climbed on; the raft was heaving dangerously, threatening to sink, its cargo grinding ominously against the deck, sliding this way and that under its fastenings.

The coffin had hit the water at an angle. The top floated free as the head end filled, pulling Tung-chi down sharply. The two soldiers who had kicked him off laughed and pointed. Aiming their rifles at him, they fired. She gasped. Both bullets hit him full in the face, blood gushing forth. As she stared, his body separated itself from the coffin; it turned over, immersing his face, bloody bubbles issuing from his mouth. Eng-chow had rushed back to her just as the two soldiers who had fired turned to her. At the same time, the argument among the raft owner, his men, the other eunuchs and the invaders was waxing furious. The forward end of the raft had been pole-braked and was within a few feet of the left bank.

Snatching Lisa up in his arms, Eng-chow jumped into the shallow water. Shouts followed them. Rifles cracked, two bullets whining over their heads. Reaching the bank, throwing her into a tangled thicket, Eng-chow dove in head first after her. They crabbed about, branches slapping them, and flattened against the ground. Looking back, they saw a rope snap mid-raft and a large crate slide overboard, dipping the craft toward the opposite bank, one of the crew and a soldier falling backward into the water. Pandemonium reigned; a man jumped off, followed by two of the boarders.

"Can we get out of here?" asked Lisa.

"Wait. Let it get a little worse. Whole thing may go down. We are lucky."

" 'Lucky'!"

He nodded. "They pleased we get off, not shoot at us, only over heads."

"How far to Tientsin?"

"Thirty mile, maybe more." He studied the sky. "No stars to follow. We follow Hun to Pei just ahead." He pushed the tips of two fingers together, pantomiming the rivers joining.

The rain was letting up now, but the storm had mired the road, so they had no choice but to avoid it, striking out overland, arriving at last at an impressive-looking marble bridge spanning the Hun. It was at this point that it veered sharply eastward to join the Pei. According to Eng-chow, the latter river ran straight through Tientsin to the gulf beyond. Well out of sight of the raft by now, they saw traffic on both rivers, but there was none on the road, the inclement weather keeping everyone indoors except those able to turn a profit and roving soldiers.

"What about your friends?" asked Lisa.

"They go back to Forbidden City."

"And you?"

"Also, but not till you are in safe hands. Can you make it? I carry you."

"I can walk, thank you."

"Too bad you lose bag."

She patted her handbag. "This is the important one, my letters of credit—though I can imagine what this dress and these poor shoes are going to look like by the time we get there."

"Travis Collier get you new shoes."

Mention of his name altered her expression just enough to betray how she felt about him. "You're a good deal more dependable than Mr. Collier."

"He help you find her."

"I sincerely hope so."

Crossing the bridge, they pressed on. The rain stopped, the clouds rolled away, the stars reappeared and the moon, round and wan-looking, as though the storm had washed away its glow. It was that interval of inertia halfway between midnight and dawn, when the world was in its deepest sleep, the loneliest, most depressing hour of the 24.

A weariness that transcended physical exhaustion had taken possession of her, a soul-draining fatigue that no amount of rest could dispel—only sight of Deirdre. And once reunited the two of them would flee China. She hated this land, its people with their hostile stares, their strange ways, the danger ever lurking, the tension it strung and knotted that made it impossible to relax, and the suddenness with which Death struck—Paul and the others in the wagon; their killers, the bandits; Tung-chi, who had journeyed from sleep to death without even opening his eyes. The pattern unfolding seemed so predictably bloody, to hope and pray that Deirdre had survived seemed almost absurdly presumptuous.

Bless Eng-chow, she thought—his cheerfulness, his unabating optimism, his protecting presence. He seemed to sense that she was becoming increasingly depressed and made her talk, about anything, to keep her mind off the black side of things. Mostly *he* talked about Travis Collier, crediting that red-haired and pertinaciously proper English gentleman with traits and attributes she herself had failed to recognize when meeting and talking with him.

On and on they hiked, stopping every half-hour to rest. She had taken to removing her shoes and massaging her feet, but now they were beginning to swell, and he cautioned her that getting her shoes back on could be painful, perhaps even impossible.

The stars dimmed and the sky began to gray, a sepulchral shade, suitable lighting to usher in the sun for the last day on earth, she mused gloomily. The sun rose, a citrine-yellow ball reflected in the distant waters of P'au-chuang Lake in the east. Gradually the two suns separated, twin yolks in an egg, the lower one drowning itself in the water.

Eng-chow pointed directly ahead. A faint pink glow softened the underside of the now-canescent-looking sky, and coming over a rise, they could see the north wall of the city stretching across the barren landscape. In its center, a small black shadow identified the north gate. People were streaming out of it, filling the causeway. They carried their belongings in little carts and wagons, in their arms, on their backs, on their heads.

"What's happened, do you suppose?" she asked.

"Who knows?" Stopping short, he cocked an ear and listened. "No shooting."

"I wish *we* had a gun."

He produced a kris from inside his belt, a beam of

sunlight bouncing off its wavy length. "This not so loud."

"Let's hope you don't have to use it."

"We rest one last time or go on?"

"Go on." She strode forward, heading for the approach to the causeway.

X

The area around the intersection of Nan-ma Lu and Tung-ma Lu streets appeared to have been the vandals' favorite target. It was still early, not yet six o'clock, and there was little traffic in the streets and no activity in the shops and marketplaces spared by the roving bands of youthful patriots. Under the sagging corner of the first floor of the British Board of Trade stood a familiar-looking red-bearded man in shorts and shirt sleeves. Conspicuous at his waist was a cartridge belt and pistol. Hammer in hand, he was fastening a crudely lettered sign to one of the few beams remaining upright:

> BRITISH BOARD OF TRADE
> TEMPORARILY LOCATED AT
> FRENCH CONSULATE, CHUNG-
> SHAN LU ROAD

"Mr. Collier!"

His hammer stopped in midstroke. "As I live and breathe!"

Hurried introductions were followed by the most beautiful words Lisa had heard in a year:

"She's at the consulate, sleeping. They've converted practically the entire upper floor into dormitories, but she's got her own private room."

"She's all right?"

"Never better."

Throwing her arms around Collier's neck, she kissed him loudly. "God bless you!"

"Don't bless me; *she's* the bloody miraculist. She

got here under her own power. She's spunky as they come, that girl!" Turning back to his sign, he gave the nail one last rap, flattening it in place. Sticking his hammer into his back pocket, he took her by the arm. "Let's go wake her up."

"I'm very happy for you, Mrs. Dandridge," said Eng-chow. "You have no further need of me, so I say good-by."

"Good-by, Eng-chow, and thank you—for everything. You saved my life."

"No." He lowered his head self-consciously.

"You did!" Seizing him by the arms, she raised herself on tiptoe and kissed him. He mumbled his good-by, waved and walked away.

"You look ready to drop," said Collier. "We'll take a rickshaw. The quicker you get out of those damp things, the less chance you'll catch bloody pneumonia."

"I'm all for a rickshaw, anything but a raft."

Eng-chow paused at the end of the street, turned and waved. She waved back and blew a kiss.

"Good luck!" she called.

Collier engaged a passing rickshaw and helped her up onto the worn leather seat, giving the driver directions. As they rode along, she pumped him with questions about Deirdre. Satisfying herself that her daughter had suffered no enduring ill effects from her ordeal, Lisa then filled Collier in on everything that had happened since they had last seen each other. She praised Eng-chow lavishly for his help.

"If he and his friends hadn't shown up, Lord knows where I'd be now."

"He's made of stern stuff," commented Collier. "He risked a great deal to help you, more than you know."

"What does that mean?"

"He's a eunuch. He's felt the birch wand and he'll feel it again for this, if not a lot worse."

"Birch wand?"

"The empresses' equivalent of the schoolmaster's

rod. Traditionally, they carry a bunch of birch wands in a satin bag of imperial yellow. The bag, you see, lends royal sanction to the beatings they administer."

If, he went on to say, a eunuch offended imperial propriety in even the most trivial respect, he could expect to be beaten on the spot. If he tried to escape the Forbidden City, he was beaten once. After his scabs had begun to form, he was beaten a second time. A second attempt to escape earned him the *cangue*.*

"A third time and he gets banished to Muken, up in Manchuria. They don't make prisons quite as dreary and foul as Muken. Oh, yes, one other thing: If a eunuch is caught stealing, he is decapitated on the spot."

"What do you think they'll do to him?"

"A double beating surely. Who knows what else?"

"How awful. You're making me feel guilty as sin."

"You shouldn't; he volunteered."

"He plans to assassinate Tz'u Hsi."

"He and two hundred others."

"I don't know about the two hundred others, but I wouldn't put it past him. He's a very determined sort."

"Not nearly as determined as a certain red-haired lady I met at my office the other day. The office . . ." He groaned. "What a bloody shambles."

"What started all this?"

He related the events of the preceding two days as they neared the consulate. The unrest, having reached its boiling point the previous afternoon and evening, had dissipated overnight, but people worrying over the possibility of future disturbances were leaving town and, according to Collier, would doubtless continue to stream out.

"Until the French leave and take their soldiers with them."

* A wooden collar that shackled the hands to the neck; the period of punishment was usually 60 days.

"And the British?"

"We're in the minority here. Tientsin is a French city."

"Oh? I was under the impression it was Chinese."

"Touché."

They turned a corner into Chung-shan Lu Road and came within sight of the consulate. Every window in view was broken. Two soldiers sat on the stone steps at the front door, playing cards. Outside the fence, early risers passed by in both directions without so much as a glance at them, although two small children clung to the fence, gaping.

Within minutes Lisa and Collier were admitted by the receptionist-clerk and were hurrying up the stairs to Deirdre's room. It was situated at the far end of a long, narrow hallway. The sun, having brightened considerably, beamed through a broken window at the far end, flooding the runner. Lisa's heart beat wildly. She was perspiring and suddenly trembling. They reached the door and Collier knocked and waited; but Lisa's patience gave way, and grabbing the handle, she swung open the door.

The room was tiny, little larger than a walk-in closet. A small hexagonal window high up in the rear wall admitted light. It appeared to be the only window in the entire building intact. There was no nightstand, no lamp. The bed was little more than a pallet. Deirdre lay sleeping, partially covered by a sheet, her arms flung carelessly across it, a tranquil expression on her face, as if she were enjoying a pleasant dream.

"Her hair!"

Collier began to explain why she had cut it, but Lisa rushed into the room ahead of him, dropping down at the side of the bed, framing Deirdre's face with her hands, then gently brushing her hair from her forehead. Bending, she kissed her lightly. The girl stirred, moving her legs and turning on her right cheek.

"My poor darling," whispered Lisa. "My poor, dear baby . . ."

Deirdre's eyelids flickered. She opened her eyes without seeing, closing and opening them again. "Mother . . ."

"Deirdre! Darling!"

They threw their arms around each other, hugging tightly, tears welling in their eyes, and began sobbing joyously, continuing to clutch each other. Standing in the doorway, Collier turned his glance from them, backing into the hallway.

"Deirdre, Deirdre, Deirdre . . ."

Lisa's voice weakened abruptly, reducing itself to a whisper. She gasped, her arms fell from their hold, and she fainted, falling across the bed.

"Mother!"

XI

Deirdre sat in the large front room off the foyer opposite the reception office. The room was shabbily furnished for so prestigious a building as a consulate, she decided, drearily furnished with a half-dozen ancient taboret chairs badly in need of polishing, a book-rack-topped desk evidently in service as a table, a hideous brass-bottomed umbrella stand and a moquette rug worn as thin as tissue paper.

She waited, nervously picking at the rickrack on the epaulet collar of the dress given her by Chancellor Débarmy's wife. It fit tightly and was years out of style, but it was the first thing she'd worn in a year that wasn't Chinese. A man walked by, glancing in inquisitively and going out the front door. Minutes passed like hours; she could hear the ticking of the clock in the other room. Then came footsteps descending the stairs. It was Travis Collier. She shot to her feet.

"He's examining her."

"May I go up?"

"Best wait till he comes down."

"It's serious, isn't it?"

"I don't know."

"She looks awful. I've never seen her so thin and peaked-looking. Those black circles under her eyes are scary." She paused, going to the window, looking out upon the fence and the street beyond. "Is the doctor any good? Is he the best we can get?"

"He has an excellent reputation. He brought our chief clerk, Pennington Joyce, round last winter in

403

remarkable fashion. Old Pen was down with pleurisy, and Martoche cured him completely. He's old school, opinionated and set in his ways, but he seems to know what he's doing."

"She's got pneumonia; I know she has. Her clothes were sopping."

"I don't know. I'd imagine pneumonia's the last thing anyone would get in this heat. I don't think she's ill, just worn out."

"I wish he'd come down."

"He will."

They waited in silence, her patience crumbling. She felt like screaming. Why didn't he come down? The clock in the other room struck eight. People came and went. The consul looked in and bade them good morning, then hurried into his office at the back of the building. He looked to Deirdre as if he'd been up all night, and probably had. Dr. Martoche came down, a somber, thoughtful look on his pale, angular face that chilled Deirdre at sight of it. He was a dapper little man, his collar crisp and white as snow, his tie knot so perfect it looked sculptured, his linen suit fitting neatly, with not so much as a single wrinkle in spite of the heat, and his blucher boots polished to a gleam. He set his bag on the desk and cleared his throat, his expression frozen on his face as if he hesitated to alter it for fear of shattering his cheeks.

"Well?" asked Deirdre.

"She's sleeping. I gave her a little something to help. She'll probably sleep all day and most of tonight. Under no circumstances is she to be awakened."

"It's serious, isn't it?"

"Very. She's totally exhausted. I don't believe I've ever seen anyone so completely drained. She barely has the strength to breathe."

"But a topping good rest is all she needs, eh?" commented Collier.

The doctor shook his head. "It's not all that easy.

How shall I explain?" He ruminated a moment, scratching one ear, deepening his frown. "Let us say a swimmer can swim only four miles, no more. At the end he's completely spent, but this one time, to keep from drowning, he has to swim a fifth, even a sixth mile."

"With what?" asked Collier.

"*Ma fait!* Where does this second strength come from?" He tapped his heart and his temple. "From here and from his imagination. He manufactures endurance. He taps the empty well and brings up a full bucket of adrenalin, because . . ."

Collier nodded. "He knows he has to."

"*Exactement.* Such herculean efforts happen all the time. But—and this is the crux—there is a price for such abuse of the physique, a high price. The muscles, the limbs, they tire, they rest, strength is restored; but the nervous system and the brain are not accustomed to such severe punishment. They do not snap back. They come back slowly, if at all."

Deirdre drew in her breath sharply. "She may never recover!"

"I'm saying she has pushed herself too long and too rigorously to come back with 'plenty of rest.' She needs weeks, months, with meticulous care and attention to diet, to surroundings—peace and quiet at all times—to daily routine. Everything in her world must be adjusted to her condition. Most important of all, nothing must happen to her to upset her. She's taken too much already; any more could be fatal."

"But if we do as you say, she'll recover?"

"Exactly as I say, to the letter, I would say her chances are very good."

"What about moving her?" asked Deirdre. "We want to leave China as soon as possible for Singapore and eventually home to America."

"There we have a problem. To weigh one against the other, to stay and run the risk of a full-scale up-

rising exploding about our ears, or should we get her
to the coast, onto a ship and away from this delightful
country? A refugee ship is coming from Singapore to
Pei-t'ang.

Deirdre brightened. "Marvelous!"

Martoche nodded. "It should be here in a day or
so. And an artillery regiment stationed in Chi-Nan is
sending two companies."

"Is it your recommendation that she leave?" asked
Collier.

"That is for you two to decide."

Deirdre pressed him. "You must favor one over the
other."

"If she were my wife or daughter, I would move her,
but only under the most favorable conditions possible.
We must see how she is two days from now when that
ship arrives."

"If we could get hold of a small boat . . ." began
Deirdre.

Martoche agreed. "Very sensible. Any other transportation is out of the question. The roads are horrendous. These people's carriages, carts and wagons
have no springs."

"We'll make the necessary arrangements," said
Collier.

"Thank you very much for coming, doctor." Deirdre
extended her hand and he shook it, snapping his heels
and bowing his head in military fashion.

"I will look in again this afternoon."

"May I go up?" asked Deirdre.

He bobbed his head back and forth, silently debating. "I suppose, but you're not to wake her. See
that you don't even go into the room."

"I won't."

"What can she eat?" asked Collier.

"For the time being, I'll take care of that. But when
I'm not around, you two are in charge. No one is to go

near her, not Chenier, Madame Chenier, nobody but you, mademoiselle."

Deirdre nodded. "Is there anything we can do for her, anything at all?"

"One thing."

"What?"

"Pray."

XII

Dr. Martoche had in no way exaggerated. Lisa slept most of the next two days and nights. During her waking periods she seemed as weak as a shadow. She perspired continuously, and her face became paler and more drawn-looking as the hours passed. It was as if the life in her was collecting itself somewhere deep within and draining the rest of her body in the process. On the morning of the second day she took a little broth but dozed off without finishing it and, awakening later, refused any more.

Deirdre was frantic with worry, and the doctor had nothing to say to mitigate her concern. What nagged more than anything else was the apparent nature of Lisa's condition. There was no way of measuring its level of seriousness, no crisis anticipated, no series of phases to which Martoche might look, as one looks to milestones along an unfamiliar road. The waiting was maddening. Early the afternoon of the second day, word arrived that the French, under La Grandière, had made good their threat to annex the three provinces of Cochin. Curiously, the seizure *accompli* failed to rouse the Chinese people a second time. In Collier's opinion, they were either fresh out of wrath or had suddenly resigned themselves to the inevitability of the piecemeal pilfering of their territory by European nations.

He and Deirdre discussed matters over tea in the room Monsieur Chenier had assigned the British Board of Trade. It was only half again larger than the one Deirdre had occupied since given to Lisa. Every pane

of glass in both windows was broken, and endless
squadrons of flies came sweeping in with the brazen
impunity of Genghis Khan's hordes of old overunning
Chung-tu. File folders had been stacked to within a
foot of the ceiling against two walls. Two of Collier's
co-workers sat opposite each other across an unsteady-
looking quarter-sawed oak table salvaged from the rubble, carrying on the business of the board.

"Madame Débarmy says that the ship has arrived at
Pei-t'ang and that most of us will be leaving first thing
tomorrow morning," said Deirdre.

"That reminds me . . ." Reaching into his jacket
pocket, Collier brought forth a slip of paper. "Keep
this. Your boat will be at the Chi-kung Ch'aio Bridge
at eight o'clock sharp. I've arranged for four soldiers
who'll be off duty to fetch her there. They'll carry her
bed as if it were a litter. That's bound to be the most
comfortable way. It's actually only a couple of hundred yards from here."

"You'll be going down on our boat, won't you?"

"I'm afraid I shan't be going down on any."

"But didn't you say . . ."

"I had hoped all four of us would be heading out,
but now that things have quieted down, it appears the
board will be staying."

"How long do you think things will stay 'quieted
down'?"

He smiled with little enthusiasm for the effort. "That,
I'm afraid, is not for the loyal troops to conjecture."

"Can't you quit? I mean, it's just a job."

He sipped and shook his head slowly. "It's considered a career, like the army. We sign a contract for
five years. I've still three to go. This is my second time
around. Glutton for abuse, eh?"

"You mean a piece of paper keeps you here until
your time is up or you're murdered?"

He pretended to shudder. "That's a grisly way of
putting it."

"That's what it amounts to. I hate to leave without you. You're the only friend we have. What if we run into trouble on the way or in Pei-t'ang? You know what the doctor said about Mother getting upset and all."

"I confess I have been thinking about that. I doubt old Chenier, Mr. Pistols, will let a flock of helpless women and children go down there without protection. There's sure to be at least a platoon going along as escort as soon as that contingent arrives from Chi-Nan."

"We're going on our own boat, remember?"

"I'll mention that to him. We'll see if we can't get you a brace of handsome young recruits."

"I'd rather four ugly old twenty-year men."

"Finish your tea and take me up to see your mother. Maybe the good news that you two are leaving will brace her and cheer her up."

XIII

Lisa had been placed on board the sampan and all was in readiness for the run down the Hai River, which bisected the city and ran to the gulf coast. The Chikung Ch'aio Bridge was crowded with people, the river aclutter with small boats and barges. The barefoot sampan owner stood patiently at his pole at the rear of his craft, his round straw hat shadowing his face from the dazzling sun. The two soldiers assigned to accompany them climbed aboard.

Deirdre shook Collier's hand. "Good-by, Travis, and thank you for everything."

"Nothing very much, I'm afraid." His eyes strayed to the curving mat roofing the sampan under which Lisa lay sleeping. "Thinking back on it, I wish I hadn't let her leave for Peking with the French chap and those others. I ought to have made a much bigger fuss than I did. To let her walk off into the dragon's mouth . . ."

"You'd never have stopped her: You know Mother."

"I might have tried. If I had stopped her, she wouldn't be like this now."

"She could be worse. There's one bright side: We're back together."

"I do hope everything will come out all right." He grinned.

"What's funny?"

"Me. I don't have any family. This thing's gotten to the point where I feel the two of you are my family. I shall miss you, Deirdre, and her."

"We'll miss you."

411

"Now she's got you back, it should help her immensely. You're better than any medicine."

"Speaking of medicine, I wonder where Dr. Martoche is."

"Running around as usual, six pregnancies, three malaria and a dozen heat prostration all going at once. Never fear: He'll catch you up before you get away from China."

The sampan man called to them. The two soldiers stood waiting at the bow. Deirdre nodded and gestured she was coming. Squeezing Collier's hands, she kissed him impulsively. His cheeks rounding above his beard reddened, but he liked it and grinned.

"Godspeed, Deirdre. Remember, go straight to Wo Sin. He's expecting you. I've sent word."

"Songkok Alley."

"Yes. Make sure you take a rickshaw. Don't walk it. Singapore's not a very nice city. And see you give that rascal my very, very best."

She nodded, smiled, boarded the boat, turned and blew him a kiss. Sitting in the stern, she waved until the red of his hair and beard and the white of his rumpled suit faded into the motley crowd traversing the bridge.

The run to the coast and then northward along the shoreline to Pei-t'ang proved uneventful. The river was crowded, the heat fierce, and Deirdre spent most of the journey sitting beside Lisa, fanning her with a tape sailor straw hat, a parting gift from Travis Collier. She would treasure it always, she thought. In spite of his reluctance to admit it, the red-bearded, disheveled, tidy-minded one with the pedantic outlook and unstinting willingness to help had practically saved both their lives.

It was midafternoon by the time their little craft reached the harbor at Pei-t'ang. Refugees were streaming into the gulf ports from all over the north, nearly half of them non-Europeans. Christians of a score of nations had been uprooted in the wave of unrest. The clerk who had let her into the consulate had blown the situation badly out of proportion. The facts since substantiated by the consul himself were that no nuns had been killed by irate students posing as patriots or by anyone else. Many people had been injured, but the only confirmed death was that of the bystander Monsieur Chenier had accidentally shot.

Deirdre's heart roused itself with music all its own as they eased slowly into the harbor, to be greeted by sight of their ship. By far the largest vessel in port, the *City of Marseilles* was no sleek China-tea clipper. Her less-than-imposing appearance was distinguished by rusty plates, scaling paint resembling shingles lifted by the wind, a well-buckled bow and a steady stream of yellowish-black bilge water gushing from her vitals. The mass of humanity already crowding her rails stirred visions of sardines packed in tight file in a can. Unprepossessing though she may have been, she symbolized the one thing Deirdre held most precious: the means by which the two of them would be getting away from China, across the seas of separation and back into their own world.

Lisa was carried up the gangplank by four sailors in crisp white uniforms and blue caps with ribbon tails. Dr. Martoche greeted them on deck, separating himself from the noisy crush of passengers sitting and standing about. There appeared to be 10,000 people on board hugging their belongings, chattering loudly, grinning in relief at their imminent deliverance. The doctor pushed through the mob, making room for the bed bearers heading toward the stern.

"We're in luck, mademoiselle: I managed to get her a state-room—nothing fancy, but as private as we can hope for, under the circumstances."

"Whatever it looks like, we'll adore it."

She craned her neck, taking in the tops of the partially rigged masts lancing the sky and the wind dirging about their main skysail yards and fluttering their pennants. Issuing from the single stack midship was a plume of smoke as thick as fur. Hands scurried aloft to unfurl the topsails and topgallants.

"It seems we got here just in time," she said.

The doctor stopped an elderly officer coming from the other direction, talking with him briefly in French. The man touched the bill of his cap and went on. "He says we're just waiting for the tide, twenty minutes, no more. I asked him to send a steward up with some decent food. God knows what manner of slop the galley will be serving up."

"How many days to Singapore?"

He shrugged. "Ten, maybe more."

"That long?"

"We have stops: first Hong Kong, then Macao, then up the Gulf of Siam to Kompong Som. Cambodia is French, you know; most of these people will be getting off there. I'm afraid Singapore's the last stop."

"Where will the ship go from there?"

"Probably back here to pick up another bunch. Look."

He pointed at the dock. The gangplank was being lifted and drawn up. The people below began screaming and waving their fists angrily. Others continued to pour onto the dock from both ends, adding to the surging mass already arrived. Even as they watched, the crush began to build, all but pushing those in the forefront into the murky water.

They got Lisa into the state-room practically battling their way to the door to do so. The room resembled a large metal box with a single salt-skinned porthole framing a clutch of curious faces outside. Soot was everywhere, as if it had been hand sprayed about the interior. The bedsheets were yellowed with age and none too clean. The bed itself had a block of wood shoved under one corner in place of a missing leg.

"All the comforts of home," said Deirdre.

"Your mother's bed is clean, bugless. I'm afraid you'll have to take your chances."

"I think I'd rather sleep on the floor. It's good for the back."

"As you wish."

Dr. Martoche indicated the two lift locks. "Keep the door closed at all times, and the porthole."

"In this heat?"

"It'll muffle the noise."

"I'd rather the noise than suffocate," said Lisa feebly, her first words since the sampan reached the dock.

"Look who's awake!" exclaimed the doctor, smiling. "How do you feel?"

"I'm all right."

"Of course you are." He laughed. "Jump up and run around the deck, why don't you? We've sent for something to eat."

"I *am* hungry."

Deirdre sat on the edge of the bed, holding Lisa's left hand tightly in both of hers as if, were she to let go, her mother would "slip back down the cliff into the sea." She kissed her on the cheek. "We'll be on our way in a few minutes. Before long, Singapore, then straight home."

Lisa snapped her eyes closed and opened them. "I can't believe it's you I'm seeing. I keep wanting to pinch myself."

"Don't talk, dear; you'll tire yourself out."

"I'll whisper." She tried to smile, almost succeeding. Her appalling feebleness frightened Deirdre so, she could scarcely mask her concern.

"What is it?" Lisa asked.

"Nothing. Oh, Mother, I've missed you so. You can't imagine. Night after night I lay awake yearning so to see you that my heart ached to bursting, imagining we'd never see each other again, you and Daddy so far away and all. Oh, Mother, I love you so!"

"My poor darling, poor little girl."

"I *feel* like a little girl." A single tear deserted Deirdre's eye, landing on the fold of the sheet.

Lisa's hand moved to touch it. "Musn't cry, darling."

"I must, for joy. These three days have been the happiest of my life!"

"I wonder what's keeping that damned steward!" barked Martoche in a self-conscious tone. "I'll go get him moving. Lock the door after me."

Deirdre did so. A whistle hooted loudly, the crowd outside cheered, orders were shouted down the deck. The *City of Marseilles* groaned and creaked and shuddered, shaking herself out of her lethargy, rousing her energies, her canvas capturing the wind, her boilers raising pressure, actuating her propeller, her rudder swinging to port, her dented and deformed bow nosing forward.

XIV

Lisa seemed to gain strength daily, inch by inch, as Martoche put it; but, to Deirdre's dismay, there looked to be no improvement in her appearance. Her sunken cheeks raised their bones, and her skin was alternately pale and flushed, as if the fever afflicting her were controlled by an unseen switch. She spoke coherently, if faintly and with effort, but eating so tired her that she invariably dozed off before she was able to finish.

Then, two days out, she began having trouble sleeping, awaking during the night. She would begin by tossing and turning. Deirdre would awake to find her with her eyes wide open, fully awake and asking for water. The first two times this occurred, Deirdre went for Dr. Martoche, but though he came at once, the damage had been done.

"She's sleeping so much during the day she's unable to make it through the night," he explained. "She's getting as much as she needs, only at the wrong time."

They discussed the situation in low tones outside the door. Like a carelessly smudged pearl, the moon inserted itself in a cloud brooch over distant Formosa, strewing its silver across a sea as flat as the deck. The refugees sat sleeping shoulder to shoulder, their knees pulled up to their chests, arms folded around them, heads bowed. A symphony of snoring mingled with the wash of the bow, the drone of the engines and the creaking of the vessel about and above them.

Martoche cocked his head and eyed Deirdre solemnly. "You're beginning to look exhausted yourself."

"I'm fine."

"Isn't everyone until they drop? Seriously, what happens to her if you collapse? You're her crutch. If . . ."

"I know; you're right. I'm not sleeping very well. I lie awake worrying. Why doesn't she start getting better?"

"She *has* started. Give her a chance; it's been less than a week. You must be patient."

"What really scares me is how different she is, like a ghost of herself. If you only knew her before . . . She was so strong, so determined and confident."

"She still is; those qualities just don't show. Not because they're not there; it's that the effort to, how shall I say, exhibit them is too much for her. You mustn't close your eyes to all that's in our favor. She wants to get better; she has patience, even if some others don't. Best of all, her mind is clear and healthy."

"I suppose." She sighed.

"What now?"

"I don't know. I guess it's me. I see her fall asleep and it's as if she were plunging down into a pit. I think to myself she's so weak she'll never wake up again. I get panicky."

He lit a cigar, a slender, crooked stick of tobacco, focusing its orange eye across the space between them. "You get some sleep, and stop skipping meals—doctor's orders. I don't want to see you carried down the gangplank in Singapore."

"You look tired yourself, you know," said Deirdre.

"Impossible! For me, this is a pleasure cruise. I have only twenty-four hundred possible patients; two babies delivered today, three more due before we get to Kompong Som; malaria, heat prostration, black fever, blood poisoning, practically every 'itis' in the medical books and six or seven other ailments ranging from the trivial to the fatal, everything but smallpox, thank God, the celestial flowers that spread like weeds. I shouldn't

grumble. I should be glad we're not ferrying this
bunch across an ocean. As it is, they have to be hosed
down from the bow to the stern every morning. Did I
ever tell you that my mother wanted me to be a
priest?"

She laughed.

"It's true. Oh, one other case I forgot about: tuberculosis."

"My 'husband' died of it. The doctor called it the
galloping consumption."

"You should have given him boiled python."

"You're funny."

"I'm serious. Chinese people eat python to prevent
tuberculosis."

"Talk about your raving primitives . . ."

"I beg to differ. I consider them one of the most
intelligent and sophisticated races on earth. They may
be badly governed and politically inept, but they're
years ahead of us in many ways, though I'm sure that
doesn't much interest you. I shall say good night,
pleasant dreams and stop worrying."

"I'll try. Good night, doctor."

The *City of Marseilles* reached Hong Kong before
dawn, disposing of fewer than 40 passengers and continuing on to nearby Macao. It would not be until Kompong Som, more than 1,300 miles beyond and the
only established French colonial port on the route,
that most of those on board would leave the ship.

Lisa's condition remained stable throughout the
remainder of the voyage, neither noticeably improving
or deteriorating. To Deirdre, she seemed to exist in a
sort of limbo, although moving, speaking and taking
nourishment, all that her doctor and "nurse" could
get into her. Martoche did not appear worried, but
there was about him an air of mystification. Deirdre
decided that a feeling of helplessness must be setting
in. There was no miraculous medicine appropriate to

the condition, no textbook treatment, and having done
what he could, all he could do now was look in on
her three or four times each day, check pulse and
temperature and murmur something in the way of
cautious optimism.

The *City of Marseilles* departed Kompong Som, her
cabins and decks all but cleared of evacuees. With less
than 48 hours to go before arriving in Singapore, the
doctor had Lisa's bed brought up to the poop deck
and placed between the locker supporting the steering
compass and the companionway to get sun and fresh
air.

Deirdre and Martoche stood with her above the
now-all-but-deserted deck. An indolent breeze skimmed
the sea, half bellying the sails, putting most of the
burden of continued movement upon the tireless
engines.

Martoche was in a cheerful and energetic mood,
although, by his own admission, he hadn't had more
than four hours' sleep any one of the preceding eight
nights. "So it seems we'll be saying good-by in Singapore, and back to Tientsin for me."

"Another trip down?" asked Deirdre.

"Perhaps more than one. It depends upon how active my colonizing countrymen are," he added, his
voice tinged with irony. "Take care of her, nurse. Get
a good doctor in Singapore, and when you get home,
raise a glass of good burgundy in fond memory of this
ship's doctor—preferably from Côte de Nuit, my
home."

"We will," said Lisa. "Depend upon it."

XV

The house was situated about 200 yards from the cityside bank of the Johore Strait. It perched upon a rise that set it regally apart from other, more conventional-looking homes in the area. At first sight, it looked a fugitive from Beacon or Nob Hill, loosed from its street block, whisked across the ocean and set down on the edge of the rain forest, a purposively distinguished Victorian mansion displaying just enough gingerbread for character without risking ridicule for garishness. It had been freshly painted white with soft brown trim. The garden beginning on one side spread around the rear, reaching into the shadow of a stand of teak heavily slung with vines and adorned with delicate ferns and orchids. Among the latter were umbrella-shaped dwarfs spattered and splashed with color, others equally showy but with broad blades unsheathed and dueling the flowers nearest them. *Borbigerum* flaunted its narrow, greenish-brown sepals and petals, its long yellow lip bearded dark purple with a purple brush of minute threads at the top that daubed the air when the breeze set it in motion.

There were star-shaped *macranthum,* blood red with yellow spilled over it, abundant and scattered, a botanical galaxy dotting the dark firmament of the trees. Other blossoms dazzled the eye, crowded in neatly tended beds interspersed among fragrant clove and jambu eugenia trees: blue giant Thunburgia, yellow black-eyed susan, holly rose, snake's-tongue, heliotrope and *pulut-pulut.**

* The twelve o'clock flower.

421

Her senses captivated by the colors and fragrances, Deirdre sat talking with Wo Sin.

Earlier, six Chinese uniformed in neatly pressed business suits and panama hats, so closely resembling one another in build and facial features that they looked to her as if one of them had so impressed their maker that he had immediately stamped out five duplicates, had met the *City of Marseilles* at the Clifford Pier in Singapore harbor. Their spokesman had introduced them as Wo Sin's aides. They had ready and waiting for Lisa one of only three spring carriages in all of Singapore (the other two in service to the governor).

The short run to the hinterlands had bypassed Songkok Alley in favor of Orchard Road. Solving a puzzle of narrow side streets, they had arrived to be greeted at the door by a beaming middle-aged Malay couple, housekeeper and handyman respectively.

Lisa had been carried into the master bedroom, where a brass bed canopied in tulle and draped with mosquito netting awaited her. In one corner of the room, boxes were stacked to the ceiling. The housekeeper had smiled at Deirdre's curious stare and proceeded to open one box after another on the floor. Out popped looped and bunched double skirts, crinolines and peplums, *casaques* and corsage postilions; sleeveless camails and *rotondes,* shawls of cashmere, silk and lace, fascinators, spoon bonnets, Empire bonnets, puff bonnets, ostrich-tipped hats; Cromwell shoes —Dangola and Vici kid oxfords, strap sandals, satin slippers. Christmas morning in September!

Shortly after they had arrived, a gig had pulled up outside carrying Wo Sin and another man. The housekeeper had ushered both into the bedroom, and Lisa greeted Wo Sin affectionately, introducing Deirdre, whom he had never met. With him was a doctor. They had left him with Lisa and adjourned to the garden.

"The clothes are beautiful!" exclaimed Deirdre. "You shouldn't have!"

Wo Sin laughed. "I'm a bachelor, child, a status that entitles me to indulge myself with my adopted niece and her mother."

"She's very ill. I'm terribly worried."

"Of course you are. But Dr. Mercer is the best in Singapore. He'll have her back on her feet in no time. She's very strong, your mother, I don't have to tell you. While she's coming around, you are to consider yourselves my guests. All I ask in return is that you allow me visiting privileges."

"You're very kind. If it weren't for you and your men, Mother and I never would have found each other. How can we ever repay you?"

"Seeing you reunited is all the payment I require. Do you like my house?"

"It's fabulous; I adore it!"

"So do I. I had it built as a retreat, but I have little time for such a luxury. No house should stand empty, though. Your living here is the best thing for it. Mr. and Mrs. Raya will wait on you hand and foot. *You* must rest, as well as your mother."

"She wants to leave for home as soon as possible. I'm afraid we're both homesick. It seems ages since I've seen Blackwood."

"I'm sure Dr. Mercer will tell you when you can leave once he's examined her."

"She tries so hard to be cheerful and patient and cooperative. She pretends she's getting her strength back, but it's all a sham. She seems to be stuck in a rut."

"The three of us must get her out of it."

"She gets depressed thinking about your friend, Lieutenant Gerard, and the others."

"A sorry business that. Travis Collier sent down a

full report." He paused to eye a green pigeon flutter to earth and twitch about, searching for seeds. "I hope she doesn't hold herself responsible."

"Oh, but she does."

"That's bad. You must change her thinking. Paul's eyes were open; he knew what he was getting into. We all have different devils prodding us. People like Paul nourish their souls with risk; it's their drug."

"I guess."

Dr. Mercer appeared at the back door, waving. He came out, bag in hand, a chesty, vigorous-looking man, his thick thatch of brown hair in need of trimming, his blue eyes lively, his gait comically awkward as he made his way toward them as if he had spent his earlier years behind a plow hunched forward, knees bent, lunging against the resistance of the blade.

"How is she?" asked Wo Sin.

"Middling. I'll tell you better in a week. I want to try a tonic: ginseng." *

"That's Chinese," said Deirdre, somewhat dismayed.

"Manchurian and Korean, actually. I've used it before in combination with aromatic bitters, sweet flag, camomile and such. Her body is, so to speak, at a standstill. She needs a boost. There is a simple regimen." His eyes met Deirdre's. "You're to see that she doesn't drink any regular tea for about a month."

"Very well. Of course, by then we'll be halfway home."

"I don't think so. I don't want her on another ship for at least two months, possibly longer. There's too much rolling, the risk of bad weather, poor food. Sea air is refreshing but can exhaust one."

Deirdre groaned. "Two months! I'd so hoped we

* No therapeutic value for ginseng has ever been established, although even today its popularity as a curative persists in the Orient and elsewhere.

could leave. Isn't home the best tonic in the world?"

"Not if it means setting her all the way back to get there. We have to take her through stages. This place, this garden are ideal—peaceful, lovely, healthful. This is a marvelous time of year, not too hot, sunny days, balmy nights. She has a comfortable bed. She can sit out here afternoons. As to treatment . . ."

She was to have 60 to 90 grains of ginseng combined with bitters daily. The root was to be cooked in a double kettle with a cuplike cover filled with rice in a little water. The ginseng would be placed in the inner vessel with water, covered, and the kettle heated.

"When the rice is cooked, the medicine's ready. She's to eat the rice first, then drink the ginseng tea."

"How often?"

"Once a day, before breakfast."

"Two months . . . She's going to hate hearing that."

"I've already told her. Go in and see her, why don't you? Both of you. Just for a few minutes, though. Getting down from Tientsin has tired her out; she needs her sleep. Wo Sin, I'll wait for you out front in the carriage."

The first thought in Lisa's mind when Deirdre and Wo Sin came into the bedroom was of Paul Gerard and the others. "It's a terrible, terrible thing, outsiders being the casualties in my war," she said soberly.

"Cheer up," said Wo Sin, "your war is over."

"Too late for poor Paul."

"And too early for you to shoulder regret you're not strong enough to carry. First you must get well. I want to see the Iron Lady back in harness."

"You make me sound like a plow mule!"

They laughed and talked until Lisa's eyelids began to droop.

Wo Sin rose from his chair. "Dr. Mercer will look

in on you tomorrow morning. Till then, sleep well, and enjoy your vacation, both of you."

He went away, his horse clopping down the dusty road, the doctor perched beside him. Lisa slept, and Deirdre returned to the garden to think and to plan.

XVI

Three days passed. Early in the afternoon of the fourth day the carriage reappeared in a cloud of red dust. Both men got out at the gate, giving over the reins to Mr. Raya. During the intervening time, the doctor had started his patient on the ginseng. Deirdre meanwhile had come upon a book in the living room that described ginseng as "a tonic to the five viscera, quieting animal spirits, establishing the soul, allaying fear, expelling evil effluvia, brightening the eye, opening up the heart, benefiting the understanding, invigorating the body and prolonging life." These modest claims did little to generate any enthusiasm for the strange-looking root, but questioning the judgment of the only doctor available did not appear to be in order.

Wo Sin brought disturbing news. Shortly after departing Singapore to return to the Gulf of Chihli, the *City of Marseilles* had blown up and sunk, with no survivors. The press attributed the explosion to fanatical Singapore Chinese patriots. Wo Sin agreed with this assessment, suggesting that one or two must have sneaked on board in port and cached a bundle of dynamite in the cold ash bed of the furnace, so that when the fire was started, with the first load of hot ashes shaken down, the fuse had ignited.

"Not a very original idea," he added, "but effective, unfortunately."

Deirdre and Lisa were heartsick at the news. That Dr. Martoche, a man who had saved so many lives, had to die in such a brutal manner.

The days became weeks, September passing the

427

world on to October. On the 20th of the month Wo
Sin came to the house alone, carrying a roll of heavy
paper under one arm, coming into the garden, where
Lisa and Deirdre sat.

"Good news," he announced. "Dr. Mercer informs
me that you two ladies may leave us any time after
Sunday."

"Marvelous!" shrilled Deirdre, jumping up.

"Of course, you're not obligated to go. And if you
do, you'll miss the Mooncake Festival and the Deepa-
vali, the Festival of Lights. Still, being neither Chinese
nor Hindu, you probably wouldn't be interested."

"What's that under your arm?" asked Lisa.

"Something that will interest you." Kneeling, he
set his hat on the lawn and unrolled a map of the
world. "Your doctor has come up with an inspired
idea." He traced with his index finger from Singapore
across the Pacific, across Mexico to Vera Cruz and
on to New Orleans and eventually Providence, the
original route followed by Lisa and Ross. "This is
fine, up to a point. To San Marcos on the west coast
of Mexico, here. But from there on it's rough traveling,
do you agree?" Both nodded. "Very well. Now let's
try the opposite direction."

"Around the Cape of Good Hope?" asked Deirdre.

"Not exactly."

The tip of his finger departed Singapore a second
time, heading northwest up the Strait of Malacca into
the Andaman Sea, past Ceylon into the Indian Ocean
and westward to the entrance of the Gulf of Aden.
"The Suez Canal," he exclaimed.

"It's not finished," said Lisa.

"It's very nearly; less than twenty miles left to cut—
twenty miles. That's a carriage ride from here to Kota
Tinggi and back and, more important, the only land
between here and Providence. One of my clerks has
done all the arithmetic. Singapore to Providence by
way of the Cape of Good Hope is twelve thousand,

five hundred miles; by the canal, ten thousand, two hundred, a saving of twenty-three hundred miles, an easier trek, taking you right to your doorstep. As for heading east to San Marcos and on, we make that much longer—fifteen, sixteen thousand. You should know, Lisa; you've traveled it three times."

"I dread to think of a fourth."

"We'll get you onto a ship heading for the Gulf of Aden, up past Djibouti as far as you can go into the Gulf of Suez, and from Bar Tawfig up the completed stretch to Little Bitter Lake. Up the lake, up the second completed stretch to Buhayrat at Timsah, up, up . . ."

His opinion was that the overland stretch could be easily negotiated by carriage or coach. A boat could pick them up ten or 12 miles south of Port Said and they could change a second time to a ship heading across the Mediterranean to Gibraltar.

"From there on, you cruise home."

"It sounds wonderful," said Deirdre, and Lisa nodded. She had picked up the map and was studying it.

"We'll plan every leg for you," said Wo Sin. "Think of it: You two are going to make history, the first bona fide travelers to use Ferdinand de Lesseps's famous ditch!"

Lisa laughed. "If he'll let us."

"It's a mission of mercy; how can he refuse? It's perfect, isn't it? All you need is a bodyguard, someone to arrange things along the way, confirm connections and keep the young sailors away from Deirdre."

"Will a ship start up the canal just to let off two passengers?" Deirdre asked. "It's awfully out of the way, isn't it?"

"Cargo ships have been using the opened southern portion lately, taking their loads as far as they can, then trans-shipping, moving them overland and onto ships waiting farther up. It is perfect, isn't it? Perfect!"

He whooped loudly and clapped his hands, looking so comical doing it that Lisa burst out laughing, so hard she couldn't stop. It rubied her face and brought tears to her eyes as she threw back her head and laughed and laughed, starting Deirdre and Wo Sin and bringing Mrs. Raya to the back door, staring curiously.

XVII

The Min River, from the Pagoda Anchorage at Foochow, was a narrow sluice boasting a current that thundered to the sea as fast as a mountain creek. It was claimed that the Min's banks were so close to each other that monkeys jumping across got their tails entangled in the brace blocks of ships passing through. But none were entangled in those of the *Phereclus* as she raced slickly out of the Min, the last of the year's tea clippers bent on beating the monsoons to fetch her cargo to de Lesseps's ditch. One hundred eighty-three and a half feet long, 31 feet across her beam and 20 feet deep, she carried 300 tons of tea down the South China Sea to Singapore, where she paused to take on 100 additional tons of tinned pineapple and three passengers and, pointing her bowsprit, bobstay and billet due south, filled sail for the long haul around the bend and westward to the Gulf of Aden.

Her tea was in 40-catty chests: cheap blacks—Bohea and congou; a superior young black—Pekoe; best black —souchong; greens—imperial and Twankay; good green—gunpowder; and superior green—hyson. Enough tea to quench the thirsts of all the peers in Parliament for the next 100 years.

The *Phereclus*'s skipper was British, a fire-faced individual shaped like the chimney on a kerosene lamp, as gregarious as a Barbary ape and devoted to beverages considerably stronger than tea. Captain Chauncey Congers was from Avenmouth, near Bristol, in contract with Albion Tea, Ltd., main offices Liverpool. He was

431

"pleased as the prior's punch" to take along two such lovely ladies and their escort.

To Lisa's surprise and delight, who should turn up as that volunteer but Eng-chow.

Wo Sin had celebrated her recovery with a farewell party at the house. He and Dr. Mercer had seen the three of them off on the *Phereclus,* and now, five days out of port, with Dondra Head, on the coast of Ceylon, off the starboard beam, the Maldives dead ahead and the beautiful weather yielding to glorious, Deirdre and Eng-chow stood at the topgallant rail while Lisa, in line with Dr. Mercer's stern injunction, napped for an hour. A sea as green as new grass slipped by as the southeast trades stoutened the canvas and a pair of square-tailed ivory gulls followed the spanker gaff, riding the wind, patiently awaiting their banquet of scraps.

"She's putting on weight; she looks so much better," said Deirdre.

"She look better than when we meet in Forbidden City," Eng-chow said. "Not tired, weak-looking."

"Best of all, she's acting like her old self again."

They stared down at the sea for a long moment; then she turned to him.

"How far will you go?" she asked.

"To big sea."

"The Mediterranean." He nodded. "Then?"

"Back to Singapore."

"Not to China?"

"No, never go back. Too hard in Forbidden City. Too much trouble."

"I bet I know who gave you trouble; Li-Lien-ying."

"He beat me once too much. I take away birch wands, beat him, nearly kill him. Then I run away, stay with friends in Pei-t'ang, come to Singapore on barrel ship."

"Barrel ship?"

"Work, lift barrels salt fish. Heavy."

"Look." Deirdre pointed off. A school of slate-blue whales was moving slowly in the direction of the ship, their long, tapering flippers flashing white at the ends, their yellowish bellies showing briefly as they curled above the surface before submerging.

"Big fish!"

"Whales. Aren't they tremendous? Mother has to see this. She must be awake by now. Be right back."

She flew down the deck and up the stairs to their cabin, which backed against the sail locker. Glancing through the porthole, she could see that Lisa had only just awakened. Deirdre banged on the glass, then the door.

"Mother, come quick!"

Lisa opened the door. Deirdre was about to blurt out word of the whales when she hesitated, seeing the strange, absent look in her mother's eyes.

"Come in, dear, I've something to tell you."

"Mother . . ."

"Sh, do as I say." She patted the bed. "Sit here beside me."

"What is it?"

"I've something to tell you, but before I do, you must give me your word you'll keep it secret."

"I will."

"Cross your heart."

She did so. "Mother . . ."

"Sh, let me talk before I burst. Remember, you mustn't tell a soul. Now, you know your father won't be back from New York until Monday night. Do you know what Tuesday is?"

"I . . ."

"His birthday! His thirtieth. You remember last year's party? It was supposed to be a surprise, but he suspected all along, though he wouldn't admit it. I made up my mind then and there it wasn't going to happen this year. So I've decided we'll have it the night before. Isn't that clever? I mean for me, who's not a bit clever. I've already started arrangements. I need your help. Can I depend upon you?"

"Of course."

"That's my girl. I should be able to, you know; you're not a little tot anymore—double numbers next birthday!"

"What can I do?"

"The decorations, of course. We can close off the dining room. We can work all day; Thursby and the maids will help. When Daddy comes home Monday night, we'll have a bite in the library. No! I've a better idea: We'll meet him at the shipyard and have dinner in town, at Larkins's or the Roger Williams Inn. Now, get a pencil and paper and write down what we'll need for decorations."

"Yes."

"Darling, look at the face on you! Why so sad? This is going to be heaps of fun. He'll be so surprised. I can't wait to see his face!"

XVIII

Lisa's outburst stunned Deirdre. It had lasted less than two minutes before the curtain dropped, ending it as abruptly as it had begun. In the conversation that ensued between the two, her mother appeared perfectly normal, giving no hint whatsoever that she was even aware she had mentioned the party plans. It was frightening, weird, almost as if another mind had temporarily substituted itself for Lisa's, unburdening itself and vanishing.

Panic struck at Deirdre and settled in her heart. There was no doctor on board. Eng-chow, as dependable as he was, couldn't possibly help, nor could the captain or anyone else. Help how? What could anyone do?

They went to bed early, as had become their custom lately. Lisa fell asleep within minutes, the steady rhythm of her breathing the only sound in the little cabin. Outside, the wind rose, flapping the spanker, and the *Phereclus* drove forward at a steady rate. Deirdre tried to sleep, but the conscious effort to do so made it impossible. Giving up after an hour's trying, she got up, dressed and wandered down the deck to the captain's cabin. She found him sitting at his chart table, spinning his compass over a map of the Indian Ocean and penciling in tiny numbers, the orange glow of his lamp lending him the look of a rotund Satan seemingly hard at work cataloging souls. She asked to borrow his medical books.

"Not feeling well?"

"I'm all right. It's just that I can't sleep. Reading

435

helps. Medicine's fascinating to me. I read everything on it I can find," she lied.

"How's your mother?"

She laughed, a brittle, humorless chuckle. "Fast asleep."

He gave her the only two books he had. From the look in his eye, he seemed unconvinced that she was asking for them because she found medicine "fascinating," but he made no comment. The book on surgery was useless to her, but the other one, Heidermann's *Encyclopedia of Medicine,* contained a brief passage that interested her. Having thanked him and said good night, she now sat by the aft-companionway skylight reading by the lamp glow from below:

Many delusions are evidently the outcome of the patient's mental state. They may be pleasant or disagreeable, depending upon whether the condition is one of elevation or depression. The intensity and quality of the delusions are largely influenced by the intelligence and education of the patient.

It went on to say that such boltings from reality were not uncommon in the aftermath of tragic loss, which was followed by a lengthy period of severe nervous exhaustion. They could best be described as a willful effort to reexperience an unpleasant period in order to refashion it, "turn an unhappy interlude or incident into a happy one."

What the article neglected to explain or even mention was the fact that the incident, happy or unhappy, had never even occurred. Plunging back nearly eight years, Lisa had created a conversation that couldn't possibly have taken place. Deirdre had not been with her mother and father when she was ten years old. She had been abducted by her Aunt Lavinia before her second birthday and had not even seen Lisa again until she was almost 16.

Deirdre closed the book, returned it to Captain Congers and went back to bed. She fell asleep beset by a tingling fear, bracing herself for the next assault against the past.

It came the next morning. During the night the *Phereclus* had cleared the Maldive Islands and was now heading into the Arabian Sea toward the Gulf of Aden some 1,600 miles distant. The wind had slackened to the whisper of a breeze, the ship ghosting along, but at breakfast the captain assured his passengers that it would pick up before noon, suggesting they watch the sea to the southeast for signs of foam and building waves.

Deirdre and Lisa had then returned to their cabin. Lisa had eaten her best breakfast in weeks and was in excellent spirits, boasting of how well she had slept. She had gotten onto the subject of Blackwood, the lands and the shipyards, considering the wisdom of selling everything and buying a small house closer to town.

"Something easier to take care of. What do you think?"

"Whatever you want, Mother."

"Whatever we both want. You'll have to live there, too. It's just that I can't see any sense at all in hanging onto the yards now that your father's gone. We'd have to depend upon others to run things. We'll have to sit down and discuss it with the lawyers. I trust Fred Muybridge's judgment. When your father was missing and we'd been told he'd gone down in the *Monitor,* Fred suggested I get rid of everything."

Deirdre was standing at the highboy, straightening things. She had picked up a comb and brush and piece of paper and was putting them in the top drawer when Lisa's hand darted out, snatching the paper from her.

"Not this."

"What is it?"

"Nothing."

Deirdre held the drawer open. "Are you going to throw it away?"

"No." The absent look had come back into Lisa's eyes.

Deirdre groaned inwardly. "Mother, what's the matter?"

"Not a thing. I'm sorry; this address belongs in my bag."

"Address?"

Lisa sighed, sinking down upon the bed, clutching the paper in both hands. "Forgive me, darling, I shouldn't do this to you. You have every right to know." She held up the paper. "It's the address of the hospital in Virginia where your father is."

"You don't have to show it to me if you don't want to."

"It's the Eastern State Hospital for the . . ." She paused, then blurted it out: "Insane. Of course, Daddy's as sane as you or I. Amnesia's not insanity. I didn't show it to you because I didn't want to upset you."

"I understand."

"Your father is perfectly normal."

"Of course."

"Amnesia's the furthest thing from insanity. Anyway, this is the address."

She held the paper up for Deirdre to read. It was, as she expected, blank.

XIX

A few days and four similar incidents later, Deirdre returned to the cabin early one afternoon to find her mother awakened from her nap and gone. The bed had been made. Deirdre rushed out and ran around the deck calling, her throat constricting, her heart tightening with fear.

"Mother!"

She found Lisa forward, standing at the railing near the catheads, talking with Captain Congers. As Deirdre drew closer, she was able to pick up their conversation.

"I've walked clear around the ship and I can't find him anywhere."

"Perhaps he's below decks, ma'am."

"It's not like him to go wandering off without me."

"Mother, excuse me . . ."

"Deirdre, have you seen your father?"

"He's back in the cabin."

"He is?" She turned to the captain, smiling in relief. "I must have missed him. Do forgive me, captain. My husband's only just recovered from an appendicitis operation. I worry."

"That's perfectly all right, Mrs. Dandridge. Ladies, if you'll excuse me . . ." He bowed slightly and withdrew.

"I'm sorry, darling," Lisa said. "It's just not like him to leave without telling me where he's going."

Deirdre took her by the hand. "Let's go back." They started down the deck. "You must take your nap."

"Nap?" Lisa stopped, confusion filling her eyes. "I thought I'd already taken it."

"You've still a half-hour to go."

"Oh."

Lisa made no further reference to Ross. Instead, she began to talk about Deirdre's hair, commenting on how rapidly it was growing. "You should never cut it, darling. When I was your age I wore my hair all the way down to my waist. My father would have had a fit if I'd cut it—not that you didn't have good reason to."

In the cabin she disrobed and got into bed. Deirdre sat reading until she saw her mother's eyes close and her breathing slow.

Closing her book, she stared at her. The pattern was clear: The lapse was always built around him, as if some small corner of Lisa's mind was holding out, refusing to acknowledge his death. But now there was another factor: She had revealed her condition to the captain, though, from what Deirdre had seen, he had played his part well, masterfully concealing his surprise. Deirdre silently blessed his presence of mind. She would have to take him aside the first chance she got and try to explain. How? What explanation could there be other than to admit straight out what he already knew, that her mother's mind was playing tricks on her?

Dear God, how she wished they were home and Lisa was in capable hands, in the care of someone who would be able to bring her back to reality to stay.

The *Phereclus* raised Sokotra Island and, putting it off her starboard beam, ran into the gulf past Suez up the completed 16-mile stretch to the Little Bitter Lake. From there they sailed into the Great Bitter Lake and on up to Lake Timsah, a total distance of some 53 miles. In Lake Timsah, Congers's orders were to turn about and discharge his cargo at Ismailia, on the northwest corner of the lake, a village of a few hundred souls and site of the Egyptian Headquarters of the Canal Company. The *Phereclus*'s pineapple and 40-pound chests of tea were to be strapped onto camels, four chests to each beast, and carried over the Jisr shelf, still to be dredged and, according to Captain Congers, a capital headache to the engineers responsible for completing the canal. The shelf, it seemed, was almost entirely of sand, and when any part of it was removed, the remainder caved in, filling the excavation back up again immediately.

Lisa, Deirdre, Eng-chow and Captain Congers stood at the rail near the lifeboat skids as the gangplank was lowered. A number of hands had begun assembling the passengers' luggage on deck. Beyond the cluster of sun-baked huts and tents and halfhearted activity of Ismailia lay the uninhabited, treeless, windblown desert, its sculptured ridges rising in perfect order, its hills and hollows neatly carved and polished by the sirocco. The heat beating down upon the area was cruel but surprisingly dry compared with that of the Peking plain and Singapore.

"How far up to the other ship?" inquired Lisa of Captain Congers.

"Less than ten miles."

"Amazing," ventured Deirdre. "We've come nearly five thousand miles and you've still how far to go?"

"Better than four more."

"And ten little miles of land keeps you from sailing clear through!"

Congers smiled. "But not for much longer—a year or two at most."

"That's a long time."

"Not compared with the last attempt to dig a canal—some pharaoh about six hundred years before Christ. Needless to say, it was never finished."

"I go to shore first to get carriage," said Eng-chow.

"There's no need," said the captain. "The road north is a disaster. You're much better off taking the train to Port Said. Look." He pointed. "On the far side of that first ridge lies the extension of the Cairo-Suez railway.

You pick it up behind the Canal office. You can be in Port Said in less than an hour as comfortable as you please."

"That's wonderful!" burst Deirdre. "How often do the trains run?"

"There's only one and no fixed schedule, but it's only a hundred miles between Suez and Port Said, and it goes back and forth and back and forth. You shouldn't have to wait too long, hopefully." He extracted his handkerchief, lifted his cap and blotted his brow and pate. "Let's get you over to the platform out of this sun."

XX

The Cairo-Suez-Port Said Railway locomotive was a "Puffing Billy," a fat, stubby, blazing blue boiler capped with a Wild West diamond smokestack, high-dome casing, domed sandbox and Belpaire fireboxes painted blood red. It looked suspiciously to Deirdre as if its various components had been gathered from all over Europe. Still, it appeared to be well riveted and bolted and sturdy enough for the flat run between the gulf and the Mediterranean.

The five wooden passenger cars trailing the tender were "kindling on wheels," in Lisa's estimation. The seats were wooden benches; there were no cushions, no lamps, no lavatory, no window glass, no baggage racks and no springs on the wheels underneath. A layer of yellow dust covered every inch of the interior of their car, save the seats and the bare floor. Their bags and boxes were piled in the seat in front of them, and Eng-chow took his place diagonally opposite across the aisle. The car was half filled with ill-clad *corvée* laborers, mostly swarthy turbaned Levantines and Egyptians with a sprinkling of Europeans of undeterminable nationality. Just as the whistle blew and the train lurched forward, a late arrival came bouncing into the car, taking the seat behind Eng-chow.

He was, noted Deirdre, a peculiar-looking man, gawky tall, slope-shouldered and ferret-faced, his threadbare suit too small for him, his hands hanging from his sleeves like fish from a torn net. His hair sneaking from under his pith helmet was blond, and a disordered excuse for a mustache was strewn across his

443

upper lip. He removed his hat, nodded and smiled at her. She looked away, past Lisa, at the landscape shriveling under the sun slipping by. The latecomer got up and came toward them, placing his hand on the knob of the upright supporting the back of their seat.

"How'dja' do, miss, madam. Allow me to introduce myself. The name's—"

It was as far as he was able to get. Like a giant demon rising from the pit, Eng-chow hoisted himself from his seat and came up behind the man. Out shot his right fist, gripping his collar, lifting him from the floor. Holding him at arm's length, he turned slowly around and carried him, kicking the air and protesting loudly, to the front of the car, out the open door and onto the platform.

Everyone gaped; not a sound was uttered. Seconds passed. Eng-chow reappeared alone. Coming back, he took his seat.

"You didn't throw him off!" exclaimed Lisa.

He smiled enigmatically but gave no indication of exactly what he had done.

"Oh, dear."

Six stops separated Ismailia from Port Said. El Ferdan was the first, 11 miles up the line. A half-dozen more passengers boarded the train. One got off, a disheveled-looking, white-faced man with a sparse yellow mustache.

Surrounded on three sides by Lake Menzala and on the fourth by the sea, Port Said was approachable by a causeway over which ran the tracks. Here at the northernmost reach the dredging was being carried on by large seagoing barges. The silt was dumped into the Mediterranean five miles offshore. The town itself had been created out of nothing on the western side of the canal on a low, narrow and desolate strip of land. A lighthouse 174 feet high dominated the few permanent buildings, the offices of the Suez Canal Company, the

British barracks, wooden and sand-brick warehouses and depots and coaling-station offices.

The crowd assembled on the station platform was even more heterogeneous than the passengers, ragged, wretched-looking and cheering derisively at the ten-minute-late arrival of the train. Assembling their bags, Deirdre, Lisa and Eng-chow got off. Then a well-dressed, well-built and good-looking young man separated himself from the crowd and came toward them, waving his hat in greeting. Eng-chow stepped into his path, blocking his way and glowering down at him.

"I beg your pardon," said the man, his cheeks flushing. Craning his neck, he looked around the obstacle, tipping his hat to Lisa. "Donald Ridgely, madam. You *are* Mrs. Dandridge and Miss Dandridge?"

Lisa nodded, unable to suppress a smile. "It's all right, Eng-chow."

Eng-chow stepped aside, letting him approach. He offered his hand to each of them. "I'm supercargo on the *Westwinder*. You sure are a welcome sight. We've been here a week waiting for you."

"A week?" Deirdre stared.

"How on earth did you know we were coming?" asked Lisa.

"Telegraph from San Francisco to New York to Newfoundland to Ireland to Dover to Calais down to Gibraltar. We've been in the Mediterranean about two weeks picking up cargo."

Deirdre and Lisa exchanged glances. "Wo Sin," they said together.

"Excuse me?"

Lisa explained.

"Anyhow, we brought over tobacco and steel and are taking back so many different cargoes I can just about squeeze them all on the manifest: phosphate from Tangier, wine from Cortagena and Palermo, figs from Smyrna, olive oil from Beirut—and you people. Our orders are to take you home to Providence."

"Well, that's good news." Lisa turned to Eng-chow. "Did you know about this?"

"No, missus."

"The *Westwinder?*" asked Deirdre.

"I've never heard of it," said Lisa.

"She was recommissioned only a few months back. That's when I signed on. The owners are Trask and MacDougal."

Lisa nodded. "Jonas Trask. I must say this is very magnanimous of the two of them."

"Mrs. Dandridge, any one of a hundred ships, sail or steam, would be honored to provide passage for you. There isn't an owner or master in the business who doesn't know and respect the name Dandridge. Mr. Trask and Mr. MacDougal are only too happy to extend the courtesy. May I ask, how was your trip from Singapore?"

"Very pleasant," said Lisa.

Donald Ridgely put his hat back on and looked about over the crowd. "Michael, Rory . . . over here!"

Four powerfully built sailors came pushing through. They picked up the baggage, and Ridgely led the way to two waiting carriages. Helping Lisa and Deirdre up, Eng-chow and he took their places in the driver's seat. The sailors followed in the second vehicle as Ridgely drove slowly through the pedestrian traffic crossing the street from both sides. Within minutes, they reached the western docks. Beyond the harbor, the Mediterranean spread its sapphire to a distant blanket of mist enshrouding the horizon. The sun continued to broil the world, concentrating its fury upon them, the air unmoving and so hot Deirdre was breathing through clenched teeth. But sight of the clipper ship waiting at anchor, her gangplank secured to the wharf beckoning invitingly, her canvas neatly furled, her sleek lines running to the tip of her bowsprit over her figurehead, a wooden-eyed, bare-breasted maid holding a gilded thunderbolt, set Deirdre's heart beating furiously.

Home! Carried by the tireless westerly across the immense harbor of the Mediterranean, out under Gibraltar's sullen cliffs, out into the mighty Atlantic. the restless blue monster conquered by and in subjugation to sail and steam, on and on to home port, to familiar sights and sounds and faces, to Blackwood.

Ridgely drew the team to a stop alongside the gangplank. Deirdre turned to her mother to sight of her staring dumbfounded.

"What's the matter?"

Her forehead clenched in a frown, her eyes slowly traveled the ship's length, pausing at her neatly lettered name below and behind her figurehead.

"The colors are different. There's no green on her figurehead. And that black stripe under the railing is new."

"Something wrong?" asked Ridgely.

Lisa shook her head slowly. "It's she. Different colors, new brass, new canvas, but . . ."

"The *Westwinder*," Deirdre said in a puzzled tone.

Lisa shook her head. "She's the *Olympia*."

"Your mother's right," said Ridgely. "*Olympia* was her name back when Baldwin and Baldwin owned her. But when they sold her to us and Mr. MacDougal had her refitted and painted, he licensed her under a new name."

The surprised look on Lisa's face had given way to an expression of disappointment. Deirdre sighed. Of all the luck! Of all the ships breasting all the oceans, sitting in front of them had to be the one on which Mr. and Mrs. Ross Dandridge, newlyweds, had crossed from England to America nearly 20 years earlier—the *Olympia*, built by the Dandridge yards for Baldwin & Baldwin, New York, and crammed from sprit to stern with ghosts, memories painful and sweet, warm and wonderful recollections carried forward through time in proper order and leading unerringly, inevitably to heartache.

Eng-chow shattered the mood, extending his great

hand to Lisa and smiling. "I say good-by here, Mrs. Dandridge, Miss Dandridge. Good luck to home."

Lisa took hold of both his hands. "Good luck to you, Eng-chow. Will you be going back with Captain Congers?" He nodded. "Take care of yourself, my friend. We shall miss you."

"I miss you. I never forget you both."

"We shall never forget you," said Deirdre.

"Godspeed, old friend," said Lisa, and kissed him on the cheek.

He beamed and stepped back, allowing them to pass and start up the gangplank. At the top, both turned to wave. He waved and walked off, joining the crowd, heading in the direction of the station.

"Dear Eng-chow," said Lisa quietly.

"That's a big man," said Ridgely in an awed tone.

Lisa nodded. "He has to be big; his heart is enormous."

XXI

They were welcomed aboard by Captain Elias Bridger, who lost no time in letting Lisa know that he had been "personally acquainted" with Cyrus Dandridge. They talked briefly; then she excused herself and, snatching Deirdre's hand, practically ran her down the deck to the cabins.

"This is it!" she burst, throwing open a door. "Your father's and my room. It hasn't changed a speck!"

Deirdre glanced about. The cabin was not large, but it was impressively furnished. The walls were paneled in rosewood and richly ornamented with imitation inlaid gold. The ceiling surrounding the lamp was as white as a wave top and framed with handsomely wrought molding with gilded beads. Two overstuffed chairs, with stout mahogany legs to match the sideboard and bedstead, occupied the open corners on either side of a lowboy attached, as was the sideboard, to a wall in the event of heavy seas.

Lisa pulled her into the room, plumping down upon the bed. "Not a speck!" Her eyes roamed about. "What a lovely two weeks we had in this little corner of paradise. That's what he called it. That's what it was. We were the only two passengers on board, the only two people on earth! We loved each other so. How my heart ached to hold him and to feel his arms around me. Seeing his eyes dance almost made me cry with happiness. And when we kissed, the heavens sang!"

"Mother, you shouldn't. Come, let's get another cabin."

"Why?"

"Please, any one but this."

"Close the door, darling."

Deirdre hesitated, sighed and complied.

"Now, come and sit. We must talk about Daddy. We haven't yet, you know."

She was right, thought Deirdre. She herself had learned of Ross's death by pulling it out of Travis Collier.

"Blame me for passing out like a love-sick schoolgirl practically the moment we met."

"Must we talk about it?"

"I want to; I have to."

"Just the passing thought of it gets me so down . . ."

"Indulge me, darling, please." She searched Deirdre's eyes, wordlessly begging understanding and an end to her resistance. "I have to and I can. No more avoiding it, no more pretending it never happened. It did. He's dead and gone. I've got to get past that; we both do so we can go on." She set her jaw muscles determinedly. "I can't stay stuck forever on this side of the truth, making believe, deluding myself. You understand, don't you?"

"Mother . . ."

There was no stopping her. "I had gone ashore to see Wo Sin. . . ."

She recounted every moment leading up to her return to the *Sea Cloud* and the discovery that Ross had been attacked and murdered. It poured out of her; she couldn't rid her mind and heart of it fast enough. It was a purging, a dispassionate documentation of the thing, a stripping away of the emotional cloak smothering it. When she was done, the relief that welled in her eyes resembled that in a person who had narrowly escaped death, perhaps by drowning in self-pity.

Deirdre took her in her arms, holding her close, gently kissing her eyes and fighting back the tears in her own.

XXII

The city slipped behind them as the brougham gained the road leading into and through the woodland. The voyage home had been too long, without incident, the weather fair but bitter cold, forcing them to stay inside most of the time. They had passed November—Deirdre's 17th birthday and Thanksgiving at sea—reaching Providence on December 9. The family lawyers, Muybridge Senior and Junior, had met them and were now lingering at the dock, collecting their things.

Ancient Enos Pryne was driving, sitting outside above them, one burl-like fist clutching the seat rail, the other the reins, flicking them over the mare's rump, increasing her pace a step. Snow had dusted the land, armoring the top sides of the limbs of the larger trees like brassards and nestling in the frozen ruts of the road. Through the window Lisa saw two squirrels jump to life, scamper across the road ahead, stop short, bunching up, contemplate the hooved and wheeled passerby and run off, their tails waving.

The wind bent the trees, the snow on their limbs sifting lightly to earth. It was creaking cold, with an edge to the wind that chilled cheeks and watered one's eyes. Lisa snugged her lap robe tighter under her and clutched the lapels of her paletot; and sneezed.

"Excuse me."

"Your cold's worse, isn't it?" Deirdre nodded, satisfied it was even before her mother could answer.

"I'm almost over it," said Lisa, sniffing, bringing out her hanky and nestling it against her nostrils. "Three

451

days coming, three days here, three days going. I make it one more day."

"That change from that broiling heat to winter is how you got it."

"I know. I promise I won't do it again."

They rode in silence, the brougham shifting from one side to the other as the wheels found and fled the ruts. Now beyond, the house could be seen overlaced by the black maples. Rising over their tops, its slate-capped granite eminence appeared patched with squares of silver, the windows reflecting the lowering sun.

Lisa's thoughts snapped back to the rainy afternoon, that milestone in memory, when, with Ross by her side, she had ridden up this very road to be greeted by the same sight. Dandridge "Castle," she remembered calling it, gazing at it with mingled fear and awe—Dandridge Castle standing firm and unconquerable against the world.

"Home," said Deirdre softly, smiling at her mother, her eyes glistening with tears, as were Lisa's.

"Look at us," she said. "Two homesick little children."

The brougham emerged from the trees, reached the turning circle and eased to a stop with a jounce before the door. As if cued by the sound of arrival, it opened. There stood Thursby and behind him the maids and cook, standing starched and prim-looking, their faces suffused with sadness. Thursby attempted to force a smile, as close to one as his feelings would allow.

"Madam, Miss Deirdre . . . welcome home!"

He knew, thought Deirdre; they all knew. She cast a sidelong look at her mother. Steady . . . steady . . .

The Muybridges had arrived, turning over the baggage to the maids. With them in their surrey came Alex Craven, bag in hand. His grin coming through the door served to dispel the self-conscious seriousness of the occasion. Lisa embraced him.

"Alex, Alex, Alex, what in the world are you doing here?"

"Where's the brandy? Aren't you going to ask me to stay for dinner?"

Lisa laughed, Deirdre, the Muybridges, Thursby and the staff laughed, and all of an instant everyone relaxed.

"I asked Mr. Muybridge to stop by and bring him up," admitted Deirdre.

"You have a cold," said Craven, cocking his head and one-eyeing Lisa accusingly. "Remember? And I have a question. Is that the best you can bring back from a trip around the world?"

"Not at all," said Lisa. "This is." Her arm went around Deirdre's waist.

He snapped his fingers. "Enough sentimental small talk. Upstairs, patient, let's have a look at you." Stealing her hand, he marched her off.

Deirdre drifted to the waiting Muybridges. "You *will* stay for dinner?" she asked.

"We'd be delighted," said Senior, removing his glasses, a gesture calculated to add sincerity.

"Good. Thursby . . ."

"Yes, miss?"

"There *will* be dinner."

"Oh, my, yes, a very special dinner for a very special occasion." His watery-blue eyes flashed and he rubbed his hands together. "Thanksgiving dinner: turkey, stuffing, cranberry sauce, the loveliest yams in Christendom, if I may say so."

"Excellent!"

Burdened with baggage, the maids scattered like chickens in a yard, Thursby barking them back to work.

He smiled fondly at Deirdre. "May I say again, Miss Deirdre, how wonderful it is to see you again. How empty this house has been with the three, er, two of you gone."

Excusing himself, he retreated to the kitchen, his

voice rising in challenge to the cook's as the door swung back and forth, slowly coming to rest closed.

Dr. Craven came thumping down the stairs, his index finger selecting one, then the other lawyer. "She would like to see you two upstairs."

Up they went, and into the study went Craven with Deirdre. She closed the double doors.

"How is she?"

"Healthy as a colt, though she does look as if she could use a few pounds."

"She's been putting on weight gradually. How bad is her cold?"

"It's nothing, the sniffles."

They sank into overstuffed chairs opposite each other. "How about that brandy you wanted?" she asked.

"Later. Deirdre, I have to tell you I'm terribly sorry. You both have my sincerest sympathies."

"Thank you."

"It's ironic."

"What?"

"Your mother was the sick one when she left here to go looking for you. She was the one we worried about. Acute melancholia. It's what kept the two of them from going after you right from Batavia. Your father was perfectly healthy."

"He was perfectly healthy in Singapore."

"It was murder, I know."

"How did you hear?"

"Fred Muybridge. Some shipping company in New York City got a telegram half a mile long."

"Trask and MacDougal."

"Whatever. But see here, young lady, you didn't fetch me up here for her cold or for my all-too-desirable company at the dinner table."

Deirdre explained. Craven listened in silence, staring at the carpet, resting his chin in his hand, taking her words in with the rapt attention of a schoolboy absorbing the lecture that follows punishment.

"You say it hasn't recurred since Port Said?"

Deirdre shook her head. "When she recognized the *Westwinder* as the *Olympia,* I nearly had heart failure. But once she got inside the cabin, it all came rushing out of her. It seems to have snapped her back to reality. Is it to stay? Is that possible?"

"Anything is possible."

"She's been herself ever since, no wandering, no fantasies, all the way home. She's over it, don't you think? It's been nearly three weeks."

"I'm no alienist; even if I were, I'd hesitate to predict she's cured. I'd be a fool to try. A friend of mine was treating her for her melancholia, Dr. Howard Cairns. He's on staff at Butler here in town. If you'd like, I'll ask him to—" He caught himself. "No, we'd better not. It could do more harm than good."

"But if he's an alienist . . ."

"Deirdre, my instincts say we should leave well enough alone. She's been through a terrible ordeal. She's not out of the woods yet. These things take months to come back from, sometimes even years. Turning Howard Cairns or anybody else loose on her at this point could be begging trouble. I say let nature have a go at it. It seems to be doing all right so far."

"We cross our fingers and hope for the best?"

"More than hope. You're to watch her like a hawk. The first sign of a lapse, six words that don't make sense . . ."

"I understand."

The doors opened. Lisa smiled at them. She had changed into a lovely rose dress with pagoda sleeves and engeanettes, her crinoline skirt tiered with flounces.

"Dinner is served."

XXIII

The bones of the bird had been returned to the kitchen, the level of brandy in the decanter lowered by half, the fires reduced to embers, the Muybridges and Alex Craven departed, and Blackwood itself, eaves and corners, wrapped in the winter night.

Lisa and Deirdre sat together in the library by the oriel window, relaxing, mesmerized by the glowing coals, comforted in the warmth and the awareness that the great adventure was ended at last.

"Tired?" asked Deirdre.

"Not very."

"I am: tired and restless, contented, down a bit, all opposites. Unwinding, I guess you'd say. This beautiful house"—she flung out her arms—"this safe harbor; it's been so long and I've been so far from it, not just in miles, but in the . . ."

"The stretch between prayer and probability?"

Deirdre nodded.

"I know what you mean. The closer we got to you, the farther away you seemed, day after day everything and everybody becoming stranger, more forbidding. Say . . ." Lisa straightened in her chair and, rising, went to the bell cord. "You, my dear, have completely forgotten your promise."

"Promise?"

She opened the doors to Thursby in the act of a stifling a yawn. "I beg your pardon. You rang, madam?"

"Yes, would you bring us a bottle of wine?"

"Any preference, madam?"

"Burgundy."

"A brand?"

"What do we have from the Côte de Nuit?"

"Ah, the classics, Chambertins, Clos de Bèze, Clos de Vougeot, Aloxe-Corton . . ."

"You decide."

"The Aloxe-Corton. Liquid silk, if I may say so."

She nodded; he withdrew.

"Dr. Martoche," said Deirdre wistfully, getting up to poke the fire. "The poor man."

Thursby returned with the Aloxe-Corton decanted and two glasses. Lisa poured. They raised their glasses and she toasted.

"To Dr. Martoche, the man and the memory. God bless you, doctor."

They sipped and toasted again, the good people all: So-leng, Eng-chow, the ship captains, the physicians, Paul Gerard and his men, Travis Collier, Wo Sin, those who had cared and helped.

"Even to giving up their lives," observed Deirdre solemnly. "Mother . . ."

"Yes?"

"Before dinner, when you talked with the Muy-bridges, did you decide about selling the house?"

Lisa refilled her glass. "Come."

She took Deirdre's hand and walked with her across the foyer and into the drawing room. The portraits of the Dandridges gazed down upon them as they crossed the Brussels carpet to Ross's picture, the Dutch painted-leather *chinoiserie* screens standing tall on either side of it serving to isolate him from the others of his family. Their arms about each other's waist, they raised their glasses to Ross.

"To you, my beloved," whispered Lisa, "my heart, my life."

They sipped.

Lisa turned to Deirdre, smiling. "To answer your question, I think—depending, of course, on how you feel about it—that we should stay here at Blackwood.

This is home. No other place anywhere could ever be the same, with all it gives us, all it stands for. Most of all, it's your father's home, where he lives."

"And always will," said Deirdre. "You're right, Mother: We belong here, the three of us, always and forever. I love you, Mother."

Lisa kissed her fondly. "My Deirdre, my darling, welcome home."

Let my voice ring out and over the earth,
Through all the grief and strife,
With a golden joy in a silver mirth:
Thank God for Life!

Let my voice swell out through the great abyss
To the azure dome above,
With a chord of faith in the harp of bliss:
Thank God for Love!

Let my voice thrill out beneath and above,
The whole world through:
O my Love and Life, O my Life and Love,
Thank God for you!
                              —James Thomson 1834-1882

EPILOG

True to her word, Lisa Dandridge never again left New England. Shortly before her 20th birthday, Deirdre was married to Donald Ridgely. In 1872 she gave birth to the first of four children—two boys, Ross Richard and Jordan Alan, and two girls, Lisa Allworth and Leslie Sharon. Their father insisted that both boys assume Dandridge as their legal surname.

Lisa Dandridge never remarried. She died in 1917, aged 87. She left four grandchildren, 13 great-grandchildren and two great-great-grandchildren. She is buried in the family vault at Blackwood. In an empty casket beside Lisa's, her daughter, Deirdre, subsequently ordered placed a sealed receptacle filled with sea water.

Much of the land accruing to the estate, including the shipyards, was eventually sold, but Blackwood and the 800 acres of woodland surrounding it remain in the family. To this day, Dandridges continue to occupy the house.

In his eulogy at her funeral, the minister described Lisa as the most remarkable woman with whom he had ever been acquainted. Said he in part: "Her courage was her weapon, her faith her shield, her love her armor."

MORE
HISTORICAL ROMANCES FROM
PLAYBOY PRESS

THIS RAVAGED HEART $1.95
BARBARA RIEFE

Lisa Allworth leaves 19th Century England to marry American shipping heir Ross Dandridge. A jealous woman tries to separate them in this searing romance that sweeps across continents and time.

FAR BEYOND DESIRE $1.95
BARBARA RIEFE

In this stupendous sequel to *This Ravaged Heart*, Lisa Dandridge embarks on a dangerous journey to the Orient in desperate search of her beloved husband, Ross, who she thought dead until now.

BLAZE OF PASSION $1.95
STEPHANIE BLAKE

A breathtaking romance that races from 19th-Century England to the Australian penal colonies, from Paris to the gold fields of California, from San Francisco to a climax of passion and revenge.

FLOWERS OF FIRE $1.95
STEPHANIE BLAKE

Ravena Wilding is torn between the passions of twin brothers in a tempestuous love story that sweeps from the Irish revolution to the American Civil War, from the slave plantations of the South Seas to the Wild West.

DAUGHTER OF DESTINY $1.95
STEPHANIE BLAKE

In this sequel to *Flowers of Fire*, Ravena's daughter, Sabrina, and a hot-blooded Irish rebel carry the torch of their passion from Ireland to India, to the powder keg of World War One and Europe.

PASSION'S PRICE $1.95
BARBARA BONHAM

In a heart-rending story set against the harshness and isolation of the vast prairies of 19th Century America, a lovely young widow and a lusty family man are victims of their passions.

PROUD PASSION $1.95
BARBARA BONHAM

The love story of beautiful and brave Odette Morel, who flees the French Revolution to face unthinkable dangers in the frontier wilderness of America.

THE DRAGON AND THE ROSE $1.95
ROBERTA GELLIS

A rich novel of the intrigue, war and struggle that preceded Henry VII's ascent to the English throne and his romance with the young, betrothed Elizabeth.

THE SWORD AND THE SWAN $1.95
ROBERTA GELLIS

Bold warrior Rannulf and gentle, radiant Catherine enter a marriage of political convenience, but from the strange alliance grows a love so powerful it challenges the will of kings.

ROSELYNDE $1.95
ROBERTA GELLIS

The first book of a magnificent four-volume romantic saga, this richly detailed and panoramic story weaves a tale of power and passion in medieval Europe—and introduces a compelling and unforgettable heroine.

IN LOVE'S OWN TIME $1.95

JANICE YOUNG BROOKS

Rich in the excitement of England's tumultuous War of the
Roses, this is a captivating tale of royal intrigue and the
tender romance of star-crossed lovers torn between duty
and desire.

ROXANA $1.95

HELENE MOREAU

Daughter, courtesan, wife and mother to the most powerful
men of ancient Persia and Greece, beautiful and brilliant
Roxana bewitches those around her as her whims and
passions alter the course of history.

WILD IS THE HEART $1.95

DIANA SUMMERS

Set against the raging turbulence of the French Revolution,
this is the compelling story of a fiery, golden-haired aristo-
crat who dazzled men with her breathtaking beauty and
ignited half the world with her flaming passion.

LOVE'S BRIGHT FLAME $1.95

SHEILA HOLLAND

Eleanor was the richest heiress in medieval Europe. She
married Louis, King of France, in a political match that
was to prove a personal disaster. But it was to Henry, King
of England, that she gave herself completely and forever.

LOVE'S GENTLE FUGITIVE $1.95

ANDREA LAYTON

In a sweeping romantic adventure set in pre-Revolutionary
America, a beautiful runaway tries to escape her secret
past—only to fall in love with the one man who could
return her to England and disaster.

ORDER DIRECTLY FROM:

PLAYBOY PRESS
P.O. BOX 3585
CHICAGO, ILLINOIS 60654

No. of copies		Title	Price
_____	E16396	This Ravaged Heart	$1.95
_____	E16444	Far Beyond Desire	1.95
_____	E16462	Blaze of Passion	1.95
_____	E16377	Flowers of Fire	1.95
_____	E16425	Daughter of Destiny	1.95
_____	E16399	Passion's Price	1.95
_____	E16345	Proud Passion	1.95
_____	E16364	The Dragon and the Rose	1.95
_____	E16389	The Sword and the Swan	1.95
_____	E16406	Roselynde	1.95
_____	E16427	In Love's Own Time	1.95
_____	E16418	Roxana	1.95
_____	E16450	Wild Is the Heart	1.95
_____	E16435	Love's Bright Flame	1.95
_____	E16455	Love's Gentle Fugitive	1.95

Please enclose 25¢ for postage and handling if one book is ordered; 50¢ for two or more but less than $10 worth. On orders of more than $10, Playboy Press will pay postage and handling. No cash, CODs or stamps. Send check or money order, or charge to your Playboy Club Credit Key #_____

Total amount enclosed: $_____

NAME _____

ADDRESS _____

CITY _____ STATE _____ ZIP _____